—From the Best-Selling Au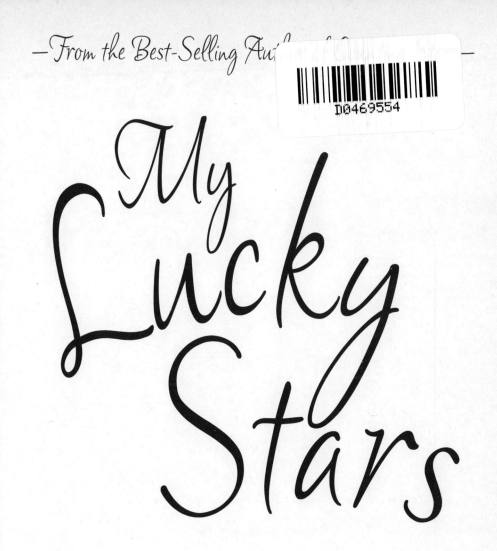

My Lucky Stars

a novel by

Michele Paige Holmes

Covenant Communications, Inc.

Cover image Red Barn and Cows © Imagine Golf. Courtesy of istockphoto.com

Cover design copyright © 2012 by Covenant Communications, Inc.

Published by Covenant Communications, Inc.
American Fork, Utah

Printed in the United States of America
First Printing: April 2012

18 17 16 15 14 13 12   10 9 8 7 6 5 4 3 2 1

ISBN 978-1-62108-035-0

To Alyssa, my goal-setting, high-achieving,
reach-for-the-stars girl—
May you discover your own testimony
and many reasons in life to thank your lucky stars,
as I thank our Father in Heaven, each day, for you.

Acknowledgments

Writing Tara's story proved a greater challenge than my previous novels, as I wanted readers to experience, along with Tara, her change of heart. Yet testimony is personal, and the way it is gained is unique for each individual. How, then, was I to write a story about Tara's drastic change of heart and her new understanding? It didn't take long before I realized I was in above my head. As a result, this manuscript sat for quite some time.

After several months, during which I continued to think about Tara—and the awful point I'd left her stranded at—I knew I needed to try again. This time, instead of reading books on plot or character, I began with the scriptures, studying particularly the Savior's ministry in the New Testament and King Benjamin's sermon in the Book of Mormon. Both helped me see clearly what Tara was missing and how she needed to change. From that point, I couldn't get the words typed fast enough. Her character became real to me, and I so wanted her to feel the joy and peace I experience in my own life. I am grateful for the heavenly help I received when working on this manuscript.

Once again, my critique group proved invaluable. Annette, Heather, Lu Ann, Sarah, Jeff, and Rob, I thank you for your time and patience, your brilliant ideas, and generosity. I continue to owe my writing career to your friendship and expertise.

I am grateful to the Covenant staff, in particular Kirk Shaw, for their help and guidance getting this story in its best possible form.

I am thankful for my family's support, especially during the long month of March 2011, when their mother all but abandoned them each night to finish this manuscript. My husband continues to be the epitome of "behind every published author is a great spouse," and I thank him for that support. He puts up with everything from piles of papers to piles of laundry while I am busy pursuing my dreams. Thank you, Dixon, for your love and enthusiasm.

Winter

"Opportunity is missed by most people because it is dressed in overalls and looks like work."
—*Thomas A. Edison*

One

OH NO, IT'S A KID. Tara Mollagen stared down at the preadolescent male sitting in the aisle seat of row twenty-seven—*her* row, the one listed on her boarding pass, the one she'd counted on having all to herself. The woman at the ticket counter had said she'd try—hadn't she? Tara closed her eyes briefly, taking a deep breath as she faced the second of her two greatest fears in less than three minutes. Stepping onto the plane, forcing herself to walk into the narrow, confined space—knowing she'd be stuck here for a good two hours—had been difficult enough.

And now she was going to have to talk to a *kid*—one of those smallish-sized people who seemed something less than human. Often sticky. Frequently whiney. And the really little ones smelled funny. At least the one sitting in her row didn't seem to have that problem.

"Excuse me," she said in what she hoped was a kid-friendly yet authoritative voice. "I believe you're in *my* seat." She held up her pass, polished nail pointing to the number twenty-seven.

"Nope." The boy didn't even glance up from his handheld video game. "I'm in C. You must have D."

Tara frowned. She looked down at the paper in her hand and saw that he was right. She was assigned to 27D, but there had to be some mistake. She'd specifically requested the aisle—had been upset enough to find out that each side of the plane had only two seats instead of three. At the very least she'd hoped to have both of those to herself.

The man behind her cleared his throat and she half-turned, dismayed to see the line of people crowded behind her. Feeling faint, she gripped the seat back, wishing more than anything that she could turn around and vault over everyone's head to the exit and get off this miserable excuse for transportation. She looked at the kid again, at the full seats in the rear of the plane, at the passengers behind her, waiting impatiently to stow their excess of carry-on luggage and find their own seats. Her hope of sitting alone vanished, and silently she cursed herself for not purchasing two tickets. Though she'd been lucky to have found a flight at all a few days before Christmas.

Expelling a breath, she attempted to remedy the situation as best she could. Even if she couldn't have both seats to herself, the aisle seat was a must. That little extra space around her on one side could make the difference of whether or not she pulled down the overhead oxygen mask *before* or after takeoff.

"How about you take the window seat?" She spoke to the kid casually, thinking he'd jump at her offer.

"Nah. You can have it."

Great. "No, really," Tara tried once more. "I bet this is your first time flying. Seeing out the window is pretty cool." *Pretty nauseating.*

"Pretty boring, you mean." The kid finally glanced up, staring at her in a way that said he thought she was as clueless as they came. "I fly all the time. My parents are divorced."

"Oh." Tara stared at the tiny space on the other side of him. There was no way she was going to survive two hours sitting there. She already felt the walls closing in on her. Having them curve a foot or so above her head wasn't going to help.

The man behind her cleared his throat again. "Lady, do you mind?"

Tara sent him a look that said, *yes*, she did very much mind his impatience and his person so close to hers.

"If you won't move over, then let me in," she said to the boy, who was absorbed in his game once more.

"Sure." He turned his body exactly a quarter of an inch.

Tara let out a huff, rolled her eyes, and proceeded to step over him. She noticed his gaze leave the video screen as her leg, with her skirt hiked up to mid-thigh, crossed his line of vision. Maybe these kinds of kids were the worst. Too big to be even remotely considered cute and definitely too young to be looking at a woman's legs. He was what— probably all of twelve? Tara resisted the urge to slap his hairless cheek.

Practically falling into her seat, she reached over and snapped the window blind shut. Though the window *should* have helped her claustrophobia, she'd found it actually had the reverse effect, making her feel like she was imprisoned in a tomb from which she could look out but never escape.

Reaching up, she twisted the knob for air, but nothing came out. She tried the one over the kid, but it too refused to work.

"Can't use those till after takeoff." The kid's tone was derogatory—as if she were completely stupid.

Tara didn't bother responding but tilted his air vent toward her so that when they *did* come on, it would flow forward, just over her face and not the top of her hair. *Serves him right—taking my seat like that.*

With the shade down, her seat belt buckled, and her bag tucked under the seat in front of her, Tara leaned her head back, closed her eyes, and tried to practice her meditation exercises. She'd been taking yoga for six months now, but so far the only thing feeling lighter was her bank account. No matter how hard she tried, how carefully she followed the instructors' commands, she *never* felt relaxed.

The whole concept of peace continued to elude her, as she was certain it would during this flight. She wished that she were up in first class, where at least you had an armrest to yourself. Right now the preteen next to her had taken over their shared one, and his elbow moved with sporadic jerks as he pushed the buttons on his handheld.

Too bad I booked so late, she thought. She'd been planning to stay in LA and spend the holiday with her mother until her mom had called two days ago to tell her she was extending her cruise into the new year. Apparently Greece held more interest than seeing her only daughter for the first time in almost five years.

Thinking about her mom, Tara felt a little sting zap at her emotions, but she brushed it away. She was thirty-four years old now. Who needed a mother at that age, anyway? What she needed right now was a *drink*. A strong one. Opening her eyes, she leaned toward the aisle, looking for a flight attendant—preferably one that was tall, dark, and handsome.

After several minutes, an attendant who was rather on the matronly side made her way down the narrow corridor, checking to make sure seat backs were upright. Tara had already reclined hers the one-point-two inches it would go back. She needed every particle of space available. *I need air.*

"I need a drink," she said as the attendant reached their row.

"We'll be by with beverage service shortly after takeoff," the woman said.

"I'd like to buy one." Tara reached for her purse. "A martini, please."

"*After* takeoff," the woman reiterated. "And please return your seat to its full, upright position." She looked at the boy. "You'll need to turn that game off until we're in the air."

"Sure," he said and continued to play.

The attendant moved on to the next row.

"But—" Tara held her wallet up. The kid eyed it speculatively, and she returned it to her purse, shoving it deep within the folds. "In first class, you can have a drink whenever you want."

"Then how come you're not sitting there?" he asked.

"I booked too late. Not that it's any of your business," she added. The last thing she needed was conversation. It was bad enough she was stuck back here, and not even in an exit row. *The exit rows!* She'd been so focused on not hyperventilating that she hadn't located them. Unbuckling the belt, Tara rose from her seat, craning her head in each direction as she looked for the emergency exits.

Her panicked gaze caught the attention of the matronly attendant as she returned, making her way toward the front of the plane.

"May I help you?"

"Where are the exits?" Tara asked.

The woman gave her a sickly sweet smile. She pointed toward the front. "The closest one to you is row fifteen. There's also one at the rear of the plane."

Fifteen. Tara felt like there was a weight pressing on her lungs. *And I'm all the way back at twenty-seven.* "Do you have *any* other seats available?" she asked. "Any aisle—or even any windows closer to an exit, closer to the front—"

"I'm sorry," the woman said. "But this flight is full. Holiday travel, you know." Her smile widened. "If you'll sit down, we'll show you a short safety presentation. I'm sure that will ease your mind."

"A drink would ease my mind," Tara muttered under her breath. She sat down again, gripping the armrest as the plane started to move. She was stuck now. There was no getting off until they reached Denver. Even worse, she was about as far from the exits as possible. *The woman at the ticket counter lied,* Tara decided. *Her hair color was so obviously fake. Shoulda been a clue.*

"Yeah. Got it!" The kid beside her jerked his arm, smashing his elbow into hers.

Tara glared at him then continued to grip the armrests and watched the safety video on the screen in front of her. She paid close attention to the segment discussing emergency landings and exit procedures. And though she was very familiar with how the oxygen masks worked, she watched that presentation too. *No problem,* Tara thought when the video instructed adults to take care of their own needs before assisting children seated beside them.

But when the film moved on to using the cushions as flotation devices, she tuned out. Unless they made an emergency landing in the Colorado River, she wasn't going to need to do anything with her seat except manage to stay in it without having a total panic attack.

Ignoring the flight attendant's instructions regarding the use of electronic devices—as her seat mate was so obviously doing—Tara took her purse from the floor and got out her iPod, as well as the soothing eye mask she'd taken out of the fridge this morning. After putting her purse away again, she stuck her earbuds in and turned up the volume, so her *Meditative Melodies* would drown out the sounds of the plane. She carefully adjusted the elastic strap of her eye mask over the back of her teased hair. The last thing she wanted was to arrive in Denver looking bad. Of course, she'd have time to freshen up before catching the shuttle to the spa in Boulder and meeting up with her friends. But she didn't like to be out in public for even a second, looking less than her best.

The mask in place, Tara reclined in her seat. She felt the plane taxi down the runway, felt it lift into the air, and she tried to mimic that same rising with her spirit as her meditation instructor had recommended the day before. The gentle tones filtered through her ears into her mind; the mask was cool and dark. Tara strived to engage her soul, restore inner balance, and refresh her spirit. But all she could think about was her need for air and the feeling of suffocation growing more intense by the second.

The plane had almost leveled out when she pushed the button to call the flight attendant and reached toward oxygen overhead.

* * *

Tara flinched, waking suddenly as something sharp jabbed her side and one of the earbuds jerked from her ear.

"*Sweet.* It's snowing in Denver!" The kid again.

She lifted her eye mask in time to see him leaning over her, his elbow digging into her side, while his other arm was outstretched, lifting the window shade.

"Don't touch that." She slapped his hand away and gave him a withering look as she lowered the shade. But the damage was done. The glimpse outside had already elevated her heart rate again. "I offered you this seat, and you didn't want it."

"But we're being rerouted to Salt Lake City," he said. "I might be able to see the salt flats from the plane. The third *Pirates* was filmed there. My dad was part of the tech crew."

"We're being rerouted?" Tara straightened her seat back, pulled the other bud from her ear, and turned off her iPod.

"They announced it a couple minutes ago." He turned away from her, muttering under his breath, "If you didn't have that lame music up so loud, you woulda heard too."

Too upset by the news to bother responding to the kid's continued rudeness, Tara unbuckled her belt and started to rise from her seat. The matron flight attendant chose that minute to reappear, collecting cups and napkins from the earlier beverage service.

"I'll need you to remain seated with your belt fastened." She pointed to the red letters overhead, lit once more.

"Is it true?" Tara asked. "Are we being rerouted?"

The woman confirmed Tara's fears. "Yes, the Denver airport has just been closed."

"*Bliz-zard*," the kid said, grinning as though that were great news.

Dismayed, Tara sank into her seat. "Now what am I going to do?"

"I know what I'm gonna do," the boy said. "I'm going to get a hotel room all by myself. No parents to bug me."

"You *want* to be alone at Christmastime?" Tara asked.

He shrugged. "Yeah. If you had my parents, you'd want it too."

Mine probably aren't that far off, Tara thought. *But I still don't want to be by myself. Weird family is better than no family.* But even that hadn't worked out, so she'd risked life and limb on this plane to be with people she barely considered friends anymore.

The pilot's voice came over the speaker, announcing their impending arrival in Salt Lake City. An inversion and a balmy thirty-two degrees awaited. It wasn't known when the Denver airport would reopen, but airline employees were ready to assist in any way possible. Tara sighed. After extra oxygen, a martini, and an hour of meditation, she'd barely begun to relax, thinking she might actually make it through the flight without losing her mind. Now she was faced with an immediate return flight, or a night alone in a hotel in the-middle-of-nowhere Utah.

Her chest tightened, and a wave of nausea washed over her. Cold sweat sprang up on her forehead as she opened her mouth and took short, panting breaths, trying to fill her lungs with oxygen while staving off the impending eruption.

Her seat companion looked over at her, seeming to notice for the first time that she wasn't well. "You look kinda green. Wanna change seats?"

Tara shook her head. "Too late." She leaned forward, digging through the seat back for the little paper bag she'd seen there earlier. The martini churned in her stomach as the plane bounced with turbulence. Tara imagined that if she opened the shade now, they'd be in the middle of a cloud. The image only intensified the feeling of suffocation.

The flight attendant returned, garbage bag still in hand.

"Can I move?" the kid asked. He inclined his head toward Tara. "'Cause I think she's gonna barf."

"Oh dear." The attendant took one look at Tara then leaned over the boy, holding out the plastic garbage bag just in time.

Tara bent over it, gagging as she emptied the contents of her stomach.

"*Gross.*" The kid leaned as far away as possible.

When her spasms finally subsided, Tara squeezed her eyes shut, mortified and miserable. A single tear tracked down the side of her face. *There goes my mascara.*

"Are you all right now?" the attendant asked.

"I won't be all right until I'm off this thing." Tara groaned as she reached for her purse. Once she'd located a tissue and a breath mint, she leaned her head back against the seat.

The flight attendant left; the boy shrank away from her. *Good,* Tara thought with the tiniest bit of satisfaction as she took over the armrest. It was only fair that he'd be as miserable as she was. *Selfish, seat-hogging kid.*

Across the aisle a woman wrinkled her nose and turned aside. Tara's face heated with embarrassment, but she still felt too sick to care much. She reached up, twisting the knobs, turning both fans on high and directing a blast of cool air directly toward her. Her carefully teased and perfected hairstyle blew out of place, but that didn't really matter now. She wasn't going to be seeing her friends in Boulder today—wasn't going to be seeing anyone she knew.

The important thing was surviving until she could get off this plane and then finding someplace to go and some way to travel so she wouldn't have to get right back on another one.

Two

Benjamin Whitmore pulled his duffel from the luggage carousel.

"Uncle Ben, Uncle Ben!"

He turned in time to hold his hands out for the six-year-old girl running straight for him.

"Cadie." Ben leaned over, allowing her to throw her arms around his neck, so he could lift her. "Umph." He staggered backward exaggeratedly. "Wow. You've grown a foot or two at least."

"You should visit more," his sister Ellen chided.

"I'm here, aren't I?" Ben set Cadie down.

"You are."

He noticed the moisture in Ellen's eyes and stepped forward to give her a hug. "Hey, Sis."

Her arms tightened around him. "I've missed you, Benji."

"I know." He stepped back, a sheepish look on his face. "At least you're moving a little closer."

Ellen rolled her eyes. "Yeah. Denver is *so* much closer to Ohio. You're the one who needs to move."

"Nah. When your kids are older, you'll be glad I live in the middle of nowhere. You can send them to me for the summer so they get that whole outdoor, farm-type experience."

A wistful look crossed Ellen's face. "Like we did."

"I want to go to the farm," Cadie said. She tugged on Ben's hand. "How many horses do you have?"

Ben looked down at her. "None. I've got something even better."

Her eyes grew wide. "*Unicorns?*"

"Uh—no. I've got—"

Someone bumped him from behind, and Ben lurched forward, nearly stepping on Cadie's foot.

"Sorry," he said, glancing over his shoulder toward the offender— a woman pushing her way toward the baggage claim, with a man wearing a shirt with an airline logo not far behind.

"I waited here over forty minutes," she said, pointing a long, polished nail toward the belt where luggage emerged. "I stood here right in front, and my suitcase never arrived."

"If you'll go to that office over there—" The man pointed to a window on the far side of the carousels. "They can help you locate—"

"I already did," the woman said. "And they wanted me to fill out a form. Paperwork isn't going to do any good. What I need is someone to actually *do something* to find my suitcase. It's got to be here somewhere. It didn't just vanish."

"I don't really—" The airline employee broke off as the woman's expression grew fierce. He ran his fingers through thinning hair. "What flight did you say?"

"Seven-sixty-nine from Los Angeles."

"Looks like you've got the wrong carousel, ma'am." He nodded toward the board listing flights. "There aren't any arrivals from California on this one."

"Of course not," she huffed. "My plane landed over an hour ago. Haven't you heard anything I've said?" She didn't wait for him to answer. "I need my suitcase. And I expect a night's hotel to be covered, since I'm supposed to be in Denver instead of stuck in—"

"Well, that's where it is." The man smiled. "Your luggage must have gone on to Denver. Happens all the time when people miss their connecting flights."

"I—didn't—miss—my—flight," the woman said, clearly enunciating each word.

Ben turned his body slightly so he had a better view of the unfolding drama. The redhead's face was brighter than her hair, and her hazel eyes flashed angrily. He was glad he wasn't the recipient of her wrath.

"The Denver airport is *closed*," she said, drawing even more attention to the scene. "I'm stuck here, and I need my luggage!"

The employee stepped away from her, hands held out, palms toward the woman, as if to hold her back. "Lady, I haven't heard that. I just barely started my shift when you caught me, but I'll check it out. Yelling isn't going to help anyone, though. It's Christmastime. We all gotta be patient. And there's a lot of kids around—" His gaze slid sideways toward Cadie, eyes large as she stared at the woman. "So let's be nice."

"It would be *nice* to have my belongings." Her voice was like acid, and Ben noticed her flexing her fingers with those dagger nails.

Yikes. Weirdos all over—even here in good old Utah. He felt a sudden longing to get on the next plane and head back home to the peace he'd found on his own green acres in the rolling hills of Ohio.

"Let's see what we can find out." Without inviting her to come along or waiting to see if she did, the employee turned and walked away, flashing an apologetic look toward Ben as he passed by.

"Do you have any other suitcases?" Ellen asked, eyeing the duffel near Ben's feet.

"Nope." He took a step back as the woman strode past once more. He watched a second longer than he should have, noticing she wore one of the tightest, ugliest skirts—a fuchsia leopard print—he'd ever seen in his life.

Ellen noticed too—or at least where his gaze ended up. "Thought you'd sworn off women," she said, a slight smirk on her face.

"I did. And *that* is exactly why."

* * *

Twenty minutes later they finally made their way toward the central elevator. Cadie had needed to use the bathroom. Then she'd wanted a drink. Ben bought her an orange soda and was sorry three minutes later when she spilled it all down the front of her dress—the *new* dress, Ellen informed him, that she'd worn especially to greet him. It had taken another five minutes for Ellen to clean Cadie up in the bathroom and dry her tears.

"I left the difficult kids at home," Ellen reminded him as they skirted the large floor map beneath the security entrance. Cadie lagged behind, dodging beneath the ropes into the mostly vacant lanes, hopping from country to country.

"You're telling me we're in for a long trip."

Ellen nodded. "Though if you'll trade off taking Cadie and Sam with you in the moving truck, I'll keep Chloe with me. She's going to be the hard one."

"How big's the U-Haul you rented?" Ben asked.

Ellen gave him a blank look. "No clue. Dallin took care of that his last trip home. That was his job, whereas I've had the minuscule task of getting the house sold and packing all our worldly goods into boxes—while being a single parent to three of the most active kids on the planet."

"Hasn't been a lot of fun?" Ben guessed.

"None at all." Ellen sighed. "Though I've sure gained a new appreciation for parents who really are single. I cannot wait for Dallin to be around for dinners, tuck-ins, middle-of-the-night episodes, church—"

"I get the idea," Ben said, grinning at his sister.

"South America. North America," Cadie called, running from one to the other on the floor map. "Want to hear my song about continents and oceans?"

"At home," Ellen said. "We're going out to eat now and to see the lights, remember?"

Cadie frowned, and Ben was afraid she'd start to cry again. He knelt beside her, intending to listen before any tears could appear, but another sound interrupted them. He turned around and was surprised to see the woman from the luggage carousel. She sat at one of a few scattered tables near the elevator, her elbow on the table, head held in one hand as she spoke into her cell phone—much louder than necessary, Ben thought.

"No. I don't have the fraud protection plan." Her lips pressed together in an angry line as she listened to the person on the other end of the call. "I see it would have been a good idea, but now I just need to *cancel the card*." The nails of her free hand drummed impatiently on the table. "Twenty-four hours? Do you have any idea the charges that could be racked up in that amount of time?"

Ben tried to look away but was too entertained by the exasperated redhead clenching her teeth and rolling her eyes. Beside him, Cadie stared openly too. Only Ellen had made it to the elevator and stood waiting for them.

"I told you I *don't have* the protection plan. So twenty-four hours *is* a problem for me." The woman stood and began pacing back and forth in front of the table.

Ben turned back to Cadie. "Sing me your oceans song."

"It's continents *and* oceans," she said brightly. "Did you know there are seven—"

"Fine. Wait the twenty-four hours," the woman behind them shouted. "But I need another card within *the* hour. I'm starving and tired. My luggage is lost, and I'm in an unfamiliar airport in a strange city."

Not my problem, Ben thought. *She looks old enough that she ought to be able to keep track of her purse.* He forced his attention to Cadie, singing her way through the oceans of the world.

"What other option would that be? That rotten kid on the plane stole my wallet, so you tell me what I'm supposed to do."

Wouldn't ask that question quite that way if I were you.

Cadie finished her song.

"Ben?" Ellen called. Behind her the empty elevator closed. "On the way over I stopped at the Garden and put our name on the list, so we should probably get going."

"I want to speak to someone else—someone in *this* country," the woman raged on.

Ben stood just as she stopped pacing. "Hello. Hello?" Her voice escalated to a frantic pitch. "How dare you—" Holding her cell phone out in front of her, she began punching numbers then stopped, holding the phone to her ear. A second passed. Her voice plummeted to a whisper. "Dead." Looking utterly defeated, she walked to the table and sank into the chair again. Leaning forward, she rested her head in both hands.

Ben started to walk past but hesitated as he saw her back tremble. Cadie slipped her hand into his.

"We should help her," his niece whispered. "Mom says we should help everyone—even if they aren't nice."

Ben's lip curved up at this bit of information. "Ellen always was a goody two-shoes."

Cadie's brow wrinkled as she looked up at him. "Doesn't everyone have two shoes?"

"Yep. They sure do." Nearly too late Ben remembered he had to watch what he said for the next few days. "What I meant was, your mom's always been a good girl. When we were kids, she was always nice to everyone, while most of the time, *I* was in trouble."

"Mom told me," Cadie said, sounding much older than her six years.

"Really?" Ben's eyebrows rose. He wondered if he was the bad example used every time Ellen's kids did something wrong. *Don't do that, Sam. You'll end up like Uncle Benji.* He tried but couldn't imagine Ellen saying that. She *was* too nice.

Raising his hand, Ben looked over at his sister and motioned for her to wait another minute. "Your mom's right," he reluctantly admitted to Cadie. "We should probably follow her example." But he wanted nothing more than to walk away and pretend he'd never seen this woman, never overheard her plight.

That's whatcha get for eavesdropping Benji, he could hear his mother saying.

This one's for you, Mom. He remembered one of the many oft-told tales his mother had shared during his growing-up years. It was about President Spencer W. Kimball helping a woman and her young child at an airport when others looked on and were annoyed instead of compassionate. Years later, President Kimball had received a letter from the woman's son—the son she'd been pregnant with during that difficult day—explaining how his mother had investigated and eventually joined the Church because of President Kimball's kindness.

Not likely that'll happen today. Ben looked at the mop of red hair slumped over the table. He glanced around to see if anyone else had noticed she seemed upset. Several people looked her way as they passed then looked *away*, hurrying by with uncomfortable expressions on their faces. *Typical.* And he was no better if he ignored her too.

With an inward sigh, Ben gathered his courage and stepped toward her table.

Three

"EXCUSE ME, BUT I COULDN'T help overhearing . . ."

Sure, you couldn't, Tara thought. *Just like you couldn't help staring when I walked past you by the baggage claim.*

"Yes?" She raised her head and looked at him, though she was already well aware of her would-be rescuer. Probably in his early thirties, sort of tall, brownish hair, faded loose-fit jeans, and a *plaid flannel* shirt. He reminded her a little of the loggers she'd seen on occasion in Washington. *Lumberjack man. My hero.*

"I'm sorry . . . about your flight . . . and your wallet," Flannel Shirt stammered. He pulled out his own wallet. "If you need a place to stay I could—"

"You can sleep on our couch. It's bouncy. We jump on it all the time. I'm Cadie." The little girl standing beside Flannel Shirt stepped forward, her hand held out.

"Benji?" A woman joined them.

Benji? He's named after a dog? Tara nearly jumped when the little girl grabbed her hand, pulling it up and down. *Sticky—great.* As quickly as possible she pulled away.

"This is my sister Ellen," Flannel Shirt said, introducing the woman who'd joined them. "And I'm Ben." He turned to his sister. "This lady's wallet was stolen, and she's sort of stranded here."

Sort of? There's nothing sort of about it, Tara thought. *Who talks like that anyway? And "stranded" seems a little mild for the day I've had. More like sucked into the very jaws of he—*

"She's gonna sleep on our couch, Mommy," Cadie said, jumping up and down. "And we can feed her pancakes for breakfast."

Tara fully expected the woman to refute her daughter's invitation, but to her surprise she—Ellen—turned to Tara with a smile on her face. "Of course we'd love to have you stay with us. Anything we can do to help."

Flannel Shirt—Ben—suddenly looked uneasy.

"Maybe she'd be more comfortable at a hotel nearby," he said. "After all, she's going to have to catch another plane to get home."

The thought of another plane ride made Tara feel as if she might be sick—again. But a hotel did sound better than sleeping on a bouncy couch in a stranger's house. And she was already annoyed with the way the guy talked about her—as if she wasn't right in front of him. She stood up as a reminder.

"I'm Tara." From somewhere she dug up a smile for the trio. "I appreciate your offer," she said, meaning it. After all, what else was she supposed to do at this point? She grabbed a pen and one of her business cards from her purse. "If you'll write down your name and address, I'll mail you a check for the hotel as soon as I get home."

The tightness left Ben's face, replaced by relief. Tara felt slightly insulted. Though she wasn't as young as she used to be, she still prided herself on looking good, and it was a rare man who didn't enjoy her company.

"Where is home?" Ellen asked.

"LA," Tara said as Ben leaned over the table, scribbling his information on her card.

Ben nodded his head as if that explained something. "Ah . . . Big city girl." He returned the card and pen to Tara.

Ellen shot him a look that said she thought he was an idiot. Despite her weariness and earlier irritation, Tara found herself starting to be amused by these two.

"Is this your first time in Salt Lake?", Ellen asked.

"Yes," Tara said. First *and* last. "I was going to Denver, but a storm shut down the airport, and we were rerouted here. Only my luggage appears to have gone on to Colorado—or possibly Alaska. No one seems to know."

"We're going to Denver," Cadie said, beginning a new round of jumping. "Our dad's already there, and we got a new house. We have to move 'cause Grandpa died, and Daddy's got to do his work for him now. Uncle Ben's gonna drive our big truck with all our stuff in it."

"I'm sure that's more than Tara wanted to know," Ben said. His wallet was still in his hand, his fingers on a credit card. He glanced around. "Maybe the easiest thing would be to find an ATM and give you the cash—"

"There's really no need for you to stay at a hotel," Ellen said. "Our house isn't that far from here. And if you're missing all your luggage too, you'll need some clothes, a toothbrush, dinner."

"Leave it to the Relief Society to bring a casserole into this." Ben rolled his eyes at his sister.

"Benji!" Ellen looked shocked. "I'm just trying to—"

"Help. I know," Ben said. "So am I, and clearly Tara would prefer a restful night's sleep at a hotel to the craziness at your house. I mean, you're *moving* the day after tomorrow."

"So?" Ellen asked. "Sure it's a little chaotic at our place, but that doesn't matter. I know I'd sure hate to be by myself in a strange city." She grinned at Tara. "Men. What do they know about what a woman wants?"

Plenty—at least this one, this time, Tara thought. There was no way she wanted to impose on this family—or have them impose on her and her space, which right now was feeling pretty cramped. The little girl, Cadie, had taken to skipping in a circle around the three of them.

"I appreciate your offer," Tara began, intending to explain that she *would* in fact prefer a hotel room to herself. But seeing Ben's stricken expression, she paused. He looked, for all the world, just like she'd felt on the plane today.

His fingers went to his shirt, as if to loosen the collar that was already unbuttoned. His face flushed as if he was suddenly hot. He was definitely annoyed, his mouth turned downward and his forehead pinching together between his eyebrows.

What's his problem? she wondered. *It isn't like I came up and started talking to him.* Though she guessed that about now he was thinking he was sorry he'd spoken to her. *Is he afraid of being around women? Of me? Or just annoyed? What did I do?*

Tara weighed the peaceful night at a hotel against the challenge this man presented. It was odd and oddly upsetting to her that he so obviously wanted her to go away. *It's less than twenty-four hours*, she reasoned. *And if he is uncomfortable around women, I could be doing him a service if I stick around.* She stared at Ben, trying to catch his eye. "Your sister is right. It would be much nicer to stay with your family than at a hotel."

She could have sworn his jaw dropped. *Thought you read me different, didn't you?* she thought smugly, feeling suddenly rejuvenated, energized with the mystery of Lumberjack Ben.

* * *

Ellen maneuvered her minivan into a spot in the parking garage then glanced over at Tara. "I'm so glad you don't mind stopping. I've been promising Cadie for weeks that we'd go see the temple lights one last time." She unbuckled her seat belt. "Now you'll be able to enjoy them too. Temple Square is usually at the top of visitors' must-see list."

Must see the back of my eyelids soon. Tara reached for the handle of the front passenger door. Ben was already there, holding it open for her.

"Thank you," she said smoothly, as if she was used to such gentlemanly behavior all the time. Silently she racked her brain, trying to remember if she'd *ever* dated a guy who'd opened doors for her.

The parking garage was toasty, as was the building above—some sort of conference center—but the air outside hit her like a thousand icicles. It had been that way at the airport too. Tara took a sharp breath and actually felt the cold constricting her lungs. *Why would anyone want to live in a place like this?* Already numb, she jammed her fingers in the pockets of her Coffeeshop trench coat and walked between Ben and Ellen. Cadie, of course, seemed completely unaffected by the temperature and skipped along beside them.

They passed the Mormon temple, which Tara supposed was a very pretty building—if buildings could be pretty. Ellen chattered on about its history, and Tara gave a cursory nod every minute or so. It was all she could manage in the biting cold. Ben remained silent, and Tara wondered about his body temperature. He wasn't wearing a coat but seemed plenty warm in that awful flannel, which she was starting to suspect might have its good points.

By the time they entered what Ellen said was the Joseph Smith Memorial Building, Tara's toes were frozen as solid as the point of the shoes they were in. Ellen led them to a bank of elevators. Tara hesitated.

"Why don't we take the stairs?" she suggested. "It might help me get my blood circulating again."

"I'll race you," Cadie said, with obvious enthusiasm for Tara's suggestion.

"Not today," Ellen said, quashing Tara's hope. "We're going all the way to the top. That's where the restaurant is, and besides, it's the best view for seeing the lights."

Half the city must have agreed with her. The waiting crowd swelled, moving forward to cram into the narrow elevator when it arrived.

"I'll wait down here," Tara offered. She stepped back, bumping into Ben's chest.

"You'd have a long wait," he said, nudging her forward, though he was trying his best to move around her.

Tara felt herself being herded into the tiny space. She turned around just in time to see the top of the doors as they shut. Ben stood in front of her. Tara squeezed her eyes shut, trying to breathe. *I hate elevators. I hate elevators.* She opened her eyes and craned her neck, trying to see if they were near the top yet. *Not even close.* The two lit up briefly then the three, indicating they were passing the third floor. She looked down, trying to relax.

Just breathe, she told herself but couldn't seem to find the air to do so. *I need oxygen—fresh air. I need to get out!* Turning sideways, she tried to push past Ben to reach the doors.

He glanced at her as she moved up beside him. "You okay?"

"No," Tara said. The doors were shut tight, and they'd only reached the fifth floor. She'd never make it all the way to the top. Her knees buckled. Ben put his arm around her, grabbing her elbow just in time to keep her from falling.

"Are you sick?"

She barely managed to nod. Sweat broke out along her forehead. Her shaking fingers found the first toggle on her coat and struggled to undo it.

Ben reached between a couple of other passengers and hit the button for the next floor—the seventh. He grasped her shoulders, turning her to him. He took over, unfastening not just the first toggle but the next three. He pulled the coat from her shoulders then pushed her toward the front as the elevator slowed to a stop.

"Excuse us. She's not feeling well." Ben pressed the open button repeatedly until the doors finally began to move. He steered Tara into the hall.

"Meet you upstairs," Ben called over his shoulder to Ellen.

Behind them the elevator shut once more. He followed Tara down the hall to the closest bench. She sat. He dropped her coat beside her then backed up, lingering a few feet away.

"Put your head between your knees. Deep breaths."

"I know, I know," she moaned.

"If you know—if you've had this happen before—then why did you get on that elevator?" he asked, his tone sharper than she'd heard previously.

"Because I was *trying* not to make things inconvenient for anyone. And I thought I'd be okay," she added. "After all, I survived a flight today."

"That must have been fun," Ben said.

Tara detected more than a note of sarcasm in his words. "Yeah. It was." She turned her head sideways, willing her body back to normal so she could glare at him. "You know what? This *whole day* has been fun. So much fun that I'd love nothing more than to crawl into bed and hope it's all a nightmare I wake up from tomorrow morning."

"Then why didn't you take my offer for a hotel?" He folded his arms across his chest and kept his distance.

She shrugged as she sat up. "I don't know." And she really didn't. What did she care if he had issues with women—with her? It wasn't like she could fix something like that in one day. And while it did bug her that he didn't seem at all interested in her—seemed the opposite, in fact—she should have let her pride take the beating instead of the rest of her. The hotel definitely would have been the better choice.

"I suppose it's too late now?" she dared to ask. "There must be something around here."

He gave a short laugh. "It's a little late to change your mind. C'mon. My sister and niece are waiting." He waved her toward what she hoped was the door leading to the stairs. "Let's get some food in you, so you don't almost pass out on me again." He started walking then hesitated, waiting when she didn't immediately follow.

She could tell he didn't want to wait for her—yet he did. It bugged her. *A sure sign of a decent guy*, she thought, feeling slightly guilty. Earlier, when she'd known he felt uncomfortable, she'd done nothing to help but had instead made it worse. She stood and met his annoyed gaze. *Why are you waiting? I know you'd love to ditch me.*

"When we were in the elevator—how did you know . . . Are you claustrophobic?"

"Hardly." He shook his head then turned around and started walking. "I guess I recognize a panic attack when I see one."

Tara wanted to know why that was but didn't have the guts to ask him when he held the door to the stairwell open for her.

Four

THERE WERE STILL A COUPLE of names ahead of Ellen's on the restaurant's list, so they waited by the large window facing the temple. Cadie ran back and forth, zigzagging through other onlookers as she covered the length of the window then back again. Tara noticed that Ellen was starting to look worn out. Ben must have noticed too, because he reached down and picked up Cadie the next time she zoomed by, headed down the hall toward the elevators.

"Up here's the best view of all." He swung her onto his shoulders as if she weighed next to nothing. The little girl squealed with delight, and Ben moved closer to the window so she truly had the best view.

Ellen let out a tired sigh and smiled at Tara. "Do you have any children?"

"Nope," Tara said, not bothering to mask the horror she felt by such a suggestion. She'd spent plenty of time the past several years wishing she had a steadier boyfriend, or even a husband, but never had she yearned for the kids that sometimes came later. No way. No-how—*never* did she want to be a mom. Some people just weren't meant to be parents. *Like my own mom. Whose fault it happens to be that I'm stuck relying on strangers in this stupid, freezing city named after a lake with salt in it. If she'd wanted to see her daughter more than the Italian coastline . . .*

"Well, kids can wear you out," Ellen admitted. She turned slightly, glancing up at Cadie, who leaned forward over Ben's shoulders, her face pressed against the glass as she gazed at the lights. "But they bring a lot of magic to your life as well." Almost on cue, a little of that magic surfaced.

"Oh, Mommy," Cadie said in a quiet, sweet voice that didn't seem to fit her overactive personality. "Isn't the temple pretty? I can't wait until I'm bigger to go in."

Tara watched as mother's and daughter's eyes met. Ellen held out her arms, and Cadie leaned forward into them. Ellen held Cadie close, her cheek next to the little girl's as they spoke in hushed whispers. Tara looked away, afraid of intruding on the private moment. As she turned aside, her eye caught Ben's. Their gazes locked for a split second, and Tara felt a jolt as she sensed the unspoken communication between them. There was a sudden vulnerability, almost a wounded look, on Ben's face, and she could tell he, too, felt uncomfortable witnessing the mother-daughter closeness. Tara wondered why.

"I'm going to take Cadie to use the restroom before we eat," Ellen said. With Cadie's hand grasped firmly in hers, she passed between Ben and Tara. There was a vacant spot at the window now, and Ben beckoned her to take it before someone else did. Tara moved to stand next to him.

They stood in silence, her eyes taking in the picturesque scene before them. The temple was astonishing by itself—a granite wonder with spires reaching toward heaven—if there was such a place. The dazzling display of Christmas lights on the grounds below only added to its beauty. When snowflakes started drifting from the sky, she couldn't help but smile. It felt like she'd stepped right into a motion picture.

"What's so amusing?" Ben asked, misunderstanding her smile.

"Nothing," she said. "It's just so strange to be here, and all that—" Her hand swept an arc, indicating the scenery below. "It's so perfect—so *unreal*."

"That's about as real as it gets," Ben said.

Tara turned to him. "What do you mean?"

He shrugged. "That temple's the real deal. The worship that goes on there, the truths that are taught . . ." He stopped abruptly as if remembering who he was speaking to.

Tara recalled his earlier, disparaging comment. *Big city girl.* "I've heard about your temples."

"Oh?" Ben seemed surprised. "Do you know someone who is LDS?"

"LD—what?" Tara frowned.

"Mormon," Ben clarified. "A member of The Church of Jesus Christ of Latter-day Saints."

"Yes. I do. Did." Tara returned her gaze to the lights outside. The snowfall was heavier now. The surreal feeling intensified. "I had a friend in Seattle who was a member of your church." She glanced at him sideways. "That is, assuming *you're* a Mormon."

He nodded. "You said *had.* This person isn't your friend anymore?"

"We haven't really stayed in touch," Tara said, feeling the twinge of sadness the admission brought. Perhaps she'd just been a coworker to Jane, an office friend, but Jane had been much more to her. She'd been the voice of reason, her shoulder to cry on during a particularly long string of bad relationships. *She was the real deal.* "She did what all good Mormons do—got married and started having a bunch of kids."

A half-grunt came from Ben. Tara glanced over again and saw he had his hands shoved in his pockets and the same, uncomfortable look on his face that she'd seen when he'd been watching Ellen and Cadie together. Too late she realized that what she'd said might have offended him. She tried to convince herself that it didn't matter, that he'd been brusque enough with her to deserve anything she dished back, but she couldn't get past the fact that he *had* been nice to her, had saved her from a miserable night in an airport chair.

"I mean, what *most* good Mormons do," she amended, trying to cover her earlier blunder. Before they'd left the airport, she'd noted the absence of a ring on his finger. "I mean, you're not married, are you?" she said sheepishly.

"Nope." The way he said it told her he felt much the same about that as she did about having children. "Then again," Ben continued, his face a complete mask, "who's to say I'm a *good* Mormon at all?"

* * *

When they'd been seated at their table at the Garden Restaurant and the waiter came, Cadie and Ellen ordered ice cream sundaes for their dinner.

"I promised her," Ellen said by way of explanation.

"Some mom you turned out to be," Ben teased before ordering a Philly cheesesteak sandwich for himself and a bowl of chicken noodle soup for Tara, who'd excused herself to make a phone call. Beneath the table, Ellen kicked him.

"Ow," he said, bending over to rub his shin. "Cadie, your mom used to kick me at dinner all the time when we were growing up."

"That's because he wouldn't ever pass anything," Ellen said. "It's a miracle I didn't starve sitting between you and Dallin."

"Daddy was there?" Cadie asked, a confused look on her face.

"Some of the time he was," Ellen said. She smoothed her daughter's hair. "He and Uncle Benji were best friends."

Were *being the operative word*, Ben thought. But Ellen was right. Back in the day before life got complicated, he and Dallin had been inseparable.

Tara returned to their table and handed Ellen's cell phone back to her. "Thanks for letting me use it. I should have charged mine last night, and of course the charger is in my lost luggage." She stepped around Ben and took the seat beside him, next to the window.

"Were you able to reach your friends?" Ellen asked. Leaning over, she snatched a sugar packet away from Cadie, who'd already opened two others and dumped them in her water. "*No* more."

Cadie frowned but turned her interest to the ketchup and mustard bottles. She took one in each hand and moved them around her corner of the table, pretending they were dolls or something.

"I left a message," Tara said. "Guess they're out."

"Chances are they haven't made it to Boulder either," Ben said. "The airport closure has got to be affecting a lot of people."

"You're probably right." Tara looked away, staring out the window again. For a fraction of a second, Ben almost felt sorry for her. He'd heard the doubt—and hurt?—in her voice and guessed there was more to the "meeting friends at a spa in Boulder" story than she'd shared. Was it a particular friend she was meeting? *A male friend?* he wondered.

"I bet the Denver airport reopens in the morning," Ellen said. "Think of this as a tourist stop on your way."

Tara nodded but made no move to face them and join the conversation. Ellen flashed Ben a concerned look. He shrugged. How should he know what was wrong with Tara? Beyond the obvious, that is— that she had terrible taste in clothing and adverse reactions to being in tight spaces.

The ice cream sundaes arrived, followed by Ben's sandwich and Tara's soup.

They all dug in, eating more than talking now. About halfway through her sundae, Cadie began to wilt. She put her elbow on the table and propped her head in her hand. Ben reached over and stuck his finger in her ice cream then in his mouth.

"Mmm," he said, grinning at her. "That's going to melt if you don't finish it."

"I don't want to. I'm tired." Cadie pushed the glass away and leaned on her mom.

"When it's bedtime, she goes downhill fast," Ellen said.

Ben glanced at Tara's bowl. Only a few noodles and some broth remained. "If you're ready, I'll grab our check and we can get going."

"Sure," Tara said. "And thanks for dinner. I'll send you some money for it when I get home."

"Don't worry about it." Ben raised his hand to get their waiter's attention. *Let's just get you home—to* your *home that is. Or to Boulder or wherever it is you're going.* Instead of getting more comfortable having her with them, he felt like things were getting progressively more awkward as the evening wore on.

Ben took care of the bill, and they bundled up and headed for the elevators. He looked at Tara skeptically. "I'll take the stairs with you if you'd like."

She hesitated as the elevator chimed then opened. Ben noted that it wasn't very full, and only two other people were waiting to get on. It wouldn't be nearly as crowded this time.

"Thanks, but I think I'll be okay."

They got on, and she stood to one side, her hands clasped in front of her, eyes shut tight, lips moving silently the whole ride down. Ben thought she was doing pretty well until she opened her eyes just before they stepped off. Wild panic filled her expression, and he realized how difficult the ride must have been for her.

"Are you all right?" he asked as they made their way toward the doors.

"I think the cold air will actually feel good right now." She tried to smile.

"Then do you mind if we stop by the nativity scene on our way out?" Ellen asked.

"Cadie can hardly walk," Ben said. His sister was really pushing things as far as he was concerned. Didn't she realize she had not one but two weary travelers, not to mention her own daughter—nearly asleep on her feet? Ben reached down and picked up Cadie, this time cradling her in his arms. She turned her face into his chest, and he experienced another glimpse of what he'd come to think of as imagined fatherhood. He could have a little girl this age, a little girl like Cadie.

But he didn't.

"It's really not that much out of our way," Ellen said. She led them down the street, through the Temple Square gate, and past the visitors' center. She found a spot in front of the nativity while Ben and Tara—limping along in a pair of ridiculously high heels—caught up.

"I love Christmas," Ellen gushed. "Love this place." When she looked up at Ben, her eyes were full of unshed tears. "I'm going to miss Utah so much."

Ah, Ben thought. *So that's what this is all about. Great. I'm going to be dealing with an emotional female the next few days. No wonder Dallin went on ahead and agreed to let me drive his family out.*

"How could anyone miss this cold?" Tara muttered, and Ben wasn't sure whether she meant for them to hear her.

Cadie stirred in his arms and began to fuss. "I want to go to bed. I need to go to the bathroom."

"Ellen," Ben said. "We need to get go—"

"In a minute, Benji." Ellen's head tilted back as she stared past the nativity, up to the second floor of the visitors' center and the statue of the *Christus* that was visible through the large glass window. "Can't you feel it—the spirit that's here?"

Ben couldn't honestly say he did. He didn't feel much of anything but annoyed right now. Ellen was wiping her eyes, getting all weepy on him. Cadie continued to whine, and she wiggled so much he set her on the ground. On his other side Tara was muttering under her breath about the cold and everything else.

"Ellen," he said, firmer this time. "Let's *go*."

"All right." She let out a long sigh and turned away from the nativity. "Don't you just love Christmas?" she said to Tara.

"No," Tara said, sounding as if she'd reached the breaking point herself. "I don't. I think it's a depressing time of year."

Ellen's mouth opened, and even in the dark Ben could see the shock in her eyes.

But he was trying to contain a smile. It was the first thing Tara had said all evening that he completely agreed with.

Five

"DOWN, COULTER, DOWN," ELLEN SCOLDED the large black Labrador that met them at the door.

Tara held her purse up in a feeble attempt to fend off the dog's curious attention, but the bag was no match for the slobbery tongue and paws that poked at her. If Ben noticed her predicament, he didn't try to help but instead carried his duffel right past them and into the main part of the house.

Left a lone hostage in the entryway, her purse held over her head, Tara stared down at the beast. It raised one paw, placing it on her skirt, and its tongue lolled from its mouth a good three inches. A big strand of dog drool rolled from the side of its mouth and landed on her shoe.

"That's it!" Tara pushed the paw away and brought her purse down squarely on the dog's nose. It let out a surprised, pathetic whimper and turned tail.

"And stay there—wherever it is you're going," Tara said. Straightening her skirt, she walked forward and found herself at the entrance of a vaulted great room. A large fireplace took up most of the wall on one end, with the kitchen opposite. Several expensive-looking pieces of furniture resided in between, and Tara felt a measure of relief at seeing them. She'd been worried—the past half hour or so—just what she'd gotten herself into. Ellen seemed mostly normal, but her kid was on the wild side, and if there were two more at home like Cadie . . . well, they could have been taking her to some run-down shack in the middle of the wilderness. That they'd driven up so close to the mountains had only made her more anxious.

Walking to the nearest sofa, Tara sank onto it then immediately jumped up when something shrieked at her. Cadie ran over and grabbed a doll from the spot where Tara had tried to sit.

"You hurt Missy." She held the doll close, examining her for signs of damage.

"Sorry," Tara said then glanced around to see if Ben or Ellen were nearby. Seeing that they weren't, she added, "Maybe you shouldn't leave your toys where people sit."

"We don't *sit* here. We bounce." To emphasize her point, Cadie stepped up on the sofa and began jumping.

"Cadie," Ellen scolded as she walked by.

Right, I'll bet you bounce, little monster. Tara gave Cadie a smug look.

"If you're going to jump on the furniture, take your shoes off," Ellen said.

Cadie flung the look right back at Tara, just before she flung her shoes across the room.

"She really is a good girl," Ben said, coming to stand beside Tara. "And Ellen's a great mom. She and I had a little—different—upbringing. We learned pretty young what was really important and what wasn't. Ellen understands that kids like to jump on furniture, and it's not such a big deal."

"We just have to make sure we buy high-quality couches." Ellen put her hand on the back of the leather sofa. "And Cadie would never jump on someone else's furniture, but this is her *home*, and she's allowed to be a child here." She and Ben exchanged a meaningful glance that Tara nearly missed, tired as she was.

Ellen handed a bundle of folded flannel sheets to her. "Most of my things are packed, but I did keep out an extra nightgown."

"Thanks," Tara said. *This is a* nightgown? *It must weigh three pounds. How lovely. I've been taken in by the flannel family.*

"The bathroom is the second door on the right." Ellen stepped back, pointing toward a hall where boxes were stacked. "I'll find a towel for you, but I'm afraid I don't have any extra toothbrushes."

"No problem," Tara said. "I keep one in my purse."

Ben arched his eyebrow at this, but Tara met his gaze without flinching. Good oral hygiene was important, not to mention one never knew when a dinner date might turn into something more. And in those situations, fresh breath could be critical.

"Well, then, if you don't need anything else . . ." Ellen said.

She looks tired—exhausted, Tara thought, noting the dark circles under Ellen's eyes. *See what motherhood does to you.* She could hear a baby crying in the other room, and Cadie was doing her best to wrench her mother's arm from its socket as she begged for a bedtime story. The dog had returned and was nudging Ellen's side, vying for attention too.

"Thank you for everything," Tara said, drudging up what little energy she had left to give Ellen a sincere smile.

Ben scooped up Cadie and carted her off down the hall. "I'll tell you a story tonight," he said. "A *really scary* one."

Cadie squealed and kicked her legs. Ellen followed. Tara made her way to the bathroom, stepped inside, and shut and locked the door. She leaned against it for a second, relishing the privacy, realizing she hadn't been alone since early that morning.

She looked around the small room, noting it was stripped bare, save for the roll of toilet paper, a soap dispenser, and a hand towel. Even the shower curtain was gone, leaving her no alternative but to clean up as best she could without a shower. Leaning forward over the sink, she turned on the water and began washing her face, freeing her skin from the excess of makeup she'd applied that morning. She had more foundation, eye shadow, mascara, and lipstick in her purse as well, so she could reapply everything in the morning—just before she caught a plane to Denver.

The water was soothing, and as her foundation washed away, Tara felt a little of her stress leave as well. She certainly wasn't at a Boulder spa as she'd planned, but she also wasn't stuck at the airport. A little sleep, a few more phone calls, and by this time tomorrow her side trip to Utah would be a quickly fading memory.

She took out her toothbrush and toothpaste and cleaned her teeth then found her hairbrush and began brushing out the self-induced ratting she'd done earlier. Mid-stroke she looked down at the flannel piled on the toilet lid. *At least I'll be warm.* With that thought, she changed her clothes quickly, slipping the nightgown over her head.

Once on, it billowed out around her, the pattern of tiny red hearts and blue flowers trailing in lines to mid-calf. The gown was probably supposed to be longer, but she had a good couple of inches on Ellen. The eyelet-edged sleeves were a little short as well. Tara stared at her reflection in the mirror, feeling like she was ten again.

"Gertrude's Mystery," she muttered, thinking of her friend Jane Warner—now Jane Bryant—for the second time that day. Tara pulled the brush through her tangled hair again and remembered those nights she'd spent at Jane's house—some more frequent than others, depending upon who she was dating at the time—when she'd often teased Jane about her flannel nightgowns.

"You'll never catch a man wearing that sort of thing," Tara had said on more than one occasion. "Where do you find those gowns, anyway? In the granny section of the store, beside the big panties?"

"Stop." Jane threw a pillow at Tara. "Be nice, or I won't let you sleep here."

"Sure you will," Tara said. "Because you *are* nice and sweet and— everything else that sort of sleeping attire implies."

"What do you mean by that?" Jane asked, frowning at her.

"I mean you're innocent—like a sweet little girl. Problem is, guys aren't looking for sweet. They're after spicy. Look how well Victoria's Secret does."

"That may be so," Jane said. "But I'm not a Victoria's Secret kind of girl, so why would I want to attract a guy who's after that?"

"Because *all* guys are after that." Tara had sat on the edge of the bed and leaned forward, earnestly wanting her poor, misinformed friend to understand *Guys 101*, which she'd so obviously missed in high school.

"And when they get that thing they're after," Jane mused, one hand on her chin, deep in thought. "That leaves you . . . here. Spending the night at my house, because you don't want to be around the guy because he doesn't treat you right. Nuh-uh." She shook her head. "No thank you to that plan. I'm more of a—" She paused then spun around, her flannel nightgown twirling with her. "*Gertrude's Mystery* kind of girl. The guy I choose is going to have to marry me before he sees what's beneath this flannel."

"Won't happen," Tara had predicted.

But it had.

Tara stopped brushing and studied her reflection in the bath-room mirror. Four years had passed since Jane's wedding. Grandma nightgowns notwithstanding, Jane had married a great guy, and she'd married him on her terms, keeping her standards.

A knocking on the bathroom door made her jump and pulled her from the memory. Tara opened the door. Instead of Ellen, Ben stood there, a towel and washcloth in his outstretched hand. He stared at her for a few seconds before speaking.

"Ellen said to tell you that you're welcome to use her bathroom since there isn't a shower curtain in here anymore."

Tara took the towel and washcloth from him. "Thanks. It would be nice to shower in the morning. I'm too tired now."

He nodded. "I understand."

Tara held the towel to her chest, waiting for him to leave.

Several awkward seconds passed, and Tara wondered if she'd missed something when Ben finally said, "Night, then."

"Good night," she said, closing the door softly as he turned to go. Despite her tiredness and the less-than-stellar impression he'd made, a slow smile formed on her lips. She glanced down at the flannel gown, swishing it back and forth.

Gertrude's Mystery indeed. Maybe there's something to Jane's logic, after all.

Because Ben Whitmore had just noticed her more in the last two minutes than he had the entire evening.

* * *

Tara rolled on her side and was surprised when her arm flopped over the side of the couch. With a California king all to herself, that almost never happened. *But I'm not* in *my bed.* Hearing the sounds of shrieking children nearby, she opened one eye, and it didn't take long for her to remember where she was—and *wasn't.*

With a silent groan, Tara flung her arm across her face. Soft flannel partially covered her eyes but not before she noticed Ben and Cadie tiptoeing behind the sofa.

"Shh." Ben held a finger to his lips, motioning for Cadie to be quiet.

"Is the grumpy lady still asleep?" Cadie asked.

"Yes," Ben said. "And we don't want her to be more grumpy, so let's be very quiet. Show me where your shoes are, and you can come with me to pick up the truck."

Grumpy lady. Ha! You haven't seen anything yet. Tara could tell by the gray light filtering through the half-closed blinds that it was still very early. And *early* she did not do—at least not without a strong cup of coffee laced with a little morning pick-me-up. Here in good old Utah, it wasn't likely she'd be getting either.

I'll show you grumpy. And who wouldn't be, being woken at this insane hour? She moved her arm so she could get a better peek at Ben. Today he wore a different plaid shirt, this one more faded than yesterday's. And even worse—the shirt was tucked into a pair of denim bib overalls. *Overalls!* Hadn't the fashion police outlawed those at least a few decades ago? "Yesterday a lumberjack, today a farmer."

"What was that?" Ben stopped mid-stride and looked back at her.

Oops. Didn't mean to say that out loud. A second ago she'd been ready for a fight, but suddenly she wasn't so sure. She was used to saying what she thought and not worrying about it, but maybe— here—that wasn't the best way to proceed. She leaned up on one elbow. "I was just noticing your overalls."

"Do you like them?" Ben came around to the front of the couch, thumbs hooked under his straps, as if he were proud of his attire.

"Sure. If you're headed out to milk cows or something." That wouldn't have surprised her all that much. She'd discovered last night that this family had a menagerie of pets—two dogs, one bunny, a hermit crab, and a tank of goldfish.

"I suppose fuchsia leopard print is more in fashion," Ben said wryly.

"Where I'm from, yes." Resigned to the fact that her opportunity for sleep was past, she swung her legs over the side of the sofa and sat up.

"And that would be . . . working as an exotic dancer somewhere?"

"No." Tara stood and met his bemused gaze with her own furious one. "That was rude."

"It was." The smile he'd been trying to contain faded. "What you said was rude too. But my mother taught me better. I apologize."

"A farmer with manners," Tara said sarcastically. "How refreshing."

"A big city girl with none, how unusual."

"I got my shoes. Can we go now?" Cadie skipped between them.

Didn't they ever teach that kid to walk? Tara noticed the little girl's shoes were on the wrong feet and tied rather strangely.

"Sure," Ben said. "Just as soon as I milk my cows."

"Ooooh. You have cows on your farm?" Cadie beamed. "Uncle Benji had a farm, ee-i, ee-i-oh. And on this farm he had some cows. Ee-i, ee-i-oh."

"I don't really have cows, Cadie."

Well that's a relief. Might have been bad if he really was a farmer. Even as the thought came, Tara wondered why it would have mattered. After today she was never going to see this guy again. If she'd offended him . . . well, he seemed plenty capable of dishing out insults himself.

"Come here, Cadie. Let's fix those shoes before you trip and fall." Ben knelt and opened his arms to the little girl. She stopped in front of him and stuck one foot out.

"If you don't have cows or horses or unicorns on your farm, what *do* you have?"

"Well . . ." Ben switched her shoes to the correct feet and glanced up, meeting Tara's gaze. She turned away, irritated he'd caught her listening.

He finished tying Cadie's shoes and stood slowly. "Pigs." He stared at Tara with a severe look that dared her to say anything negative—anything at all.

"I have pigs—on my farm."

Six

BEN FLIPPED THE PIANO BENCH upside down and stacked it on top of the piano in its spot in the moving van then headed back to the house for more boxes. Ellen passed him on the way, followed by two men from her ward, each laden with a box or two.

"That's the last of the furniture," he called to her.

"Great. Thanks, Ben." Ellen walked up the ramp, and Ben entered the house through the open garage door. He passed through the kitchen, where Tara paced back and forth, one hand pressed to her ear while the other held the phone.

"You don't have *any* idea when it will reopen?"

Ben pressed his lips together to keep from chuckling until he'd left the kitchen. He wasn't sure why, but Tara was really starting to amuse him. He knew it was wrong—*so wrong, Benji*, his mother would have said—to have fun at another's expense, but he couldn't seem to help himself. The woman was simply so . . . bossy, arrogant, and needy. And none of her many needs were being met at the moment. *Probably for the first time in her life.* For some reason it did him good to see her brought down a notch. Too bad he wasn't going to be around long enough to see the end result.

After the shock last night of seeing her without a pound of makeup, with a normal hairdo, and wearing something besides her ridiculously flashy clothes, he'd begun to think that maybe there was a regular person in there. But, nope, he'd been wrong. The Wicked Witch of the West whom he'd accidentally woken that morning showed no signs of normal human behavior. And when she'd discovered that Cadie had gone through her purse and gotten into her makeup . . . *whoa*. Tara's true colors had come out, along with her dagger fingernails. The way she'd twisted up her lips and squinted her eyes had scared even him, and it had sent Cadie bawling to her room. All over a lipstick or something.

Ben retrieved a box from the stack in the hall and retraced his steps through the kitchen.

Tara was still on the phone, really giving it to the person on the other end.

"You expect me to believe you don't know your supervisor's name? Do you even know your own name? What kind of—"

He had one foot on the garage step when her verbal tirade turned serious, unleashing profanity that made his face red—with anger. He could only imagine what it would do to Sam and Cadie—watching a DVD in the next room—if they overheard it.

Pivoting around, he walked across the kitchen and placed the box on the counter. Leaning across the sink, he grabbed the phone cord and yanked it from the wall. Tara, facing away from him, did not immediately realize her call had been disconnected. She continued to berate the airport employee another ten seconds before pausing then holding the phone away from her ear and frantically pushing buttons.

"Great. I lost the call."

"What you *lost* is your temper." Ben picked up the box again.

Tara whirled to face him. "Excuse me?"

"Those kids in the other room don't need to hear your potty mouth."

"My *what*?"

"You heard me," Ben said. "The toilet around here is cleaner than your language. I don't appreciate the profanity and neither would my sister who's been very generous with you."

Tara planted one hand on her hip and gave him a completely unapologetic stare. "I'm sorry if Miss Jump-on-the-furniture-and-steal-my-makeup overheard me, but sometimes swearing is the only way to get through to people. The guy at the airline wasn't getting it."

Ben shook his head in disbelief. "I think you're the one who doesn't get it. Haven't you ever heard the saying about catching more flies with honey than vinegar?"

"I'm not after flies. It's a *flight* I need—right out of this godforsaken place."

"Of all the many places God might be inclined to forsake, I'm pretty certain Bountiful, Utah, isn't at the top of the list. Now LA, on the other hand . . ."

"Don't start," Tara held her hand out, palm facing him. "Just because I don't live on a farm."

"This isn't about where anyone lives." Ben took two steps closer to her so that the box he held was the only thing separating them. He lowered his voice. "This is about those kids in the other room and my sister who's been so kind to you. You don't deserve her kindness, and if you expect it to continue, you'd better watch your language. Either that or get out."

Ben turned to leave the room and ran straight into Ellen, just coming in from the garage.

"Benji! What do you mean by telling our guest to get out?" Ellen looked from Ben to Tara, whose face was a mask of shock.

"She—" Ben started, but Tara cut him off.

"It's my fault," she said to Ellen. "He didn't do anything. It's me. I'm sorry." Blinking back tears, she pushed past him, headed for the family room.

Ellen started after her, but Ben put a hand on her arm, holding her back. "She's fine. Let her be. You've got a houseful of boxes to load."

"What happened?" Ellen said.

"Nothing worth rehashing. C'mon." He handed his box to Ellen and went to the hall for another one. A few minutes earlier and he would have gladly tattled on Tara, no doubt scandalizing his sister, who hadn't heard words like that in a very long time.

But—as she had last night—Tara had surprised him. She'd apologized—sort of. And he could have sworn there were tears in her eyes as she walked past him. He'd have never pegged her for a crier. Or, if he had, he'd have bet she'd use those tears to her advantage. But she hadn't . . . at least not yet. Still, her apology unsettled him more than the profanity he'd heard come from her mouth in the first place.

He was surprised and, against his better judgment, intrigued.

* * *

By late afternoon Tara had given up on getting a flight to Denver anytime soon. The airport was still officially closed as the snowstorm continued, and she'd been told that when it did reopen, there were so many flights that had been canceled, and so many people stranded, that there was no guarantee she would be able to get on a flight for another day or two. As she poured sodas and set out pizza slices for those who'd come to help Ellen move, Tara mulled over the idea of renting a car. She could take a couple of days to drive home, maybe stop in Vegas on the way, and forget the whole doomed Boulder spa plan.

When she really thought about it, she didn't feel all that sad at missing the trip. The whole point had been to avoid being alone for Christmas, which she could do just as easily if she timed her driving so she was in Las Vegas for the holiday. The thought of being surrounded by slot machines on Christmas Day was depressing, though not as depressing as being alone in her condo. She wondered what the chances were that she might meet someone in Vegas. Someone decent enough to spend Christmas Day with, anyway. She let out a weary sigh just as Ben and Ellen came into the kitchen.

Ben grabbed a slice of pizza and lifted it toward his mouth.

"We haven't prayed yet," Ellen said.

He stopped, the pizza millimeters from his mouth. "Sorry."

Tara watched, both amused and surprised that he let his sister boss him around like that. At the least she expected him to roll his eyes, but instead he set the pizza on a paper plate and folded his arms, waiting as the rest of the helpers filed into the kitchen. When everyone had gathered around the island, they bowed their heads. Tara closed her eyes briefly as Ellen started praying.

During the prayer Tara peeked, checking out the crowd—mostly guys—surrounding her. They all appeared to be middle-aged and not in particularly great shape. She'd noted earlier that most had rings on their fingers, not that it would have mattered if they didn't. Honestly the only one who seemed to have any potential in the whole group was Ben. And since his earlier announcement that he was a pig farmer, that potential had washed right down the drain.

When the prayer ended, she slipped from the kitchen, away from the sweaty, hungry swarm attacking the pizza. She walked to the far end of the family room, near the fireplace radiating warmth into the now-empty space. Standing at the picture window, she looked at the mountains that rose up steeply behind the house, practically in the backyard.

Snowflakes fell, adding to the layer of white already on the ground and providing a stark contrast to the brown, rocky mountain.

Ben was right, she thought. Even with her dislike of snow, she had to admit this place was beautiful, not a place God had forsaken.

Maybe Ben was right about LA, too. Or me, at least. "Forsaken" certainly described the way she felt right now. Christmas was two days away, and not only was she stranded here, but there was no one who even cared—or knew, for that matter. The girls in Boulder hadn't returned her call, and she doubted they would. Her mother probably wouldn't call over the holiday at all, using the excuse of poor reception or the expense of calling from the ship. Her father—wherever and whoever he was—wouldn't be searching for her either. Though that had been her fondest wish each and every Christmas since she could remember.

Tears stung the back of her eyes again, and Tara angrily blinked them away. What had Ben started, scolding her like that, making her cry? She hadn't cried in a long time—not since she'd moved from Seattle. She'd left both the rain and her tendency toward tears behind, vowing that LA would bring more sunshine to her life, both literally and in her relationships. Too bad she hadn't figured on the smog.

A lone tear trickled down her cheek, but she didn't bother to wipe it away since she wasn't wearing any makeup. Cadie had all but destroyed her mascara, giving it to the dog to chew on. Her foundation and lipstick hadn't fared any better. Ellen hadn't been much help, offering only a new tube of Chapstick as replacement.

Chapstick, flannel, kids, and overalls . . . only in Utah. Maybe someday she would laugh about this, but right now none of it seemed remotely amusing. Breathing in deeply, she tried to pull herself together and began mentally practicing the request that she was going to have to make. She hadn't been able to get her credit cards replaced yet, nor had she been successful in getting money wired from her credit union. And with tomorrow being Christmas Eve, she didn't imagine her luck would change. Which left her having to ask Ellen or Ben for enough money to get a hotel tonight and a rental car home. She'd worry about money for Vegas later. Somehow she just knew Farmer Ben wouldn't be on board with that plan.

"It's not looking good, Sis."

Speak of the devil. Tara kept her position facing the window as Ben's voice, followed by Ellen's, drifted from the kitchen.

"Oh, where's your faith, Benji?" Ellen's voice was light, but even this far away, Tara could detect a stressed undertone.

"Where's your common sense?" Ben retorted. "Colorado's one giant blizzard right now, and you expect me to drive a woman and her children right into the middle of it?"

"You're exaggerating," Ellen said. "The blizzard is in Denver, and I'm sure it will be cleared up by the time we get there."

"Portions of the highway have been closed."

"They have. *East* of Denver." Ellen sounded defensive now. "I've been checking too, you know."

But Ben wasn't backing down. "If we had another guy, El, but we don't. How do you think Dallin would feel if I let something happen to his family?"

Ellen let out a frustrated groan. "Is that what this is about? You're still worried what Dallin thinks of you, how he sees you?"

A lengthy silence met this remark, and Tara dearly wished she could see their faces. After a good minute had passed, Ben spoke again.

"I'm worried about getting my sister and her children safely over the Rocky Mountains. And with the weather the way it is right now, it seems mighty foolish to attempt such a thing with a moving truck and a minivan. If we get stranded—even if we just need to put chains on, I wouldn't have anyone to help me. You'd need to stay in the van to take care of the kids."

"But it's Christmas. Dallin can't be without his family on Christmas. And would you have Cadie and Sam and Chloe spend it away from their dad? Here, in this empty house?"

Tara heard Ben's sigh and tried to decipher if it was one of frustration or defeat. "If we had another adult . . ."

"Well, we don't. And no one's going to want to join us on a road trip the day before Christmas. I mean they'd have to be going to Denver themselves, and where are we going to find—hey, what about Tara?"

Tara's head snapped up at Ellen's suggestion.

"She was headed to Colorado, anyway, and the airport still hasn't reopened. Maybe she'd be willing—"

"Have you lost your mind?" Ben let out a sound that was half-laugh, half-choking. "'Cause I'd sure lose mine, being in a car with her all day."

That'd be because you don't have much mind to lose. Tara's earlier melancholy disintegrated in a burst of anger. *Like I'd want to go with you, anyway.*

"You wouldn't have to ride with her," Ellen said. "She could come in the van to help me with the kids."

"Lot of help that would be," Ben said sarcastically.

He's got a point, Tara admitted to herself. She had no desire and no clue how to play nanny to a bunch of kids confined in a car. *But how hard could it be? And it would get me to Denver.* The possibility of still making the spa trip tempted her. At least she'd be with people she knew for the holiday. In Vegas it'd be up to her to find someone. And that would take energy and effort. Effort she didn't feel like putting forth right now.

"You're not being fair—or nice," Ellen said.

And you're just figuring this out? Tara turned away from the window, heading toward the kitchen, intending to join them. Ben's disparaging comments aside, she decided the idea was worth discussing.

"I'm being completely fair," Ben said. "I should have said, 'If we had another *man* to come with us.' Because if we hit a storm, I'm the one who'll end up needing help. And I'm pretty darn sure that woman couldn't change a tire to save her life."

It was the nudge she needed to make up her mind.

"Actually," Tara said, smiling sweetly as she stood in the wide doorway between the family room and the kitchen, "I can."

Seven

"Have fun," Ellen called, waving from the front step.

Fun. Oh yeah, shopping with Farmer Ben should be real fun. Tara picked her way down the icy driveway. She'd hinted to Ben that he might want to change his overalls before going out, but his only response had been a rude comment about *her* attire.

"I can't believe I'm doing this." Ben didn't bother to hide his irritation as he climbed into the van and started the engine.

"That makes two of us," Tara said, getting in on her side. *But I'm desperate, and hitching a ride with you will get me to the girlfriends in time for Christmas.* But she couldn't hitch a ride dressed as she was now. If she was freezing here in the city, traveling through the mountains might literally kill her—or give her frostbite on her legs, anyway. She reached for the seat belt, buckling herself into the front passenger seat of Ellen's minivan as Ben backed it out the driveway.

He drove in silence and a little too fast, winding his way through holiday traffic to the nearest mall. Privately, Tara was impressed with his skill. He could have held his own during rush hour in LA. Not bad, considering he probably spent most of his time driving a tractor.

A few minutes later she lurched forward then back as the van came to an abrupt halt in front of Sears. Her heart sank. She couldn't remember ever having shopped at Sears, but she was pretty certain they were known for things like drills, saws, and riding lawnmowers.

"You want me to wear a tool belt?" She wasn't trying to be funny.

"They sell clothes here," Ben said.

Eying his plaid shirt, she imagined just the kind of clothing he was talking about. Turning around in her seat, she searched the store names on the building, hoping against hope there was a Saks or Nordstrom nearby—or at least a Macy's.

"I'll be back in an hour." Ben pulled out his wallet and thumbed through it, taking out the few bills inside. "Here's forty-seven dollars." He slapped the cash into her hand. "I'll meet you here at 7:30."

She stared at the money. *He's kidding, right?* "*One* hour? *Forty-seven* dollars?" *And Sears?* she wanted to add but didn't. "You can't be serious."

Ben gave her a look that said he was. "Fifty-nine minutes," he said, glancing at the dashboard clock. "I've still got to help Ellen with some things, and I want to get to bed early. We have a long drive tomorrow."

Tara shook her head. "I'm sorry, but what you're asking is impossible. Do you know nothing about shopping? First of all, look at this parking lot. The line at the register is going to be a half hour by itself."

"Better choose your clothes fast, then," Ben said unsympathetically. He rolled down the driver's side window, waving another car around them. "I'm blocking traffic, and you're wasting time."

Tara didn't budge. "When was the last time you set foot inside a mall?" she demanded. "I'll be doing good to get socks and underwear for forty-seven bucks. There's absolutely no way I'll be able to get jeans and a sweater too."

"At Sears you can." Ben's forehead wrinkled, and he pressed his lips together as the driver behind them honked. "And if by chance I'm mistaken, then I suggest you get long johns. Now are you going to get out or not?"

"Not." Tara folded her arms across her chest. "I know you think I'm being difficult, but you really don't understand."

"You're right. You're extremely difficult—a real pain." Ben drove forward. "And I don't understand how I let my sister talk me into taking you with us. But if she wants to do this so bad, *she* can take you shopping. I'll stay home. Dealing with three cranky kids beats this any day."

Tara felt her anger rising to match his, but she tried to remind herself he was just an ignorant farmer. It was up to her to educate him on the ways of the world—or the way of the mall, at least.

She reached out, placing a hand on his sleeve. "I'm grateful you're taking me shopping. Really, I am. And I know I must seem unappreciative."

"I'll say." Ben turned to look at her then her hand, which she hastily removed from his coat sleeve.

"I'm sure that wherever it is you buy your overalls, they probably don't charge much. But women's clothing is different. A decent pair of jeans, a sweater, socks, shoes—and everything else I'll need for a day or two—is going to cost *at least* $200." *And that's really pushing it.* She couldn't remember the last time she'd purchased an outfit for so little. "I'll repay every penny—with interest, if you'd like. I make good money. In the last quarter alone, I—"

"You don't have to tell me what you make." Ben pulled the van into an empty stall at the far end of the lot.

Right. It'd only hurt your ego. Tara wondered what the average salary for a pig farmer was. If money was really tight for Ben, then this could be a problem. She'd tried talking to Ellen about borrowing a little money for clothes, but every time, one of her needy kids had interrupted.

Ben turned to face Tara. "You're telling me that clothing you wear for one day is going to cost me two hundred dollars?"

"At least," Tara said. "But you'll get your money back. Think of this as a loan."

"It's not the loan part that's bothering me," Ben said. "It's ridiculous that you'd spend so much on jeans and a sweatshirt."

Tara shrugged. "Sorry. But that's the way it is. In the city, things are different. As I said, I'm sure farm country—or wherever it was you got your overalls—isn't the same."

"The place I bought—" Ben paused, then a slow, sly grin lit his face. He turned away, put the car into gear, and drove forward.

"Oh, no," Tara said, alarmed by his sudden smile. "No overalls for me."

"Of course not," Ben said. "You can have your jeans and sweatshirt."

"Sweater," Tara amended. She wasn't about to show up in Boulder wearing fleece.

"Sweater," Ben agreed, turning toward her. "Maybe even cashmere, if you'd like. And we should get you a jacket, too. A nice leather one. Maybe some shoes as well; those heels aren't going to be practical if you end up having to change a tire."

"You're scaring me," Tara said, noting the positively evil glint in Ben's eye, reflected by the stoplight.

"Don't worry." Ben reached out, touching her sleeve as she'd touched his. "I'm grateful you took the time to educate me on what it costs to outfit a woman from LA. And now I'm happy to show you what it cost to outfit my mother here in Utah."

* * *

"One hour. Forty-seven dollars," Ben repeated as he parked in front of a large, white building.

"What is this place?" Tara asked, once again not making any move to get out of the van.

Your first lesson in humility. "It's a great store. Lots of name brands." Ben hopped out of the van and came around to Tara's side. He intended to walk her into the store—partly so he could make sure she didn't slip and fall in her ridiculous shoes and cause him even more trouble, and partly so he could see her reaction when she realized where he'd taken her.

He opened her door and held a hand out.

She continued to look at him suspiciously but allowed him to help her from the car.

"Deseret Industries," she read as they made their way to the building.

"DI for short. You can find anything here."

"I've never heard of it," Tara said. "Must not be a chain."

"Oh, they've got them in Utah, Idaho, Arizona," Ben said. "The Church runs them. People donate their clothing and other items, and the employees are often people who need job training or other support."

"Wait." Tara stared at him. "Did you say *donate*? People *donate* their clothing? Is this a—a *thrift* store?"

"Yep. You'd better get going. Sometimes it takes a while to pick through things here. It isn't every day you come across a real find— like these overalls—right off the bat." Ben nodded toward the store.

"You want me to shop here for—*used*—clothes?"

"The correct term is *secondhand*, and yes, I do. You'll be able to get everything you need for forty-seven dollars. And I expect change when you're done."

Tara was speechless as they continued to walk toward the entrance. Ben was grateful for the slushy parking lot and glad he'd held on to her arm after she got out of the van. It made half-dragging her a little easier. Oh, how he'd love to see her shopping in there. *Why not?* he thought. He'd planned to go to the auto parts store and look at chains for the moving truck while Tara shopped, but they could do that afterward. The opportunity to see Ms. Stuck-up having to shop secondhand was too much to resist.

As soon as they'd made it inside the store, he let go of her and went to get a cart. When he returned a minute later, she stood in the same spot, a dazed look on her face as she took in the racks of merchandise, the shoppers, the cashiers. Her gaze settled on a family with about a half dozen ragged-looking kids. Their cart was piled high with clothing and toys, and the children clamored around their parents excitedly as they made their way to the register.

Tara's eyes followed them through the entire checkout process, right up to the point when the father handed the cashier a commodities form.

So she's not just rude to me, she's just plain rude, Ben thought. *Has no one ever taught her it isn't polite to stare?* He was about to explain it himself when she turned to the right and the women's section. They both stopped short as she caught him watching her, and he caught her once again with misty eyes.

Cry all you want, sweetheart. Those tears won't work on me. "Nothing here is going to bite, you know."

Tara nodded, her lips pressed together as if she didn't trust herself to speak.

Was she really that appalled that it brought her to tears? *Good grief.* He felt more disgusted than ever with the female by his side. It was tempting to steer her toward the ugliest stuff he could find. Heck, she *deserved* overalls. Muck-covered, filthy ones at that.

"What size are you?" he asked, as they reached the first rack of jeans.

"I can find my own clothes," she said, but her voice was shaky.

"I doubt it." He looked her over quickly then began sorting through the racks, throwing things into the cart every so often. Years of back-to-school shopping with his large family had made him a pro. Shopping at DI had always been a group effort. He well remembered finding clothes to fit him, as well as helping to find things for his siblings. And, of course, that help had been reciprocated. *Many hands make light work*, his mom had always said on those trips. Thinking back on those days, he remembered that it hadn't seemed like work at all, but an exciting once-a-year opportunity for "new" clothes, with a trip for store-bought ice cream afterward.

When he had a good ten pairs of jeans for Tara to choose from, he led her to the dressing rooms. "Try these on. I'll go find some sweaters."

Surprisingly, she obeyed, grasping the hangers and going willingly into the tiny room. Ben searched the sweaters nearby, purposely avoiding the especially gaudy ones, though, given the outfit she'd arrived in, the more outlandish things might have been more to her liking. He'd found a brown cardigan and a navy V-neck, when a soft pink pullover caught his eye. He checked it for stains and, seeing none, threw it in the cart and headed back to the dressing rooms. He dropped the sweaters over the door.

"I'm going to look for shoes now. You want to tell me your size for those?"

A weary sigh came from the other side of the door. "Eight and a half. Please tell me you're not going to pick out my panties next."

Ben nearly laughed but caught himself just in time. He pictured Tara leaning her head against the wall, imagining the worst.

"Thanks for reminding me. I'm on it," he said then walked away before he *did* laugh.

The boots were really picked over, and there was nothing remotely close to her size, so he had to settle on a decent, though ugly, pair of sneakers. Before returning to the dressing room, he snuck over to the women's lingerie—just for fun. He hadn't really believed Deseret Industries sold used underwear, but there amid the slips and other articles was a circular rack of some particularly unattractive women's panties. *Gross.* Even he drew the line there. But Tara didn't know that, and the thought of teasing her was too much to resist.

Feeling more than a little embarrassed, Ben made his way around the rack, picking out the ugliest underwear he could find, a sickly green pair that would have easily accommodated two Taras. With a twisted smile, he stuffed them in one of the shoes and handed them under the dressing room door. Less than five seconds later, it flew open, nearly smashing his nose. He jumped out of the way just in time.

"Absolutely not." Tara shoved the underwear at his chest. "Jeans are one thing, but if you think I'm going to put on someone else's—"

Ben burst out laughing. Tara's eyes narrowed as she glared at him. "Is this all a big joke to you? Do you think it's funny I have no clothes to wear, that my wallet was stolen, my credit is in jeopardy? Is it amusing the airport closed and stranded me here? Is it simply *hilarious* that I'm at your complete mercy, with no one else to turn to?" Her voice cracked. "Do you find it hysterical that I'm not only impoverished right now but all alone? Even that family over there—" Her gaze drifted to the registers. "Even they have more than I do. They have each other."

Her eyes were flooding with tears again, but before Ben could say or do anything, she'd pulled the dressing room door shut and locked it.

Sorrrry, he thought. He should have known she couldn't take a joke.

You should be sorry. His mother's voice spoke in his head. *That was mean, Benji. And you're not a mean boy.* The first nigglings of guilt began. *But she annoys the heck out of me.* He knew exactly what his mom would have said to that.

You don't have to make the situation worse. Rise above it; don't stoop to her level. He didn't think it was possible to stoop to whatever level—or planet—Tara was on. He didn't live like her—in some ridiculously fast lane where profanity motivated people and underwear cost forty-seven dollars. But, by his own admission, he hadn't tried to make things easy. If anything, he'd hoped to dissuade her from coming with them tomorrow. It was going to be awkward enough seeing Dallin again tomorrow night, and he didn't need a grumpy female getting on his nerves all day leading up to what was bound to be a stressful reunion.

"I'm sorry," Ben said, after a minute. "I *was* joking. You don't have to wear used underwear. I'll take you someplace else to shop."

"Just go away," Tara said. "Give me my hour like you promised."

Ben stared at the door, feeling bad and wondering if she really wanted him to leave. A second later, when the shoes sailed over the door and hit him on the head, he decided she did.

Eight

ELLEN SAT ON THE FLOOR and ripped open a bag of marshmallows. "Who wants a s'more?" she asked then began placing them in the small hands waving in front of her.

"Me. Me. Me. Me. Me," Sam, her three-year-old, chanted.

Ellen caught Tara's eye. "Would you help him with one?"

Tara shrugged. "Sure." She scooted off her sleeping bag and onto the tarp Ellen had spread in front of the fireplace.

"Bring your marshmallow to Tara, and she'll help you." Ellen's voice was calm, even with all three children and the two dogs clamoring around her.

Tara took a roasting stick from the hearth. "Do you do this often?"

"About once a month in the winter," Ellen said. "The rest of the year we use the fire pit outside. The kids love it." She sighed. "One of the many things we'll miss about this place."

Sam plopped himself in Tara's lap and shoved a marshmallow up near her nose. Tara gasped. "So I see."

"Just don't let him get that close to you once he's eaten one," Ellen warned. "He'll be a big, sticky mess. Remember, kids, you *have* to stay on the tarp. Mommy won't have time to clean up any messes in the morning."

Is she kidding? Tara thought, wondering how they could possibly pull this off without graham cracker crumbs in the carpet, chocolate on the walls, and melted marshmallow goo everywhere. She stabbed Sam's marshmallow onto the stick and held it toward the fireplace, only to have one of the dogs snap the marshmallow off.

Chloe, the eighteen-month-old, laughed hysterically and fell back on the tarp, her diapered bottom landing on the plate of crackers Ellen had just set down. Sam screamed and jumped up to go after the dog.

Ellen reached out, snagging Sam by his pajama bottoms. "Let Coulter have it. We'll get you another one." She handed him two more marshmallows and sent him back to Tara.

Sam stuffed one in his mouth and gave the other to Tara. This time she held the stick out of reach until there was a clear line to the fireplace. Cadie, her cheeks puffed out like a chipmunk's, hopped around the perimeter of the tarp.

"How many marshmallows do you have in there?" Ellen asked, reaching out to pat Cadie's puffy cheeks.

"Four." Cadie opened her mouth to show her mother the sticky balls of white stuffed inside. Tara looked away, disgusted.

Chloe still half sat on the graham crackers and was doing her best to get the chocolate bars out of their wrappers.

"No more," Ellen said, sounding amused. She took the chocolate and marshmallows and put them on the mantel.

Sam sat beside Tara, his eyes large as he watched the flames. Tara found herself mesmerized by them too. All in all, she had to admit this was a cozy little gathering. Ben was outside getting the truck ready for tomorrow, so she didn't have to deal with him. And the kids were quieter right now with their mouths full of chocolate and marshmallow and their eyes drooping with sleep.

When she'd fixed two s'mores for Sam and he'd toddled off to brush his teeth, Tara roasted a marshmallow for herself and enjoyed a treat she hadn't had in years—if ever. She really couldn't remember. Camping hadn't exactly been her mother's thing.

"Hey, did ya save any for me?" Ben asked, coming in through the front door, stamping snow off his boots.

"There's plenty," Ellen said. "With Dallin not here, we haven't even used half a bag."

"I miss Daddy," Cadie said, returning from the bathroom with Sam.

"We'll see him tomorrow." Happiness lit Ellen's face.

"Yep." Ben didn't seem as enthused. "With a little luck and prayer. The chains I bought will fit the truck tires. If we don't have to use them, we'll just return them in Denver." He walked toward the fire, and Tara stiffened and looked away. But she needn't have worried about another confrontation. Ben seemed equally eager to avoid her and sidestepped so as not to come anywhere near.

They'd barely spoken since the DI incident, though he had taken her to Target so she could purchase new underwear, socks—and a tube of mascara, which she hadn't mentioned to him.

Cadie plopped down in front of her mom. "I want to see Daddy now. I want him to come *here*. I don't want to go to Denver. I don't want to move." Her voice grew whinier with each statement. Over her head, Ben and Ellen exchanged concerned looks.

Ellen stood and took Cadie's hand, leading her to one of the sleeping bags spread in a circle around the family room. "You're tired, sweetheart. Let's tuck you in bed."

"This isn't my bed." Cadie folded her arms across her chest and pushed her lip out.

Tara finished the last of her s'more as she observed the drama from the sidelines.

"I don't want to sleep here. I want to sleep in my room. I want my things back. I—"

"Shhh." Ellen pressed a finger to her lips then used her hand to smooth away the hair from Cadie's forehead. "We talked about this, sweetheart. I know it's hard. But it's what we needed to do. And tomorrow we'll be with Daddy again. We'll be in our new house. And all your things will be there."

Instead of responding positively to her mother's soothing words, Cadie reacted with anger, trying to hit and kick her mom while alternately sobbing and yelling.

Tara looked on, her decision to never have any children solidified. But Ben did more than watch. He strode forward and plucked Cadie right from the floor and her temper tantrum.

He carried her across the room to the bar separating the family room and kitchen. Setting her down on the high counter, he leaned forward, one hand on either side of the hysterical child.

"Cadie." His voice was firm. "Stop crying and look at me."

She shook her head.

He straightened and backed up, as if ready to walk away. Cadie's response was immediate, her slender arms reaching out to him. But

Ben didn't move any closer. Tara watched, wondering what he'd do next. For the second time that evening, she found herself captivated by family drama.

At the store earlier, she'd been baffled by the attitude of the family as they made their simple purchases. The children had been happy and excited—grateful, even, as she'd heard several thank-yous as they watched the cashier ring up their toys and clothes. The parents had seemed happy too, though how they could be—living in such destitute circumstances that they had to shop at a place like that—was beyond her.

It had been such an odd moment, an odd experience—unfathomable a few days ago. But there she'd been, Tara Mollagen, in a thrift store in Utah, watching a poor family and being struck with the realization that they were *happy*. While she was not. She wasn't even just *un*happy. She was miserable. It had been enough to bring tears to her eyes—again.

She'd tried to figure out why, to get a grip and decipher what was wrong with her, as she tried on jeans alone in the dressing room. And the realization she'd come to had hit painfully. She wasn't sad because she was buying used jeans—though that certainly didn't make her list of great experiences. Nor was she miserable because she was in Utah—though that wasn't great either. She was depressed because her life was disappointing. Because nothing ever changed. Because she did the same things year after year after year, and no one ever noticed or cared. None of it mattered.

I don't matter . . . to anyone.

I *don't matter to anyone.* The sentiment repeated itself in her mind as she watched Ben and Cadie. The little girl obviously mattered to him—or Ellen did at least, as he was taking the time to help out with her daughter. But Tara sensed it went beyond that and that he really did care about his niece, a six-year-old whom he saw infrequently.

He wasn't her father, and Tara wondered if he should have even interfered. She glanced at Ellen and saw that she'd moved on to tucking in her two younger children. She didn't appear to mind Ben's assistance. Tara swung her gaze back around to Ben and Cadie, who was now sniffling.

He stepped closer to her, speaking in a quiet tone. Tara strained to hear what he was saying. *Sure. Talk all nice to the bratty kid. But when you were talking to me earlier . . .*

"Here's the thing, Cadie," he said. "Do you have a mom?"

She nodded.

"Does she love you?"

Nod.

"Lots?"

Bigger nod.

"And do you have a dad who loves you lots too?" Ben took another step toward her.

"Yes." Cadie's voice trembled.

"That's right," Ben said. "And you have a brother and sister who love you. And two dogs, and a bunny."

"And a crab and fish," Cadie added, starting to perk up a bit.

"I'm sure they love you too," Ben said. "And they're all traveling with you to Denver. And you'll have a great house and meet new friends. Cadie—" He leaned close, his eyes level with hers. "You have a *great* life. You have all those people and animals who love you, plus you know who loves you most of all—don't you?"

"Heavenly Father and Jesus." Her immediate answer surprised Tara.

Why would anyone teach their kid that some unseen being loves her more than her own parents?

Ben picked her up. "You're a smart cookie."

She giggled. "I'm not a cookie."

He sniffed her hair. "Nope. You aren't." He carried her over to her sleeping bag. "But you *are* a princess, a real daughter of God. Here and in Denver."

You tell her that now and when she grows up and realizes she's just a regular person, you're going to have trouble. Tara shifted uncomfortably and averted her gaze as they drew closer.

Ben set Cadie beside her sleeping bag then unzipped the side and helped her climb in.

"Heavenly Father knows you and loves you, Cadie. He'll help you. He's always here, even when your dad isn't."

Oh, please. Tara rolled her eyes.

"I know Heavenly Father loves me," Cadie said matter-of-factly, a grin on her face as she reached up to pat Ben's cheeks.

"That makes you much more blessed than a lot of people, than your mother and I were at your age." Ben bent over, placing a kiss on her forehead. "You have it all." He leaned back, still on his knees beside her. "And you ought to thank your lucky stars."

Nine

ELLEN SLID THE VAN DOOR shut, partially drowning out the sound of her crying toddler. "It's your choice," she said, giving Tara an apologetic smile. "You can come with me and Sam and the dogs and the bunny and the fish and the screaming baby—or you can ride with Cadie, the hermit crab, and my insensitive brother."

Tara stared, bleary-eyed, through the van window. "Some choice," she said, though she couldn't help but return Ellen's smile. Ellen was a genuinely nice person. *Too bad for her, she's surrounded by the rest of us.* Tara included herself on the list of those who were likely a pain for Ellen. After yesterday's disastrous shopping trip, Ellen had played referee between her and Ben the remainder of the evening, providing a nice buffer during the stilted conversations and awkward silences. Fortunately, Ellen had taken Tara's side and given Ben a good scolding for taking her shopping at a thrift store.

"How long do you think she'll cry like that?" Tara asked, peering at the little girl pulling at her car seat straps and screaming her lungs out.

"Chloe's record is two hours, eleven minutes. She hates the car—a lot of eighteen-month-olds do. But she's also cutting two molars right now, so it could be longer. I'm thinking I need to look up crying in Guinness and see if I might have a world record contender on my hands."

Tara wondered how Ellen could be so lighthearted when looking forward to two or more hours with a screaming child. She knew she certainly couldn't. She couldn't handle much of anything right now, tired as she was. For the second night in a row she'd had virtually no sleep. A screaming kid would drive her nuts.

"In that case, I guess I'm going to have to choose the truck and Ben. I'm not very good with little kids." *Any kids.* The thought of sitting beside Cadie wasn't appealing either.

"Good luck," Ellen said. With a farewell wave, she walked around to the driver's side and climbed into the van. Tara turned toward the truck. Ben's gaze met hers through the windshield as she looked up. He was obviously wishing she'd chosen to drive with Ellen.

I know—how about Ben takes all the kids and pets in the van, and Ellen and I drive the truck? It was a brilliant thought and made Tara smile for a half-second before she realized Ellen would never go for it. She was the kindest, most attentive mother Tara had ever seen, and even if her children were jumping on the furniture, covered head-to-toe with marshmallow and chocolate, or screaming, Ellen still seemed to want to be close to them.

Reaching up, Tara grabbed the handle of the passenger door and hoisted herself into the truck.

"*You're* coming?" The dismay in Cadie's voice echoed what they all felt.

"Yep," Tara said as she settled in next to Cadie's booster seat. "And I'm planning to sleep." *So don't bother me,* she added with a look. She put her purse on the floor beside the hermit crab's cage and reached for her seat belt. The truck had good-sized windows, and with the cold air seeping through them, she'd probably be okay. As long as she could see out and get air.

She buckled the seat belt over the pink sweater Ben had picked out the previous evening. That he'd chosen a decent pair of jeans and a nice sweater for her should have earned him some points, but for some reason it had made her more irritated. Farmer Boy wasn't supposed to be right about things—especially finding cheap women's clothing.

Last night's incident with Cadie had bothered Tara too. Ben had handled the situation perfectly, as though he had a dozen kids of his own. It irked Tara to see him so kind to the whiney little girl when he'd been so curt with her yesterday. And that bit he'd said to Cadie about thanking her lucky stars. What, was Ben the male Pollyanna or something? She'd never met a guy like him before, and she still couldn't quite believe he really was as he appeared to be. He was so different—unusual—weird.

Fascinating. And she did *not* want to be fascinated by a pig farmer.

Less than ten hours, and you'll never have to see him again. That brought a smile to her lips. *This nightmare's almost over.*

Ben started up the truck, and they were off. Cadie leaned over Tara, straining for a last look at her home.

"It'll be okay, kiddo," Ben said kindly. "Knowing your dad, he's picked out a really cool house for you in Denver."

Cadie just nodded and swallowed, doing her best to hold in despair. Tears filled her eyes, and her lips were pressed tightly together, as if she were holding back a sob or scream. Tara could relate. She'd been doing a bit of that herself the past few days.

* * *

"Will you paint my nails?" Cadie asked, her face about an inch from Tara's.

Tara opened her eyes and blinked then leaned back so she could focus. *What's the kid doing, getting in my space like that?* She shook her head. "No. Can't you see I'm sleeping?" She edged toward the door, as far away from Cadie as possible.

"But yesterday I saw nail polish in your purse. It was purple. I like purple. Please?"

"No." Tara shut her eyes, hoping that was the end of it.

"Will you paint my nails, Uncle Ben?"

"Can't. I've got to drive. Why don't you take a nap, and maybe when you wake up, we'll be there."

"How long have we been driving?" Tara sat up and looked hopefully at her surroundings.

Ben chuckled. "Forty minutes."

She frowned at him. "That's not funny. And why do grown-ups tell kids things like that anyway? It's mean. Like she'll really sleep for eight hours."

"Like you can't share a little of your purple nail polish?" Ben glanced over, arching an eyebrow.

Tara frowned. "It'll make the truck smell."

"Doesn't bother me," Ben said. "I'm used to bad smells—living on a farm and all." He grinned.

"Please?" Cadie said again. "You're not sleeping now."

"That's because your uncle tricked me."

"Not on purpose," Ben said.

Cadie tilted her face, leaning close to Tara once more. "Please."

"Fine." Tara bent down to get her purse. She found the polish quickly—with her wallet and makeup gone, there wasn't much left in her purse to search through. "Let me see your hands."

She held out a set of stubby, chewed nails.

Tara grimaced. "Not much there to paint."

"Shouldn't take long then," Ben said.

He was right. It took less than two minutes for Tara to paint Cadie's *nails*, though it was a stretch to call them that. When she was finished, Cadie held her hands out, admiring them.

"They're pretty. Thank you."

"You're welcome," Tara said, surprised at the little girl's sudden courtesy. "Hold your hands very still for a few minutes or you'll smear the polish—and I *won't* paint your nails again." She put the bottle back in her purse and leaned her head against the window, intending to go back to sleep. She'd scarcely had the thought when Cadie tapped her on the shoulder with one of her still-wet fingers.

Tara cracked an eyelid, checking her sweater for polish. "What did I just tell you?"

"I'm sorry I used your makeup on the dogs and bunny." The little girl's face was solemn.

"The *bunny*? Didn't hear about that one," Tara said.

"Mommy said not to tell you or you'd yell again."

From the corner of her eye, Tara saw Ben biting his lip, likely trying to repress a smile. Yesterday she'd been right to yell at him for being amused by her misfortunes.

"Snowball needed some lipstick," Cadie continued. "She's all white like Snow White, so she needed blood-red lips to make her prettier."

The laugh Ben had been trying to hold back escaped in a kind of a coughing bark. "Glad you didn't go for real blood there."

"I'm going to try for a real *nap* here, so if you don't mind . . ." Tara leaned her head against the window once more. One thing she'd learned for sure on this trip—kids were even weirder than she'd thought.

Trying to forget about the one a foot away from her, Tara pulled one knee to her chest and leaned against the door. The cab was warm, but the window felt cold against her head. The contrasting temperatures only added to her drowsiness.

Cadie poked her again.

Tara didn't open her eyes. "What now?"

"I apologized, so you're supposed to forgive me."

"What if I don't want to?"

"But you have to if you want other people to forgive *you*." Cadie sounded worried.

Where does the kid come up with this stuff? "Maybe I don't need anyone to forgive me."

"Uncle Ben needs to forgive you," Cadie said. "He was mad last night, and I heard him tell Mommy that you're the most 'noying woman he's ever met."

"Cadie," Ben said sharply.

She continued as though she hadn't heard him. "And Mommy said it was his fault for letting you get under his skin. But I don't know what she meant by that. It sounds gross." Cadie pulled at the skin on her hand, as if trying to see how one might get beneath it.

"What else did you hear Uncle Ben say?" Tara asked, fixing a look on the subject of their conversation, his hands gripping the wheel and red creeping up his face.

"Nothing," he said. "Cadie, I think you should check on your crab."

"Uncle Ben couldn't say anything," Cadie said. "When Mommy's talking mad at you, she doesn't like you to talk back."

"I see," Tara said, a smirk on her face. Oh, what good it did her to see Farmer Boy brought down a notch.

"But Mommy said lots more," Cadie continued, eager to have an attentive audience. "She said Uncle Ben should grow up. That he shouldn't be grumpy with you 'cause he's worried about seeing Daddy."

"That's *enough*, Cadie." Ben put a hand on her leg.

"I want to hear what she has to say." Tara moved Ben's hand and put her arm around Cadie, pulling her closer to her side of the truck.

"Mommy said you don't know any better, so Uncle Ben shouldn't blame you. And she said it's Christmas and we have to be nice to you no matter what."

"No more," Ben said, his voice quieter but just as firm.

This time Tara agreed and pulled her arm away from Cadie's shoulders. Turning to the window, she stared out at the white landscape, retracting her earlier, nice thoughts about Ellen.

I don't know *any better? What—does she think I'm one of her kids or something?*

"It's time for you to take a nap now," Ben said, presumably to Cadie. No one needed to tell Tara to sleep.

A hand tugged at her sleeve. "Will you forgive me?"

Hearing that Ellen didn't really like Tara either hadn't put her in a forgiving mood, but she wanted sleep—or at least to be left alone. She shrugged Cadie's hand off and curled up in her corner of the cab again.

"Sure, kid. Why not."

Ten

TARA STRETCHED AND YAWNED SIMULTANEOUSLY. The yawn turned to a frown as she heard the deep, crooning voice coming from the radio. "What are you listening too?"

"Sinatra." Ben glanced over at her for a second before returning his attention to the mountain road.

"Only reception we can get right now?" she guessed. "Want me to try to find something else?" She reached toward the dashboard radio.

"It's from my iPod."

"Oh." Tara leaned back in her seat. The voice continued . . . *our troubles will be miles away.* "Wouldn't *that* be nice," she said under her breath.

"What?" Ben asked.

"Nothing." She shook her head.

"There's no accounting for taste, huh?"

"I didn't say that."

"But you were thinking it."

She yawned again. "Maybe. Though I'm hardly awake enough to think."

"It's nine forty-five," Ben said. "What time do you usually get up?"

"Not this early. It's only *eight* forty-five in California."

"Seriously, that's early to you?" Ben really couldn't believe it. But then there wasn't much about this woman that was believable.

Tara nodded. "I'm a terrible sleeper, so I get up as late as possible. Which isn't all that late when you don't fall asleep until two or three in the morning."

"Must be some nightlife you have there."

"Now who's jumping to conclusions? I said I don't sleep well, not that I party all night. But I suppose you're awake before the rooster on your farm crows."

"No rooster," Ben said. "But I've got a particularly loud pig that usually wakes me up. And it is often before the sunrise."

Tara shuddered. "Pigs and sunrise. Sounds lovely."

"It is," Ben said. "You ought to try it sometime."

"No thanks." Silence, thick and awkward, followed her comment. Ben wished she'd go back to sleep, but she kept her eyes focused on the road stretching out ahead of them. He supposed there was nothing else to do but apologize—that or endure the uncomfortable feeling between them for the next six or so hours.

"I'm sorry about earlier."

"You're sorry Cadie tattled," Tara said, looking at him over the head of the sleeping child.

"Well, yeah," Ben admitted. "But I'm sorry I said those things about you."

"What things would those be?" Tara asked innocently.

She's really pushing it. He swallowed another dose of humility, though she was the one needing that medicine a whole lot more than he did. "I'm sorry I said you were annoying."

"*The most* annoying, if I recall correctly."

"Yep," Ben said. "Kind of like you're being right now." He threw her a look.

She ignored it. "I guess I'd better forgive you." Tara waved her hand in the air. "Who knows who else I've offended and need to be forgiven by . . . The pizza guy, the dogs, Ellen."

Ben caught the hurt in her voice when she mentioned his sister. "I think you're okay," he said. "Ellen isn't upset with you, and if you did anything to the dogs, it was probably well deserved."

Silence descended again, and this time Ben didn't try to change it. He'd done his part, and it wasn't like Tara had apologized. If they didn't say another word to each other the entire drive, it was fine by him.

"So you and your brother-in-law don't get along?"

Should've known it was too good to be true.

Tara leaned back, like she was settling in for a while. She turned to Ben, clearly waiting for his answer.

"We get along fine. Dallin and I were best friends when we were kids."

"But not anymore? Was it too much when he became more interested in your sister than you?"

Nosy females. "Something like that."

"Hmmm." Tara brought a hand to her chin as she stared at him. "Or did you know some twisted fact about Dallin's past that made you think he wasn't good enough for your sister? Did you try to interfere?"

"No." Ben kept his answer curt, his tone neutral, though he was bothered by the way she'd put that scenario together. It was all too close to the truth—if the tables were turned, that is.

"So is doing this huge favor for Dallin, moving his family for him, your way of trying to fix things?"

"Nope." *Maybe.* He hadn't thought about it. Guys *didn't* think like that, making everything they did some complicated emotional deal. Ellen had asked for his help. He'd said yes. It was that simple. "Next subject," Ben said. "What are your plans in Boulder?"

"In a minute." Tara said. "That you *don't* want to talk about this tells me it *is* bothering you."

"Might be." Ben looked at her. "But I'm not a woman and discussing it for three hours won't fix it."

"You never know. It could." She smiled the first real smile he'd seen from her. It was pretty—and flirty and coy. No doubt she'd used it on numerous other men.

"I don't think so. You want to talk? Then tell me what's in Boulder."

She shrugged. "A spa, shopping. The usual."

"Have you been there before?"

"Never. I hate flying, so I usually go somewhere tropical for my trouble."

"But not this time. Ah . . ." Ben gave her the same speculative look she'd used on him. "You must be meeting someone *important.*" He remembered her panic on the elevator and could only imagine what it had cost her—and what could have possibly motivated her—to get on a plane for two hours.

"Oh yeah," Tara said without much enthusiasm. "I'm meeting the love of my life."

Lucky guy, Ben thought sarcastically. Poor sap, was more like it. And maybe the guy had realized that too. Ben knew Tara had tried and been unable to get in touch with the person she was supposed to meet. He felt the tiniest particle of sympathy for her if his hunch was right and she had been or was about to be dumped. Having experienced that himself right around the holidays, he knew it wasn't something anyone—even the most annoying woman on the planet— deserved. Maybe that was *why* she'd been so incredibly annoying. It would certainly explain a lot. He wondered what she was going to do if her guy wasn't around anymore.

"So you're off to a romantic, snowy holiday." He tried to imagine Tara cruising downhill on a snowboard and couldn't. She was more of the sit-by-the-fire-and-look-pretty type.

Tara sighed. "Not really. There isn't a guy. Just some girlfriends. We were supposed to meet at a spa."

Girlfriends? A spa? She's got to be kidding. He didn't buy it for a minute. "Really?"

"Really." She shrugged as she met his gaze for a second before turning away, her eyes downcast, shoulders slumped. She looked almost sad—dejected. His theory flew out the window.

"Must be some spa or some friends for you to have boarded a plane three days before Christmas, at the height of crowds and airport congestion."

She shook her head. "Neither. Pathetic, isn't it?"

Yeah. "No. I mean, friends are important. Sometimes we're closer to friends than family. I can see why you'd want to be together for the holiday. I'm just surprised, remembering how bad your claustrophobia was. I can't imagine you felt real great on the flight."

"I threw up." She smiled again as she looked at him. "Almost all over the obnoxious kid sitting next to me—the one I'm pretty sure took my wallet, the little brat." A spark of anger flickered in her eyes.

Ben struggled to keep up. In the space of a few seconds he'd witnessed three major emotions from her. If nothing else, Tara was proving to be good entertainment on the drive.

"Almost? You didn't get him?" He returned her grin, hoping to avoid the rage he knew was there, just below the surface.

"No. The flight attendant brought a bag just in time. It took her half the flight to get my drink, but she got there fast enough to save the kid's designer jeans. Still, he was pretty disgusted—that was something."

So by the time I met her at the airport, she'd really had an awful day. "Well, you're a good friend," Ben said. "And I bet after this experience, you'll insist your girlfriends spend Christmas at your place next year."

"Maybe," Tara said, vague again. "But I don't want to think about next year right now. It's too depressing."

He knew what she meant. With both of his parents gone now, and things strained between him and Dallin, he'd spent the last few Decembers alone. *Like every other month of the year. True enough*, he admitted to himself. Though most of the time the solitude didn't bother him. His work was often a lone venture, and he could only say that the time afforded him had been good for building up his business and reputation these past few years. And of course he wasn't completely by himself. He had the pigs, who, it turned out, were quite good company.

"I usually fly first class," Tara was saying. "It makes a big difference. Had I known how awful I'd feel on the flight, I would never have come."

"What would you have done instead?" Ben asked, his curiosity overriding his earlier feelings about not talking to her the entire trip. He wanted to know what other single people did at Christmas. And why were the holidays such a big deal, anyway? He always enjoyed the opportunity to remember and celebrate the birth of his Savior, but in spite of that, why did it always have to be such a melancholy time of year?

"I wanted to visit my mom. But . . ." Tara breathed in then exhaled heavily, "she's on a cruise."

"You should have gone too," Ben said. "That is, unless you've got motion sickness to match your claustrophobia."

"No." Tara leaned her head back against the seat and closed her eyes.

Ben glanced at her and saw the sadness was back. Without her animal-print clothing and gobs of makeup, she didn't seem to be the same brash woman he'd offered to help at the airport. Even her red hair appeared toned down, turned to a dark auburn, on mellow mode with her temper at the moment.

"It couldn't have been too expensive." He wouldn't soon forget the uppity way she'd behaved when he'd offered her forty-seven dollars and an hour in Sears.

Tara shook her head, sending strands of that long auburn hair floating around her face. "I told you, I make plenty of money. I didn't go because I'm tired of being the inconvenience in her life."

Ben wasn't sure how to respond to that. A long time ago he'd known what a bummer it was to have a mom that thought he was an annoyance. But he'd been just a kid. He could only imagine the hurt that might cause an adult. He glanced at Tara and caught her looking at him—and looking nothing like the woman he'd argued with last night.

"I hate that feeling, that *un*wanted feeling." She paused, her face coloring ever so slightly, as if she'd just remembered where she was and who she was talking to. Turning away, she said, "But I don't suppose you know what I mean."

You'd be wrong there. But Ben wasn't about to tell *her* that.

"Boy, how did we get here—you extracting my life story from me? We are definitely discussing your issues with Dallin after this." The insecure Tara of a moment before was gone, the sassy woman back. Ben wasn't sure whether to be relieved or not. But there was no way they'd be discussing Dallin or anything else personal.

How did *we get here, in the middle of a civil conversation?*

"I think I liked it better when you were annoying," Tara said. "At least you spoke to me then."

"*I* annoy *you*?" Ben asked. "*How*?"

"Oh yeah." Tara smiled at him once more, this time without appearing coy.

"Tell me how I'm annoying."

"You're just different, the first farmer I've ever known," she said.

"I don't usually hang out with big city girls."

"*Really?*" she said with mock astonishment. "You prefer to stay at home and play with your pigs."

"I do." *Pigs don't talk back.*

Tara shook her head again, this time in a confused, I'll-never-understand-it sort of way. "Guess it takes all kinds."

"Yes, it does," Ben agreed. *It most certainly does.*

Eleven

SHORTLY AFTER TARA TOLD BEN much more than she should have, Cadie woke up and had to use the restroom. Ben radioed Ellen, and they all stopped at the nearest rest area, where the bathrooms were not only freezing but beyond disgusting as well. Tara decided she could wait until they stopped for lunch.

They got back on the road again, this time with Sam for company. Tara was both glad and sorry for the exchange. Sam kept to himself for the most part, so long as she continued providing whatever snack or toy he demanded from the backpack Ellen had sent with him. But with Cadie not around to distract Ben, Tara worried their conversation would stray back to her pathetic life. And she didn't care to share any more of that with Ben. She wasn't even sure how he'd gotten her to open up as much as she did in the first place.

Since moving to LA, she hadn't really been a talker, mostly because there was no one to talk *to*. The friendships she'd formed down there were superficial at best.

And what did that say about Ben? He wasn't exactly her best buddy, either. Worst enemy came closer to the truth when she thought about the previous day and night. Yet for a good half hour they'd enjoyed each other's company, and she'd trusted him enough that she'd started to share her personal angst.

No more, she promised herself. *At least not unless he spills the beans about Dallin.* And she knew that wasn't likely. Ben might have been a good listener, but so far he wasn't much for talking about himself.

Interesting. A guy who listens to me and doesn't spend all day bragging about himself. When was the last time I dated someone like that?

Never. She chalked it up to old-fashioned farm values. The image of Ben bending low in his overalls then holding out his hand to help her into a buggy made her smile.

"What are you smirking about over there?" Ben asked, giving her a curious look.

"Not much," Tara said. "Just wondering how to get you to open up. So I'll feel like things between us are a little more even, you know."

"My lips are sealed." Ben pressed his together to prove his point.

"All right." Tara moved to plan B, the more indirect route. Ben didn't realize who he was dealing with. She was expert at getting guys into a conversation. It was the first law of dating. Even if she didn't like the guy and could tell things were going nowhere, she could always get a man to talk long enough that she got a dinner out of the evening, making it worth the time and effort she spent getting ready.

"Forget your brother-in-law. Tell me about the rest of your family. Where do your parents live? Is your dad a farmer too? Do you have any siblings besides Ellen? Does this penchant for numerous pets—" Tara nudged the hermit crab cage away from her leg for about the twentieth time "—run in your family?"

"Man. Twenty questions." Ben made a face.

Tara shrugged. "There's nothing else to do."

He stared at the road ahead of them. "Guess you're right. Hmmm." His brow wrinkled as he considered her questions.

"My parents are both deceased, but they lived in a little town called Richfield. My dad had a lot of acreage, but he didn't do much farming, though my mom had a garden that could feed the whole block."

"Go on," Tara said.

"There are fifteen children in our family."

She gasped. "*Fifteen?*"

"Yep."

"No wonder your mother is dead—no disrespect," she hastily added.

"No offense taken," Ben assured her. "As for pets, if you count the chickens, we had at least a dozen of those, too, though not all at the same time. And I think that makes us just about even on family history."

"You can't stop yet," Tara protested. "You have to at least explain the fifteen kids. Are you the oldest? In the middle? Boys, girls? Were your parents *crazy?*"

"Second youngest," Ben said. "Ellen came about a year after me, though we're only eight months different in age."

"Huh?" Tara gave him a confused frown.

He grinned but didn't offer anything else.

Tara thought about what he'd said. "Ellen was adopted?"

Ben nodded.

Sam shook his empty cracker bag in her face. "More."

"I agree," Tara said, taking the bag from him. "Ben should tell us *more* about his family." She dug through the backpack Ellen had put in the truck that morning. Finding the goldfish crackers, she refilled Sam's bag.

"More, *please*," she said, holding the bag just out of Sam's reach and imitating the way she'd heard Ellen speak to him.

"More, please," he repeated, reaching for the treat. Tara handed it to him, thinking it was the first satisfactory dialogue she'd had with a child since her arrival.

"Can you hand me one of those water bottles, *please?*" Ben asked, pointing to the still-open container.

Tara gave one to him, opened one for herself, then drank over a third of it at once. She hadn't realized how thirsty she was. *Better be careful*, she warned herself. Who knew how long till they stopped for lunch, and already she felt like she could use a bathroom. After taking one more tiny sip of water, she put the bottle back in the box and crossed her legs.

"How long have your parents been gone?" she asked.

"Dad's four years now. Mom is three. She died almost a year to the day after he did. We all know it was because she missed him so much."

Tara was silent for a minute. "What was it really? Was there an accident or something?"

Ben shook his head. "No accident. They both just got old. Mom was fifty-four when I came. Dad was fifty-six."

"Your mom had a baby when she was *fifty-four?*" Ben's family sounded weirder by the minute.

"She *adopted* me when she was fifty-four. I was seven."

"Oh. So both you and Ellen are adopted?"

"All of us were adopted. All fifteen kids, plus a few more that were temporary over the years."

"What do you mean?"

"Our parents did foster care. Some of the kids they cared for eventually went back to their families. The ones who didn't stayed and got adopted."

"Wow. That's amazing." And it was. Tara found herself wishing she could have met Ben's mom. It would have been interesting to find out what had possessed her to adopt fifteen kids and then what had kept her sane through raising them all.

Her mind jumped tracks fast, circling around to Ben's issue with his brother-in-law. *If Ben and Ellen aren't related by blood . . .*

"So when did you meet Dallin?" she asked casually.

But Ben was on to her. "You're not even close," he said. "Ellen is my sister, blood or not. She always has been and always will be."

"Can't blame a girl for trying." Tara smiled in spite of her frustration at being foiled again.

"I thought you were going to try to get some sleep today."

"What? Are you tired of me?" she asked in a wounded voice that wasn't entirely pretend.

Ben looked over at her. "No. Actually I'm not. You're pretty good company. Better than old Sam here." They looked down at Sam and noticed, for the first time, what he was doing with his fish crackers.

Tara watched, somewhat disgusted, as Sam put the cracker in his mouth, got it good and slimy, then removed it and stuck it on his jeans.

"Whatcha doing there, buddy?" Ben asked.

"Lake." Sam pointed to the ring of fish on his pant leg. "Fish swimming in the lake."

"Of course." Ben slapped the steering wheel and let out a snort. Tara had to look away to keep from laughing.

"Why?" she asked. "And *how* could your parents raise *fifteen* children? Fifteen fish-on-the-jeans kids, fifteen pairs of feet jumping on the couch, fifteen sticky marshmallow-on-the-face kids? Why would anyone do that? And how did your mother stay sane while she did?"

"That's a valid question," Ben admitted. "And the only thing I can tell you is something I heard my mother say over and over again throughout her life."

"Yes?" Tara leaned forward, eager for this paragon of wisdom, this deep family secret, he was about to impart.

"It's all about joy."

"That's it?" she asked. "What does that even mean?"

"I suppose we have to figure that out for ourselves. But for my mom this—" He inclined his head toward Sam and his pant leg lake of fish crackers, "—was the joy."

Twelve

SHORTLY BEFORE NOON TRAFFIC BEGAN to back up and slow on the highway. They'd made good time to that point, but within a few minutes they were bumper-to-bumper with the cars in front and behind at a complete standstill.

This isn't good. Tara had hoped they'd be stopping for lunch—and more importantly, a bathroom—soon.

Ben put the truck in park. "Be right back." He opened his door and jumped out, letting in a blast of icy air in his place. Tara reached forward, twisting the knob on the heater to high.

As he watched his uncle leave, Sam began fussing. He reached down swatting at the fish stuck to his pants, sending many of them Tara's way.

"Don't do that." She grabbed for his hand. "I don't want any fish. You keep them."

"No fish. No fish," he cried, letting out a howl like a wolf. Tara peered out the window, trying to see how many cars in front of them Ellen's van was. If Sam was going to whine, maybe they could trade back for Cadie.

Ben's door swung open, and he climbed in the truck. "I'm not sure what the delay is, but it looks like a long one. Cars stopped in front of us as far as I can see."

This is so not good. Tara crossed her legs again and tried not to think about the water bottle and two cups of hot cocoa she'd consumed that morning.

Sam continued to fuss, so Ben unfastened his car seat and picked him up. "You want to steer the truck for a while?"

The little boy nodded. Ben turned the ignition off, sat Sam in front of him facing the wheel, and let him go for it, adding sound effects as necessary.

Tara rolled her eyes at them. "I'm surprised you don't have fifteen kids of your own. You're very good with them."

"No kids. Just pigs—which sometimes don't seem too different."

Remembering the way Ellen's kids had attacked the marshmallows and chocolate the night before, Tara agreed.

"What made you decide on pigs—on Ohio?" she asked. "That's clear across the country. I'd think you'd want to be near family."

"I did until a few years ago. But after my parents died, I needed to get away. I'd served a mission for my church in Ohio, and I liked it a lot. It seemed the logical thing to go back."

"Do you ever wish you hadn't?" Tara asked. Once, the logical thing to her had seemed moving to LA, but there were times she wasn't so sure that had been the right choice.

"There are some things I miss—the mountains, for instance. About the tallest thing you get in Ohio is a hill, but it is green and beautiful there. I've got a great piece of property."

"It's amazing what people will do for property," Tara said. "I sell real estate, and I've seen the need to own land do some pretty strange things to people."

"That's not why I moved," Ben said. "If I'd just wanted land, I could have stayed in Richfield and taken over my parents' place."

"Why didn't you?" Tara asked. "Not enough room for pigs?"

"Not enough room for me," Ben said then instantly looked as if he wished he could take that statement back.

Ahh. Now we're getting somewhere. "You and who else?" Tara asked.

"I don't want to talk about this." Ben reached for the key and turned the truck on again.

Kudos to you for not lying and saying, "No one else."

"Dallin," she guessed.

"Give the whole Dallin thing a rest, okay?"

"Sorry," she muttered then turned and looked out her window, feeling a little of the apology she'd just given. It had been kind of fun talking with Ben.

Wish I hadn't ruined it.

* * *

"Tara." Ben gently shook her shoulder.

She rubbed her eyes and sat up, coming out of a surprising dream where she and Ben weren't fighting but were—

She glanced at his hand on her shoulder. "I fell asleep again? Where are we?"

"Same spot we were twenty-five minutes ago." He pulled his hand away. "I'm going to take Sam up to his mom and walk a little farther to see what I can find out."

"Okay." *If you see anyone with a motor home . . .* she almost added. Wasn't that what people always did in the movies when they needed a bathroom?

Ben bundled Sam up and left the truck. "Lock the doors behind me, okay?"

She nodded, touched that he thought enough of her to give her safety advice. *He probably would have told anyone the same thing.* She needed to let go of the dream she'd been having. *But he didn't tell anyone, he told* me. *And it was nice.*

Her fingers rested on her shoulder where his hand had been. *Don't go there,* she warned herself, but found it impossible not to— for a minute or two, anyway. Out here in the snow-covered Rocky Mountains, a guy in a plaid flannel shirt seemed just about perfect. It had been a nice dream.

When Ben disappeared from view, Tara did what she'd wanted to all morning, since his confession about having Sinatra on his iPod. She was dying to know what else he listened to and took the opportunity to find out, reaching for the iPod on the dashboard. She began scanning through songs, many of which she'd never heard before. A lot of Ben's music seemed to be from another era, and while it wasn't unpleasant, it also wasn't what she'd imagine a man in his thirties would listen to. After about fifteen minutes and twice that many songs, she turned it off and went back to worrying about finding a bathroom.

Though it was only about twelve thirty, the sky was beginning to darken. They were in a pass, with steep mountains rising up around them, blocking much of the sunlight that was probably out there. The feeling of darkness coming on only intensified her need for a bathroom.

"This is ridiculous," she told herself. "You're thirty-four years old. You can hold it."

Her little pep talk did absolutely no good. Tara slunk down in her seat, true misery starting to sink in as quickly as the windows were fogging up. She rubbed the one closest to her with the sleeve of her sweater, knowing now was not a good time for her claustrophobia to kick in.

Still Ben didn't return. The truck was getting cold now, so she reached over and turned the key, bringing the engine to life. She rubbed her hands briskly in front of the heater vents, willing the air to get hot, hoping that once she was warm again, her need for a bathroom would subside a bit.

The minutes ticked by with agonizing slowness. At last, when she thought she might die of boredom or a full bladder, Ben came into view. He had something in his arms, and he was stopping at each car, handing whatever it was to the drivers. When he neared the truck, she leaned over in his seat, unlocking the door. He pulled it open and climbed inside.

"No kids?" Tara asked, feeling grateful she didn't have to deal with whining or crying right now.

"They're watching a DVD in Ellen's van." Ben held out his hands. "But I brought ice cream. The good stuff—Ben & Jerry's."

"Ice cream? Is that what you were handing out to everyone?"

"Yep. This is what caused the delay. About a quarter mile ahead of us a semi slid on some ice and jackknifed. The trailer tipped over, and there's ice cream all over the road. The driver's telling people to take as much as they want. It won't be saleable now." He lifted the pint containers, staring at the labels. "Chunky Monkey or Cherry Garcia?"

"It's, what, ten degrees outside, and you're offering me ice cream?"

"I am. And where's the gratitude?" Ben pouted. "I had to hike down an embankment for these."

"I'm sorry," Tara said. "*Thank you* for hiking down an embankment for me."

"Oh, I didn't do it for you." The pout was gone. "I love ice cream. You're just lucky I'm in a sharing mood." He popped the lid off one of the pints.

"How were you planning to eat that?" Tara asked. "My fingers are already chilled, and I don't think I'm up for completely freezing them."

"You can't eat ice cream with your fingers." Ben rolled his eyes at her then continued with a hillbilly accent. "Not even us farmers are that backward." He handed the ice cream to Tara then reached in his pocket, pulling out what looked like an over-accessorized pocket knife. From this he produced a fold-out metal spoon.

"Basic tool of any Boy Scout—and farmer," he said.

"You were a Boy Scout, too?"

"Oh yeah. Half the time my parents had us recite the Scout Oath with our prayers. They lived and breathed it." He took the open carton from Tara and dug in with the spoon. She expected him to take the first bite, but he held it out to her instead. Feeling suddenly self-conscious, she leaned forward, allowing him to put the bite in her mouth.

"Mmm. Thank you."

Ben took the next bite for himself then offered her another.

She shook her head. "I actually need something else first—before I can fully enjoy the ice cream."

"You want a sandwich? Ellen packed some this morning. Do you want me to go get one from her?"

"No." Tara shook her head then looked away. She felt her face starting to go red and tried to remember the last time she'd felt embarrassed like this. "I need a bathroom," she finally admitted. "Is there a rest area nearby I could walk to? Or someone with a motor home, maybe?"

"Oh, boy." Ben leaned back in his seat, staring out at the cars and road ahead of them. "I didn't see anything up ahead, and we haven't passed any rest areas in a while. I guess I could walk back and look for someone with an RV, but generally you don't see a lot of those on the road this time of year—especially on a highway with a ten-thousand-foot summit and lots of snow."

"I didn't think about that." *Because about the only thing I can think about right now is my bladder that's about to burst.*

"You could use an empty water bottle," Ben suggested.

She felt her face go redder. "In case you haven't noticed, I'm not a guy. It's a little more complicated for me."

Ben laughed.

She didn't see what was so funny.

"Fair enough. I guess the only other thing to do is to go outside."

"*Outside?*" she asked, certain her face was a mask of horror. "I'd have to—"

"Squat?" Ben suggested.

She looked away, too embarrassed and appalled to continue the conversation.

"It can be done, you know. When we went camping, my mom and sisters—"

"I'm not your mom and sisters," she snapped, angry now.

He shrugged. "Then hold it. I was just telling you your choices."

Tara folded her arms and kept her gaze straight ahead. *Some choice. I haven't had a decent choice since I stepped on that plane three days ago.*

Ben continued to eat his ice cream, whistling between bites. When he'd had enough, he put the lid on the carton and put both cartons outside on the hood of the truck. His whistling resumed once he was back in his seat.

"What are you so happy about?" Tara asked.

"I don't know," Ben said. "It's Christmas Eve, I'm here in a beautiful canyon with a pretty woman sitting next to me, and I just had some awesome ice cream. Things could be worse."

She ignored his compliment. "You're happy about the delay, aren't you?" she accused. "This means more time before you have to see Dallin—and probably less time with him."

The whistling stopped. Ben turned to her, fixing his eyes on hers. "What is it with you? Why do you feel the need to pry into my personal life?"

"I don't know," she admitted, feeling somewhat bad that she'd brought it up again. *What* is *with me?* she wondered. "Maybe it's because you seem so good, so perfect in every other way, that I want to know about this one thing in your life that isn't right. There are a whole lot of things in my life that aren't right, and being around you—Mr. Happy, Helpful Farmer—is kind of depressing. But if you give me some dirt, I might feel better."

Ben shook his head. "I'll never get females."

"Get as in *understand*, or get as in *get*?" Tara asked.

"Both." His serious tone told her he wasn't about to elaborate.

After a minute, Tara spoke again. "I think you could—the latter get, I mean. You're not bad looking, and if you lost the overalls . . ."

He turned to her. "I'm not wearing overalls today."

"I know. You look good in cords." There. She'd said it. She admitted to checking him out. She'd played another one of her cards, when he'd played none of his.

Their eyes met again, and she shifted uncomfortably in her seat. This was getting good—it was getting like her dream. Except that in her dream she hadn't cared about finding a bathroom more than anything else in the world.

Ben must have realized she was becoming seriously miserable.

"I'll help you find a place where no one will see you," he offered.

Mortified was not usually a word in her self-describing vocabulary, but it pretty much summed up her existence in that moment. She was going to have to take him up on that offer. She was going to have to climb out of this somewhat warm truck and go out in the freezing cold. She'd have to walk down the road, out onto the embankment. And the people in the cars would know exactly what was up. She squeezed her eyes shut. *I can't do it.*

"You take care of your . . . problem, and I'll tell you about Dallin."

Tara's eyes popped open. "Are you serious?"

He nodded. "Serious and stupid, probably."

"No." She gave him a smile of gratitude. "It's like I said a minute ago. You're just good. Too good to be true."

Thirteen

BEN CAME AROUND AND OPENED Tara's side of the truck. He held his hand out to her and helped her get down.

"Are you going to be able to walk for a bit? You didn't wait too long, did you?"

"No. I'm not three. And I can walk." She glared at him.

He tried hard not to smile, not to be amused at her latest predicament. If she'd only used the bathroom earlier, but no—she'd been too uppity for such a humble facility. Well, she was going to have to pay for that now—with frostbite on her backside if she wasn't careful. Ben wondered how many times a similar scenario—Tara thinking herself above something and then ending up with humbling circumstances later—had been repeated in her life. Obviously not enough, or else she was a slow learner. But his sister was right about one thing. Tara didn't seem to know any better. And after learning that she had a mother who saw Tara as an inconvenience, he felt a little more empathy.

Ben shut the door behind her and pulled a fleece hat from his pocket. He'd seen it when they were in line at Deseret Industries last night and had thrown it in the cart on a whim, thinking maybe Cadie would want it. But it had been too big for her. It would probably fit Tara fine. *Big head that she has.* He stepped in front of her and grabbed her shoulders, stopping her for a second.

"Wear this. It will help you stay warm." He jammed the pink and purple Minnie Mouse hat over her head. Flower petals poking out at ridiculous angles sprang every which way, and the embroidered Minnie rested just above her eyebrows.

Tara looked up, trying to see the hat. "It's not my head I'm worried about."

Ben chuckled. "I'm glad to see you haven't lost your sense of humor. Come on." He took her hand so she wouldn't slip in her tennis shoes.

They walked along the road for a couple hundred yards until they came to a spot where the bank steepened and sloped off into a ditch of sorts. He led Tara down the slope to a lone juniper.

"This is it."

She looked at the tree with such despair that Ben almost felt sorry for her.

"Take it or leave it," he said.

She sighed. "Get going, then." She tugged her hand from his and started to walk behind the tree.

"I'll just wait up here," Ben called. He climbed back up to the road and stood waiting, wondering if he ought to go get some more ice cream since they'd come this far.

Two minutes passed. Then three. Then five. She really *was* going to get frostbite if she didn't hurry.

"Ben," a forlorn voice finally called.

He turned around. "Yeah? Want some help climbing up?"

She shook her head but beckoned to him.

Probably wants me to fetch her some Charmin or something. He trudged down the bank again, stopping a few feet away from her. Her teeth were chattering, and her nose was excessively red—from more than the cold, it seemed. Unshed tears hovered, just waiting to spill from those big, beautiful eyes.

What now? "What's wrong?"

"My zipper's stuck. I tried and tried to unzip it, but my fingers are frozen, and I can't get it to move." She shivered then pulled her legs close, doing a little hop up and down. "This is all your fault," she wailed, striking out at him suddenly, pushing against his chest. "Because you wouldn't buy me n-n-ew jeans." Tears started to trickle down both sides of her face.

"You're serious?" He still suspected she could turn on her faucet whenever she wanted.

"Yes, I'm serious!" she screamed. "I'm freezing to death and in pain and my stupid zipper is stuck."

"All right, all right." He held his hands up. "You, uh, want me to try it?"

She nodded and wiped her cheek with one hand. Still shaking, she leaned forward, arms folded across her middle. "Please hurry."

It was the first time he'd heard her say please, so he knew she must be desperate. Feeling awkward and embarrassed and just plain bad about the situation, Ben gripped the top of her jeans with one hand, pulling them as far away from her body as possible. With his other hand he worked at the zipper, tugging as hard as he could, twisting it every which way, trying to get it to move. After a couple of minutes, he realized it wasn't going to happen.

"Great," Tara muttered. "Just great."

"I don't suppose they'll slide down over your hips?" he asked.

She shook her head. "If you'd gotten a size larger they would have, but these are good and tight."

Ben felt an inkling of guilt. He'd picked those jeans thinking about how her curves would look in them. *And she thinks I'm "good."* He reached into his pocket and took out his knife again. "The only thing I can think of is to cut them. Just slice right alongside the zipper."

"Fine. Give that to me." Her tears were gone, and she was snappy again. Ben continued to be amazed at how fast her moods changed. He was starting to wonder if she had multiple personality disorder or something.

Unfolding the scissors, he held the knife out to her.

Tara grabbed it from him and ran behind the juniper. He hurried back up the embankment and had barely reached the top when he heard a repeat of yesterday's colorful language.

This time he laughed.

His laughter was cut short by Tara's bloodcurdling scream.

Fourteen

BEN WHIPPED AROUND, STARING AS Tara ran out from behind the tree, screaming. One hand held her pants up, the other flailed in the air. He took a step toward her then slid halfway down the embankment.

"It's alive!" She ran straight into his chest, nearly knocking him over just as he'd caught his balance.

"What's wrong?" He put his arms around her, trying to steady them both.

"There's something alive back there. A wolf maybe. It tried to take a bite out of me." She pushed past him and tried to climb toward the road.

Ben doubted a wolf would venture so close to the highway, especially with this much activity up there right now. His curiosity got the better of him, and he started toward the juniper only to see a white jackrabbit hop out from behind the tree.

Ben chuckled. "Some wolf." He turned to Tara. "It's a bunny."

Tara watched, disbelieving, as it hopped away. "Told you there was something alive," she huffed, walking along with a strange gait, one hand swinging wildly, the other clutching the front of her jeans.

"Lots of things are alive out here," Ben said. "And most of them won't hurt you. In fact, they're more afraid of you than you are of them."

"Want to bet?" She glared at him for a second before continuing her march.

"So did you, uh, take care of your problem?" he dared ask.

"One of them," she retorted. "The other is walking right beside me."

"Hey." He grabbed her free arm, stopping her. "You need to knock off the attitude. I didn't have to get out of the warm truck to help you, you know."

"You were a *ton* of help," she said sarcastically. "I don't even have pants that stay up now."

Ben couldn't believe this. "You asked for the scissors."

"Because there was no other choice." Tara stomped her foot childishly. "I haven't had a choice about *anything* for three days. I'm sick of this. I need my wallet back, my clothes . . . my *life*."

"You can have it." Ben let go of her arm and walked past her. "I'll be happy to drop you off at the nearest gas station. You can get yourself to wherever it is you want to go. Or maybe your fairy godmother will come rescue you, since you're such a spoiled princess."

"*What* did you say?" Tara struggled to keep up. She reached out, grabbing his arm just as she lost her footing and started sliding backward down the hill.

Ben caught her. "I said you're spoiled. In fact, your name ought to be *Tiara* instead of *Tara*. You're a pampered . . . privileged . . . brat."

She gasped and pushed him away. "Well, Benji, at least I'm not named after a *dog*."

Ben narrowed his eyes. He was partial to his name. Once, around the time he was getting adopted, he'd wanted to change it along with his new last name, but that was before his adoptive mom had taken the time to explain it to him. He loved her for that, and he loved his name because of it. "I'm not named after a dog. I'm named after a king. King Benjamin was one of the finest men who ever lived."

He turned and walked off, thinking that he wasn't acting so much like his namesake at the moment. What was it about this woman that brought out the absolute worst in him?

He expected to hear her behind him and braced himself for another volley of insults or another physical assault. But neither came. When he reached the road, he reluctantly turned around again and saw her standing in the same spot. *Literally frozen? Nah. It'd be too good to be true.*

Gritting his teeth, he retraced his steps until he stood in front of her. Her nose and cheeks were red with cold, and her lips appeared to be turning blue. "Come on. You're freezing."

"What do you care?" she asked.

He was the one who felt like swearing as he noticed her eyes starting to well up again. "I said I'd leave you at a gas station. Not in the middle of nowhere—without even a decent pair of pants." He suddenly found it hard not to laugh. She looked so forlorn, standing there holding up her jeans and wearing Minnie Mouse plastered across her brow. The flowers were lying on their sides now, pressed down by the moisture from the lightly falling snow.

Tara shivered again, sending a little tremor from her head to her toes. Ben smiled. He couldn't help it. His anger of a moment before melted in the face of such a tragic figure. He realized his moods were becoming as erratic as hers and hated to think what would happen to him if they spent much more time together.

"Come on," he said again. He reached out, touching her shoulder, pulling her toward him.

"I'm cold," she said. "I just want this to be over. I want to go home."

"I know, Princess. You gotta move first, though."

She did, stepping closer until they were less than a foot apart.

Ben reached down, tilting her chin up, so he could see her eyes. They were swimming with tears and full of hurt.

"Hey, I'm sorry—okay? I was outta line. I shouldn't have said those things."

She shook her head. "They're true."

Ben wasn't sure what to say to that. What he'd said to her *was* true. She was spoiled and stuck up and . . . shivering and vulnerable, and very, very pretty with her head full of tousled curls and her hazel eyes shining up at him.

His mother had taught him that sometimes actions were better than words. King Benjamin had been a man of action too. He'd worked alongside his people instead of just giving them lip service. *Lip* service. The fleeting thought was enough to prompt him to a sudden change of course. *If you can't beat her . . .*

Ben took Tara's rosy cheeks in his hands and bent down, brushing his warm lips over her chilled ones.

. . . kiss her. He closed his eyes, savoring for the brief moment the softness of her skin, the touch of her lips against his, the long-forgotten feeling of having a woman in his arms.

He was just about to pull away when her hand came around his neck, drawing him to her. For a split second he stiffened, surprised that she was accepting his offer, that she hadn't pushed him away.

Instead she clung to him, moving her lips over his with a desire he'd have never guessed was there. Vaguely aware of his own matching desires, Ben responded, kissing her tenderly, a sort of apology for all the mean things he'd said and done since he met her. He couldn't remember why he'd been angry, couldn't imagine being upset with the warm, giving woman in his arms. Her lips were sweet, her fingers caressing, as they wove their way through his hair.

Breathless, he finally pulled away but kept her tucked tight in his embrace. He kissed her forehead then pressed her face against his chest, wondering if she could feel the thundering of his heart.

The question *What just happened?* hovered below the surface, and he knew he would—*they* would—have to deal with it in a minute. But for now he wanted to hold her, to enjoy this moment of peace when all was in accord between them.

Snowflakes fell, melting in her hair and on his nose, and still they didn't move. Then the sudden sound of car engines from the road above ended the spellbinding moment.

"The truck," Ben said. He grabbed her hand and started up the embankment. She climbed with him to the top then pulled away.

He looked back, struck by how beautiful she was, how much he wanted to kiss her again. But she wasn't smiling at him, didn't look happy at all.

"Thank you for everything, Ben," Tara said. "But I think it's best if I ride with Ellen now."

Fifteen

ELLEN GLANCED AT TARA, HANDS held out in front of the heater, shivering in the passenger seat. "My brother must have really turned on the charm to make you choose the zoo van over him."

Tara felt grateful Ellen had refrained from commenting on her cut-down-the-front pants. "The truck seat was uncomfortable," Tara said quietly. It was a lousy excuse though at least not a complete lie. The plastic seat had felt hard and springy, but *everything* in the cab of that truck would have been uncomfortable after the kiss she and Ben had shared. She'd either have bawled and clung to him. *Wow. Being in his arms felt so good.* Or spilled more of her soul and begged him to kiss her again. *Who'd have guessed that Farmer Ben . . .* Her lips were still tingling—or were they just defrosting after being cold for so long?

"Mmm-hmm," said Ellen, glancing over at Tara, not sounding the least convinced of her excuse. Fortunately, her attention was quickly diverted to the drama in the backseat.

Tara turned around to see if she might help and thought the better of it. Chloe was straining against the straps of her car seat and screaming. *Has she stopped since this morning?* And now Cadie was yelling too, her head bent at an odd angle as her sister pulled her hair.

"*Girls,*" Ellen snapped, sounding rather near the end of her own rope.

Feeling bad for her, Tara climbed in back. One hand held up her pants while the other pried Chloe's fingers from Cadie's head. When she'd separated the girls, she handed Cadie a tissue from a box on the floor. When Cadie just held it in her hand, Tara helped her wipe the tears and even the snot from her face. *Disgusting.*

Chloe's screaming ceased for a second as she watched them, but Tara could tell she was just catching her breath to start up again. Seized with sudden inspiration, she handed the toddler the tissue box, showing her how to pull the tissues out, hold one up to her nose, and make a pretend sneezing sound. To Tara's great surprise, the little girl laughed. Tara repeated the action, and Chloe laughed louder—a sound much more pleasant than her previous screams.

Ellen looked in her rearview mirror. "You're a genius."

Facing away from her, Tara shook her head but privately smiled at the compliment. "We'll see if you say that when there are—" She glanced at the supersized box of tissues "—one hundred and fifty pieces of Kleenex on the floor of your van."

"It'll be worth it. Besides, I'll get Ben to clean it up."

Tara turned around and made her way to the front passenger seat. "He probably would if you asked him—good guy that he is."

Ellen sent her a funny, eyebrows-raised, questioning kind of look. "Oh, he'll do it but not because he's particularly good. He'll just be glad for an excuse to stay out of the house, away from Dallin."

Dallin. How could I forget? On the other hand, I'm surprised I even remember my name after that kiss. "So what is it between those two?" Tara asked casually. It wasn't like she was prying into big family secrets when Ben had promised to tell her anyway.

"Too much is between them, I'm afraid," Ellen said, her voice heavy with regret. "Too many memories. Too much distrust. Too much hurt."

"Aren't you the least bit worried about having them together, then?" Tara was dying for Ellen to elaborate on the memories, trust, and hurt but knew she had to play her cards well here. Ellen was female, after all, and likely knew a thing or two about the art of conversation. She also didn't seem the type to spread gossip or be disloyal to the two most important men in her life.

"I *am* worried," Ellen said, her hands, tense with the reminder, tightening on the steering wheel. "But I'm also hopeful, you know. It's Christmas. Miracles happen. There's peace on earth, goodwill toward men."

Tara snorted. "If you believe in all that."

"I do." Ellen looked over, her eyes serious. "I believe in it very much, and not just at Christmastime."

Instead of responding, Tara looked out the window. *Is there no one I can ride with who won't make me feel weird about who I am and what I believe? Peace, goodwill . . . joy.* The memory of Ben's lips on hers filled her mind. *Okay, so that might have qualified as joy.*

"So what are your plans to bring about this peace and goodwill between the two of them?"

"Lots of prayer?" Ellen shrugged. "To tell you the truth, I haven't really planned anything, other than I know Dallin is going to take Ben aside and apologize again . . ."

For . . . ? Tara silently prompted.

". . . and McKenzie is going to be there."

Tara sent Ellen her best blank look.

"She's Dallin's sister and Ben's ex-fiancée," Ellen said without missing a beat. "They were engaged back when Dallin and I were dating and engaged. It was supposed to be a double wedding."

Tara turned slightly in her seat, trying not to appear overeager. This was getting good. "But it wasn't." She stated the obvious, hoping the tactic would keep Ellen going.

"No." Ellen shook her head. "And in a way, it was Dallin's fault. Though at the time he was only trying to protect his sister." She let out a sigh filled with regret. "Even *I* had my doubts about Benji for a little while there."

"Doubts about what?" Tara asked.

Ellen's grip on the wheel tightened again, and she waited a moment before answering.

"His sanity."

* * *

They made their last bathroom stop about an hour outside Denver. This time Tara didn't say a word about the freezing seat, lack of toilet paper, or smelly condition of the facility. A toilet was a toilet, and holding her nose beat holding her pants any day of the week.

After the stop, she summoned her courage and asked Ben if she could ride with him again.

"Sure," he said and walked around the truck without so much as offering her a hand or opening her door as he'd done before. Though he *had* produced a piece of rope for her to tie her pants up with.

"Boy Scout," Tara grumbled with a hint of affection in her voice. It hadn't been her plan to ride with him again—not after that kiss that sent her head spinning and her heart racing. But by the time she'd heard the whole Dallin-Ben-McKenzie story, she had changed her mind. Ben had no idea he was headed for a weekend that included not only his ex–best friend, but his former and recently divorced fiancée. Talk about the makings for a nightmare family get-together. This was the kind of stuff screenwriters in Hollywood made movies about.

Tara knew she couldn't send him into that—to face the woman who had rejected him literally days before their wedding—without letting him know how she felt about their kiss. It was going to mean humbling herself big time, but she'd have to do it anyway. It was the only decent thing to do. *Not to mention honest,* her conscience added.

Remembering that earlier she'd told Ben she wanted to know some dirt about him, she felt very, very bad.

She climbed into the truck and buckled up. On his side of the cab, Ben did the same. The space between them remained vacant, as the kids had all chosen watching cartoons in the van over riding with their uncle.

Ben surprised her by asking, "You have a nice visit with Ellen?"

"In between the kids screaming, you mean?"

"Yeah." One side of his mouth twitched. "Chloe still going, then?"

"Actually, no," Tara admitted. "I taught her how to blow her nose, and she quieted right down. Ellen says it's worth the seventy-five pieces of tissue Chloe shredded in the backseat."

"Who knew you'd be so good with kids?" His tone was teasing.

It was the perfect lead-in for what she wanted to tell him. *Who knew you'd be so good at kissing?* Her courage faltered. "Not me."

Ben didn't say anything else, and the conversation effectively died when she couldn't think of a way to say what she wanted. The thing was, complimenting him went against every female instinct. Never *ever* was a woman supposed to tell a guy—after their first kiss, and after he'd just hurled insults at her—that he'd made her spine tingle, sent her head reeling, and made her feel something she wasn't sure she'd ever felt before. Stuff like that didn't happen, anyway. She knew better. She'd kissed a whole lot of men, and a kiss wasn't really a big deal. Even the sweet, gentle kind Ben had given her.

It was *only* a kiss. *Then why is my heart racing just thinking about it?*

She concentrated on the lights of the approaching city, knowing she ought to be worrying about how she'd pay for things in Boulder and how she'd get home from there. She'd have to call the airline again. *I'll have to say good-bye to Ben.*

He spoke up suddenly. "I'm sorry about earlier—kissing you, I mean." He sent an apologetic glance her way. "And the things I said—I was way out of line."

Leave it to Farmer Boy to apologize.

"Well, I'm not sorry," Tara said. Ben's eyes narrowed in irritation. Too late she realized her blunder. "About the kiss, that is," she added hastily. "I am sorry I said you were named after a dog. But all things considered, that wouldn't be too bad. Benji was a sweet dog, kind of like you."

Ben shot her a look of disgust and turned away. "I'm not sure if I've just been complimented or insulted even worse."

Stupid. Stupid. Stupid. Tara felt like beating her head against the dash. *This is ridiculous.* It had been a very long time since she'd felt flustered in front of a man. These days she was always in control. She said what she felt and didn't think another thing about it. *Because that usually involves telling a complete jerk of a guy off.* Expressing a sincere compliment was turning out to be more difficult—especially when that meant putting herself out there for . . . *rejection, humiliation, complete mortification. All things Ben must have felt and will likely face again this weekend.*

After thinking about it that way, thinking of Ben before she thought of herself, she suddenly knew exactly what to tell him.

She turned to him, reaching out to touch his sleeve. "Ben, the kiss you gave me was the nicest one I've ever had . . . and I've had a few," she added, a sheepish look on her face.

"I imagine you have."

"What's *that* supposed to mean?" Her eyes narrowed.

"That you're a very beautiful woman. That's *all*." Ben looked at her, and they both burst out laughing. "It was a lot easier to argue with you, you know."

"I know." The laughter left her eyes. *Why is that?* It was a troubling question. *Why can't I get along with a nice guy like Ben? Why'd it take me so long to realize he is nice?*

"I'm sorry about your pants, DI, the whole thing."

"Don't worry about it." Tara waved her hand in the air. "It'll make for a great story when I'm back home."

"Just what I always wanted—to be watercooler talk outside an LA boardroom." He grinned.

"If it'll make you feel better, you can tell the pigs all about me."

"You can bet I will." Their eyes locked for the briefest second, sending Tara's heart rate skyrocketing again.

What will you tell them? she wanted to ask but was saved from making a further fool of herself by Ben's ringing cell phone. It was Ellen, reminding him that their exit was coming up.

Tara withdrew to her side of the truck and tried to focus on where she'd go from here. *To Boulder, obviously. This thing with Ben . . . isn't a thing.*

Ben too seemed somber after the phone call and withdrew into himself.

Mentally preparing to see Dallin? Tara wondered and felt for him again, knowing what—and who—was waiting.

Fifteen minutes later, they entered an upscale neighborhood, even by Tara's standards. The gated community boasted enormous homes, tree-lined streets, and lavish, over-the-top Christmas light displays. From the corner of her eye, Tara studied Ben, wondering what he was thinking. Was he comparing his humble farm to his friend's obvious success?

They made a right-hand turn, and Ben slowed the truck, leaning forward to scan the addresses. Three homes down, he turned into the driveway and came to a stop.

"Well, this is it."

"Yes," Tara said. "Thank you again, for everything. I really appreciate your help, and I *will* mail you a check."

"You planning to walk to Boulder?" he asked. "I've taken you this far. Another thirty minutes isn't going to—"

"It *might* kill you." Tara smiled. "Better quit while you're ahead. Anyway, I'm going to call the rental car company. I was supposed to pick a car up in Denver. I paid for it in advance with my credit card, so they should be able to bring me one."

"Make sure it's a four-wheel drive." Ben stared past her at the snowy yard.

Is that concern *in his voice?* "Good idea."

His face was tense as he pulled the key from the ignition.

Tara glanced up at the house and saw the front door open, a tall, well-dressed man standing on the step. Beneath the porch light, Tara could see he was about Ben's age, though his hair was turning to salt-and-pepper gray. *See what kids do to you.*

He started down the walk and intercepted Cadie, swinging her high in the air and enfolding her in a big hug. Suddenly uncomfortable, Tara turned away.

Ben's eyes were still riveted to the scene, filled with a hurt Tara hadn't seen before. A split second later the hurt vanished, replaced by shock then anger as his lips pressed into a thin line.

"No way," he said under his breath.

Tara followed his gaze, though she was pretty sure she knew what had him ruffled. A petite brunette stood hesitantly behind Dallin, a hopeful smile on her face as she watched the family reunite.

Some reunion. Tara felt her ire rising on Ben's behalf. *How unfair. How mean. How . . . fortunate I'm still here.* Without stopping to examine her motives too closely, Tara leaned toward Ben, pulled him close, and crushed her lips to his once again.

Sixteen

Los Angeles, January

Tara crossed her legs and bent down to adjust the leather lacing on the back of one of her Lucchese black calf boots. She loved these boots and usually felt a little thrill each time she pulled them from her closet and slipped them on. She'd loved them from the moment she first spotted them in the store window and hadn't batted an eye at the $389 price tag. Of course the $184 leather, knee-length skirt with matching ties on the side had to be hers as well. And normally wearing them both was enough to brighten even the gloomiest winter day.

But that was before "normal" ceased to exist. Before an annoying pig farmer messed with her mind. These days—since her Christmas holiday that wasn't—nothing about her life felt normal at all. Today even the boots brought no pleasure.

"Tara. Tara? I know you're not going to let us down." An Armani suit coat flashed briefly in her line of vision.

"Of course not." Tara pulled her fingers from the soft leather, sat up straight, and opened the portfolio on the table in front of her. She cleared her throat before looking at the three other people sitting at the conference room table. Her coworker Gabby flashed her a thumbs-up.

Tara turned her attention to the man standing at the head of the table. "Over the past twelve weeks, I've closed sales on five properties: two condominiums, one retail property, one half-acre—"

"I'm aware of your stats," Jonathan, the evil one from corporate, said. "I've got your sheet right in front of me. And while your sales are definitely down, you're to be commended for doing this well in such tight times. It's people like you who'll keep this company afloat in the coming months."

"Umm—thanks." Tara tried to give Jonathan an appreciative smile before sending a confused glance at her colleagues. Jonathan wasn't exactly known for kind words, so something had to be up. *Talk about abnormal.*

"As each of you well know, the real estate market, especially here in California, is taking the biggest hit in this economy. Homes are losing their value faster than we can reduce—and sell—them. As a result, we've got to lose some personnel who aren't making the grade. Prime Properties isn't going to continue to pay prime benefits for those who can't perform."

Try saying that three times fast. Prime, properties, pay, perform. Tara rolled her eyes when Jonathan wasn't looking.

"Tough economy or not, we need performers. And many in this office simply aren't."

Here goes, Tara thought. *Odd that he chose to do it that way—the compliment before the axe.* Strangely enough, she found she didn't care that she might be about to lose her job. Like the boots, somehow the high-powered world of Southern California real estate had lost its appeal too.

"Max, you're staying because you've managed to land a big sale when *supposedly* no one is buying ten-million-dollar homes anymore."

Ever the cool one, Max continued to recline in his chair and barely gave Jonathan a nod.

"Cynthia, you're staying on because . . ."

Because lechers like you can't keep your eyes—or hands—off her. Once, this had really bothered Tara. Wasn't she supposed to be the woman men couldn't help noticing? When—and how—had that changed? She wasn't sure, but it had. *And I can only be thankful.* Since meeting Ben, *since that incredible kiss in the middle of a swirling snowstorm*, the thought of another man's hands on her was strangely unwelcome.

"And Tara's proven her ability to do what it takes to get a sale." She suppressed a shudder when Jonathan placed a hand on her shoulder as he walked past.

Tara forced a smile and tried to imagine it was Ben's hand on her shoulder. Ben's fingers pulling that ridiculous cap over her ears. Ben's lips . . .

"So you're my dream team." The hand left her shoulder. Jonathan's voice droned on.

"We'll be closing this branch by the end of the month and relocating you to the main office. It'll mean more commuting for everyone, but I know you're all up to the challenge. Cynthia, since you're so far out of the city, we'll make some arrangements for housing closer in."

I'll just bet you will, Tara thought, noting the way Cynthia was batting her eyelashes and Jonathan was staring at her—like a hungry wolf. *Ben would never look at a woman that way—like she's a piece of meat to be devoured.*

"That's everything, then," Jonathan continued. "I'll leave it up to you to let the others know I want them out by tonight."

Others? What's he talking about? What did I miss? Reluctantly Tara left the image of Ben standing on a Colorado mountain and focused on Jonathan snapping his briefcase shut. His Armani suit strode past one last time, and then he was gone.

"I'm outta here too," Max said less than ten seconds later.

"Oh, no, you don't." Gabby reached out, trying to grab his coat as he walked past. "You can't leave *us* to break the news."

"And hearts," Cynthia muttered.

"Of course I can," Max said. He paused in the doorway. "Females are always better at this sort of thing, being the compassionate, gentler sex and all."

"That's sexual harassment," Gabby called after him.

"Don't you wish, sweetheart." Max's voice echoed down the hall.

Gabby leaned forward over the table, head in her hands. "Great. Just great."

"What?" Tara finally dared ask. "What did I miss?"

Both Cynthia and Gabby stared at her. "You sure you didn't bump your head snowboarding or get hypothermia or something on your trip?" Gabby asked.

"No. I'm just tired," Tara said. "I must have fallen asleep for a minute while Jonathan was talking."

"Well, you didn't miss much." Cynthia rose from her chair, slinging her purse over her shoulder. "Basically we have until this evening to clear the office of all *nonperforming* personnel."

"Which would be everyone but the three of us and Maximilian." Gabby sighed.

"You're kidding?" Tara's mind wandered up and down the rows, calculating how many people they had in the office. It was one of Prime Properties' larger branches. "You must have misheard Jonathan," she concluded. "There's no way he'd—"

"You want it in writing? It's right here." Gabby tossed a folder across the table. Tara grabbed the file and opened it, quickly scanning the paper that verified Jonathan's edict.

"Convenient of him to leave the dirty work to us," she said.

"He's left *all* the work to us," Cynthia said. "We've got just one secretary between us, and we'll have everyone's listings to cover."

"There actually aren't all that many listings right now," Gabby said. "And I'd gladly take on more than that if it meant I could avoid telling someone she's fired."

Tara nodded in agreement. She didn't know the others in the office all that well, but that didn't mean she wanted to be the one to deliver bad news.

"We don't have to tell anyone anything." Cynthia leaned over the table and took the folder. "I'll just make copies of Jonathan's memo and hand them out to everyone. Easy as pie." She smiled broadly and gave a little shake of her hips as she headed toward the conference room door.

"I don't think that's such a good idea," Gabby said. "I think Jonathan wanted us to actually speak with—"

"You want to tell them in person? Go ahead. Here comes Herb now." Cynthia leaned out the doorway. "Oh, Herb. Could you come here for a second?"

Though Tara couldn't see Herb, she could imagine his reaction to Cynthia's request. Where many men in the office were only too eager for her company or attention, Herb went to extremes to avoid her. More than a few times, Tara had seen him start to enter the break room then head back out when he realized Cynthia was there.

Or was it because I was there? The thought bothered Tara, and she wondered why she hadn't considered the possibility before. There'd been a time or two when both she and Herb needed to go to corporate, and always he'd deferred the office car to her, telling her he'd take his own vehicle so he could pick up his kids—or run some other errand—afterward. Until now she'd never considered that he might be avoiding her too.

"I am so not doing this. No way." Gabby sent Tara a stubborn look.

"That's not fair," Tara said. "You guys aren't gonna dump all of this on me."

"Technically, he *is* on your team," Gabby said just as Herb appeared in the doorway. He shuffled into the room, eyes darting back and forth suspiciously. Cynthia stood behind him, fanning the folder in front of her face.

"What do you ladies need?" Herb asked. He reached up, scratching his nearly bald head, disturbing the few remaining hairs combed strategically across the top. When his pathetic hairstyle was sufficiently destroyed, he started on his too-wide, too-short tie, tugging at the sloppy knot.

Seeing he was uneasy, Tara tried to sound friendly, hoping she could somehow soften the you've-lost-your-job speech. "Come in for a sec, Herb." She pulled the chair next to her out and motioned for him to sit down.

"I really don't have time, ladies."

Unfortunately, you do. In fact, you're going to have a lot of free time. Tara glanced around the room, hoping someone else would speak up. But Gabby pursed her lips, shook her head back and forth then looked down. Cynthia stood in the doorway, still holding the folder. She shrugged and gave Tara a falsely bright smile. Herb hadn't moved from his original spot, two feet inside the room.

Tara silently cursed Jonathan and Max, Cynthia and Gabby. And anyone else who had contributed to this sudden predicament. *Best to just get it over with.*

"Here's the thing, Herb," she began. "Jonathan was just here, and he wasn't pleased with the sales coming out of our office. He wasn't pleased with any of the team stats and pointed out that the only ones who've really done much of anything this past quarter are Gabby, Max, and me." She purposely excluded Cynthia. The only thing *she'd* done was swing her hips the right way.

"Go on," Herb said.

Tara met his gaze and noticed the corners of his eyes were crinkling. She could tell his unease was starting to melt into worry. She paused, racking her brain for anything she knew about him, any way she might let him down easier. His desk was only a few away from hers, and when she'd first come to work here, he'd been very welcoming—in a fatherly sort of way. She thought back over the past couple of years, remembering snatches of conversations she'd overheard, conversations she hadn't taken the least bit of interest in.

He was married. She knew that much. And the photos she'd seen crammed on his desk reminded her that he had a couple of kids.

That realization hurt her chest in a funny sort of way. *What if it was Cadie and Sam's dad who was about to lose his job?* The thought surprised her. Hadn't she been thrilled to get away from them? And what would it matter to her if their dad did lose his job? Why should she care about Cadie getting sparkly shoes for Christmas, or Herb—and whatever his kids needed? But something akin to guilt began to nag at her.

She remembered suddenly that one of his kids had braces, and the other had some skull condition. What if it was serious—life threatening? Tara's dread rose a notch. Herb wasn't just about to lose his paycheck. He'd be losing his medical insurance too.

"How's your daughter with the skull problem?" she asked against her better judgment, giving in to her sudden need to know what losing this job was going to do to his family.

"Melanie doesn't have a *skull* problem." Herb's head tilted slightly, and he gave her a strange look. "She's got *scoliosis.* She wears a brace that's helping to straighten her spine."

"Ah . . . that's right." Tara nodded her head up and down. *Braces, skull problems—I was close.* She thought it pretty amazing she'd remembered that much.

"I've got a lot of work to do," Herb reminded them.

"Going to make copies." Cynthia waved the folder in the air and walked down the hall.

Gabby continued to look down at her hands, folded together on the table in front of her.

Tara sat up straighter and took a deep breath, ready to continue now that she realized the news she was about to deliver wasn't going to kill a kid.

"Herb, how many sales have you made this last quarter?"

"None of my listings have sold, but I got one and a half percent off a townhouse sale in—"

"As Jonathan just noted in our meeting, one and a half percent off someone else's listing doesn't do much for the company. Did you know that during the same amount of time, I've been able to close on five listings? That's *five* different commissions that have come back to this office—to pay *your* benefits."

Herb shrugged. "Everyone has good and bad months."

"Maybe so," Tara said. "But some people's worst months are consistently better than your best." *He's making this so easy. Poor, pathetic, middle-aged man.* "Those five sales I had didn't just fall into my lap. I had to *work* for them. Long hours—long after you'd gone home most of the time. I had to invest the time into getting to know my clients' needs and wants."

Gabby snorted. Tara glared at her across the table, but Gabby only arched an eyebrow, challenging her. *See if I share any more of my secrets with you,* Tara thought. That Gabby's own sales remained high, that she was one of those selected by Jonathan to stay, was largely due to the things she'd learned from Tara.

And they were all good, Tara rationalized. *I haven't done anything wrong, haven't broken any laws—technically speaking.* She'd only made suggestions and hinted at things that might or might not have been true. Sure, there was something in the Realtor's creed that mentioned honesty with all clients, but her own mother had taught her that a little white lie wasn't really bad, so long as no one got hurt. And no one ever did. They got properties. The ones they wanted. The ones they might have believed they were going to lose if they didn't bid a bit higher or act quicker. But in the end everyone was always happy. No one was complaining when she handed out a celebratory bottle of champagne, along with keys or a big, fat check. And the end result was all that mattered.

She'd first discovered her gift of persuasion years ago when trying to help her friend Jane close one of her own listings. Tara's little trick had gotten her a lecture from Jane—*the ingratitude*—whereas Jane had ended up with a great house and a handsome husband. And it had all started with a little fib. But still, Jane had been upset with her. Some people just didn't get it.

Like poor Herb.

Tara leaned back in her chair, studying him. "What do you think it would take for you to have sales like I do?" she asked, fully expecting to render him speechless. And then, when he couldn't answer, she'd have her way out. After all, how would he be able to argue with being let go when he'd just admitted to being an underachiever?

"Well," Herb said thoughtfully as his eyes met hers. "I suppose I could ignore my wife and children for several months. I could flirt with clients. I could fudge a little on the stats. But I don't imagine wearing short, tight leather skirts would help me the same way it seems to work for you."

Gabby laughed then tried to cover it with a fake cough. Tara didn't bother looking at her but stared at Herb, shocked at what she'd just heard. He brought a hand to his chin as if further considering.

"I could kiss up to the boss. Work absurd hours, have this—" He held his hand out, indicating the posh conference room "—be my only life."

Dead silence met his comment for a full ten seconds, then Tara found her voice.

"That's enough. You're fired."

"I figured as much," Herb said calmly and turned to leave.

Tara stood, her eyes shooting daggers his direction. "Why'd you want to be a Realtor anyway? You're a lousy salesman." She tried to think of another insult that would hurt as much as the ones he'd so passively flung at her.

"I didn't." Herb paused long enough to send a look full of sympathy her way. "I wanted to be a good dad, and I figured real estate would be a flexible job for that. Until now it has been. It's been enough to pay the bills, and I haven't missed any ball games."

It took Tara a second to realize what ball games he was talking about. Then she remembered the times Herb had left early, mentioning Little League, soccer, or some other kid-related event.

"But don't you *want* to be successful? Don't you want to get ahead?" She'd seen the dumpy car he drove—a Nissan from the early nineties. "Don't you ever want to go anywhere—besides some field where your kids are playing?" She stepped closer to him, having momentarily forgotten his insults in her desire to understand.

He shook his head and continued to look at her sadly. "Not if success is this . . . you, Gabby—" He looked her way. "Max, Cynthia. If corporate decrees the four of you are the kind of success this company wants, then you don't need to fire me. I quit." Herb left the room and walked down the hall, out of sight.

"That went well," Gabby said.

"Shut up." Tara returned to her chair and began gathering her things.

Cynthia came back in the room, a stack of papers in her hand. "All in favor of my brilliant idea?"

"Aye." Gabby waved her arm in the air.

Tara didn't say anything but hurried to shove her portfolio into her oversized Coach bag.

"Don't mind her," Gabby said to Cynthia. "She's pouting. Herb quit before she could fire him."

Tara whipped her head around to look at the two women. "Technically I fired him first."

"What's it matter?" Cynthia sat on the edge of the table, her legs, bare to mid-thigh, crossed. "He's gone. One down, how many to go?"

"Don't you feel just a little bad?" Tara asked, disbelief on her face. "I mean, these people have lives. Some have families. They have their own mortgages to pay."

"Not my problem," Gabby said.

It echoed one of Tara's frequent sentiments and stopped her cold.

One hand held her purse while the other reached for the back of the chair to steady herself. She felt as if a bucket of ice water had just washed over her. Almost like the icy air that had hit when she'd first stepped outside in Salt Lake City.

Not my problem . . . I could kiss up to the boss . . . Have this be my only life . . . If corporate deems you four the best . . . Your name ought to be Tiara . . . You're such a spoiled little princess . . .

A huge lump formed in her throat, and Tara knew she was going to cry—again. She still wasn't quite certain why, but tears were imminent. She stared at Gabby—cold, calculating, selfish Gabby. *Just like you taught her to be,* an inner voice whispered.

And Cynthia? Out to use her body to get whatever she wanted. *And I've been jealous.* Along with the threat of tears, Tara felt nauseated. Angry. Disgusted.

With herself.

"Twenty-seven," Tara said.

"What?" Cynthia wrinkled her pert little nose.

"Twenty-seven people you have left to fire," Tara said. "I've taken care of two for you."

"Two?" Gabby asked. "There was just Herb."

"And me," Tara said. "I quit."

Seventeen

Tara walked around her living room, picking up glasses half-full of champagne and plates with half-eaten hors d'oeuvres.

"What a waste," she mumbled, conscious, for the first time in a long time, of the money she'd thrown away on a party that was . . . pointless.

The people who'd come weren't really her friends. Sure, they'd go to lunch with her or shopping or to a club, but that was where it ended. As deep as it got. They wouldn't slow down long enough— take time from their own self-centered, fast-track lives—to listen when she wanted to talk, to care about something she cared about, to help her when she'd practically begged them to. *Recommend me to your boss for the job that's opening in your office. Introduce me to a guy who's decent. Come over just to hang out and talk. Help me figure out who I am—what I'm doing here.*

"What *am* I doing here?" Tara stopped at one of four vases of red roses scattered throughout the room. She bent over, inhaling their fragrance, and found they didn't smell sweet to her at all. "Stupid holidays," she muttered then picked up the vase and dumped it, water, flowers, and all, in the trash.

"Hey, babe." Doug appeared in the bedroom doorway, his shirt-tails hanging open above a pair of unbuttoned khakis.

"Oh." Tara glanced at him then returned to her work. "You're still here."

"Well, yeah. It's Valentine's. I assumed you'd want me to stay over."

Do I? Tara examined her thoughts for a moment. She could spend the evening alone, *or* she could share it with a guy who didn't really care about her. *Some choice.* She was tired of pretending, tired of being with people who only used her to get what they wanted.

"Nope. I don't want you to stay."

Doug's mouth opened and he held out his hands, palms up. "Did I do something? Was it because I was talking to Lisa all evening? She and I used to have a thing, but it's been over for a long time. We're not—"

"Out." Tara pointed a polished nail toward her front door. "Just get out." She dumped another plate full of food in the garbage. *So much for the splurge on catering. Better not use that company again. Do I want to do this again?*

Behind her, Doug expressed a few choice words about her hospitality then left, slamming the door behind him.

"Love you too," Tara said bleakly. She dropped the trash bag on the floor and sank onto her plush, white sofa. Grabbing up the nearest flute of champagne, she leaned her head back and drank the entire thing. Added to the alcohol she'd already consumed, she was starting to feel a little light-headed. Not an entirely great feeling, but it was a whole lot better than her usual Valentine's Day misery.

She found an open bottle and drank some more. The room was beginning to spin a bit now, a little like the Tilt-A-Whirl at Knott's Berry Farm when it first started going. She'd had a date there last year. She'd been furious at first, when her date—*what was his name?*—had told her that's where they were going. But surprisingly she'd had a really good time. Until the end of the evening, that is, when the guy had accidentally let slip that he took his kids to Knott's Berry Farm a lot. She'd had enough fun and liked him enough by that point that she might have attempted to give the he-has-kids issue a chance, but then she'd discovered he also had a wife to go with the kids—a wife whose season pass Tara happened to be using.

"Jerk," she muttered then brought the bottle to her lips again. When it was empty, she tossed it toward the trash bag but missed. Instead, the bottle hit the corner of the wall, shattering before it fell in pieces to the floor. *What a mess. Like me.*

Grabbing up one of the heart throw pillows she'd purchased as part of her decor for the ultimate Valentine party, Tara lay on her side, curling herself around the pillow. Instead of being soft and comforting, like a stuffed animal might have been, it was stiff and unyielding.

Like a real heart. Or the ones I *encounter, anyway.* She lay there a long time, staring at the empty room, the *emptiness* surrounding her. For weeks planning this party had been the thing she'd focused on, the thing she'd looked forward to, the thing that kept her going. Now it was over, leaving her feeling emptier and even more alone than she had before.

"It's over," she said to herself and knew she was talking about much more than the party. The life she'd planned out for herself, the posh condo, the six-figure income, the social scene in LA. None of it mattered anymore. In fact, she couldn't stand it, couldn't stand being here. She wasn't sure why it had appealed to her in the first place.

What's a girl to do? she wondered. According to Fergie, crying wasn't an option. And she hadn't cried once since the day she quit. But she was tired—oh so tired—of feeling lost and empty. Tired of being here. There had to be something better. Some *place* better.

Her eyelids closed in sleep, the last images floating before them— water, a snow-capped mountain, a quaint island, a place she'd once considered home . . . a friend she'd once considered true.

Spring

"*Restlessness is discontent, and discontent is merely the first necessity of progress.*"
—*Thomas A. Edison*

Eighteen

Seattle, Washington

DR. CHASSON ADJUSTED HER GLASSES as she stared at the lines on the hospital monitor. "How much longer will Peter be out of the country?"

"Eleven weeks, four days." Jane pulled her gaze from the screen to her doctor's face. "He just left on Monday. We thought he'd make it home in plenty of time for the babies' birth."

"He will if I have anything to do with it." Dr. Chasson glanced at the IV line going down to Jane's arm. She walked around the side of the bed, checking the bag and adjusting the drip. "Hmmm."

"Hmmm what?" Jane asked. She pushed the button on the remote, raising the bed, and herself, to more of a sitting position—no easy feat with her bulging stomach and the various things currently attached to it.

Dr. Chasson met her concerned gaze. "You're going to have to be on strict bed rest. And with your husband gone, I'm thinking that means you need to stay here for a while."

"But the labor has stopped."

"But will it stay that way when you're off the terbutaline?" Dr. Chasson pulled up a chair and sat beside Jane.

Jane looked over at her, trying not to panic and trying not to feel envious of her doctor's trim figure and stylish outfit. *Swollen ankles have a payoff in the end*, she reminded herself.

"You're weeks away from the safe zone, and this was a close call."

"I know," Jane said. "But Maddie needs me, and—"

"My point exactly," the doctor said. "You're a mom, and from my experience, moms don't rest when they're at home with their kids."

"*Kid*. Just one," Jane reminded her. "And she's a great little helper. Plus I've got family who can pitch in." But even as she spoke the words, doubt filled her mind. Her mom and dad were out of the country too, serving a mission. Her closest sister, Caroline, was in Arizona, trying out a job possibility with her husband. And her other siblings were scattered miles apart up and down the northern coast of Washington. It had been months since they'd gotten together for a family dinner, and Jane knew they each had busy, full lives with their own spouses and children. It wasn't likely she'd be able to get any of them to stay with Maddie. And the thought of sending Maddie away—when Peter was already gone—was unbearable.

I've got to be home. I'll work something out.

"You do have a big family," Dr. Chasson said.

Jane could tell she was wavering. "And you've delivered how many of their babies? My sisters know a thing or two about being pregnant. They'll watch out for me."

"Hmmm," Dr. Chasson said again, this time writing something on the papers on her clipboard. "You know what complications can happen if you don't make it to thirty-six weeks?"

"I know," Jane said. And she did, probably more than any other first-time pregnant mother. The twins she and Peter had adopted five years ago had been born two months premature with a host of health problems. Mark hadn't been strong enough to withstand them and his heart condition and had died shortly after his first birthday. Though time had softened the constant sorrow she'd felt after his death, she would never forget the precious little boy he'd been and how he had suffered. She would do just about anything to keep these twins from coming early. *Even sending Maddie away, if I have to.*

"I'll find a way to stay down, or I'll check myself back into the hospital," Jane promised. "I'll find someone to stay with me, and I can direct things from the couch."

"Lying down is best," Dr. Chasson said. "And I'll want to see you every week. You'll have to call an ambulance if you have any more spotting or cramping. This isn't something we can mess around with. First time or not, labor can progress quickly, and we might not be able to stop it next time."

"I understand," Jane said, trying her best to stay calm.

The bleeps monitoring her babies' heartbeats remained steady.

"Of course, all this is based on the next twenty-four hours. Your IV is almost finished, and then we'll wait and see what happens. If there is no activity tonight or tomorrow, I'll release you. Though I think it's best if we keep you on preventative medication for the duration of your pregnancy."

"Thank you." Jane waited until Dr. Chasson left the room, then she rested her head against the pillow and closed her eyes. But she wasn't thinking of sleep. She had twenty-four hours to pray for a solution—a minor miracle. She'd had a few miracles before—big ones—like her husband being found in the Iraqi desert after his helicopter was shot down.

Jane had no doubt her Father in Heaven would hear her prayer again this time. The Relief Society on Bainbridge was mighty, but it was also few in numbers, and Jane knew they could only do so much. It would be taxing on them—and her—to have Maddie farmed out for the next eleven weeks. What she needed was someone who could stay at the cottage with her, someone who could take over the responsibilities of the house and yard while caring for Maddie.

Not much that I'm asking for, she thought with a wry smile. But her parents had taught her that the first step to solving a problem was prayer. It was always the place to start.

Lying there in the quiet room, Jane folded her arms and bowed her head, beginning by thanking her Father in Heaven for the many blessings he'd granted her these past five years. *So many times You've answered my prayers. And now I ask again.* In earnest she pled for the safety of her husband, their babies, and Maddie's care for the next nearly three months. Tears trickled down her face as she felt overwhelmed with the worry that was hers—the things that could go wrong and all that could be taken from her. But on the heels of that fear, Jane felt a sudden peace wash over her, a comfort that was almost tangible. It filled her mind and heart, carrying away her worry.

It had taken a miracle for her to get pregnant with these babies, and Heavenly Father was going to help her get them safely here. He would provide the care she and Maddie needed. She knew it without a doubt.

Nineteen

TARA PUT THE TOP DOWN on her convertible and cranked up the radio as she drove onto the Golden Gate Bridge. She'd timed her drive right, and the midday traffic wasn't bad. The breeze blew her hair from her face and the sun sparkled on the water as she looked out at the ocean below. The morning fog had already burned off, revealing an exceptionally beautiful, clear day for April. The sixty-degree weather was a bit cool for having the top down, but she knew things weren't going to be any better up north. Best to enjoy what sun she had while she had it.

Glancing behind her, she checked to make sure her various boxes and suitcases were still wedged tightly in the backseat. Goosebumps worked their way up her arms beneath the sleeves of her sweater, the pink one Ben had bought for her in Utah last December. She hadn't worn it since that ill-fated drive through the Rocky Mountains, but she'd reasoned that it was the perfect attire for moving day. After all, it hadn't cost a fortune, so it wouldn't matter too much if something happened and it got ruined.

In the two and a half months since she'd quit her job, she'd decided that much of what she owned didn't really matter to her. She'd sold her condo at a loss, sold all of her furniture to help cover some of that loss, and given much of her clothing to charity. She'd tried to find a Deseret Industries in Southern California, but they didn't exist there, so she'd had to settle for taking everything to the Goodwill.

The things she had left were her absolute favorites. Three suitcases of shoes in the trunk, several garment bags full of her best pant-suits and skirts, and two large bags and one box of accessories. Her makeup case took up the front seat. What little else she'd decided to keep she'd shipped to Jane's house on Bainbridge, a little island near Seattle.

Thinking about those packages she'd mailed yesterday, Tara felt the only nervousness she had about this move surface. She felt confident she could get her old job back—after all, she'd been one of their top sellers before she left. She also knew she could find a place to rent. Paying off the mortgage on her condo had taken most of her savings, but she had enough to cover first and last month's rent and a security deposit, so she was probably good there too. But for those first few days, while she found a place, she'd hoped to stay with her old friend Jane.

It used to be—when Jane had been single—no problem to pop in for a night or two. Jane had always said her door was open, and she'd come through with that offer on many occasions.

But what if that isn't the case now? Tara worried. Marriage and children might have changed that scenario. *Might have changed it a lot. I should have called.* But she hadn't wanted to, hadn't been willing to risk a rejection that might have changed her mind about coming home, or somewhere as close to home as she'd ever had.

Jane might not welcome her with open arms, but Tara really hoped she'd welcome her just a little. More than a night or two on the couch, she needed a friend, someone who would encourage her and help her figure out what to do next. Jane had always been that kind of friend, and above all, Tara hoped that hadn't changed.

Twenty

Jessica handed her aunt a glass of lemonade. "What if I skipped the backpack trip and hung out with you next week?"

"Absolutely not," Jane said. "But nice try." She took a drink and looked out across the backyard, watching Maddie and her cousin climbing on the play set. "Your last year of girls' camp is the *best*. Being a youth leader is a lot of fun. You don't want to miss that. And I know you need this backpack trip to certify."

"*You* need me." Jessica poured lemonade into two miniature pink plastic teacups then set them on a matching tray. "Be right back." She carried the cups, along with a plate of animal crackers, across the yard to the little girls.

Jane smiled as she watched her niece. Jessica would be a great mom someday, and no doubt that day would be here before she knew it. It was hard to believe Jessica was already seventeen. It seemed to Jane like just yesterday she'd been singing karaoke at Jessica's twelfth birthday party.

"Time flies," she said as Jessica returned to the patio.

"What?"

"I was just thinking about how much you've grown up, how fast time goes—except when your husband is out of the country and you're five and a half months pregnant." Jane patted her round tummy. "Then it slows waaaay down."

Jessica looked at her with concern. "Don't you think you should lie down and take a nap? I'll stay out with the little girls. You go inside and sleep for a couple of hours."

"You sound like Grandma—and that nurse I had at the hospital," Jane said, laughing as much as her constricted airflow allowed these days. "You've got the bossy part down pat."

"Not bossy enough," Jessica muttered, sinking into the chair beside her. "If I were, you'd be in *bed*, not out here on the patio. That's why they call it *bed rest*, you know."

"I know." Jane nodded. "But it's the *rest* part that's important, and I'm doing that. Besides, I feel so much better when I'm out here. I'll go crazy if I have to stay indoors the next two months. Out in the yard I can see the garden and the trees—" She paused mid-sentence, eyes glued to a peach tree laden with buds. She hadn't gotten around to pruning it, and when the fruit began to grow, some of the branches were going to be overburdened. Her gaze shifted to the shed, and her fingers flexed involuntarily as she imagined the pruning shears in her hands.

Jessica noticed. "Don't even think about doing yard work. I forbid it. I'm going to drive down to the store and buy a new padlock for that shed so you can't get to your tools."

"Bossy and *controlling*." Jane grimaced. "You've definitely got the traits to go into nursing."

"Bet you don't know any nurses who give pedicures," Jessica said. "How about finishing those toes?"

"You mean I've still got them?" Jane said in mock seriousness. "It's been so long since I've seen my feet." She raised one leg as high as it would go—not far at all—straining to see her half-painted toenails.

"What'll it be today?" Jessica held up a sheet of decals. "Hearts? Flowers?"

Jane lowered her leg. "Do you have any stars?" She leaned her head back, a wistful smile on her face as she stared up at the cloudy sky. "I miss them. It's been so long since I've used the telescope."

"It better be a lot longer," Jessica said. "Tell me you're not thinking of going up on the roof anytime soon."

"Oh, I *think* about it all the time," Jane said, longing in her voice. "Then I get up off the couch and remember how much effort just a simple movement like that takes."

"I'll look at the stars for you next week," Jessica said. "I should be able to see tons at camp."

"Lucky." Jane nodded her agreement. "Are you all packed?"

"I was packed before I came. My carry-on bag had stuff to wear at your house. The suitcase I checked has my backpack in it."

"I'm so glad you get to go." Jane knew the past few months had been difficult for Jessica. Her parents were going through a tough time, and this sudden move in the middle of her junior year of high school couldn't be easy.

"I wish Mom could have come too," Jessica said. "We always wanted to go to camp together, but . . ."

All of your little brothers came instead, Jane silently finished Jessica's thought. For all the effort she and Peter had had to go through to have a baby, it seemed the opposite for Caroline. Though she and Ryan had planned to be *done* having babies, they just kept coming.

For the past couple of days, Jane had the recurring thought that perhaps Caroline was going to come visit as well, though not to camp but to stay with her. Jane had continued her prayers, asking for the help she needed, and she still felt every reassurance that everything would work out. And, of course, it had worked out so far.

First, Jessica had flown in a few days early and had been able to help Jane with Maddie and also with Allison, the niece Jane had committed to babysitting months ago. Allison's parents were on a once-in-a-lifetime trip to Israel and Egypt and had farmed their children out to various family members for three weeks. It was unfortunate that the second day of their trip had been the day Jane ended up in the hospital with preterm labor.

But even from a distance, Caroline had come to the rescue, changing Jessica's ticket and flying her out that night. But with the backpack trip only two days away, Jane knew something else had to happen soon, and she felt strongly that the something might be her sister. Along with the reassurance that all would be well, the Spirit was also whispering to her that there was something *she* could do to help someone too—even having to rest as she did.

Caroline was the only one Jane could think of who needed help, that shoulder to cry on, a listening ear, as she tried to hang on to her marriage and make it through an extremely trying time. Jane's prayers now included a plea that she might be prepared and know how to help, what to say and when to listen. Though she was concerned about her sister, Jane was grateful for the distraction from her own problems. Between worrying about Peter and anxiety over their unborn babies, she'd dissolve into a ball of nerves if she wasn't careful.

"What are you going to do Thursday morning if you don't have any help?" Jessica asked, pulling Jane from her thoughts.

"I *will* have help." Jane gave Jessica a reassuring smile. "Trust me. Some things you just know."

"Wish *I* knew it," Jessica muttered.

"Hello, anyone home?" a high, falsely bright voice called through the gate.

Jessica jumped up to see who it was while Jane's mind raced with memory. She hadn't heard that voice in—

A blur of red—hair, sweater, leather pants and boots—stepped through the gate as Jessica pulled it open. Jane's mouth dropped in astonishment then curved in a smile.

"Tara!" she exclaimed as she struggled to get up from the chaise.

Tara took a hesitant step then practically bounded across the yard. She stopped a foot in front of Jane and stared at her stomach.

"You're *huge*. What has Peter done to you?"

Jane laughed and threw her arms open, engulfing Tara in an awkward hug. "I see you haven't changed at all. You still tell it like it is."

"And it *is*, Sister. Holy cow. You *look* like you swallowed a cow."

"That's not very nice," Jessica said. Arms folded and a frown on her face, she stood beside them. "Aunt Jane, you shouldn't be up. You need to lie down."

"I didn't swallow a cow," Jane said, letting Jessica help her back to the chair. "Just a couple of pills that increased our odds of getting pregnant—and having *twins*."

"Twins? You're having more twins? But you've already got a set." Tara took the chair Jessica had been sitting in.

"We have Maddie," Jane said, the faintest trace of sadness in her voice. "Mark died. It wasn't very long after Peter and I married."

"I'm so sorry," Tara said. Her smile faded, and her bubbly manner seemed to deflate. "I didn't know. It must have happened after I left for LA."

"Probably," Jane said. She could tell Tara was uncomfortable with the sudden change in subject. "Let me introduce you to Maddie. Girls," she called. "Come here for a minute." She raised her hand, beckoning Maddie and Allison over.

Maddie poked her head out from the fort at the top of the play structure, waved at her mom, then slid down the slide and ran across the yard to join them.

"This is my daughter, Madison." Jane pulled her close, kissing the top of her sweaty head. "Maddie, this is Mommy's friend Tara."

"Hello." Madison walked up to Tara and held her hand out.

Tara shook it. "Nice to meet you."

"I like your red clothes," Maddie said, her eyes roving up and down Tara.

"Thank you very much."

"I have to go now." Maddie pulled her hand away and spun around. "Allison won't come down the slide unless I catch her."

"You have *another* one?" Tara asked.

"Just borrowed. She's my niece. And this is another niece, Jessica." Jane motioned for Jessica to pull up another chair and join them. "She's here visiting. Her family recently moved."

"Oh?" Tara turned to Jessica. "Where to?"

"Arizona," Jessica said stiffly. She shot Jane a look full of questions.

"Tara and I used to work together," Jane said. "On our lunch hour, we'd share our dating woes over extremely fattening baked goods."

"Ah . . . orange rolls," Tara remembered. "Those were the days."

Not really, Jane thought, glad she'd moved on with her life. *But has Tara?* She glanced at her friend's hand, noting the absence of a ring.

"How is California?" she asked.

"Smoggy and crowded," Tara said.

"Oh." It wasn't the answer Jane had anticipated. Knowing Tara, she'd expected to be regaled with an hour's worth of stories about ritzy events, fabulous parties, and the like. She felt the first inkling that something wasn't quite right—that perhaps Tara's dropping by was more than a social visit. But things with Tara had never been predictable. Her lifestyle choices made for a wild ride, and Jane wasn't one to judge her for that. She'd always felt bad that she couldn't help Tara figure out the things that would bring her true, lasting happiness.

"Has real estate taken a beating down there like it has here?" Jane asked.

"Worse," Tara said. She pointed to the lemonade. "May I?"

Jane nodded, and Tara took a Zoo Pals paper cup off the tray and filled it with lemonade.

"So is your job okay?" *What if it's Tara? What if she's the one you've been thinking of who needs your help? No-o.* Jane pushed the ridiculous thought aside.

"It was fine," Tara said. "But then corporate wanted me to fire a bunch of people on my team, and . . ." She took a deep breath, squared her shoulders, and met Jane's eyes. "I refused to do it, so I quit."

"Good for you," Jane found herself saying. *Bad for me? What does this mean?* "So are you here visiting?"

"Nope." Tara shook her head. "I'm here to stay. LA wasn't the place for me, after all. I'm going to see about getting my old job back, and I'll find an apartment. Hey, mind if I use your bathroom?" She jumped up, heading for the patio doors.

"Sure," Jane said. "You remember where it is, I guess."

When Tara had entered the house, Jessica leaned in close, whispering loudly, "Aunt Jane, she left a suitcase by your gate. I think she's planning to stay."

"Of course she is," Jane said, her lips curving with a speculative smile as the puzzle pieces seemed to fall clearly into place. "A long time ago I told her my door was always open, and I meant it."

"But you can't play hostess right now. You have to rest."

"I plan to," Jane said.

"But she—she can't take care of—"

"She'll have to." Jane felt the sudden need to laugh out loud.

"What's so funny?" Jessica asked warily.

"Nothing. Everything." Jane shook her head and wiped the corner of her eye. "Sometimes the Lord works in mysterious ways, that's all."

Twenty-One

"Thanks for driving Jessica to the ferry," Jane said, looking up from her spot on the couch between the two little girls snuggled beside her as they watched *Cinderella*.

"No problem," Tara said as she walked past Jane and went into the kitchen. She placed three bags of groceries on the counter and returned to the car to get the rest, along with the takeout she'd ordered for dinner. *Thanks for doing the grocery shopping too. Buying dinner was so thoughtful of you. You're the best, Tara.* In her head she tacked on a few extra words of praise that would have been nice to hear.

She loaded up both hands then closed the car door with her hip. Of course she was driving her own car too and using up her own gas, because Jane needed her car ready for her next doctor visit.

She'll probably ask me to drive her there and fill up her Jeep while I'm waiting, Tara thought with no little amount of irritation. She'd been there less than forty-eight hours, and in that time she'd barely had two seconds to herself.

Yesterday, before she had worked up the nerve to ask Jane if she could stay a few days, Jane had asked *her* if she'd be interested in staying the next eleven weeks while Peter was gone. Of course she'd jumped at the offer—it was even better than the week or two she'd hoped for . . . or so she'd thought.

So much for being the houseguest. Tara set the bags on the step and opened the door. *What she needs is a nanny and a maid. She practically tricked me.* The old Jane never would have done something like that. Tara had always heard that pregnancy made women wacko, and that certainly seemed the case with Jane. She couldn't even get up for a glass of water anymore, and she was always putting her hands on her stomach and talking to herself—or rather those *things* growing inside her.

It was unnerving.

"Did you get pizza?" Jane's five-year-old and her two-year-old cousin were already sitting at the counter, rummaging through the bags she'd brought in.

"Fruit snacks?" Allison asked.

"Chinese," Tara said. "It's better for you."

"Would you mind fixing the girls some plates?" Jane called from the other room.

"Sure," Tara called back. She took two plastic, divided plates from the cupboard above the dishwasher. *Sure I mind. I would have liked my dinner hot.* She began pulling little boxes from the restaurant bag.

"Oooh. Those are cute. Can I have them when you're done?" Maddie asked.

Tara shrugged. "If you want them."

"Thank you." Maddie beamed at her.

"You don't have to thank me all the time."

Maddie looked confused. "Please and thank you are the magic words."

"Never mind," Tara said. "Just eat your rice." She plopped an egg roll on each plate next to the rice she'd already scooped out. After taking another plate from Jane's cupboard, she began serving herself. When she turned back to the counter to get some silverware, she found both girls staring at her.

"What?"

"We haven't prayed yet," Maddie said. Allison held her folded arms up as evidence.

"Well, go ahead." Tara waved her hand at them. "No one is stopping you."

They continued to stare at her.

"It's your turn," Maddie whispered. "You haven't said a prayer since you got here."

Tara leaned over the table, close to the little girl's face. "That's because I *don't* pray."

Maddie gasped, jumped off her stool, and ran into the other room.

"Fine. Go tattle." Tara stabbed her fork in the egg roll and took a bite while Allison looked on with big eyes. A minute later Maddie returned to the room.

She climbed up onto the stool, folded her arms, and said a prayer. When she was done, she looked at Tara as if the incident had never happened. "Thank you for dinner."

"You're welcome." Sometimes she wished Jane's kid was more like Cadie instead of Miss Manners. It was difficult to be gruff with a five-year-old who was always thanking you.

"Mommy says thank you too," Maddie added.

Jane. Tara glanced at the open boxes on the counter then reluctantly set her own plate aside to fix one for Jane. *She's got to eat too.* When she had it ready, she carried it into the living room where Jane was resting, eyes closed, hands folded over her bulging belly.

Uncertain whether to awaken her, Tara spoke softly. "Jane?"

She opened her eyes, sat up a little, and accepted the plate from Tara. "Thanks," she said. "I'm so glad you're here."

Tara could see she meant it, and she felt just a little guilt for her earlier grumbling. She couldn't help but return Jane's smile. "Me too."

* * *

Tara walked into the living room and sank into the nearest chair. "They're finally asleep." *Little devils.* She ran a hand across her cheek, still trying to wipe away the excess slobber from Maddie's good-night kiss. She'd brushed two sets of teeth, read three bedtime stories, brought in two drinks of water, checked for monsters under the bed, and helped wipe a bottom in the last hour since Jane had asked her to put the girls to bed. Who knew such a simple thing as getting a couple of kids in bed could be so . . . complicated and exhausting?

"Great. Now we can watch a movie. And how about making some popcorn?" Jane said, all enthusiastic.

She's not tired. She's been resting all day. Tara glared at her, irritated Jane hadn't even thanked her or noticed how drained she was. Grumbling under her breath, she hauled herself out of the chair and walked toward the entertainment center. "You certain you're up to watching one of these?" Tara asked as she glanced through the shelves of Jane's favorite romance DVDs. She wasn't sure *she* could handle it tonight. For some reason, being back in Washington had increased her melancholy and restlessness instead of curing them, and she didn't know why. But she could almost bet that watching an over-romanced chick flick was not going to remedy the problem.

"Why not?" Jane asked.

"For starters, your husband is seven thousand miles away. And aside from that, you won't possibly be able to imagine yourself as the heroine looking like you do."

"Thanks for reminding me how very fat I am right now," Jane said. "I'd nearly forgotten. It's been about three hours since you last mentioned it."

Tara shrugged and said flippantly, "If your friends aren't honest, who can you count on?"

"Good question," Jane said. "Speaking of friends and honesty and all, why don't we pretend it's old times? Step into my cubicle and talk. We can watch a movie later."

"All right." Tara sauntered across the room, taking a chair opposite Jane's couch. "What do you want to talk about?"

"Hmmm." Jane brought a finger to her chin, pretending to consider. "How about what you've been up to the past five years since you literally disappeared off the map."

"*I'm* not the one who vanished," Tara protested. "You're the one who quit your job then went and got married and started having all these kids."

"*All* these kids?" Jane laughed, reminding Tara that her once-single and once-fun friend was still in there somewhere. "Maddie is five and still waiting for a sibling. In my family that's practically cause to be disowned. If I was like my mother or sisters, I'd already have three children with another on the way."

"Looks like you're making up for lost time," Tara said, staring at Jane's stomach. "There could be three in there."

Jane attempted to kick her. "You're gonna give me a complex. When did you get so mean?"

"Corporate real estate in LA does that to you."

"Is that why you left? Was it brutal?"

"It was pretty bad, but that's not why I left. I just—just wanted a change of scenery, I guess."

Jane's eyebrows rose speculatively. "Did that change have anything to do with a man?"

Yeah, but not like you're thinking. "I didn't leave anyone, if that's what you're hinting at. I haven't lived with anyone the entire time I've been there." *Except for that two-week stint with Mario—what a disaster.* Tara grimaced, trying to push the painful memory to the back of her mind.

Mario was the first guy she'd dated in LA. She'd met him at the pool of their apartment complex her first week there. He'd shown her around, taken her to all the ritzy clubs, sent her flowers and jewelry regularly . . . swept her off her feet and swept every last cent out of her bank account by the time she'd discovered the fraud he was, less than a month into their relationship. After that she'd been careful, picky—wise, even. But eventually the sting of his betrayal had faded and the persistent loneliness that was her only companion had compelled her to start dating again. And she'd followed the same pattern as always . . . one miserable man after the other.

Long ago she'd decided there must be some magnetism in her that attracted the less-than-desirable, a stamp on her forehead that advertised, *Looking for a loser—someone who will use or abuse, take advantage of and stomp all over what's left of my fragile heart.*

She'd dated dozens of guys just like that. Every single one of them, in fact.

Except Ben, and that wasn't exactly dating. Tara sighed aloud. She didn't want to think about or talk about her life. It was too depressing.

"I didn't come back up here for anyone, either. I'm not dating Zack again. Yes, I still love painting, though I haven't done any in a long time. No, LA wasn't what I thought it would be. There. All caught up now?" She stood again. A movie was starting to look real good.

"Hardly." Jane pulled the oversized cushions off the back of the sofa and did her best to scoot in then beckoned for Tara to come and sit beside her. "You *used* to want to talk all the time."

"That was before you were married and got all fat on me." *Everything is weird now. Different. I hate it.*

"Ah, Tara, I've missed you. Nobody could ever make me feel quite so bad about my out-of-control hair." Jane ran her fingers through her ever-present natural curls. "And now you've got even more things to insult me about. I'm not sure I'd make it through the rest of this pregnancy without you." She held out her arms, and Tara reluctantly came over, bending down for an awkward hug.

"Now stay," Jane ordered, patting the empty spot beside her again.

"Oh, fine." Tara sat—or tried to—but it was a precarious perch. Jane took up more space than she realized.

"I'm the same person I used to be," Jane said. "And I'd really love to hear what's going on in your life. I'll even throw in a box of tissue for free."

"We're probably going to need it," Tara said after a minute. *If I get started . . .* Still, she hesitated. "This feels so weird. Maybe if we had orange rolls from the bakery?"

Jane shook her head. "They're closed. Besides, I'm already too fat, remember?"

Tara giggled. "You are." *I am never having children. Never. Never. Never.*

"Glad my weight gain is providing amusement. Now what gives? You can't just show up on my doorstep after years of being gone and not tell me why."

"Well, you see . . ." Tara took a deep breath then launched into her story. "I met this guy."

"And?" Jane prodded.

"And that was it," Tara said. "I met him at the airport in Salt Lake, and we spent a couple of days together pretty much hating each other's guts. Then I started to see some things I liked about him. Then he kissed me—totally messed with my mind—and I left. The end."

"What were you doing in Salt Lake?" Jane asked.

Tara threw her hands up in exasperation. "I tell you this whole thing about a guy, and you want to know about the geography?"

"Sorry." Jane smiled sheepishly. "I was just curious. I never imagined you in Utah, that's all."

"I never imagined me in Utah either," Tara said and proceeded to tell Jane her nightmare-flight-and-getting-stranded story. Jane listened attentively, gasping and oohing in all the right places, so that by the time Tara reached the end of her tale, she felt things were a little like the old days.

"Ben sounds terrible," Jane said. "Though Ellen sounds like a really nice person."

"She is," Tara said. "And her husband turned out to be nice too."

"So did you ever find out what the deal is between him and Ben?"

Tara nodded. "Of course I did. You know that when Tara wants to know something—"

"Tara finds out," Jane finished. "I remember. Boy, do I remember. There was the day you stole my plant with the note in it from Paul, and the time—"

"Yeah, yeah," Tara said. "Do you want the rest of this story or not?"

"Definitely."

"So I asked Ellen on the last part of our drive, and she told me all about Ben and Dallin being best friends from the time they were about ten until they went on their missions. Ben came home a few months before Dallin, and he started dating Dallin's younger sister, McKenzie—also Ellen's friend."

"I follow," Jane said.

"By the time Dallin got home, Ben and McKenzie were engaged. Dallin and Ellen started dating too. Everything was great. That's when Ben's birth mother showed up."

"He's adopted?" Jane asked.

Tara nodded. "They all are. Ben and each of his fourteen brothers and sisters. I forgot to mention that part." Tara hurried on. "Anyway, Ben's mom had big problems. Alcoholism, schizophrenia—some very *serious* stuff. And she expected Ben to take care of her."

"Did he?" Jane asked.

"He tried," Tara said. "He got her some help, paid for her therapy, drove her places. Things like that. It was hard, and it took its toll on him and on his engagement. By then Dallin and Ellen were engaged too. Ben and McKenzie decided to postpone their wedding and get married at Christmastime with Dallin and Ellen. But then Ben got sick."

"What kind of sick?" Jane asked, worry in her expression. Tara was glad to see it there. She was afraid she'd painted Ben in too harsh a light, and she wanted Jane to like him, wanted her to understand what a good person he really was.

"He started having some . . . mental problems. Breakdowns, panic attacks. Behavior similar to his mom's. Suddenly it was his adoptive parents taking *him* to counseling."

"Is he better now?" Jane asked.

"He's been better for a long time. Ellen said the doctors thought it was his interaction with his birth mother that triggered his anxiety. She'd been very abusive—the reason Ben was removed from the home and placed in foster care—and being around her again brought back a lot of repressed stuff, or something like that."

"Very plausible," Jane said.

"Yeah." Tara turned to her. "You'd know, wouldn't you, Mrs. Bachelor's Degree in Psychology."

"Bachelor's nothing." Jane angled her head toward a frame on the far wall. "I've got my master's now. Check out my diploma."

"You did it? You went back and finished?" Tara jumped up and went over to the wall, reading Jane's diploma. "I'm glad one of us has been doing something productive—no pun intended—" She stared pointedly at Jane's stomach "—all this time."

"I'm sure you have too," Jane said.

Tara pursed her lips together and brought a finger to her chin as if considering. "Nope. Not really."

"Let me decide. Come finish your story."

Tara sat down again, this time in the chair so Jane could have the whole couch. "So Ben had these repressed memory, psychotic incidents. But he got counseling, his parents got rid of his mom—not literally," she clarified. "But they sent her somewhere else and told her she had to stay out of his life. Everything was better, but McKenzie had cold feet. Dallin advised her *not* to marry Ben, because he was afraid Ben would be an unstable husband and have recurring mental problems and tendencies toward alcoholism like his mother. So the week before the wedding, she called it off."

"Wow." Jane leaned back against the couch cushion. "Poor guy."

"I *know*," Tara said. "When Ellen first told me the story, I thought I'd probably have to punch Dallin when I met him."

"Why?" Jane asked. "Wasn't Ben rude to you all weekend? Why care so much about his problems?"

"Because he cared about mine."

"I don't see how," Jane said. "At the airport he may have offered you money for a hotel, but beyond that what did he do except insult you? Wasn't it Ellen's idea for you to come to her home and then with them to Denver?"

"Ye-es," Tara said. "But Ben went along with it, even though he didn't want to. He helped me off the elevator when I was sick. He bought me dinner, opened doors for me, took me shopping—though his idea of shopping was very different from mine—shared his spoon and his ice cream. He even walked with me out in the cold when I'd waited too long for a bathroom break."

"And then he kissed you," Jane finished.

"There was that," Tara said quietly. "But it was more than just his kiss—great as it was—that made me want to stick up for him. Ben is a completely decent guy, this wholesome farmer type, and he didn't deserve what he got. It wasn't fair."

"Life is seldom fair," Jane observed.

"Don't I know it." Tara attempted to laugh, but a funny, choking sound came out instead. "But in spite of what life had dished out to Ben, he was still a nice guy. And all those times we fought, when he called me on the carpet for my behavior, I deserved it. I *wasn't* nice."

"Hmm." Jane placed her hands on her stomach and stared up at the ceiling. "That's quite the admission. Most people wouldn't be able to see themselves in that light." She sounded impressed.

Tara shrugged but didn't say anything. It had taken being around Ben and Ellen and then the contrast of being back in the boardroom at work for her to see how awful she'd behaved. And just because she did see it didn't make it any less painful. Nor did she quite know what to do about it. *I am who I am, and Ben is who he is, and life goes on.*

"So maybe you wanted to punch Dallin as a way to make up for being less than nice to Ben on the trip." Jane was twiddling her fingers, and Tara could tell she was entering serious therapist mode.

"I wanted to punch him because Ben didn't deserve such a crummy best friend, but I didn't because I could see right away—from the way Dallin treated his wife and kids, and Ben, and even me—that he's a nice guy too. Ellen says he has a lot of regrets about what he said to his sister. Ben moved far away and lives all alone, and McKenzie ended up marrying someone else and is going through this awful divorce."

Jane sighed. "I hate sad endings."

"Me too." Tara snorted. "It's the story of my life."

"It doesn't have to be." Jane lifted her head, looking at Tara. "If you liked Ben, why did you leave so abruptly? Why not keep in touch?"

"Because," Tara said miserably. "I knew we were too different. He was too much like . . . you. And I was too much like . . . me."

The room was quiet after Tara made this observation. She waited, wanting Jane to chime in with some other positive, false comment about how things could work out and everyone could live happily ever after. But Jane had always been an honest friend too.

After several minutes had passed, she finally spoke. "And you aren't particularly happy with *you*."

She's still got it, Tara thought. *Uncanny how she's always seemed to be able to read my soul. Wonder if she's going to charge me now that she has her master's?*

"No," Tara said, looking at the carpet. "I'm not happy at all."

"Ben isn't the real issue here," Jane said. "What's bothering you is your dissatisfaction with your own life—with yourself."

Ouch. "If I say you're right, then what do I do?" Tara asked.

A slow smile blossomed on Jane's face. "*If* you agree that I'm right, and *if* you really and truly want to change . . ."

"Maybe." Tara leaned forward slightly.

"Then you take a deep breath, roll up your sleeves, get ready to work, and trust me. You've come to the right place."

Twenty-Two

"TARA, YOU PROMISED." JANE'S VOICE held a slight reprimand as she looked down at the bed and Tara's toes poking out beneath Maddie's My Little Pony blanket. Jane nudged the mattress with her knee and put her hands on what used to be her hips. "Could you *please* get up now?"

It's 10:15, after all. Jane vaguely wondered just how long Tara *would* sleep if no one bothered her. "It's important for the girls to go to church each week, and I can't take them."

"Jessica already said she would." Tara's reply was muffled beneath the pillow she'd pulled over her head.

"And what happens next Sunday when Jessica is gone?" Jane asked. "She flies home tonight, and then you're on your own. If you go with her today, then you'll know how to get to the chapel, where Maddie's Primary classroom is, the schedule . . ." She leaned forward, tugging on the blanket. "Oooh—ow." She straightened, eyes closed, as she brought a hand to her stomach.

Tara threw back the covers and bounded out of bed. Wild-eyed, she stared at Jane. "What? Are you okay? Are you having those kids now?"

"No." Jane turned away but not before noticing Tara's outlandish and immodest sleeping attire—hot pink-and-black-striped booty shorts trimmed with black fur, a matching chemise, and a sleeping mask that was tangled in a knot of her hair.

Where does she find this stuff? Doesn't that furry trim itch? Jane shook her head as she waddled toward the door. "It was just a kick, but I'd better go lie down. Jessica is helping Maddie wash her hair, and then I'm sure she'd love some help dressing the girls."

Tara grimaced. "No, thanks. Miss Perfection and I don't get along so well—in case you haven't noticed."

I've noticed. Jane suppressed a grimace of her own. Last night she'd spent the evening acting as referee between them. She paused in the doorway and turned to face Tara again. "Cut her some slack. She's had a rough year and been hurt a lot. She's just trying to protect me."

"From what?" Tara asked. She yawned and stretched, her long, almost clawlike nails reaching toward the ceiling. Between her stripes and wild hair, she did look a little like a predatory cat.

"From you." Jane met Tara's surprised gaze.

"That's the dumbest—like I'd do anything—"

Jane held a hand up, stopping her. "There are many ways people can get hurt."

"Don't I know it." Tara fell back onto the bed. "No worries, though. I'll stick around long enough for you to have those kids."

"I wasn't thinking about that," Jane said, catching Tara's eye again. "But more about what can happen between friends when one really cares—and the other doesn't."

* * *

"I think," Tara's shrill voice carried down the hall, "that at thirty-four years of age I should be able to pick my own clothes."

One would think so. With a sigh, Jane closed her scriptures then braced herself for what was sure to be another confrontation. A few seconds later, Tara breezed into the room and turned a circle, showing off a skirt that had a slit almost all the way up to her hip. On closer inspection, Jane saw that the skirt was actually a dress—of sorts—the top being the perilously low-cut halter variety.

Oh boy. For the past week she'd done her best to ignore Tara's immodest clothing. Maddie was still young enough that she hadn't questioned things *too* much. But Jane knew there was no way she could send Tara to church dressed—or *not* dressed—as she was right now. The ward members, as good as they tried to be, were bound to feel uncomfortable with such blatant immodesty, and likely there would be more than a stare or two directed her way. The last thing Jane wanted was Tara's first church experience to be uncomfortable.

"Aunt Jane, the bishop will kick Tara out if she shows up wearing that."

"The bishop won't kick anyone out," Jane quickly corrected. "Nor would he ask her to leave."

"See." Tara shot an I-told-you-so look Jessica's direction. "Where are the girls? Let's go."

"They're on the back porch, but—" Jane raised herself to a sitting position on the sofa. "Uh—actually there *is* a problem with that dress. It's likely you'd attract some unwanted attention."

"Why?" Tara asked. "You said all the women would be wearing dresses or skirts."

"They will." Jane hesitated, wanting to proceed with caution. She tried to imagine what it would be like if she hadn't had modesty ingrained in her from the time she was a very little girl. If she'd really had no concept of her body being sacred.

"The top is slit down to your belly button," Jessica blurted. Like her mother, Caroline, she had no problem being bold.

"Is not," Tara said, looking down. "That's just a birthmark I had embellished a little."

"Ugh." Jessica turned away, looking repulsed.

Jane found herself fighting the urge to laugh, though the situation really wasn't funny. Tara saw nothing wrong with the way she dressed, and Jane wasn't sure she knew how to help her realize that the way she displayed her body was only serving to attract the wrong kind of men.

"It's just that because the top is so low, because we can see so much . . . real estate . . . people are going to feel uncomfortable. The dresses most women will be wearing today are a bit more—"

"Appropriate," Jessica finished. Her arms were folded across her chest, and she had a rather smug, self-righteous look on her face.

"*Conservative.*" Jane frowned at her niece. "Jess, why don't you wait outside with the girls."

A brief flicker of hurt crossed Jessica's face, but she marched past the two of them and went outside. Jane knew she'd have ruffled feelings to smooth over there later, but right now her bigger concern was Tara. *How can I help without hurting her?*

"I'm glad to see you've taken my side. That little snot has been on my case all morning. She even did some lame head, shoulders, knees, toes routine about not showing your ankles in public."

This time Jane did laugh. She could only imagine Tara's reaction to the modesty rhyme the young women of the Church were often taught. "Ankles are okay." She glanced down at Tara's slender ankles, shown off by strappy sandals and an anklet that coordinated with her toe ring.

"But if your shoulders are bare, it's a shirt you shouldn't wear." Tara wagged a finger and did her best to imitate Jessica. "Seems like your church is kind of hung up on body parts."

"I can see how you'd think that." Jane sent a silent prayer heavenward that she'd say the right thing. "We believe our bodies are a gift from God. We're made in His likeness—he has a body too—and we have the greatest respect for Him and His gift." When Tara didn't say anything, Jane forged ahead. "To show that respect, we dress modestly, reserving the privilege of sharing our bodies with only our husband or wife."

"So, I am like, the biggest sinner ever?" Tara's voice wavered between hurt and haughty.

"No—I mean, it's different when you haven't been taught."

"I'm not five, and I don't appreciate being treated like that," Tara shot back. "First Ellen, now you."

"What did Ellen do?"

"Nothing—never mind."

"You're breaking our deal to trust me," Jane reminded her, but her tone wasn't scolding. She knew pain when she saw it, and beneath Tara's contempt, Jane could see misery.

Tara shrugged and sat on the arm of the sofa. "Ellen told Ben that I didn't *know* any better. Like I was some little kid or something. I'd kind of forgotten about it—until now. Thanks a lot."

Jane reached over, taking Tara's hand in hers and squeezing. "She didn't mean it that way, and neither did I. You have to understand that Mormons are raised differently. We grow up constantly hearing that how we dress affects who we are, and the kind of people we'll attract and ultimately be with."

"Dress for success," Tara muttered. "I think I figured that out somewhere along the way."

"Did you?" Jane looked into her friend's sorrowful gaze. "Have you had much luck attracting good, decent guys? Or—" Jane lowered her voice. "Is it possible you got mixed up about what real success is?"

"Don't criticize me," Tara warned. "Don't you dare try to tell me that success is *this*—a lovely three-bedroom home—white picket fence included—a husband who's off flying his helicopter in a war zone, a goody-two-shoes little girl who says her prayers every night, and being big and fat and miserable with more brats kicking around inside you."

Ouch. In her younger days, Jane knew she would have gotten up and marched out of the room at such a speech, leaving Tara to stew in her own problems. But she'd learned a thing or two about patience the past couple of years.

And answers to prayers—strange though they may seem. Jane hadn't imagined the feeling—no, *knowledge*—that she and Maddie would be taken care of the next few months. And while Tara certainly wasn't the answer she'd been expecting, Jane knew that Tara was supposed to be here as much for herself as to help. She took a deep, calming breath before she spoke again.

"Okay. I won't tell you that's success. But I'll tell you it's happiness."

"Sure it is." Tara let out an indelicate snort. "Taking care of everybody and everything all the time. Making sure they eat and say prayers and have clean clothes and go to church. I'm not even you, probably not doing half of what you usually do around here and for your daughter, and I've hardly had ten seconds to myself since I walked through your door."

"I never said it would be easy."

"*Easy?*" Tara snorted again. "It's exhausting. And then your church adds all this modesty and—*this.*" Tara threw her arms out, making a point to look at the Proclamation on the Family, the Living Christ, and the pictures of the Savior hanging on the wall. "It's nuts, that's what it is, what you are now, Jane." She turned to her, a pleading look in her eyes. "Don't you miss the old days when you could come and go anytime? When you could eat out, spend money how you liked, fit into something besides a bathrobe?"

"I do miss wearing the clothes in my closet," Jane admitted, but she patted her stomach affectionately as she spoke. "As for the rest of it, though . . . I *don't* miss coming and going everywhere *alone*, eating out by *myself*, having no one to talk to, share with, plan with. Sure, I had a lot more free time then, but life was empty."

"So those are my choices—empty or exhausted. I guess I'll stick with empty, thank you very much." Tara rose from the sofa then walked down the hall to her room.

Jane followed, arriving in time to see Tara retrieving her suitcase from the floor.

Jane sighed. "What happened to staying until the babies are born?"

"Sorry. I can't handle this. I don't know why you want me here, anyway. I'm not good with kids—even yours, who is super nice—and I can't change my life for some farmer in Ohio I'll never see again." She plopped the suitcase on the bed and started scooping things into it.

"Well, that's a relief," Jane said. "I was afraid that's what this was all about."

"What?" Tara paused, hands on hips as she stared down at Jane.

"I was afraid that you quitting your job, leaving LA, showing up here—it was all so you could figure out how to get this guy, Ben. And I knew that would never work. A person can't change for someone else. If you want to be different, be truly happy, then it has to be *from* yourself, *for* yourself."

"I want to be left alone."

"Done." Jane took a step backward, into the hall. "But I really do need you right now. I wish you'd stay."

"*Need.* There it is. There's that word I keep hearing." Tara yanked several hangers full of clothes from the closet and tossed them toward the suitcase. She mimicked Maddie's high voice. "Tara, I need a drink. Tara, you need to go to church. Tara, you need to get some milk at the store. Tara, you need to change your wardrobe. I'm not used to all this *need*. It's making me crazy. And what about me? What about what *I* need?"

"What *do* you need?" Jane asked quietly. "Tell me, and I'll do anything in my power to get it for you."

"I need—I—" Tara faltered. She pulled another dress from the closet and held it close to her heart. "I don't know anymore. I just— don't know."

"What if *I* do?" Jane whispered. She walked into the room again, stopping a foot away from Tara.

They stood across from each other, Tara in her size-seven revealing dress, Jane in her stretched-to-the-max bathrobe. "Trust me," she pled. "I care about you, Tara. I love you. I want to help."

"Why should I trust you? Look what you've gone and done to yourself since I last saw you. You're a mess."

Jane grinned. "So are you."

"I am," Tara agreed, tears suddenly spilling from her eyes. Jane held out her arms. Tara only hesitated a second then stepped into Jane's embrace, crying on her shoulder.

Twenty-Three

"YOU SHOULD WASH THAT BATHROBE," Tara said, frowning as she looked down at the black smeared across the shoulder of Jane's robe.

"You should wear less makeup," Jane said, her mouth twisting in a familiar smile.

Tara resisted the urge to hug her again. Being in her embrace, hearing Jane say she cared about her, *loved* her even, had been the best moment she'd had in a very long time.

Since Ben's kiss. Tara froze, her fingers on the keys to Jane's car. *That's what was different about Ben's kiss.*

When other men had kissed her, usually after a date (sometimes before), there hadn't been any emotion—*aside from desire*—involved. But Ben's kiss had conveyed so much more. He'd felt bad for her situation. He'd been sorry for giving her a hard time. Somehow, in spite of all their arguing, he'd liked her too. She'd felt all that. *And when he held me afterward . . .* She remembered the comforting feeling of her head against his chest, his arms around her.

She remembered how it had scared her a little. And the hurt in Ben's eyes when she'd told him she was going to ride with Ellen. *He felt something too.*

"You okay?" Jane asked. "You look like you've seen a ghost."

"Just trying to talk myself into going out in public like this." Tara splayed her fingers across Jane's white sweater that she'd borrowed. It was so . . . *plain.* Her thoughts slid back to Ben's kiss. *He kissed me because he cared about me. As much as I'd annoyed him, he still cared about me. And when I kissed him in the truck, it was because I cared about him. Wow.*

It was with this startling revelation still in her mind that Tara loaded the girls in the car and drove to church. Even Jessica's brooding silence couldn't cast a pall on the glorious feeling coursing through her. *Ben cared. I cared. It was magic. Could I have that again? Is that what Jane and Peter have? I should trust her. Maybe, as with her Gertrude's Mystery nightwear, she's on to something.*

The glowing feeling Tara felt inside lasted all the way until they entered the chapel full of strangers. There were children everywhere. Teenagers. Babies. Families. People who dressed like Jane, in stuffy suits and dresses with sleeves. Tara knew at once that coming had been a bad idea. *No way I'm going to blend in here.* Only Maddie's insistent hand, tugging her inside, kept her from bolting.

The little girls wanted to sit up front on a middle pew, but Tara insisted on taking a side bench near the doors. If escape proved necessary, she wanted a quick one.

The meeting began with some guy—Jessica said it was the bishop—talking, and then there was a song and a couple of prayers. After that, the older boys in the room walked around bringing trays with little pieces of bread to everyone. Tara couldn't help but notice the difference between these teenagers—with their white shirts, ties, and respectful manner—and the kid she'd sat next to on the plane. The phrase "doesn't know any better" came back to her. She couldn't imagine the annoying kid on the plane reverently serving bread to everyone like these kids were. He wouldn't begin to know how. *Am I so different?* she thought uncomfortably. Just being in this building felt so foreign.

As the boys reached the row in front of theirs, Tara whispered to Jessica, "Should I take one?" She imagined that everyone's eyes were on her, seeing through the disguise of Jane's modest sweater to the inner woman who clearly did not belong in this holy place.

Jessica shrugged. "You can if you want to, but the sacrament is about renewing our baptismal covenants. And since you haven't been baptized . . ." Her voice trailed off as the tray was passed to them.

Baptized or not, Tara decided the path of most invisibility was to do what everyone else was, so she stuck a piece of squishy white bread in her mouth. As she chewed, she noticed that Jessica, along with much of the congregation, sat with their heads bowed and their eyes closed.

Tara didn't feel the need to do that too. After all, if everyone else was closing their eyes, it was a good time for her to check them out.

Her nonchalant perusal of the crowd did not yield any potential Bens but rather a ton of little kids and a fair amount of elderly people. Apparently the Bainbridge Ward, as Jane referred to her congregation, wasn't a real hip and happening place.

After the bread came trays with little cups of water—so small it was hardly worth the drink. Then the bishop stood up again and announced who would be speaking. Tara listened a little after that, but between people-watching and keeping the girls' crayons from rolling off the bench, she didn't really get a lot out of the sermons.

When it was over—*finally*—an hour and fifteen minutes later, Jessica showed her where to take Maddie to her class. Next they dropped off Allison at the nursery, where Tara had to extricate herself from the crying little girl.

"What now?" Tara asked after she'd managed to get out of the roomful of howling toddlers.

"Sunday School," Jessica announced. "Come on. It's probably in the Relief Society room. I'll go with you."

"Where else would you go?" Tara asked, following Jessica down the crowded hallway.

"There's a class for youth my age," Jessica said. "It's usually more fun than the adult class, but since you don't know what you're doing, I'll go with you."

There it is again. Even Jane's holier-than-thou niece doesn't think I know anything. Tara slid a sideways glance at her as they found seats in the back of the room. *Let me tell you something, sister. I know a whole heck of a lot more about the world than you probably ever will.*

And that's a good thing? The surprising thought caught her off guard as much as Allison's reluctance to leave her had.

Yes, it's good, Tara defended herself from the traitor that had invaded her mind. *I've been places. I've made big money. I've done a lot of things.*

That didn't matter.

She forged on past the negative voice. *I know lots of people.*

Who don't care about you at all.

I've been in several serious relationships.

That all ended badly. Tara's hands shook slightly as she signed the roll and passed it to the woman seated beside her. She resisted the urge to put her hands over her ears to try to stop whatever was nagging her. Maybe it was just this place, this building for Latter-day Saints, as it said on the outside, that had her feeling so lousy and questioning everything she'd ever done in her life.

It was a relief when class started and the teacher asked everyone to open their scriptures. Tara held the ones she'd borrowed from Jane, determined that she could do this part right, at least.

"We're getting ready to begin those chapters that deal with the Savior's earthly ministry," Brother Bartlett, the middle-aged man who was teaching, said. "Before we begin, what are some of your thoughts about the time Christ spent among the Jews?"

It was a long time ago? Tara was glad she knew that much, at least.

Several people raised their hands and said various, intelligent, introspective things. *I don't know. I don't know,* seemed to chant in her head over and over again.

She felt herself getting angry, just sitting here in this room with people smarter than her.

"Those were all excellent comments," Brother Bartlett said. "And we'll delve into many as we look closely at the Savior's teachings. But today we're going to look at the overarching themes Christ taught. There are several that we can see when looking at the Savior's ministry as a whole."

Themes? This is like being in English class all over again.

"But the overlying one I want to focus on today is one applicable to us all and perhaps the one the Savior most wished to impart. If you'll turn to Luke, chapter nine, verse twenty-four."

Tara stared down at Jane's scriptures and the thumb tabs on them. There were easily a couple of dozen, each with about three names on them. *How am I supposed to find Luke?* From the corner of her eye, she noticed those around her with their scriptures open, flipping purposely through the pages. She opened hers to the middle, thinking that was as good a place to start as any.

Jessica leaned over. "It's in the New Testament, not the Book of Mormon."

"Hmm?" Tara asked, trying to sound as if she really didn't care. *I really don't care, do I?*

But she had to admit she was curious. What was this one thing that was applicable to everyone—even her? She flipped toward the back of the book.

"The Bible," Jessica whispered louder. "You know, Old Testament, New Testament?"

Tara shook her head slightly. "Never read it; never had one."

Jessica's face softened a bit, and she reached over, turning the pages in the opposite direction. After a minute she said, "Here. Verse twenty-four."

Tara looked down and began reading along with the teacher. "'But whosoever will lose his life for my sake, the same shall save it.'"

"If you'll follow the cross-reference at the bottom of the page, we see also that Matthew, chapter ten, verse thirty-nine reads similarly. 'He that loseth his life for my sake shall *find* it.' The teacher looked up expectantly. "So. Thoughts?"

That's it? What does that even mean? All around her hands shot up, and people started explaining their interpretations of the scripture. She tried to follow, but her head was starting to hurt.

"Thank you," Brother Bartlett said after several minutes of discussion. "If you get one thing from studying the Savior's ministry, I hope it is this—that in losing ourselves, we truly can find ourselves."

Yes. You said that already. But what does it mean? Tara felt her irritation growing. How was she supposed to know anything about religion if no one ever explained it?

Brother Bartlett went on. "The Savior did not lose His life while here on earth; He gave it willingly for each of us. But that is not what He asks of us, and it's not what He is talking about here."

Tara fidgeted in her seat.

Brother Bartlett left the podium and walked around the front of the table. "I believe He said this for those times when we feel lost, overwhelmed, or unsure where to go next or what to do with our lives. We become discouraged and disillusioned with everything around us."

Tara looked up from her clenched hands. Brother Bartlett glanced around the room, his gaze passing hers then returning suddenly.

"The Savior knew we would encounter discouragement and loneliness here on earth."

Where else would we encounter those things? Mars?

"So He gave us the scriptures and prophets so we'd have specific instructions about how to live, how to stay on that strait and narrow path that will lead us back to Him."

Back to Him, where—how? This makes no sense.

"But at times," Brother Bartlett continued, "all of the difficulties of life can seem overwhelming. We feel discouraged and lost and don't really know what to do next."

He's got that right. Tara thought about the mess that was her life. She had no job. No home. No family. No purpose or plan. No idea what came next.

"At those times I suggest starting over, with this very scripture as our guide. 'He who will lose his life, will find it.'" Brother Bartlett leaned back against the table. His arms were folded, his face serious as he looked around at the class, as if considering his next words carefully. After several seconds his gaze drifted to the back of the room again, to Tara.

"Brothers and Sisters, I challenge each of you who are feeling a little lost or in need of direction to give this scriptural promise from the Savior a try. Forget about yourself. Focus on others. Do all you can to serve and love them, and you'll be surprised with the results. You'll find yourself as you never have before."

Tara found herself unable to look away from his kind yet piercing gaze. *Does he know how lost I feel? Am I imagining this . . . connection?* A warm sort of comfort seemed to envelop her at the possibility that someone might understand.

A corner of Brother Bartlett's mouth lifted in a smile, as if he'd heard her thoughts. He turned away and walked around the table to the chalkboard to point out some additional scripture references.

Tara stared at his back, wishing he'd look at her again, wishing she'd somehow been able to record what he'd just said—to her. *To me. He was talking to me. I felt it.*

She hardly moved for the rest of class, hardly breathed, but tried desperately to hold on to the peaceful feeling that had flooded her soul when he'd spoken. Over and over again she repeated the scripture in her mind. *He who will lose his life, will find it.*

It still didn't make complete sense to her, and it wasn't as if any of her concerns about her future had been solved. But still, in spite of that, she felt more hope than she had in a very long time.

Twenty-Four

Sunday afternoon seemed one continuous round of Candy Land, Sorry!, and Chutes and Ladders, and Tara thought she'd kill herself if they played one more game where Gloppy Gumdrop, a ten-inch colored slide, or a "return to start" card sent her back to the beginning of the board and added another thirty minutes of play. Each time this had happened, she'd grown progressively grumpier, which only added to Maddie's and Allison's delight. By the time four of her markers started over, both girls were rolling on the floor in a fit of giggles.

"You should have had Allison on your team," Maddie said. "She wanted to be with you, remember? But you said no and now her and Jessica are winning."

"*She* and Jessica," Jane corrected from the couch, where she lay relaxing, reading a magazine.

Tara made a face at Maddie that started her giggling again.

Rolling her eyes, Tara said, "What we should have done is play a *real* game like poker where you get cards that—"

"I don't think so," Jane said, correcting Tara this time.

"No real fun around here," Tara muttered. The kitchen timer went off, saving them from further discussion and Tara from further torture. "Lasagna's done," she said jumping up. "Who wants to help set the table and make a salad?" The words, inviting "help" from Maddie and Allison, were out of her mouth before she'd realized what she was saying. *I'm starting to sound like Jane. Scary.*

"I will. I will." Both girls jumped up and started to follow her. Tara sighed, wishing she hadn't opened her mouth. She could have had ten minutes of peace in the kitchen by herself.

After dinner Jessica helped the girls get in their pajamas and settled them down with a movie while Tara did the dishes in the relative quiet of the kitchen. Clearing the table and loading the dishwasher by herself seemed a great luxury. No one was hanging off her leg. No voices chattering a mile a minute in her ear. It was a welcome break.

Jessica's ride would be here soon, and then tomorrow Tara would be doing the dishes *and* putting the girls to bed. She was tired just thinking about it. Maybe it would be easier as soon as Jane's other niece went home. Tara sure hoped so. It wasn't that the little girls were poorly behaved, but they wore her out just the same. Not to mention that taking care of them and Jane's house all day hadn't left her any time to look for an apartment or a job. *I have a job—about ten of them*, she thought, though she didn't feel as resentful about all the work as she had this morning. Jane couldn't do much right now, but she'd proven she was still a good listener. Having her to talk to at night almost made the crazy days worth it. *Almost.*

"Night," she said awhile later, waving casually at Jane as she headed down the hall. She planned to take a long, hot shower then curl up with something from Jane's plentiful selection of romance novels. She walked into the guest bedroom, flipped on the light, saw someone on her bed, and screamed.

"Hey." The giant bubble that had been coming out of Jessica's mouth popped. She sat on the edge of the bed, swinging her legs.

"You scared me," Tara said, holding a hand to her thumping heart. "What are you doing in here? Don't you need to pack or something?"

"Already did. Aunt Jane asked me to meet you in here."

Tara's eyes narrowed with suspicion. "She did?"

"I did." Jane said, right behind her. Tara moved into the room so Jane could fit through the door. She walked over to the bed and sat beside Jessica. They both smiled up at Tara.

"What?" she asked, putting her hands on her hips. "You two look about as innocent as a pair of crocodiles."

"Snap. Snap." Jane moved her arms, imitating a crocodile's mouth. "*Actually*, we're here to help *you* look innocent."

"The first step in your personal makeover," Jessica chimed in.

"I don't want a makeover," Tara said. She'd hoped Jane had forgotten the deal they'd made this morning, after the pre-church dress debacle, but apparently that wasn't the case. Tara wondered if she could plead foul play, as Jane had unfairly caught her in an emotional state and a moment of weakness. *Anyone getting a much-needed hug from a friend would have succumbed.*

"I didn't mean the regular kind of makeover," said Jane.

Jessica rolled her eyes. "You're already gorgeous. You don't need any help that way."

"Thank you—I think."

"It's true," Jane said, nodding her agreement with Jessica's compliment. "Now that we've established this has nothing to do with your looks, let's get busy. How you dress has the potential to help you have a more meaningful life, get a better job—"

"And to date some *nice* guys," Jessica added.

Tara glared at her. "I don't need a teenager telling me about dating. And I've had plenty of high-paying jobs." *Not that I'd really classify them as good.*

Ignoring the two of them, Jane continued. "Showing off, *revealing* your . . . assets . . . isn't really the best way to attract the right kind of man." She stood and went to the closet.

Tara groaned. "Is this about that head, shoulders, toes thing again?"

"It's about you looking your best and treating your body—the body God gave you—with respect. If you show respect for it, others will too."

"I respect it," Tara said defensively. "I work out."

"That's good. That's part of it," Jane said. "But another part is the way you dress."

"Or *don't* dress."

Tara caught the words spoken under Jessica's breath.

"Listen, Miss Know-it—" She stopped, remembering that Jane had asked her to be nice to the teen.

And, she admitted grudgingly, *Jessica* was *nice to me church. She'd answered all the questions from the nosy leader of the women's relief meeting. She even introduced me as Jane's longtime friend and a real answer to prayer.*

Remembering her relief at not being given away as the imposter she was, Tara felt an inkling of patience for the girl in front of her. She grabbed a pillow from the bed and tossed it at Jessica. "Just because I don't know the New Testament from the Bible doesn't mean—"

"The New Testament is *part* of the Bible," Jessica said in mock exasperation.

"Whatever," Tara said. "You people have a lot of books."

"You have a *lot* of clothes." Jessica's eyes were wide as she stared at the open closet. Jane had thrown back the doors, revealing the rod, crammed with hangers and all of Tara's favorite things. Rows of shoes lined the bottom of the closet. "Wow," Jessica said. "I've never seen so many pairs of high heels."

"Too bad you guys have something against showing off your toes."

Jessica giggled. "Toes are fine. See?" She lifted her own flip-flop-clad foot.

"It's the ankles that are bad?" Tara asked. "In Jane's case, completely understandable. Those things are disgusting."

"Leave my cankles out of this, please," Jane said, following Tara's lead, her own voice lighter.

"Ankles are fine too," Jessica said. "It's when you start getting above the knee that you get into trouble."

"I see." And Tara did—kind of. How many times had she dressed according to the clientele she'd be dealing with? Too many to count. If she'd wanted a male client to be distracted and willing to spend a little more than he should, then she'd worn a low-cut blouse and tight skirt. *Playing up my assets*, was how she'd always thought of it. *Working with what I've got.* But thinking about the things Jane had said this morning put using her body that way in a different light. One she'd never before considered.

Tara studied her skirts hanging in the closet. She doubted there were any that came below her knee or even to it. How was she supposed to stop wearing everything in her wardrobe, to give up the few material possessions she'd chosen to keep?

"Well?" Jane asked, glancing from Tara to the closet then back to Tara again.

"My clothes are my friends," Tara said, her light tone gone. "You can't really expect me to give them up. I'll wear your skirts to church, but the rest of the time—"

"The rest of the time is important too," Jane said gently. "And I thought *I* was your friend."

Her simple statement stopped the protest on Tara's lips. She remembered standing beside Ben, looking out at the Salt Lake Temple, talking about—and missing—her friendship with Jane. *Now, here I am with her again. And she called me her friend.*

Tara also remembered the dream that had given her the courage to abandon LA and return to Washington. She thought of the last week here at Jane's home—the chaos, the exhaustion, the talks late into the night. She had to admit, she was in a much better place than she'd been a month ago. Perhaps, in exchange for all that, she could give up *some* of her clothes.

She remembered the Sunday School teacher's challenge. *I could lose them,* she thought. *I could lose my old life and trust Jane with my new one. I can do this for Jane. I can think of her instead of myself.*

Tara ran her fingers across the skirts clustered in the closet as she considered. *It isn't as if my old life is great, anyway.* She'd already decided to give it up, to change, when she moved here. So why not try Jane's version?

After all, what do *I have to lose?*

* * *

About ten thousand dollars' worth of clothes. That's what I have to lose. Forty-five minutes later, Tara stared dismally at the enormous pile on the bed and then at the few, sparsely populated hangers still in the closet. The remnants of her once-glorious wardrobe.

"Don't cry," Jessica said, putting an arm around Tara's shoulders. "If you'd like, we can go shopping when I come back next month."

Tara felt oddly comforted by Jessica's sympathy. Maybe kids weren't all bad. Maybe by the time they became teens, they could sort of be fun to hang out with. "I'd like that," she said, meaning it. "And I'm pretty sure it'll be necessary, because I don't think being completely naked fits in with your standards, either. And that's about where I'm at with what I've got left here."

"This pink sweater is nice," Jane said, holding up the pale-pink angora Ben had purchased at the thrift store.

"I'm rather attached to that one." Tara took the sweater from Jane and held it close. *What was Ben doing right now? Had he gotten together with his ex-fiancée? I wonder if he'd be surprised if he could see me now and know what I'm doing.*

Twenty-Five

"How was church this week?" Jane asked after Tara had settled the girls at the kitchen counter with peanut butter and jelly sandwiches.

"Not bad," Tara said. In truth, it *had* been a little better than the previous Sunday. During the past week Jane had taught her how to navigate the scriptures, so she hadn't felt like a complete idiot during Sunday School. She also had to admit to enjoying today's lesson on Jesus. She wasn't certain about Him being the Son of God and all that, but He definitely had some good stuff to say. He seemed genuine, unlike the Pharisees who seemed to be all show.

Jesus certainly had that losing yourself thing down. She'd started a count to figure out just how many people He'd healed. From what she could understand from the scriptures, the healing business had been brisk, but the pay poor. Sometimes He didn't even get so much as a thank you.

Kind of like me, Tara thought, noting that no one had thanked her for taking the girls to church, fixing breakfast *and* lunch, and cleaning up the kitchen. *Then again, if Jane were to thank me for everything I'm doing around here, she'd be saying thank you all day long.*

But a thank you once in a while would have been nice. This week Tara felt like she'd left any semblance of the houseguest status behind and moved full-on to being "the help." Jane was spending an awful lot of time lying in bed, leaving Tara to spend an awful lot of time with the two kids, the washing machine, and the dishwasher. It would have been nice to be appreciated.

And they have their reward . . . The scripture about the Pharisees came to mind again, making her feel uncomfortable. *Am I like that? Can't I help Jane just to be nice—without needing constant thanks?*

"Tara, you okay?" Jane waved her hand back and forth, trying to get her attention.

"I'm fine," Tara said, wishing she were. "Just thinking." She pushed the troublesome thoughts from her mind and concentrated on easing Jane's. "I went by the nursery to check on Allison, and they were doing that head, shoulders, knees, toes thing. I can't believe how early you guys teach this stuff. Like she even realizes she's *wearing* clothes yet."

Jane laughed. "I think the song they were singing was probably a little different, but yeah, we do teach modesty early."

"Modest is hottest," Tara said, mimicking Jessica. "No kidding. My other clothes had way more ventilation than these." She pulled at her new blouse and pencil skirt. "It's awfully hot for April."

"I've been thinking," Jane said, changing the subject in a nonchalant tone that cued Tara that something big was up.

"What now? Do I need to dye my hair a nice, respectable brown? Do I have to take out my extra piercings and wear more modest underwear?"

"Eventually," Jane said, nodding her head.

What? Tara worked to keep the milk she'd just swallowed from coming back up. "I was joking."

"So am I." Jane flashed her a grin.

Tara stuck out her tongue. "I hate you. Don't freak me out like that. I like my red hair."

"You can keep your red hair forever," Jane assured her. "And we can talk about the other stuff later."

"Hmm," Tara said. "How many more weeks until Peter gets back? At the rate we're going, I won't be recognizable if it's too much longer."

"About nine weeks," Jane said. Tara heard the note of longing in her voice. "Plenty of time for the missionaries to teach you."

"Who're they?" Tara took a bite from her own sandwich and kicked off her heels.

"They teach the gospel full-time. Most of them are young men, but some women serve too. They spend eighteen months to two years as full-time missionaries, teaching people who want to learn more about our church."

"Oh. Do I want to learn more about your church?" Tara asked around a second bite of sandwich.

"Yes, you do," Jane said emphatically. "You want to find meaning and purpose in your life, remember?"

"Vaguely," Tara said with a wave of her hand. *Guess I did say something like that. But it was during another moment of weakness.* "So when do I meet with these guys? I do get the guys, right? I think I'd like them better. And how young is young? Any in their early thirties?"

"Try nineteen and twenty," Jane said. "And you'll get sisters if there are any in the area. They don't like the guys teaching single women."

"Well, that's no fun." Tara took a sip of milk and leaned back in the rocking chair. "I suppose I could do that. Maybe they could clarify some of the stuff I hear in Sunday School."

"I'm sure they could," Jane said. "Why don't you make a list of questions, since they'll be coming over after dinner."

* * *

"Do you believe in God?"

Taken aback by such a direct question, Tara stared, dumbfounded, at the two young women seated on Jane's couch. They'd been here less than five minutes, and Jane had barely excused herself to go into the other room to read to the little girls.

Leaving me on my own with virtual strangers. "Maybe I'm misunderstanding, but I thought *I* was the one who was supposed to ask the questions."

"Oh, you can. Anything you want," Sister Ayer, the brunette from New Hampshire, said. "But if you can give us an idea of your current beliefs, then we know where to start in teaching you about the gospel of Jesus Christ. It may be that we already share many of the same convictions."

"I doubt it." Tara studied the women, trying to gauge their sincerity. *If they can be this direct, I can too.* "What made you choose to give up two years of your life to do this?"

"Eighteen months," Sister Henrie, the blonde from Michigan, corrected. "But I'd stay for two years if I could. The men get to."

Sister Ayer nodded in agreement. "The time goes so fast, and there's so much to do."

"Like what?" Tara asked. "And why do *you* have to do it? You could be in college or starting your careers or—"

"Starting a family?" Sister Ayer asked, a knowing smile lifting the corners of her mouth.

"O—oh. I get it." Tara nodded. "This kind of puts off the inevitable get-married-and-have-a-bunch-of-kids thing."

"Only if we choose it," Sister Ayer said. "And I'm very much looking forward to that stage of life too. My boyfriend still had six months left on his mission when I turned in my papers—when I applied to go," she added, seeing Tara's confused look. "And I really wanted to serve."

"All of my older brothers went on missions," Sister Henrie said. "And I always heard how great they were—the best two years of their lives. I wanted the same opportunity."

"But what is that opportunity exactly?" Tara sat up straight, eager to hear their answers.

"*You* are." Sister Ayer's smile was big—and genuine. "We get to share what is most precious to us with you. What could be better?"

Tara shrugged. A flippant, "I don't know," was on the tip of her tongue, but she was tired of admitting that to everyone—especially herself. "I still don't understand."

Sister Henrie scooted forward to the edge of the couch. "Let us teach you, and you *will*."

"All right." Tara lifted her hands in surrender. "Teach away. I'm listening."

"Do you believe in God?" Sister Ayer's tone was softer when she asked the question this time. "In an exalted being who is your Heavenly Father and who created the earth and all the things on it—including you?"

"No," Tara said. "I don't believe in anyone or anything like that. But I *am* confident that my parents created me. You know, the whole sperm-meets-egg thing."

A tiny sound that might have been a laugh escaped Sister Henrie's lips before she pressed them together tightly. She pretended to cough into her hand. "Of course. Your parents *did* create your physical body. But what about your spirit? We believe that, in addition to our earthly parents, we have Heavenly Parents, a Mother and Father who are the creators of our spirits."

"*Everyone's* spirits?" Tara asked.

"Yes," Sister Henrie said. "Heavenly Father is the parent of everyone who has ever lived and will ever live on earth."

Tara gave a low whistle. "No wonder Mormons are so into big families. You have a lot to live up to."

This time it was Sister Ayer who laughed, and she didn't try to cover it up. "I can see we're going to have a great time teaching you." Her eyes sparkled with amusement and . . . something else. Tara wasn't sure what, but she could almost feel the happiness exuding from her. She really did seem to be having the time of her life.

Go figure. Maybe New Hampshire is a really boring place.

"Of course, our earthly parents are wonderful."

"Not mine," Tara said then instantly wished she hadn't.

"I'm sorry." Both young women spoke at once, their eyes turning sympathetically toward her.

Sister Ayer gestured to one of the documents—The Family Proclamation—hanging on the wall. "The family is central to Heavenly Father's plan, but not every earthly family functions the way Heavenly Father intended it to."

"That is one of the reasons it's important to know we have a Heavenly Father who loves and cares for us," Sister Henrie said. "He knows each of us by name. He sorrows when we suffer and rejoices when we choose to do right. He is always there."

"And while our earthly parents might let us down, Heavenly Father never will. His love is constant and unconditional. But to feel that love, you have to know Him." Sister Ayer paused. "Would you like to get to know Him, Tara?"

"Why?" Tara asked. "I mean, why is it all up to me? He's the parent, right? Shouldn't the parent look out for the child regardless of whether the child is paying attention or not?" She thought of the past two weeks, the way she'd kept an eye on Maddie and her cousin. Often the girls lost track of time, and she'd have to call them in from playing outside to eat lunch. She'd held their hands when they would have run in front of cars, in the busy church parking lot. She'd given them baths and made them brush their teeth because it was good for them. And while they might have sought her out for things like ice cream cones and bedtime stories, when it came to taking care of them, she'd been the one dishing that out on her own—like any good parent would.

So *if* she had a Heavenly Father, why hadn't He done the same and watched out for *her*?

She voiced the question. "If I've got a Heavenly Father, shouldn't I *already* know Him?"

"Excellent questions." Instead of being deflated by Tara's response, Sister Henrie seemed excited by it. "Before we came to earth, we lived with our heavenly parents, but we were only spirits. In order to gain a body, we had to come here."

"We also came to learn and grow," Sister Ayer added. "To prove ourselves. So we could return to Heavenly Father's presence and become exalted beings as He is."

"Exalted?" Tara asked. "And we were alive before we were born?" Not only had they *not* answered her question, but they'd confused her more.

"We're getting ahead of ourselves," Sister Henrie said. "The important thing here is that we are spirit children of Heavenly Father. We came to earth to get a body and to be tested and to learn about Him and His gospel. For us to do that, there had to be a veil between this life and our premortal life with God. We had to forget."

Tara's forehead wrinkled as she tried to follow their logic. "Forget what?"

"Think about it for a minute," Sister Ayer said. "If we remembered God and knew all that was to happen on earth and afterward, it wouldn't take any faith to get back to Him."

"And faith is what He requires," Sister Henrie said. "He wants us to pray and read and study and believe."

"And then the miracle happens." Jane stood in the doorway. Tara thought her eyes looked sad.

"Are you all right?" Tara asked, worried that Jane wasn't feeling well or that she'd just heard bad news from Peter.

"I'm fine," Jane assured her. "No. Actually, I'm not. I am sorry. Very, very sorry." She came into the room and sat carefully in Peter's recliner. When she'd eased her awkward body into the chair and raised her feet a little, she turned to Tara.

"You *should* know your Heavenly Father already. Because *I* should have introduced Him to you years ago."

"No, Jane." Tara shook her head. "I didn't mean it that way. I meant that He—*if* He's really there—should have let me know it."

"How do you think He does that?" Jane asked. "With lightning bolts and messages written across the sky?" She shook her head and gave a short, false laugh. "It doesn't work that way. He asks *us*—people like me who were fortunate enough to have been blessed with parents who taught me about God—to tell you, to share the gospel."

"But you didn't," Tara said, more than a little taken aback at seeing Jane so distraught over this.

"I didn't," Jane said. "I'm so sorry. When we worked together I had every opportunity—"

"I wouldn't have listened." Tara cut her off. "I had no need or desire for something like that, like this—" she gestured to the missionaries "—in my life."

"How about now, Tara?" Sister Ayer sat back a little, looking like she had all the time in the world to wait for her answer.

The room went silent, as if they were all holding one, collective breath. Tara closed her eyes, wishing herself away from there, from them, from their questions, so she could think.

Do I want this? Do I want to find out if God is real? And if He is, do I want Him in my life?

A yearning, keener than the one she'd felt all the years she'd wanted to know who her father was, began deep inside. She felt it building, filling, warming, and comforting her in a way she'd never experienced. It was almost as if a kindling of desire had lit in her heart. *I am ready. I do want to know*, she was about to say, when a sudden memory halted her.

The closest thing I've felt to this warmth was the time Danny Iggleton poured whiskey down my throat when he wanted me to be friendly with him behind the portables after school. She hadn't thought of that in years and wondered why such a painful image had to flash into her mind just when she'd been feeling something new and profound—and *good*.

A dozen more memories followed, her worst episodes of misery and shame. The time she'd done more than just dress seductively to make a big sale . . . The time she'd pinned losing an account on a coworker, when she'd known the fault was hers . . . The way she'd railed at Ben last December, when he'd called her out for swearing with Ellen's kids nearby. All the many times when she'd been less than nice yet somehow justified her temperamental, impatient behavior.

You're not worthy to know God. You don't deserve a father. He doesn't love you. The thoughts screamed through her mind, and the gentle warmth of seconds before slipped away.

Tears burned behind her eyes, and she ached with inexplicable loss. It wasn't as if she'd had anything—or anyone—in the first place, so why did she feel such a void now?

"I . . ." Tara tried to speak but couldn't express her desire, and she couldn't make the wretched feelings consuming her go away. Through hazy vision, she saw Sister Ayer flipping through her scriptures. Jane was trying to get up. Sister Henrie had gone as pale as her light blonde hair and was giving her a look of genuine concern.

"Are you all right?" she asked.

"I don't know," Tara said. She gripped the arms of the rocking chair, as if hanging on for life—or her sanity, at the least. "I feel so awful. I don't think I can do this. I *am* awful."

"'But when Jesus heard *that*, he said unto them,'" Sister Ayer began reading in a strong, sure voice, "'They that be whole need not a physician, but they that are sick. But go ye and learn what *that* meaneth, I will have mercy and not sacrifice: for I am not come to call the righteous, but sinners to repentance.'"

The Sunday School scripture. That one had been part of the lesson today. Tara had liked it then, and now . . . Peace began edging its way into her heart, pushing aside the awful memories, the feelings of worthlessness.

Sister Ayer looked up from her scriptures. "Tara, we've all made mistakes, but Heavenly Father and His Son love us just the same. They *want* us to know them. It's Satan who makes us feel unworthy."

"They do love us—*all* of us. *You*," Sister Henrie said. "'As the Father hath loved me, so have I loved you: continue ye in my love.' What you felt a minute ago—and we all felt it with you—was

Heavenly Father's love. But the adversary, Satan, doesn't want you to know that love. He wants you to be miserable like him."

"He's real *too?*" Tara wasn't surprised that she sounded hoarse—and afraid. Whatever it was that had just happened to her, the two forces she'd just felt—and *adversary* seemed an appropriate term—had been real. *So very real.* She suppressed a shudder and swallowed. Her throat hurt, as if she'd crammed all of the emotions of the past few minutes roughly down it.

"I've been miserable for as long as I can remember," she said and strangely felt as if a burden lifted from her shoulders with that admission. "I'm not happy. I—I don't know how to fix it, how to have peace."

Both missionaries leaned back against the couch cushions, as if limp with exhaustion. Happy relief lit their faces. Jane had finally managed to get out of Peter's chair. She waddled over to Tara, reached down, and took her hand.

"You've already started," she said. "Recognizing that you're not happy, that things could be better, is the first step."

What are the other steps? Tara wondered. She wanted that warmth and comfort back. And she *never* wanted to feel the fear and despair that had overpowered her moments before. But still, she was leery of what she was committing to. "What does getting to know God involve?"

"Some reading." Sister Henrie rose from the couch, crossed the room, and handed her one of the books of scripture she'd been holding. "And prayer."

"Do you think that over the next week you could read some scriptures we've marked for you?" Sister Ayer asked. "And then pray about what you read?"

Tara looked down at the blue copy of the Book of Mormon. She liked to read, and the book wasn't overly thick. *And if it might lead me to that feeling again . . .*

"Sure," she said at last.

I always wanted a father. I guess one up in heaven is better than not having one at all.

Twenty-Six

ALLISON APPEARED IN THE DOORWAY of Tara's room, thumb in her mouth and a much-loved doll in her other hand. Tara adjusted the magazine she was reading so that it covered her entire face and pretended she hadn't noticed the little girl.

"Tra," Allison gurgled.

Tar-a. How hard can it be, kid? But I'm not here, anyway. Not here. Not here. Not— A tiny hand patted her arm, making Tara start and drop the magazine.

"Tra." Allison repeated. Grabbing Tara's arm—and the hairs attached to it—she pulled herself up onto the bed.

"Oh no, you don't." Tara sat up and gathered the little girl in her arms. "You nap in *your* bed, missy, not mine." She trudged down the hall, returning Allison to Maddie's room, where she was supposed to be sleeping. Maddie, too old for naps now, was in the other room watching a movie. Jane was at a doctor's appointment.

How did it come to this? Me, alone with two kids? Jane so owes me.

She deposited Allison on the bed then turned to go back to her room. She looked forward to this hour of peace every day, and no one was going to take it from her.

"Tra." Allison's little fingers clutched at Tara's legs before she'd even made it halfway down the hall.

"Listen, kid." Tara removed them, along with what felt like a chunk of her skin. "It's naptime. You need a nap; *I* need a nap. So—"

"Trrrrrraaaaaaaa," Allison wailed, sliding to the floor, going into meltdown mode. Maddie arrived a second later, apparently having decided the scene in the hall was better than her movie.

"Can you tell what she wants?" Tara asked, her voice a mixture of irritation and panic.

"You," Maddie said. "She wants you to rock her or snuggle with her in bed. That's what Jessica did when she was here and what my mom does when Allie can't sleep at night."

Tara stared down at the little girl. "You want your mom?"

Allie nodded.

"Mom says Allie misses her parents and needs extra loves."

"We all do, Sugar." Tara blew a stray hair from her eyes then bent down and scooped a now-screaming, kicking Allie from the floor. With purposeful steps, she returned her to Maddie's room, this time not letting her go when she set Allie down. Looking into the toddler's eyes, she searched her mind for possible ways to handle the situation—aside from rocking or cuddling, which weren't her thing. Unfortunately, there wasn't much in her life experiences to draw on.

"Allie." Tara spoke firmly. "You need to take a nap."

More wailing—accompanied by kicking—met this announcement. Still keeping an eye on Allie, Tara stood and backed away.

"Listen," she said, "your mom and dad will be back in a couple of days, and Aunt Jane will be here tonight. I'm sorry, but I don't do that rocking thing, and my bed is just for me, so you're gonna have to deal with this on your own. It's time to put on your big-girl panties and grow up."

Covering her ears so she wouldn't hear the little girl's continued screams, Tara practically ran back to her own room. Maddie stared curiously after her a moment then went to her bedroom with Allie and closed the door behind her.

After a few minutes more, Allie's crying ceased, and Tara let out a relieved, satisfied sigh. *Both girls must be lying down now. There's something to be said for being firm.* She tucked the victory away for future incidents and to share with Jane. *Poor Jane has been getting up at night, letting that squirmy kid in her bed, when all she needed to do was be a little tougher.* Tara felt a new kind of satisfaction. *Of course I can take care of a kid. I've been in the boardrooms of corporate America. What's so different?*

Setting the magazine aside, she closed her eyes and allowed herself to doze lightly. Every few minutes she would open her eyes and look at the clock. Ten then twenty then thirty minutes passed with no noise from Maddie's room.

They must both be asleep. I am so good.

Invigorated by her success, Tara got up and went to the kitchen to start dinner. Tonight she'd make something nice—something besides tacos or spaghetti or burritos. If the little girls didn't like it, well too bad. She'd tell them it was what she served or nothing. They'd come around.

She was assembling the ingredients for chicken parmesan, angel hair pasta, and a spinach salad when both girls started screaming. Tara set a pot on the counter and ran down the hall. She flung open Maddie's door and found the girls sitting on Maddie's bed, each with their mouths open and howling.

"What?" Tara asked. "What is it? What's wrong?"

"My bed is wet," Maddie wailed. "Allie pottied all over my bed—and me."

"She did? *You did?*" Tara stared at Allie, her legs slightly raised over the wide, dark spot on the comforter beneath. "Did your Pull-Up leak?" Tara marched across the room, grabbed each girl by an arm, and hauled them from the bed.

"She's not wearing one," Maddie said. "I let her wear my panties—my pretty flowered ones—and she *wet* them." Fresh tears fell from Maddie's eyes.

"Why did you do that?" Tara stepped forward and yanked the blanket off the bed.

"Because," Maddie said, "you told Allie to put on her big-girl panties, but she doesn't have any. So I shared."

"You shared," Tara repeated. *I have to clean this up—seriously?* Hands on hips, she frowned at the little girls. Allie stood awkwardly, her legs spread wide, a look of abject misery on her face. Maddie, on the other hand, looked disgusted and angry.

With me, Tara realized. *She's ticked at me.*

"Don't look at me like that." Tara wagged a finger in her face. "I'm not the one who peed in your bed."

"Why are you so mean?" Maddie yelled. "I snuggled with Allie 'cause you made her sad, and now my bed is all wet. This is *your* fault."

You want to see mean? Tara thought. But the accusation stung. Biting her tongue so she wouldn't be *meaner*—and get tattled on to Jane—Tara ignored the girls and began pulling the sheets off. They bore a similar round stain, as did the mattress beneath.

"Great. Just great." She gathered all the wet bedding, stepped around the girls, and headed for the laundry. "Stay right there," she ordered. "You're both going to have a bath."

Before she could get to the laundry room or start the water running in the tub, the phone began ringing. Tara glanced at the caller ID on the kitchen counter as she walked by. *Harrison Medical.* As the name registered in her mind, she dropped the laundry and reached for the phone.

"Hello?"

"Hi, Tara." Jane's voice was tired.

"Are you okay?" Tara asked, trying not to sound worried. *Please don't tell me you're going to be late. I can't take another hour. I—*

"I've got to stay overnight," Jane said. "They want to monitor the babies for several hours, and I have to take a stress test in the morning."

You think you're *stressed?* "Um—okay," Tara said. What else *could* she say? *Come home right now? These kids are driving me nuts?* Pushing aside her own concerns, she tried to think about what Jane must be dealing with. "Is anything wrong with the babies? Are you having contractions again?"

"Little contractions, but their heartbeats are strong. My doctor's just being cautious. How are the girls?" Jane asked.

"They're—" *Naked.*

Maddie and Allison streaked across the hall and into the bathroom.

So much for staying right where I told them to. Tara imagined their wet, smelly clothes sitting on Maddie's carpet. "They're fine. I, uh, I'm getting ready to give them a bath."

"Oh, did they get really dirty playing outside?" Jane asked.

Tara caught the wistful note in her voice. To Jane, the most difficult thing about bed rest was not being able to work out in her yard.

"They're pretty dirty," Tara hedged. "But don't worry about it. I'll make sure they're all clean. I'll take good care of them."

"Thanks, Tara. I *really* appreciate it. I owe you."

No kidding. "No problem. Feel better, okay?"

They said good-bye and Tara headed down the hall. She entered the bathroom to find both little girls sitting in the tub with no water but about a million toys and a big blob of something pink between them. An empty bubble bath container lay on its side on the floor.

"We waited to start the water," Maddie said, as if she were the authority here and had taken over the bathing process because Tara was incapable.

I am capable, Tara thought. *Just because I messed up on the panties thing . . .* She turned the faucet, and as the cold water hit their skin, both girls squealed.

"Sorry," Tara said in a cheerful voice, feeling slightly better about the mess awaiting her in the other room. She held her hand under the water until it reached the right temperature then sat on the edge of the tub as it filled, a giant mound of strawberry-scented bubbles rising ever higher.

While the girls played, she decided to clean the bathroom. *One less thing to do later*, she reasoned as she scrubbed out the sink. Now that she thought about it, she wasn't exactly certain *what* she would do "later" with Jane gone tonight. They'd settled into a familiar routine of eating ice cream and talking about life, a routine that she looked forward to. A hint of loneliness tugged at her heart, but Tara pushed it firmly aside. She was too busy to feel sorry for herself.

Overworked and underpaid . . . just like—Jesus. She thought of the New Testament scriptures she'd been studying the past few days. The missionaries had left her with a copy of the Book of Mormon, but she preferred reading from the four Gospels—as Jane referred to them. There was something about reading of Jesus's life, the words He spoke, that spoke to her. Again and again she returned to the message from the first Sunday school lesson she'd attended.

He who will lose his life, shall find it.

She hadn't really tried that yet. It was hard—all this giving and serving and doing unto others. Maybe that's what impressed her so much and drew her to reading about Jesus. The way He'd continuously given of Himself. She didn't understand how He could. *Or why he would.*

The girls laughed and a second later, water splashed over the edge of the tub. Tara turned a reprimanding frown on them. She opened her mouth, intending to scold, but something about the looks on their faces stopped her.

They're just little. I was little once. Did Mom scold me when I splashed in the tub? Knowing her mother, probably. It was an unhappy thought, one Tara didn't wish to act out. Surprising herself more than the girls, she cupped a hand under the sink faucet and filled it. "You want to splash, do you?" she asked, tossing the water at the girls.

Maddie's eyes widened and her mouth opened in a shocked O. Allie laughed and sent another wave over the side of the tub. Tara gasped and jumped back, as if the water had just missed her. It *had* succeeded in soaking the bath mat, but Tara held back a groan. *I'll just add the mat to the wash I'm already doing.*

Pushing the wet rug aside, she knelt beside the tub. She scooped up a handful of bubbles and plopped them on Allie's head. "Bet I can make you look like Ashton Kutcher when he's growing a beard." She proceeded—to Allie's delight—to sculpt a full bubble beard.

"Would you like one too?" she asked Maddie.

Maddie's eyes were still huge, and she stared at Tara as if seeing her for the first time. Tara couldn't blame her. *I've been impatient and grumpy and . . . What is wrong with me? This is* Jane's *daughter. My friend's child.*

"I'm sorry, Maddie. I'm sorry I made Allie cry and your bed got wet." *And for everything else I've said or done since I've been here.*

"That's okay." The corners of Maddie's mouth lifted in a smile. "I forgive you."

Tara remembered when another little girl had asked her forgiveness, when Ben's niece had tried to tell her why forgiving others was so very important.

"Thank you, Maddie." Tara felt another lump in her throat and wondered if she was developing some condition she ought to have looked at.

Her symptoms—the frequent inability to swallow and watery eyes—were troubling.

Twenty-Seven

MADDIE RESTED HER HEAD ON the counter, an inch from the newspaper Tara was trying to read. "I miss Allison."

"Me too," Tara said. She didn't miss the messes, but she'd been surprised to discover the way Maddie latched on to her now that her cousin was gone. From the minute she came home from kindergarten every day, until she finally dropped off to sleep at night, Maddie followed Tara around, seeking constant attention. Jane did what she could to entertain her daughter, reading stories, and playing those never-ending games, but Maddie was like Jane, always wanting to be outside. She wanted action.

"Want to play ball?"

"Not really." Tara scanned the want ads. Reading the newspaper classifieds wasn't nearly as efficient as looking for jobs online, but she checked every day just to make sure she hadn't missed something. Since she'd had to partially replace her wardrobe—she couldn't begin to purchase substitutes for everything she'd packed up and promised not to wear—her bank account had shrunk even more. She worried that if she didn't have a job by the time Peter came home, she wouldn't have enough to pay first and last month's rent and a security deposit, let alone anything left to tide her over for a month or so until she had a regular paycheck.

"How about jump rope?"

"Nope." At five, Maddie had not yet mastered jump rope. She *had* mastered jumping up and down, singing loudly, and snapping the rope repeatedly—on Tara's arm, shoulder, and head. Once had been more than enough for that game.

"Tea party in the playhouse?" Maddie's voice was pleading. "We can pretend the prince is coming again."

Tara set the paper aside and looked down at the little girl. "You know what you need?"

"A sister or a brother to play with?" Maddie suggested.

"Yes," Tara said. "That's exactly what you need." *So this is why people have more than one kid—to keep the first one from driving them nuts.* "Lucky for you, you're going to get both."

"I know. I know." Maddie excitedly bounced up and down on her toes. "And Mommy says I can help feed them bottles, and I can rock them, and when they get bigger they'll play outside with me."

"I'm sure they will." Tara imagined Jane in her element, outside with a spade in her hand, the flower beds bursting and children running over every inch of the yard.

"Will you play with me now? We can have real cookies outside." Maddie put on her most hopeful expression. "I'll let you have the china cup," she offered, as if that were enticement beyond what Tara could resist.

"All right," Tara said, holding her hands up in surrender as she got off the stool. "Tell you what. You can have the china teacup if I get to answer the playhouse door when the prince arrives."

"Deal." Maddie's grin was huge.

Tara grabbed a package of Oreos from the cupboard while Maddie skipped down the hall to get her play dishes. When she returned, they filled the tiny teapot with water then headed outside. It wasn't as warm as the previous day, but the wind wasn't nearly as bad as it had been last night. Tara glanced up at ominous clouds overhead. "I think this had better be a quick tea party, unless we want to get soaked."

Maddie ran ahead, leaving Tara to bring their feast. "Mommy thinks it's fun to play in the rain."

"I'm *not* your mommy," Tara grumbled. She reached the play structure and handed everything up to Maddie, who'd already scaled the side. Tara moved more slowly, taking care not to snag her pants on any rough pieces of wood.

She arrived at the top and ducked under the canvas roof, only to find that Maddie had climbed down the opposite side.

"What are you doing?" Tara called to her. "I thought we were eating up here."

"Look at the birds!" Maddie shouted. She squatted in the grass behind the sandbox and beneath the big tree that grew next to it. "A whole nest of them—look."

Tara stared down at the nest and the three bald baby birds peeping loudly. Following a straight line up from the ground, into the high limbs of the tree, she thought she could tell where the nest had fallen from—probably in last night's wind.

"Where is their mommy?" Maddie asked. "Will she come back?"

"I don't know. Maybe," Tara said, though she was doubtful. The nest appeared to be pretty battered. Maybe something worse had happened to the bird who'd made it. "Don't touch them," she called to Maddie. "Come back up here, and we can watch for her."

Maddie stayed beside the nest a minute more then climbed up to the play loft again. Tara got busy passing out the Oreos and pouring water in the miniature cups.

"Come, mommy bird, come," Maddie chanted as she kept her eyes glued to the nest below.

"Maybe she'll only come if we're quiet," Tara suggested.

Maddie nodded and brought a finger to her lips. "Shh," she said, as if Tara had been the one making all the noise. She pressed her face between the wood slats, staring at the nest below.

Tara ate an Oreo then leaned her head back against the railing and closed her eyes, enjoying the cool breeze and fresh air. Times like this, it was easy to understand why Jane liked being outside so much. All this open space gave Tara a sense of freedom and something almost akin to peace. The worries that had seemed so omnipresent in the big city all but vanished in the quiet and beauty of Bainbridge.

"She's not coming," Maddie whispered after what might have been a whole two minutes.

So much for peace. "We haven't been quiet long enough," Tara said, opening one eye to look at her.

"What if the mommy bird doesn't know where her nest is?" Maddie asked.

"She knows," Tara said. *Smart bird, staying away from all that whining.*

"No. She doesn't." Maddie shook her head. "We have to tell her."

"I don't speak bird," Tara said.

"Me neither." Maddie's brow furrowed so deeply that Tara had to bite her lip to keep from laughing. She had to admit that kids were amusing, especially Maddie, the way she took everything so literally.

"We could pray," Maddie offered. "And ask Heavenly Father to help us talk to the mommy bird."

"I don't know," Tara said. "It's the middle of the day. He's probably kind of busy right now." She picked up an Oreo and held it out to Maddie. "Let's have our tea party." From watching Jane, she had learned the highly effective parenting technique *distraction*. With Allison it had worked every single time.

Unlike Allie, Maddie didn't fall for it. She knelt on the floor of the playhouse, folded her arms, bowed her head, and began to pray. Tara sat across from her, feeling awkward, as Maddie pled for the mommy to find her baby birds.

No sooner had Maddie whispered, "Amen," then she jumped up, a joyous look on her face.

"I know what's wrong. I wasn't *loud* enough," she announced.

"Huh?" Tara frowned. "I don't follow."

"It's okay," Maddie said. "I can be loud, and we're up high—" Her mouth opened in a little gasp and her eyes widened—"Just like King Benjamin. We learned about him in Primary. I have a tower like his."

"No clue what you're talking about," Tara said, but Maddie had already run out from under the canvas, onto the bridge that connected the play fort to the swings. She flung her arms wide.

"Mommy bird! Come get your babies." Her shouts carried across the yard. Tara was pretty certain that if *any* birds were nearby, they wouldn't be for long.

"Under the big tree. By the sandbox," Maddie yelled. "Oh, mommy bird!"

"I think you're scaring the babies," Tara called to her. *You're scaring me, kid.*

"But this is what the king did when he wanted the people to hear him. He stood on his tower and talked loud. For *three* days. We played that in Primary. David got to stand on the chair instead of me."

Tough luck. Tara decided to employ another parenting tactic she'd learned from Jane—*ignoring.* After all, what did she care that Maddie was acting a little weird? She was finally entertaining herself, and that was all that mattered. Tara decided she'd run in the house and grab a book to read on the patio.

She'd no sooner crawled out from beneath the shelter of the canvas when a cold, fat raindrop hit her forehead. Another splashed onto the bridge of her nose before she'd had a chance to retreat.

"Time to go in," she announced, gathering up the Oreos and dishes.

"Mommy bird, mommy bird." Maddie's voice took on an urgent note.

Tara peered down at the nest. One of the baby birds had ceased to chirp and sat quite still.

"Will it die?" Maddie asked.

"I don't know," Tara said. "But *you* might get sick if we don't get inside before it starts pouring." She held her hand out. "Come on."

Maddie turned away and pressed her face between the wooden slats of the railing again. "I can't leave them."

"I can." Tara climbed down the ladder and ran across the yard to the patio. Once sheltered from the rain, she turned and saw that Maddie remained right where she'd left her—on the bridge and getting soaked.

"This one's all Jane's," Tara muttered as she entered the house. Her own limited parenting tactics had run dry, and she had no problem calling in the expert. Tara deposited the remains of the tea party on the kitchen table then went to Jane's room and discovered she was asleep.

Of course. Tara stood in the open doorway of Jane's beautifully decorated bedroom, debating what to do. Jane was curled on her side in the middle of the king-sized bed and looked small and vulnerable all by herself. Tara knew Jane hadn't slept well last night, but on the other hand, it was *her* responsibility to deal with her child.

Tara glanced out the window at the pouring rain. Part of her— like ninety percent—was ready to let Maddie stay outside and get hypothermia. But another part, small though that might be, thought of Jane and the added worry she'd have if her daughter were sick.

Last night Tara had overheard Jane talking to Peter on the computer. She'd envied the love and concern in their voices, the way they laughed easily, the plans they made for their future together. But she hadn't envied the worry in Jane's voice or the tears she'd seen fall when Jane laid her head on the desk and wept at the end of the call.

Knowing she couldn't add to that burden, Tara reluctantly left the bedroom and returned to the backyard.

"Madison!" She tried for the tone of voice she'd heard Jane use with her daughter exactly twice during the past few weeks. "Come in this house right now."

Maddie paused for a moment, stared at Tara, then shook her head. "Not until the mommy bird comes."

"Don't be ridiculous," Tara called. "You've got to come inside and get dry."

"Mommy bird." Maddie acted as though she hadn't heard her.

Tara looked up at the angry sky and swore. Then she ran out to the swing set, climbed the ladder partway, and grabbed Maddie's arm. "You'll get a chill if you stay out here, and then your mom will be upset with us both."

Maddie turned, and Tara saw that, in addition to the rain, tears were dripping down her cheeks. "We can't let them die."

Tara leaned to the side and stared down at the nest. The baby birds were silent now—and unmoving. "I think they're already dead," she said as gently as possible.

"No!" Maddie ran to the side and swung herself over before Tara could stop her. With all the agility of an active five-year-old and the passion of a tender heart, she descended in seconds, dropping to the ground beside the nest.

"Don't die, birdies. Please don't die." Eyes pleading, she looked at Tara. "Help them—*please*."

With a half-sigh, half-groan, Tara climbed down. Grassy, muddy water squished around her Jimmy Choo sandals with each step as she made her way over to Maddie, squatting beside the nest. Tara broke a twig from the nearby bushes then bent over and used it to touch the birds, trying to determine if they were alive.

The first bird was stiff enough that it fell over when she poked at it. *Definitely dead.*

"Nooooo," Maddie wailed.

The second's eyes were open and unmoving. "I'm sorry, Maddie," Tara said.

The little girl was now near hysterics. "Is-is tha-at one . . ."

Tara reached the twig out once more then paused, offering a silent prayer—of sorts—of her own. *God, if You're really there, please give Maddie a break and let this bird be alive.*

The third baby bird let out a pathetic little cheep when the twig touched it.

"Oh!" Maddie cried and stretched out her hand to pick it up.

"No," Tara said, her own hand stopping Maddie. "We shouldn't touch it. We should just—just—" *What?*

Maddie raised two solemn eyes to hers. "What would Jesus do?" she asked. "Would He leave a little bird alone in the rain?"

It was on the tip of Tara's tongue to say that she wasn't Jesus and had no aspirations to be, but she couldn't seem to say the caustic words. She knew that it was partly the hopeful smile Maddie bestowed upon her, but there was something else too. Some other force held her here in the mud and cold and rain, messing up her hair, ruining her shoes.

I can't say stuff like that anymore, she realized with a sort of bewilderment. *Because I know about Jesus. I know who He was and what He did. Who He is.*

She'd used both God's name and His Son's in common conversation for as long as she could remember. But Maddie's question made her think. She couldn't brush it off because she *knew* what Jesus would do. For the past few weeks she'd been reading about the many things He had done. And somehow, that knowledge translated to responsibility. For her language and attitude. And—

For this bird.

Tara threw the stick aside and, gritting her teeth, picked up the wet, slimy, disgusting nest. Walking as fast as she dared, she returned to the patio and set the nest on a chair, safely out of the rain.

"It's too cold out here for the bird. And she's hungry. Plus she's sad sitting next to her dead sisters." Maddie stepped toward the chair, hands outstretched.

"*Really*," Tara said. But she picked up the nest before Maddie could and took it inside the house. "As if I wasn't doing enough already. Now I've got to play veterinarian."

Once inside, she set the nest on a piece of newspaper on the floor.

"Find a box," Tara ordered. "And some tissues." Maddie scrambled off to do her bidding.

Sure. Now she obeys. Tara tore a paper towel from the dispenser and used it to remove the one, live bird from the nest. She held it carefully, doing her best to wipe the rain from its almost nonexistent feathers. A hint of compassion stirred in her soul as she stared at its tiny eyes. The poor thing really was cold. And no doubt terrified too.

"I'll bet she's hungry," Maddie said as she entered the kitchen, the pink box from her Easter shoes in hand. "We have good worms in our yard. Want me to go find some?"

"No. Go change your clothes. Then we'll worry about feeding the bird."

"Her name is Fran."

"Wonderful. Go change your clothes." Tara placed the bird on the pile of toilet paper in the box. As soon as she set it down, its pitiful cheeping began again. Ignoring it, she went to her room to change her own soaked clothes and to have a moment of silence to mourn her shoes.

After removing the drenched, muddy, grass-stained sandals, Tara sat on the bed and tried to wipe them off, but the damage seemed pretty permanent—and thorough. Her favorite and funky Phyllis-printed leather wedges were officially dead. *Another $375 down the drain. Could have rented a penthouse for what living here is costing me in clothes and shoes.* She placed the shoes in the box with far more care than she'd carried Maddie's precious nest.

Feeling frustrated and sad, Tara stared at the floor of the closet for a few moments then finally decided that her other pair of Jimmy Choos—cosmic snakeskin platform pumps—would have to do as a substitute for now. There was no way she could afford to buy new shoes—good ones, anyway—until she was working again.

By the time she returned to the kitchen, Maddie was there peering over the box, probably breathing on the bird, she was so close. Tara was about to tell her to back off so she wouldn't catch some bird disease when she saw Jane, looking tousled and sleepy, already pulling Maddie away.

"Nice nap?" Tara asked in not the nicest tone.

"Yes," Jane said. "Though I see I missed the excitement."

Tara shrugged. "I don't know what to do with it now. I'm sorry, but I draw the line at digging for worms."

"You don't have to," Jane said. "Mix a little ground beef with some cottage cheese and a little bit of dirt. Warm it just a little—to room temperature—and I'll feed the bird."

"How do you know—never mind." Tara waved off her own question.

Jane answered anyway. "When you spend as much time as I do working outdoors, you're bound to come across a baby bird or two."

"Have any of them made—" She stopped, watching Maddie from the corner of her eye.

"None," Jane said sadly. "But we have to try, you know?"

Tara watched Maddie's sweetly hopeful expression as she leaned across the table, singing to the bird. "I know."

* * *

Tara sprawled on the sofa while Jane sat in Peter's chair, a pair of tweezers in her gloved hand as she fed the baby bird for the eighth time since they'd rescued it that afternoon.

"I'd forgotten how often baby birds have to eat," Jane said, carefully maneuvering the particle of food into the bird's open beak. "I'm afraid this is good practice for what's coming."

"Times two," Tara said, reminding herself that she *had* to have a place of her own by the time Jane's babies were born.

"I'm sorry Maddie gave you such a hard time today," Jane said.

"It's okay," Tara said and meant it. "She's your daughter, all right—ready to dig worms, completely content being outside in the middle of a major downpour . . . She was actually pretty cute out there in the rain, standing up on her fort pretending to be some king."

"She got the idea from Primary last week. Maddie told me all about the lesson they had and how they got to dress up and pretend to listen to King Benjamin."

"Mmm-hmm," Tara murmured. She could feel herself falling asleep and knew she should get up and go to bed. Peter would be calling soon, and she didn't need to eavesdrop on any more intimate conversations.

Must be nice to have even a phone call to look forward to. I wonder what would happen if I called Ben. She indulged in a memory, as she did more often than she knew she ought. She'd never see Ben again. He might as well be a figment of her imagination. He might as well be, but he wasn't. When she allowed herself to think of him, to remember, she always returned to that spot on top of a snowy Colorado mountain, just before he had kissed her. He was telling her she was a spoiled princess.

At least I wasn't named after a dog. Tara cringed, remembering the awful things she'd said. In her mind, she could still see Ben's face, indignant, and hear the anger in his voice.

I wasn't named after a dog. I was named after a king. King Benjamin was one of the finest men . . .

Tara's eyes popped open, and she sat up and turned to Jane. "What did you say that king's name was?"

"Benjamin," Jane said. She paused, the tweezers poised in midair. Beneath them, the baby bird's open beak waited expectantly.

"Who is he?" Tara demanded.

"A prophet in the Book of Mormon." Jane studied Tara curiously. "Are you all right?"

"I'm fine." Tara swung her legs over the side of the couch. "That's the book the missionaries gave me?"

"Yes. The one you haven't opened yet," Jane said, resuming her task.

"I've been busy," Tara said. "Do you know of any other kings named Benjamin?" She'd thought about it a few times since Ben had mentioned the name but never seriously or for very long. It was obvious this Benjamin wasn't some well-known historical figure like Napoleon or George Washington, but still, she'd been kind of curious. It had never occurred to her—until now—that he might be someone in the scriptures.

"He's the only King Benjamin I know," Jane said. "A good guy, too. You ought to look him up."

"I'll get around to it," Tara said, her voice nonchalant. She stood and stretched then walked toward the hall.

"Good night," Jane called.

"Night," Tara said, walking a little faster as soon as she was out of the room. She intended to *get around to it* right now. Before she'd taken three steps, Jane called to her.

"Yes?" Tara said.

"Try Mosiah."

Tara backed up then leaned her head through the doorway. "What?"

"Mosiah," Jane repeated. "It's the book in the Book of Mormon where you'll find King Benjamin."

"Oh. Thanks." Tara's eyes narrowed. "How did you—"

"Just a guess." Jane smiled sweetly. "Ben. Benjamin. I figured there might be some connection. Something that—*interested* you."

Tara shook her head as she gave half a laugh. "You keep this kind of intuition up, and Maddie is going to hate you when she's a teenager."

Jane laughed. "Good luck," she said. "I hope you find what you're looking for."

Twenty-Eight

TARA SAT CROSS-LEGGED ON HER bed, the closed copy of the Book of Mormon on her lap. For the past five minutes she'd been staring at it but hadn't found the courage to open it. For all her earlier eagerness to read about Ben's namesake, she was suddenly afraid to do so.

Which is ridiculous, she told herself. *What's so scary about reading about some old, dead king?*

Nothing. A shiver of apprehension accompanied the thought. There was a feeling in the room—not quite like either of the feelings she'd felt during that first meeting with the missionaries, but a strange sensation just the same. And somehow she knew it had to do with this book. She was afraid that if she opened it—

Things will never be the same.

She stared at it another minute then picked it up—still keeping it closed—and gently bent the soft-covered volume back and forth like a wave.

It shouldn't be a big deal. After all, she was enjoying the New Testament. Reading about Jesus was interesting and brought a sort of peace—like she'd felt when she'd been outside this morning before it rained. Her own problems and concerns seemed to dissipate in the vast, overall picture the scriptures presented. They had opened up her world by a couple thousand years and several thousand miles. It was impossible to feel despair when reading them. It was easy to feel courage and hope.

To feel my burdens lightened. Just as Jesus promised. I love that feeling.

There. She'd said it—or thought it, at least. She was pretty sure that not even Jane knew this about her. The missionaries certainly

didn't. Sister Ayer and Sister Henrie had been more than patient the
past few weeks, but Tara could tell they were frustrated by her lack of
progress.

*I haven't followed through with what they asked. I haven't opened this
book.* Her fingers traced the small, gold lettering beneath the title.

Another Testament of Jesus Christ

She would find Jesus in this book, as well, she knew. *And King
Benjamin too.* What was his role? Was he a man of position like the
Pharisees in the Bible, who knew of Jesus but didn't *know* Him? Or
was he like the disciples who had left their nets straightaway and
followed Christ? Since Ben was named after him, Tara knew it had to
be the latter. And she wanted to read the story, wanted to know and
understand it for herself.

Even if it means that some things will never be the same. She thought
of this morning again, the way Maddie's question about Jesus had given
her pause. Tara realized that some things had already changed.

But nothing that I can't live with. Changing her vocabulary wasn't
too difficult. She could always change it back. And all of her clothes
that hadn't passed the head, shoulders, knees test were still in boxes in
the corner. She could always unpack them. She could leave. She could
get in her car, drive to LA or anywhere else she wanted, and start over,
on her terms.

I can do anything I want. Agency had been one of the first lessons
the missionaries taught. Right now, she wanted to use it to read. With
hands shaking slightly, she opened the book.

* * *

King Benjamin was one exemplary guy. Tara lay on her bed and stared
at the ceiling. She felt exhausted, drained to the point of being light-
headed as she came back to the present after spending two hours
in ancient America. She'd read the Words of Mormon—beginning
where she'd found the first reference to King Benjamin—through
Mosiah chapter six, when King Benjamin died—four times. Using
the colored pencil Sister Henrie had given her, Tara had marked scriptures—a lot of them—that she wanted to remember.

King Benjamin's story was inspiring, but it was his beautiful words that still echoed in her mind and heart and made her eyes water. Equal parts of shame and longing rolled over her. She would have been one of those he chastised. She longed to be one of those who repented and had a . . . Tara held the open book above her head near the beginning of chapter five to read it again.

"A mighty change in us, or in our hearts, that we have no more disposition to do evil, but to do good continually."

Her own heart literally ached with the same desire. She'd been lying here for some time, doing as King Benjamin had suggested and considering— She flipped back to chapter two.

"On the blessed and happy state of those who keep the commandments of God."

Jane and Peter did seem to be blessed in all things, though Tara knew their life was no picnic. They worked hard. They served. They loved. All things that King Benjamin himself had done.

All things that Ben did too. Surprisingly, she hadn't thought of Ben much while reading. King Benjamin's tale had consumed her. But now that she made the comparison, she could see that Ben was aptly named.

From the moment she'd first met him, he'd worked and served, from helping out with Ellen's kids, to packing up a houseful of stuff that wasn't his responsibility, to driving it all across the mountains, and then unpacking the truck. She'd left him that way, snuck out like a coward to her rental car, while he labored carrying a piano into the house.

Then there were all the things he'd done for her during those few days. First he'd offered to help—when no one else around bothered. *On the elevator he saw that I was ill and took care of me.* He'd taken her shopping, when clearly it had been the last thing he'd wanted to do. *He walked with me in the snow when he didn't have to.* When she thought back to those three days, she couldn't think of a time Ben *hadn't* been serving someone.

Like King Benjamin, he used the strength of his own arm but relied upon the strength of the Lord. Also like King Benjamin, he'd used bold words in chastising those who needed it.

I needed it. Tara squeezed her eyes shut, as if that somehow might shut out the shame she felt at the way she had acted. She'd used terrible language in front of Ellen's kids, and she'd complained and whined and thought of no one but herself during that entire weekend.

It's a miracle Ben didn't dump me at the side of the road somewhere.

Tara wondered why he hadn't, but it didn't take long to guess the answer to that, either. It had to do with Maddie's question. *What would Jesus do?* It was something she herself was just starting to consider. But people like Ben and Ellen and Jane had likely been considering it for years. *That's why Jane was so hard on herself about not telling me about her church when we worked together.* She must believe that sharing her beliefs is what Jesus would have done.

That's why Ben helped me in the first place. Because it was what Jesus would have done.

How many times has he read the scripture about serving men being the same as serving God? Ben had understood the concept. And suddenly Tara understood too. The story she'd just read—King Benjamin's—was a perfect example of what Brother Bartlett, the Sunday School teacher, had been trying to get at these past few weeks. Losing oneself in service was the way to find oneself, and happiness.

Tara knew that, on some level, she'd been fighting against that and against Jane's efforts the entire time she'd been here. Change was hard, especially this kind of change. And service was . . . *work.* She flipped through Mosiah again, rereading the marked passages once more. King Benjamin had labored "with all the might of his whole body and the faculty of his whole soul." He hadn't cared for riches, and he'd given thanks to God for all he had. Love and service was what it came down to. Jesus had been all about the same thing. His words had lasted over two thousand years. King Benjamin's were even older than that. The idea of all of that time passing, and all of the millions of people who had read their words, was awe inspiring.

Tara closed the book and held it close to her heart, knowing she already loved it as much as the New Testament. It was time to take the Sunday School teacher's challenge seriously. It was time to try to do as Jesus—or King Benjamin—would have. It was time to go to work.

Summer

*"If we all did the things we are capable of doing,
we would literally astound ourselves."*
—*Thomas A. Edison*

Twenty-Nine

Tara woke to the sound of insistent chirping coming from the kitchen. *That bird!* Tossing aside the covers, she got up and went to Maddie's room. It was empty, so she went to the kitchen and wasn't surprised to find Maddie standing on a chair, leaning over the table, doing her best to feed the always-starving fledgling.

"Good morning," Maddie said sweetly. "Look at Fran today. Isn't she pretty? I brushed her feathers."

Tara opened her mouth, a flippant comment on the tip of her tongue about how Maddie should have used the brush on her own tangled hair. But she caught herself just in time. *Take a second. Start over. Start the day right.*

"Morning, kiddo." She gave Maddie's shoulders a quick squeeze. "Fran looks great. Be right back." Tara retreated to her room, closed the door, and knelt by the side of the bed.

Heavenly Father, she began then paused. She'd been praying morning and night for the past two weeks, but it still didn't feel any more natural than the very first time she'd knelt awkwardly beside her bed. *I'm grateful for the good night's sleep.*

A little more would have been better. Why do little kids and birds have to get up at six thirty every day?

I'm grateful for this home to stay in.

Really, thank You for that one. I've been checking apartments around here, and the average rent is through the roof.

I'm glad that Jane and Peter are well. Thank You for Jane's friendship. She paused again. This was where it got tough each time.

Thank You for the scriptures and the things I'm learning. Help me to know they are real. Help me to know You.

She waited, eyes closed and face pressed to the side of the mattress. A minute or two passed, but Tara didn't hear any still, small voice. She didn't quite feel the tenderness inside that she'd experienced lately either.

Probably because I was grumpy this morning. She added one last supplication to her prayer and knew she'd likely have to repeat the request throughout her day. *Help me be nice.*

She closed her prayer then stood and went to the closet, staring at the paper she'd taped there. In a minute, she'd open the doors and quickly find something to wear. It wasn't too difficult, as her choices remained limited. These days instead of spending the colossal amount of time she used to in putting the perfect outfit together, she was doing something new. She was working on putting together a better Tara—perfection being completely out of her reach.

Her inspiration for betterment had started with her study of Christ's life. It seemed impossible to Tara that *anyone* could read about Jesus and not want to be better. One of her favorite hours of the week had become Sunday School and Brother Bartlett's lessons that clarified what she'd read in the New Testament that week. She looked forward to his lessons, learned from them, and always left the room feeling uplifted.

But inspiring as learning about Jesus was, being like Him also seemed unattainable. *Enter King Benjamin—and his namesake.* Tara's lips curved in a smile as she thought of Ben. Reading about King Benjamin had changed her life—or rather made her want to change it. *Really change.* No longer was her reform about pleasing Jane, or even Ben, but about being a better person.

For myself—to myself.

Easier said than done. Tara thought of the way she'd almost snapped at Maddie first thing this morning. She remembered the scripture about the natural man being an enemy to God.

No kidding. My natural woman is positively wicked. From the moment she woke up each morning, to the minute she fell asleep at night, being a better person was proving incredibly difficult.

Even my dreams are bad sometimes. Tara sighed. Changing, really changing, was really hard.

She studied the list on the closet door, took a deep breath, and committed to one more day of being obedient to her commandments. She'd made her own list, since most on Moses's tablets weren't a problem for her. She might *say* she was going to kill something sometimes. *Like that stupid bird that chirps day and night.* But she knew she'd never actually do it. Stealing wasn't a problem either. Honoring her mother and father . . . She couldn't really go there yet. But most of the Big Ten, as she'd come to think of them, weren't a worry. It was the other stuff she wrestled with. Tara faced her list with courage.

"No drinking." She took a pencil off the dresser and added another tally mark next to the first item on her list. *I've gone thirty-six days. What's one more?*

"No swearing." No tally marks were next to this item. Tara sighed. *This one may be hopeless.* Though she'd ceased using Deity's name, she still found too many other words lingering in her vocabulary.

"No cheating." *Nothing to cheat* at *around here except Candy Land.* And she didn't count strategically placing certain cards near the top of the pile so the game would be shorter as dishonest. *It's not like I win*, she thought. *I always make sure Maddie ends up with Queen Frosting, or whatever her name is, at the top of the board.*

"No lying." She checked that one off too. With only Jane to talk to, it was pretty much an impossibility. *Besides, Jane loves me—faults and all.*

"No falsifying information." That one was easy right now, but its challenge loomed large. Tara felt genuine fear about being an honest Realtor in this economy.

"Serve others. Got that one down." Tara added three tally marks. She did that all day long from Jane to Maddie to Fran the bird. And yesterday she'd even made an amazing Italian dinner—homemade breadsticks, salad dressing, the works—for the missionaries. She added an extra tally and considered the possibility of upgrading to gold stars like Maddie's kindergarten teacher used.

"Be nice." Her fist clenched around the pencil, and she fell backward on the bed. *Why is that so hard?* The more she'd tried to change, the more she worked on this one goal in particular, the more it bothered her. She was, apparently, not a nice person at all—as evidenced by her near-caustic remark to Maddie just a few minutes earlier.

Discouraged, Tara read the last item on her list.

"Get to know Him." The *Him* she referred to was God, her Father in Heaven, the missionaries liked to say. She liked that better too. God seemed like a title, but Father was someone she could relate to—or wanted to, anyway. After the first couple of weeks of messing around, she'd finally taken the missionaries' challenge seriously. She was going to find out if He was real. Writing *Get to know Him* on her list implied that she already believed He really was out there—somewhere—listening to her, watching over her. And she wanted Him to be real. She wanted it more than she could believe or dared tell anyone.

She wanted it all to be true.

Thirty

THROUGH THE OPEN DOORWAY LEADING to the kindergarten classroom, Tara stared at the rows of tiny chairs crammed into the space.
Four rows with ten chairs each.

They expect to fit forty people—in here? She felt claustrophobic
already. With a sigh she stepped through the doorway and took a seat
in the middle of the front row. Jane had advised her to come early, to
avoid being squished in the back, and Tara was grateful she had taken
that advice. As it was she'd be doing good to survive an hour this close
to so many—

Kids.

The morning kindergarten filed in, many of them hot and sweaty
from recess. Their teacher gathered them around her desk for a
minute then sent them all out to the hall to get a drink and use the
restroom before the end-of-the-year program began. As Maddie
walked by, she stopped in front of Tara then leaned forward and gave
her an impulsive hug.

Tara hugged her back while thinking that Maddie was well on her
way to being as sweet as her mother.

The seats around Tara began filling, and soon all of those in the
front two rows were taken. In addition to the twenty sets of parents
being squished in the small space, many had brought younger children with them, and a couple had babies with strollers. Tara was
pretty certain they were exceeding fire code with this many people in
the classroom, but she decided that in order to keep to her resolution
to be nice, it was best she not say anything.

The class returned, this time taking their places on the risers. The teacher spoke for a moment about how much she'd loved her class this year and was going to miss them.

It takes all kinds, Tara thought, impressed that the woman was able to spend six hours a day, five days a week, nine months of the year, *year after year*, with twenty five-year-olds.

The program began, and the class sang several songs. Tara recorded them all with Jane's video camera. When it came time for Maddie to walk across the floor to receive her kindergarten diploma, Tara held the camera as still as possible while her other hand flashed a thumbs-up. Maddie returned the gesture, and behind her Tara heard someone murmur, "How cute."

She does look cute, Tara thought with a touch of pride. Yesterday she and Maddie had gone shopping and gotten their hair done. Maddie's was cut in a cute bob—at Jane's request, so she wouldn't have to worry about doing too much to it in the coming baby-filled months. Maddie wore a new dress—white with cherries on it and all "twirly," as she had described it when she'd twirled around and around in front of the dressing room mirror.

"She's adorable," the woman beside Tara whispered. "But she must have your husband's hair. Not a strand of red on her."

Two months ago—one month ago, even—Tara knew she would have been quick to clarify that Maddie was not hers. *No way. Not mine. Never.* But now . . .

Maybe one child, a nice one like Maddie, would be okay someday.

Tara acknowledged the woman's comment with a half nod and continued filming while Maddie marched toward her seat. Jane would want to see every minute. Tara knew how much she'd wanted to come. During her last two doctor's visits she'd been contracting a little—in spite of her medication—and was under strict orders to stay completely down or report to the hospital.

Consequently, Tara found herself doing more and more around the house and with Maddie.

Surprisingly, she was enjoying it.

Diplomas in hand, the kindergartners all sang one last song, and then the program was over. Maddie came down from her spot on the risers.

"You're a big first-grader now," Tara said, giving her another hug. Absently, she wondered if she would ever attend another kindergarten graduation, would ever set foot inside an elementary school again— with her own child.

"Want some cookies and punch?" Maddie asked, pointing to the mob of school children and their younger siblings attacking the refreshment table.

Tara eyed the cluster of sticky fingers waving in the air. One cookie went flying, and someone had already spilled a cup of red punch. The baby who had been sleeping in a stroller a few feet away began to wail.

"I have a better idea." She unfolded herself from the tiny chair and turned toward the door as her sudden need for air became urgent. *What was I thinking a minute ago? I don't want kids!*

"What?" Maddie asked, taking her hand. "What's your better idea?"

"Ice cream," Tara said. "Any flavor you want. My treat, and we'll bring some home for your mom too."

"Two scoops?" Maddie asked, looking wistfully at the refreshment table.

Even she knows how to work things. "Well, you are only going into *first* grade." Tara pretended to be considering. "But I guess two scoops would be all right today."

"Yeah." Maddie skipped ahead, out the door to the playground, also overrun with little kids.

Tara resisted the urge to run too—far, far away. Instead, she said a silent prayer, an earnest plea that she might hold it together and not freak out around all of these short people.

She made it halfway across the blacktop without any of them touching her, though one came very close when his ball bounced past. The noise on the playground was deafening, and Tara wondered how the teachers could stand it. *Why do they send them all outside at the same time?* Hundreds of little bodies swarmed over every surface, all of them with high-pitched voices at full volume.

Somehow she made it to her car without breaking into a sweat.

"How about we ride with the top down today?" she asked Maddie as she helped her buckle her seat belt.

"Yes. Yes." Maddie bounced up and down in her booster. "But won't it mess up our hair? Yesterday you said that good hair is really important."

"It is," Tara said. "But some things are even more important than that."

"Like what?" Maddie asked.

Tara closed the back door and looked up at the clear, blue sky. She climbed in, started the ignition, and hit the switch for the roof to retract. "Fresh air."

* * *

It was close to one o'clock by the time Tara and Maddie returned home. Maddie's face had telltale evidence of the chocolate chip mint ice cream she'd eaten, but her dress remained clean. She ran ahead, eager to tell her mom all about the program.

Tara carried five different pints into the house and put them in the freezer, hopeful that at least one of the flavors would cheer Jane up. During the past few days she'd seemed particularly melancholy. Tara knew the increased dosage of terbutaline wasn't making her feel great, but she'd tried to encourage Jane, reminding her that there were only two more weeks until Peter came home and less than a month until she could deliver their babies.

Less than a month for me to find a place of my own. On one hand, it was strange to think of moving out, but on the other . . . She was ready. To move on with her life, to take the next step. Scary though that might be.

Tara closed the freezer door and opened the fridge, examining the choices for dinner. One thing for sure, after the enormous two-scoop, oversized waffle cone Maddie had just consumed, she wasn't going to want to eat anytime soon.

Tara was feeling an avocado to see if it was ripe yet when a scream echoed down the hallway from the bedroom.

"Maddie!" Tara dropped the avocado and raced to Maddie's room, but she wasn't there.

She wasn't in Jane's room either, but a second scream came from the master bathroom.

Tara ran to the doorway and looked in. Maddie stood next to Jane, who was lying on the floor, her eyes closed, spots of blood on the bath mat by her legs.

Thirty-One

"Mommy," Maddie wailed.

Tara dropped to her knees beside Jane. "Get the phone." She reached across Jane, grabbed Maddie's arm, and pulled her toward the doorway. "Hurry!"

Still sobbing, Maddie ran from the room. Tara leaned over Jane and almost cried herself when she felt the faint breath escaping between her lips.

"Wake up, Jane," Tara ordered and shook her gently. Her gaze left Jane's overly pale face and traveled to her stomach, which suddenly didn't seem as large as it had this morning. *She didn't*— Tara glanced around the room, half afraid she'd see a baby somewhere, though that was impossible. *Wasn't it?*

"I got the phone." Maddie thrust it at her, and Tara punched in 911. Before anyone picked up, she ordered Maddie from the room again, telling her to get her mom a blanket and pillow.

"911 Dispatch," a man answered. "What's your emergency?"

"My pregnant friend is on the floor, and she won't wake up, and it looks like she's bleeding," Tara blurted.

"You're calling from 12468 Sunrise Court, NE Bainbridge?"

"Yes." Tara took Jane's hand in hers and began rubbing it.

"Is she breathing?"

"Yes," Tara said. "But she's cold and really pale."

"Is there any chance your friend is just asleep, or—"

"I found her on the bathroom floor. She's not responsive when I talk to her or touch her."

"How many months pregnant is she?" the dispatcher asked.

"I don't know. Wait." Tara racked her brain, trying to remember what Jane was always telling her about how far along she was and what her babies were doing now. "She's having twins, and the doctor said she could have them in another month, and it would be okay. Could you please just send an ambulance?"

"One is already on its way, ma'am."

Maddie returned, holding Jane's pillow under her arm and dragging Jane's comforter behind her.

"You said you think your friend is bleeding?" the operator asked.

"Yes," Tara said. "There's blood on the rug near her hip."

"Is there any other liquid? Is the rug wet?"

Tara let go of Jane's hand and touched the bath mat. It was soaked, though there was no sign of any water having been run in the shower or tub recently. "It is wet," she said. "Is that bad?"

As if in answer to Tara's question, Jane moaned.

"Mommy." Maddie tried to push her way past Tara.

"No," Tara said. "I need you to watch out the window for the ambulance. They're coming to help your mommy."

When Maddie hesitated to obey, Tara gave her a little push. "Go! That's what your mommy needs you to do."

Maddie dropped the blanket and pillow and ran from the room.

"It's likely her water broke," the dispatcher was saying. "What I want you to do now—"

"They're here!" Maddie shouted.

"Already?" Given the distance to the nearest fire station, that seemed impossible, but Tara heard the sirens out front. "Thank goodness." She wasn't sure how they'd managed to come so quickly, but she was grateful. "They're here," she said to the operator.

"I'll stay on the line until they're with you," he said.

"Let them in," Tara called to Maddie. To Jane she spoke softer. "Help is coming, Jane. Don't you have those kids yet or do anything scary. You hear?"

Less than a minute later, two paramedics entered the room. Tara jumped up and moved out of the way as the first one knelt next to Jane. The second, a woman, set down a large box and opened it, revealing a tray of sterile instruments.

Tara backed out of the room and almost backed into Maddie just as the first paramedic untied Jane's robe and threw it wide, revealing her blood-soaked underclothes.

"Mommy," Maddie cried. "Why is he taking off Mommy's clothes?"

Tara turned to Maddie, picked her up, and carried her into the bedroom, where a third paramedic was rolling in a gurney.

"They're going to check on your brother and sister," Tara explained to Maddie. "And to hear their heartbeats, they have to listen to your mommy's tummy." Tara carried Maddie out of the room, down the hall, and into the living room. She set her on the floor but kept her hand. "Let's say a prayer."

Maddie nodded and knelt beside Tara at the side of the couch. Tara bowed her head and began. "Heavenly Father. We are grateful the ambulance came so quickly. Please bless the paramedics. Please bless Maddie's mommy and her baby brother and sister. Help them be okay." She was about to close, when Maddie nudged her and reminded her to bless her dad as well. Tara added Peter to her list of requests and closed the prayer. When she'd finished, Maddie threw her arms around her neck.

"I'm glad you learned to pray."

"Me too," Tara said, hoping the little faith she had was enough. *If not, let Maddie's be sufficient.*

Unsure what to do next, she sat on the couch and held Maddie tight. That the paramedics had not whisked Jane away in the ambulance frightened her. *She was breathing—and* bleeding. *How bad is it?* Tara strained to hear any sounds from the bedroom, while at the same time hoping Maddie wouldn't.

None of the three paramedics had emerged yet, but the sound of another car in the driveway startled Tara into action. Keeping a hold of Maddie, she went to the still-open front door and saw a woman from the Relief Society, the one who had asked a million questions the first week Tara attended church, emerging from her Oldsmobile.

"Is everything all right?" the woman, Sister What's-Her-Name, asked.

"No," Tara blurted, suddenly glad to have someone else here with her. "I think Jane fell. We found her when we came home from kindergarten graduation." *And ice cream*, her conscience shouted. *Why didn't I call Jane first?*

"The paramedics are here, but they haven't come out of her room yet. I thought they'd probably take her right to the hospital, but . . ." Tears flooded Tara's eyes. "I don't know what to do."

"Addison," the woman called, turning to her car. Tara followed her gaze and saw her elderly husband emerge slowly from the passenger side. She'd asked Jane about them once, and Jane had explained that they *were* married, though it was a second marriage for both, and Addison was ten years his wife's senior. Tara thought he looked about twenty years older. Jane had said that was because he'd had a stroke two years ago that he had never fully recovered from. Also according to Jane, the Sheffields—*ah, that's their name*—were two of the nicest people in the ward.

Tara watched as Addison shuffled toward them.

"We were on the way home from the doctor a few minutes ago," his wife explained. "But I had a feeling we should stop by and check on Jane."

"Oh, thank you," Tara said and had never meant a thank-you more in her life. She stepped back from the doorway so they could come in.

"Which way?" Brother Sheffield asked then looked toward the hall and started that direction before Tara could answer.

She wasn't at all certain he should be going down there. *Shouldn't we stay out of the paramedics' way?*

Sister Sheffield took Maddie's hand and led her to the kitchen. "You graduated from kindergarten today? How exciting. Will you tell me all about it?"

Tara hesitated a half second then followed Addison. She reached Jane's room just after he did then stopped in the doorway and brought a hand over her mouth as she gasped at the scene within.

The paramedics had moved Jane to the bed, and all three were around her, each working frantically—two on Jane, the other one on the blue, unmoving *baby* that had just emerged from her.

This wasn't supposed to happen. *It's too early.*

"No," she cried, reaching toward Brother Sheffield as he moved toward the bed.

Her hand missed the back of his shirt, and before she could try again, he'd pulled his keys out of his pocket and was untwisting a vial of something that dangled from the chain.

"Clergy," he said to the paramedics working on Jane, then he edged around them to the top of the bed.

"Hurry," one paramedic said. Tara wasn't sure whether he was speaking to Brother Sheffield or his coworker. A minute later, the second, dead-looking baby was delivered.

Tara stood transfixed and horrified yet unable to tear her eyes from the two blue babies, Jane's still form, and the blood everywhere.

Brother Sheffield put a drop of whatever was in the vial on top of Jane's head, then he placed his hands on her head and began a prayer different from any Tara had heard before. He called upon God to bless Jane through him and the priesthood. He blessed her that the bleeding would stop and she would live. It was a simple, urgent prayer. Brother Sheffield finished quickly and moved on to one of the babies, placing one finger on its tiny head.

In the distance, Tara heard another siren wail. Before Brother Sheffield had finished with the second baby, another team of paramedics rushed in. Tara backed into the wall but couldn't seem to leave the room.

The babies, already being hooked up to tubes and wires, were whisked away by two separate teams as Brother Sheffield said, "Amen." Another female paramedic joined the man already working on Jane.

"Placental abruption. Still hemorrhaging," he said. His tone indicated how serious this was.

Two paramedics lifted Jane on the gurney and wheeled her from the room while the other two continued to work on her. The IV bag brushed Tara as they passed.

"I want to go! I want to go too! Mommy!" Maddie was thrashing against Sister Sheffield's grip as she watched them wheel Jane away.

As soon as the gurney was out of her way and had cleared the front door, Tara ran to Maddie. "It's all right," she said, folding her in her arms. "They're taking her to the hospital." *She'll be all right.* As she thought the words, Tara glanced over her shoulder and saw Addison Sheffield making his way toward them. A moment ago he had stood straight and spoken clearly. Now his limp seemed more pronounced than usual, and his words were garbled as he called to his wife. *Will Jane be all right?* she wanted to ask. *Did you just heal her—like Jesus healed people? Is it real? Does that power still exist?*

Halfway down the hall, Addison stumbled and fell.

Sister Sheffield ran to her husband, exclaiming over him.

The first ambulance, carrying one of the babies, tore out of the cul-de-sac, its siren screaming. The second one was right behind.

"Is he all right?" Tara asked.

Sister Sheffield nodded. "He's not used to so much excitement and doesn't usually move so fast. He'll be okay, but I need to get him home." She waved her hand toward Tara. "You go now. See to Jane. As soon as I can, I'll send someone for Maddie."

Tara took a split second to decide whether or not she should take Maddie to the hospital. She weighed inflicting more trauma on the little girl—who had already seen more than enough—with not being there for Jane, and decided it was more important they were both there. *Just in case she*— The thought was too appalling to finish.

"Thank you," Tara called to Sister Sheffield, promising herself she'd never again think of her as the nosy question lady. Tara took Maddie's hand, grabbed her purse off the counter, and ran to the car. She scooped up Maddie and dumped her into her booster. "Can you buckle yourself?"

Maddie nodded and began pulling the belt across her lap. Tara jumped into the car and started it. She pulled out of the driveway and drove after the third ambulance—the one carrying Jane—which was still in sight but quite a bit ahead.

Maddie's sobs continued from the backseat. Tara had to slow for a red light, so she hit the button for the top to go up.

"Mommy had her babies," Maddie managed to get out between sniffles.

"She did," Tara said, not wanting to elaborate or even think about the way those babies had looked. She couldn't imagine that they'd make it. But *Jane . . . Jane has to.*

"Daddy needs to give them a blessing," Maddie said.

"Brother Sheffield did that." Tara stepped on the gas the instant the light turned green.

"He did?" Maddie leaned forward, gripping the back of Tara's seat.

"Are you buckled tight?" Tara asked. She watched in the rearview mirror as Maddie nodded.

"Brother Sheffield blessed Ella and Easton?"

"Yes." Tara changed lanes to pass a slower car so she wouldn't lose sight of the ambulance.

"And Mommy too?"

"Your mom too." Up ahead another light turned yellow. Tara swore under her breath and hit the brake.

The crying from the backseat ceased. "Then they're going to get better." Maddie sat up tall in her seat. "Heavenly Father will fix them. Let's go see Mommy now."

Tara looked up and met Maddie's eyes in the mirror. They were bright from her tears, but there was a calm assurance there too.

Oh, to be like a child, Tara thought, remembering the scriptures in both the Bible and the Book of Mormon that she'd read about that. She never really understood those references, or that concept before, but now she did. She turned in her seat and reached for Maddie's hand.

Please help me have the faith of this child.

Thirty-Two

TARA THANKED THE TEENAGER WHO had stayed with Maddie for a good part of the night then watched from the doorway as she walked to her mother's car. Half wishing the girl would have stayed longer—*Who's going to stay with me?*—Tara closed the front door and wandered into the kitchen. The last thing she'd eaten was ice cream with Maddie at noon. In more ways than one, that seemed like a lifetime ago.

Absently, Tara took a clean glass from the dishwasher then opened a cupboard and stood up on tiptoes, reaching for a bottle on the highest shelf. After a couple of tries, her fingers grasped the neck, and she pulled it down, only to discover it was empty, a note rolled up inside replacing the original contents—a bottle of sherry she'd brought with her from Los Angeles. Tara stared at the bottle a moment, as if not quite sure of what she was seeing, then unscrewed the lid and tipped the bottle, carefully reaching a finger inside to retrieve the note.

Tara,

I don't know why you are feeling so discouraged at this particular moment, but whatever it is, you can't let it beat you. You've come so far. This isn't what you need or want. You're stronger than you think you are, and you know where to go for real help.

Love,
Jane

Tara crumpled the note in her hand then instantly smoothed it flat and held it close to her heart as her tears began again. *Oh, Jane. I turn to you for help.* She tried not to think of the last time she'd seen Jane—after two transfusions and just before they rushed her in for an emergency hysterectomy. Tara had stayed at the hospital all during the surgery, waiting to hear better news, to know that her best friend would be all right. But even after the surgery Jane wasn't all right, and the doctors hadn't been able to say when or if she would be.

Tara placed her hands on the counter and leaned over it, sobbing silently. She'd never felt more alone or afraid in her life. Never had she needed Jane more.

The computer in the family room chimed, and Tara looked at the clock, realizing suddenly what the noise meant. Peter was calling.

Oh no. How was it that she'd all but forgotten him today? She'd explained Jane's situation to the hospital staff and somehow hoped they would take care of contacting Peter, though she'd known that wasn't really the case. *And now I'll have to tell him—the person who loves and needs Jane even more than I do.* Wiping her eyes, Tara hurried to the computer and logged on to Skype.

Peter's face appeared a moment later. He was wearing his army fatigues and smiling—until he saw Tara's face instead of Jane's. He spoke first.

"What's wrong?"

Tara didn't know where to begin. She opened her mouth twice before a rush of words finally came out. "Jane fell, and her water broke, and the placenta tore away." She knew she was telling it all wrong. She should have started elsewhere—with the babies. "Ella and Easton are doing well. They're early, of course, and it was close at the beginning, and it's too early to know if—" *I shouldn't tell him about that now.* Tara searched for the most encouraging thing she could say. "Jane had been taking that medicine for the babies' lungs, so they're doing pretty good . . . all things considered."

"How is Jane?" Peter's face had crumpled from the handsome, confident man Tara knew to someone completely terrified.

"Pretty bad." Fresh tears fell from Tara's eyes, and she brought a hand to her mouth, trying to contain her sobs. "But she's got the best doctors. She's had two transfusions, and—and she had to have surgery." Tara doubted any of that mattered to Peter. Like her, what he wanted to hear was that Jane would be okay. *She has to be*, Tara thought for the hundredth time today. This was the twenty-first century. Women didn't die from childbirth—

Very often. The doctor's chilling words came back to her. Jane had an unusual set of circumstances working against her. She'd been carrying twins. It was her first pregnancy. She was thirty-five. Preterm labor had been threatening for weeks. All things adding up to an unthinkable chain of events that started with a fall, her water breaking, and the placenta tearing away from the uterine wall.

Leading to severe hemorrhaging, a coma, and possible death. Tara couldn't bring herself to repeat those awful words to Peter.

But she wiped her eyes, took a deep breath, and told him the facts as simply and delicately as possible. By the time she'd finished, his eyes were watering, his brow creased, and the pain lining his face made it look like he had aged ten years.

"How is Maddie taking all of this?" Peter asked after he had taken a couple of minutes to compose himself.

Tara smiled through her tears. "Your daughter is amazing. She has the faith—"

"Of a little child," Peter finished, nodding his head as if he knew exactly what Tara was talking about.

"She wanted you to come home and bless Jane and the babies," Tara said. "When I told her Brother Sheffield had already done that, she was very relieved."

"I'll get the next flight possible." Peter's voice was gruff again.

"In two weeks?" Tara asked. She was pretty certain Jane had said that, regardless of circumstances back home, Peter had to stay to complete his assignment.

"Tomorrow or the next day," he said. "I'm not here to fly missions." He held up his scarred hand, reminding Tara of the many surgeries he'd had to fix it after a crash in the Iraqi desert several years earlier. "My reflexes aren't quick enough anymore. I've been here instructing, and they can all do without me now."

"Let me know when your flight comes in," Tara said.

Peter shook his head. "I'll get someone else to pick me up. You've got enough to do. Just take care of Maddie—and Jane."

"I will." Tara felt tears building again and could see that Peter was in much the same state. They ended the call, and once more, she was left alone in the dark house.

For several minutes she sat, numb and unmoving, staring at the blank screen of the computer. Jane's note lay beside it on the desk, and Tara picked up the paper again, doing her best to smooth out the earlier wrinkles.

You know where to go for real help.

Jane's words seemed to jump off the page at her. *Jane wasn't referring to herself. She meant for me to pray. How many times today have I already prayed?*

For Jane.

Of course, for Jane. Tara scoffed at her own thought. Jane was the one who needed the help, who needed a miracle.

As do you.

Tara froze, her fingers still covering the paper. Beneath her blouse, she felt her heartbeat escalate. The voice she'd just heard wasn't hers.

You know where to go for real help. I'm here. I'm listening.

You are? Desperate to know if this was only her overtired imagination, Tara practically slid from the chair then crawled over to the couch, where she buried her head in her arms.

"Father?" she spoke out loud, not caring if she sounded ridiculous—not feeling ridiculous but desperate for the answers she sought. "I need Thee," she pled. "I believe in Thee. Please, please bless me with Thy Spirit . . ."

Thirty-Three

TARA FELT A NUDGE, AND the next thing she knew, Maddie was sneaking beneath her arm—still folded across the couch.

Sunlight streamed through the patio doors, warming the room and making everything seem far better than it had been the previous day. Tara moved her head and realized she'd been kneeling at the sofa all night. *Or what was left of it after Peter's call.*

"Tara?" Maddie laid her head sideways on the couch and looked into Tara's eyes, her own features watchful with childish concern. "Are you still crying?"

Tara blinked rapidly, trying to clear her vision and come fully awake. She sat up straight and then enfolded Maddie in her arms.

"Are you still sad?" Maddie asked.

"Not anymore." Tara considered the question, and her answer so readily given. She *didn't* feel sad. The oppressive weight of yesterday—of *all* of her yesterdays—had lifted. In its place there was a new feeling inside, wrapping her in comfort and love and *peace.*

"I'm not sad, either," Maddie said. "Can we have waffles for breakfast? We could bring some to Mommy at the hospital."

Jane. Worry for her rushed to the front of Tara's mind, yet even that wasn't enough to overcome the peace and . . . lightness . . . enveloping her. Tara was almost afraid to move, afraid that if she got up and started her day, the feeling would vanish.

She chose her words carefully. "I don't know if your mom is well enough to eat waffles this morning." *But she is well.*

All is well.

Tara didn't know how she knew this, but she did. She hugged Maddie briefly then got up on stiff legs, exercising her faith that the goodness she felt wouldn't disappear but would follow her to the kitchen.

"I'll call the hospital and ask." Tara grabbed her cell phone from her purse and called the direct number she'd added yesterday. The nurse who answered was the same one who'd been on duty when Tara had left around one in the morning.

The news wasn't as heartening as Tara had hoped. There was little change in Jane's condition, though she was stable now. Her bleeding had finally stopped.

She just needs to wake up, Tara thought, then she explained the situation to Maddie exactly that way.

"Your mom is really tired. Having those babies wore her out, so she's going to sleep today." As she spoke the words, Tara thought they really did make sense. She could almost believe them herself. She hesitated, waiting to see Maddie's reaction to hearing that she couldn't see her mom.

"O-kay," Maddie said after a few seconds. "Can we draw her a picture? And make cupcakes for Ella and Easton?"

Tara nearly laughed. "Yes. Absolutely." *To be like a child* echoed through her mind again. She felt almost like a child this morning— free, somehow, from the cares of the world, though she knew they were still there.

Maddie was already hauling out the waffle iron and the cupcake tins.

"One thing at a time," Tara said, taking the heavy iron from her and putting it on the counter. "First we need to—"

"Pray," Maddie said.

"You're right." Tara stared at her across the counter, remembering a day, not so many weeks ago, when she'd looked across that same counter and told Maddie that she didn't pray.

"We need to thank Heavenly Father for the miracle," Maddie said.

Tara nodded then smiled through her sudden tears. "We need to thank Him for a few of them."

Thirty-Four

MADDIE CARRIED THE SHOE BOX carefully across the patio. "I'm going to miss you, Fran."

I won't, Tara thought, feeling liberated at the possibility of not having a bird to feed almost around the clock. She hoped Jane was right, and it really was ready to be on its own. Though she *was* glad it had survived this long and guessed it was probably Maddie's tender heart and care that had seen the creature through.

"You saved Fran's life." Tara knelt beside Maddie at the edge of the patio. *Kind of like your mom saved mine.* Telltale moisture formed in Tara's eyes. For the past week and a half, it seemed she'd done nothing but cry.

"Good-bye, Fran." Maddie's own voice sounded teary as she lifted the bird from the box. "Fly and be happy," Maddie whispered. She uncovered the bird and held her palms flat and steady.

Fran hesitated a half second then spread her wings and took off, soaring into the air, flying across the yard to the tree where her life had begun.

Maddie waved, and a smile lit her face. "She flew!"

"Yes, she did." Tara hugged Maddie a little tighter. A new feeling, *another* new feeling—one that had been building for the past several weeks—seemed to burst from her chest. Sudden understanding filled her mind, accompanied by one simple word.

Joy.

* * *

"Mommy's coming home today. Mommy's coming home." Maddie skipped ahead of Tara, toward the hospital entrance. Peter had left earlier to take care of paperwork at the hospital and to help Jane dress the twins, who were also being released. Tara had promised to bring Maddie so she could be part of their homecoming.

Tara had to hurry to keep up with Maddie as she skipped toward Jane's room. After having her mother gone for nearly two weeks, the little girl was more than ready to have her home again. Tara was eager for Jane to return too, though she knew that the magical time they'd shared together the past few months was over. Peter was home, and Jane—and her time—belonged to him and their children.

Lingering purposely behind, Tara watched Maddie run into her mother's hospital room. Tara readied the video camera for the grand exit then stole forward and peeked inside, hesitant to intrude yet also wanting to witness the reunion. Jane sat on the bed with Maddie beside her. Each of Jane's arms held a baby. Peter stood behind them, his hand beneath Maddie's arm, supporting little Ella's head.

Something that she could only guess was longing hit Tara hard as she turned on the camera and tried to focus the lens. The feeling surprised her. She *didn't* want what Jane had. The thought of being responsible for two babies was terrifying. Yet she *did* want what Jane had. She wanted someone who loved her, the way Peter loved Jane, and she wanted someone *to* love. She'd learned that thinking of others before herself, *serving* them, wasn't such a bad thing after all. When it came down to it, she had to admit . . .

I'm really going to miss that kid.

Tara knew she needed to find something to fill her life. Maddie was going to leave a pretty big void.

Jane caught sight of Tara at the door and waved her in. Tara paused the camera and entered the room.

"I hear Fran made it." Jane's smile was triumphant.

"She flew beautifully," Tara confirmed.

"Success all around, or so I hear," Jane said, handing Easton off to Peter. "Congratulations on the new business."

"Well, it's only a start," Tara said. "But I am officially licensed and legal now." After selling her old wardrobe on eBay last month, and making quite a bit of money, she'd realized what potential there was in the used clothing market—especially designer labels that many people liked and were familiar with but couldn't necessarily afford to buy in this economy.

She'd done some research, placed a couple of ads, and before she'd even fully developed the idea, she had clients on both ends, some wanting her to sell their items, others looking to purchase specific things. She'd become a broker again, this time of used clothing, purses, shoes, and the like. The potential was endless. Already she was thinking about other markets she could expand to. And to be fair, she had to admit that the idea had begun with a trip to Deseret Industries in Utah.

The correct term is secondhand, Ben had first informed her. Tara couldn't help but grin as she remembered that shopping trip and the ill-fated jeans.

"What are you thinking about?" Jane asked.

"How Ben would laugh if he knew I now sell secondhand clothing for a living."

"You should tell him," Jane said. She turned sideways on the bed so Peter could put on her shoes. He knelt in front of her and carefully slipped each foot into a sandal.

In just watching that simple act, Tara felt her eyes start to moisten again.

"Look, I have ankles again." Jane raised a foot and pointed her toe.

"You look great," Tara said. And Jane did. After emerging from a coma three days after she'd given birth to the twins, she had surprised everyone by how well she seemed to feel, both mentally and physically. Only a few setbacks with recovering from her hysterectomy had kept her in the hospital this long.

Jane returned the compliment. "You look great too, Tara. Ben really should see how you've changed. Call him," Jane prodded. "Invite him to your baptism."

"I don't know," Tara said. The idea of calling Ben was equally terrifying and exciting. "That's not really something I can ask on the phone. I don't think he'd believe me." She sighed. "I was so awful last December."

"So *show* him you're different. Go see him," Jane said.

Tara shook her head. "No way. I can't even fly from one state to another without having a panic attack. I can't afford a first-class ticket right now, and I'd never make it across the country in coach."

"You could drive," Peter suggested. He finished putting on Jane's shoes and stood. He held his hand out to Jane, helping her from the bed. "Trust me. Guys love coming home and finding strange women in their backyard." He pulled Jane close and hugged her.

"Kiss her, Daddy," Maddie said, looking up from her post, sitting between the babies in their car seats.

"I think I will." Peter bent his head and brushed his lips to Jane's.

Tara looked away, feeling the intruder again. Yearning hit her once more, and this time she indulged it, reliving Ben's kiss, wondering what it *would* be like if she saw him again. If she shared with him all that had happened this summer, the way she felt, her desire to be baptized.

"I could ask *Ben* to baptize me." She spoke the thought out loud.

"That's a great idea," Jane said. She and Peter stepped apart as a nurse with a wheelchair entered the room.

"Ben's the one who first . . . piqued your interest, right?" Peter asked.

"Yeah." Tara put the video camera away and stepped out into the hall while everyone got ready to leave. She wondered how many miles it was from here to Ohio. How many days of driving that would be, how long it would take.

I must be crazy. She couldn't believe she was even considering it. A trip like that would cost money. It would take planning. It would be—

Amazing. She'd never done anything like it before, had never really traveled anywhere other than big cities. Yet she loved Bainbridge—the space, the fresh air, visiting Jane's home.

But this is *Jane's home, not mine.* Long ago, Jane had taken her own leaps of faith that led her here. She had worked to make her own happiness.

The nurse wheeled Jane out to the hall. Peter followed, a baby carrier in each hand. Maddie took up the rear, cooing at the twins. Tara followed, a smile on her face as she remembered, all too well, a time she'd told Jane she was the crazy one.

Perhaps there was something to be said in favor of following her example.

Thirty-Five

TARA PULLED THE BLANKET CLOSE around her and lay back on Jane's roof, gazing at the sprinkling of stars overhead. A few feet away, Jane had her eye pressed to the telescope as she studied the night sky.

"Dinner was great," Tara said. "Thanks for having me over."

"I figured a farewell dinner was a good way to make sure you really left on your trip tomorrow," Jane said. "And as a follow-up, I'm going to expect a full star report from Ohio."

Tara laughed. "I'm going to have to see how strong the farm aroma is there before I commit to hanging around outside."

"Well, I'm glad it's clear tonight," Jane said. "It's been forever since I've been up here."

"The sky is beautiful," Tara agreed. *The heavens*, she thought, wanting to know more about them and excited because—finally—she knew where to turn for answers. "What do you think heaven is like?" she asked, when Jane had left the telescope and was making her way toward her.

"Like Bainbridge," Jane answered without hesitation. "It's beautiful, and I'm surrounded by the people I love."

"Guess I'll be lonely there too," Tara said, feeling disappointed.

Jane turned to her. "You won't. Because heaven is also a place where we're free from our sorrows. It says so in the scriptures. You won't be lonely. We'll be free of care, and any physical or other ailment we suffer on earth is also lifted from us."

"You sound so sure," Tara said. Her own testimony felt fragile. She longed for Jane's security, for her years of learning and understanding.

"I'm not sure about everything," Jane said. "But this . . ." Her voice trailed off, and she lay back on the roof beside Tara. For a few minutes neither spoke.

"I saw Mark," Jane said suddenly.

"Who?" Tara turned her head to look at Jane.

"Maddie's twin—our little boy." She brought a finger to her lips and swallowed. In the dim light, Tara could see the tide of emotion rippling across Jane's features.

"When I was in the coma," Jane said. "I was with him—with Mark."

Tara's eyes widened. "Is that—*normal?*"

Jane made a sound that was half-laughter, half-choking. "Not that I know of. But I was with him. Really. And he was *well.*"

"What else?" Tara asked, eager to hear and believe what Jane was telling her. "Did you see Peter's brother? Where were you? What—"

"I didn't see anyone else," Jane said. "Just Mark." Her voice grew wistful. "I couldn't even tell you where he—we—were exactly, but I was with him."

Tara wasn't sure what to say to this, though she could tell Jane spoke the truth. "How amazing—what a miracle."

Jane nodded. "I've had more than my fair share, it seems." She smiled. "I'd better be careful from here on out."

"I should say so," Tara agreed. Above them a universe of stars twinkled, making miracles seem a real possibility. "Who says there has to be a limit?" The past few months flew before her in a blur. Stepping back to look at them, she saw miracles too—many of them.

She'd arrived, just when Jane had needed someone to stay with her. All the things Brother Bartlett had taught . . . *Just for me.* The way the missionaries had been so in tune with her feelings and needs.

Miracles had happened with Jane and her babies. An ambulance had been nearby, returning from another call. Sister Sheffield had felt prompted to check on Jane. *Brother Sheffield's blessings.* Tara realized that all of it had helped build her fledgling faith. She knew she would cherish this time, this summer, for the rest of her life. It was when she had first read about King Benjamin, had first discovered she had a Father in Heaven.

All because I happened to meet a good man named Ben.

Tara hugged herself, feeling both warm and shivery at the same time. "I know one thing." She spoke with as much conviction as Jane had moments ago. "We've both been blessed, and we ought to thank our lucky stars."

Autumn

*"Good fortune often happens
when opportunity meets with preparation."*
—*Thomas A. Edison*

Thirty-Six

TARA WATCHED THE ODOMETER TURN over another mile as the Jeep bumped along a dirt road. She glanced at the GPS again, hoping once more that the computer knew what it was doing. In the rearview mirror she saw a cloud of dust forming in the wake behind her and wondered how long it had been since it had rained. Certainly not that long. The October air smelled crisp and clean, and the lush, green hills were dotted crimson, pumpkin, and gold. Leaves stirred in the slight breeze as they sailed toward the ground.

"Arriving at your destination," the GPS announced after she'd passed a third farm. Tara slowed as she came to a sturdy-looking wooden mailbox with *Whitmore* stenciled across it. The flutter of nerves that had been building inside since she'd crossed the Ohio border now seemed to erupt in her stomach, and for a split second she felt a wave of suffocating panic, though the windows were down and there was space all around her.

Through her mind scrolled the many possible scenarios she had imagined about her reunion with Ben. Now that she was here only one seemed a real possibility—that he'd think she'd completely lost her mind when she explained that she'd driven over two thousand miles to ask him a question.

A really important question, the Spirit reminded her, and Tara felt her newfound peace return along with a boost of courage. She drove past the mailbox and followed the long gravel drive toward a nondescript white two-story farmhouse. Resisting the urge to back up and turn the Jeep around so it would be facing the road, ready for a quick escape, she parked, shut off the engine, and said a silent prayer.

A quick glance in the rearview mirror showed what she had suspected—her windblown hair looked nothing like the long, shiny locks displayed by models. And the face staring back at her seemed almost foreign. Her new less-is-best look still surprised her sometimes.

Automatically her hand went to her purse on the seat. In the past it had always held an array of products she could cover up with and hide behind at a moment's notice. Not so anymore. Of course, cutting her daily makeup routine in half didn't really have anything to do with her new religion—she'd seen plenty of women at church who believed strongly in too much eyeliner and bright lipstick—but was more about her new belief in herself. She was Tara Mollagen, thirty-five years old, been kissed way too many times, with a few too many freckles for her liking. But that was okay.

I'm okay. Ben had thought so before when she'd likely looked her worst—and had certainly acted it—on that mountaintop, so what was to keep him from being her friend now? She smiled at her reflection and stepped out of the Jeep.

The house wasn't any more impressive up close, though it wasn't bad either. She'd known a few career bachelors who were total slobs, and from the look of the yard, at least, Ben didn't fall into that category. Remembering the way she'd seen him work during those few days at Christmastime, she wasn't surprised that the patch of lawn was neatly mowed, the flower beds groomed, and the walk swept.

More important was the surprising lack of farm smell. She'd caught more than a few whiffs of animal on her way here and was pleasantly surprised that she wasn't reeling with the stench of dozens—or hundreds—of pigs.

How many does Ben keep, anyway? Looking in either direction past the house, she didn't see much indication of farming at all, aside from a rather battered cornfield, which even she knew was long past due to be harvested. Since everything else appeared so tidy, this puzzled her.

Maybe he's better with animals than he is with crops. But looking around, she couldn't see any indication of the animals, other than an enormous red barn on the side of the house opposite the cornfield.

On unsteady legs—from the long car ride, she told herself—she made her way to the front porch and climbed the few steps. She ran her fingers through her hair once more then took a deep breath. As she lifted her hand to knock, she heard the sound of glass breaking, followed by a shout. The front door banged open, just missing Tara as she jumped out of the way. An enormous, pink potbellied pig lumbered past, grunting loudly with each step.

He keeps them in the house? Her eyes followed the pig as it left the porch and crossed the yard, headed toward the barn.

"Ben's not out there, either, you stupid—" A man in the doorway stopped abruptly, his eyes sweeping over Tara. "Oh, hey. I didn't realize anyone was here. Sorry for shouting."

"That's okay," Tara said. She tried not to gawk at the pig, which was shaking its head savagely and running circles in the drive.

The man followed her gaze. "Persephone's been a real pain today. She gets upset when Ben's not home."

"Oh." *Pigs have moods?* She turned her attention to him. "So, Ben isn't here?"

The man shook his head. "He and Deb went shopping, but they should be back any minute."

Deb?

"C'mon in and wait. I'm sure you're better company than the pigs," he added, grinning at her.

"I'd hope so." Instead of accepting his offer, she looked toward the Jeep—and the large pig standing between her and escape. While she wasn't eager for a confrontation there, she wasn't sure she wanted to stay. In all the possibilities she'd considered about her reunion with Ben, she hadn't imagined one where other people would be there when she first saw him. This guy and someone else—a woman.

My mistake, she thought glumly.

Ben had never said that he lived alone, but that was the way she'd thought of him. She'd imagined driving into his yard and seeing him out on his tractor—or possibly a horse—then looking at her and . . . What? What had she really expected him to do? She sighed inwardly. *This is what comes of reading too many of Jane's romance novels over the summer.*

"I should be going," she said. "Maybe I'll come by tomorrow."

"Can I tell Ben you stopped by? I'm sorry, I didn't even ask your name."

Jane. Old friend from school. The lie was on the tip of her tongue. In the past, lies had never hesitated to roll right off, saving her from unwanted attention or getting her out of dates she didn't care to go on. Occasionally, she'd used one in reverse to get access to someone she otherwise wouldn't have been able to meet. But now . . .

"Tara," she mumbled. "I'll write down my cell, and maybe Ben can call." She reached for the pen in her purse. It would be better this way. He could call her. They could arrange to meet somewhere by themselves, and she could ask him then.

"You're Tara?" The man sounded surprised. "On-the-way-to-Denver Tara?"

Her face heated under his gaze. "Yep. That's me." She could only imagine the things Ben must have told his friends about her. She hurriedly scribbled her number on a scrap piece of paper. No way she was coming back tomorrow. She'd just talk to Ben over the phone. And if he had a problem with her request, then she'd ask Peter to baptize her.

What I should have done in the first place.

"Here." She held the paper out.

"Oh, no." He grabbed her hand and pulled her through the open doorway. "Ben would kill me if I let you walk away. I'm sure he had no idea you were coming, or he wouldn't have gone to town. Don't you live in California?"

"Used to," Tara said. *I used to do and be a lot of things that I'm not anymore*, she wanted to add. Though she didn't know this guy at all, she hated that he obviously knew her—or the past her—based on whatever Ben had told him.

"I'm Josh." He shook the hand he still held. "Come on into the kitchen. Persephone broke a glass, so watch where you step."

"Persephone is the pig I saw?" Tara's hand dropped back to her side, and she followed Josh through a front room and into a spacious kitchen. Just inside, she paused, taking in gorgeous maple cabinets, what appeared to be an antique farm table, and wide-plank oak flooring. "Wow. This is nice." *Nicer than I expected.*

"Well, you know, Ben and his wood."

She didn't know, but with a backward glance at the room they'd passed through, she started to guess. Resting above a large stone fireplace was one of the most beautifully carved mantels she'd ever seen. Matching crown molding ran the perimeter of the room, and an antique rocker rested in the corner opposite the fireplace. Ben's home might be plain on the outside, but the inside was impressive. With regards to furniture, at least, he had good taste. *But this place could use some art on the walls.*

"He's friends with the Amish?" she said, only half joking as she rolled a solid wood pocket door back and forth.

"Most of the time." Josh grabbed a broom and began sweeping broken glass from the floor. "I sensed a little more than friendly competition at the fair last month."

"Oh." She imagined Ben parading around a center ring, his best, shiny pink pig at his side. "How did he do?"

Is there a big prize for winning? Does he count on that for part of his income?

"He beat out everyone," Josh said, as if that were a normal occurrence.

While he continued sweeping, Tara walked around the room, looking at the few pictures on the walls. She recognized one that had to be Ben's family. At *least* fifteen kids were crammed into the photo, gathered around a couple that appeared more like grandparents than parents. Ben, looking tall and gangly, and with a mouth full of braces, stood beside a teenaged Ellen. Fascinated, Tara moved closer, staring at the photo, wondering how it would be to have a family like that, to be connected to so many people.

Leaving the picture on the wall, she walked closer to the mantel and noticed another framed photo on the end. It was a recent picture of Ben, his arm looped around the shoulder of a pretty blonde. *Deb?*

"No one can come close to touching what Ben's got in that barn," Josh was saying. "And, in spite of that, everyone around here loves him."

"I'll bet." With a last look at the picture, Tara turned away from the mantel and walked into the kitchen.

Josh opened the pantry door, and another large pig lumbered out. "Ham! You big *pig*. Have you been eating the cookies again?"

Ham rolled his head around and grunted a reply that sounded a lot like laughter. Josh swatted him lightly with the broom before putting it away.

"Does Ben name all his pigs?" Edging to the side of the kitchen, Tara kept her eyes glued to the animal. It had to weigh a couple of hundred pounds easy. She wondered how fast pigs could move, if their teeth were sharp, and if they were prone to biting.

"He does. That makes it a little harder when they're gone—he misses them, you know. But while they're here, he treats them like family."

"Naming a pig *Ham* is treating it like family? Seems kinda sick to me." Thinking of the pig parading around in front of her being turned into a Christmas ham *did* make her feel sick. She made a mental vow to swear off all pork products. It'd be easy compared to everything else she'd given up lately.

Josh laughed. "Not *that* kind of ham. He got the name because he's always *hamming it up*; Ham's a clever pig—and a mischievous one too."

As if to prove Josh's point, Ham came up to Tara and nudged his snout under her purse just enough to lift the strap from her shoulder and send it sliding down her arm.

"He's hoping you have mints," Josh said. "Deb always keeps some in her purse, so now he expects that."

Tara clutched her purse to her chest and looked down. Ham nodded his head and grunted as if to say, "Well?"

"Tic Tacs okay?" She looked to Josh for approval.

"He'll be your friend forever."

"Just what I always wanted." Tara lifted the tiny plastic box from her purse and held it up. Ham stuck his tongue out, and she shook a few mints onto it. Ham slurped them into his mouth, let out an appreciative grunt, and trudged off.

She watched him go, wondering what kind of pigs Ben had in the barn that the other farmers around here couldn't touch. The pigs she'd met so far were smart enough to miss people when they were gone and to steal cookies from the pantry. Who knew what the rest of them were capable of?

"Lemonade?" Josh offered as he pulled a pitcher from the fridge.

"Sure." Tara took a seat, and Josh poured two glasses and set them on the table.

"So what exactly has Ben—" Tara's question was cut off by a beeping horn and the sound of a car on the gravel drive. She tensed, her eyes on the doorway leading to the front room.

Why didn't I leave when I had the chance? Why did I even come in the first place? A flurry of butterflies erupted in her stomach. Feeling the need for fortification, Tara automatically reached for her drink before remembering that it was only lemonade. Though, if it had been a martini, she wouldn't have had any.

"One hundred and . . . twenty-six days," she reminded herself. She'd gone that long without drinking any type of alcoholic beverage, and she wasn't about to let herself down now. It was nice to be free of that crutch, and she'd learned there were better ways to deal with stress.

But man, sometimes this new gig is hard. Right about now, her nerves could have done with some soothing.

Josh flashed her a grin from ear to ear. "This is gonna be great. I couldn't have imagined a better surprise if I'd planned it myself."

"I could." Tara was dismayed to hear the croak in her voice.

Outside a car door slammed; seconds later footsteps sounded on the porch. She heard the front door swing open.

Ben was home.

Thirty-Seven

TARA WAS STILL TRYING TO decide whether or not she should stand up when Ben came into the kitchen. He carried a couple of bags of groceries in each hand and headed straight for the table then stopped abruptly when he spotted her.

"Hello, Ben." She tried to smile but wasn't quite sure she was successful.

"Tara?" The bags' momentum shifted, slamming the groceries back into his sides. Ben didn't even flinch but continued to stare at her in a very confused, disbelieving sort of way.

So this is what someone looks like when they think they might have seen a ghost. She knew she was smiling now. "I'm real, and I won't bite. Come put your groceries down."

He made no move to follow her instructions. Expressions scrolled across his face, as easily readable as if he'd been shouting them out. Shock. Disbelief. Curiosity. Suspicion. And for a fraction of a second—happiness? *Please let him be glad I am here*, she prayed silently.

At last he returned her smile, and she nearly sagged against the wall with relief. He came forward, put the bags on the table, and held out his hand.

"Tara."

She took it, remembering the last time she'd touched him, when she'd grabbed onto his shirtfront in the moving van as they were parked in Ellen's new driveway. She'd pulled him close then and planted her lips on his, not because she felt any overwhelming desire—well, maybe she'd felt a little—but because she'd wanted to give him a boost of confidence just before he had to face a Christmas with both his ex–best friend and ex-fiancée.

Thinking of that kiss brought a blush to her face, so she pushed the memory aside and studied Ben as he stepped back from the table, hands in the pockets of his faded jeans, an untucked flannel shirt fitting nicely across his well-toned arms and chest. What had she found wrong with that attire last December?

"I can't believe you're here—in my kitchen."

"You guys are going to have to move the feed." The woman Tara had seen in the photo on the mantel entered the kitchen. "It's too heavy for me to lift."

"Ben's got a visitor," Josh said, reminding Tara that he was still in the room.

"Hi," the woman said. She moved around Ben and set the bags she was carrying next to his on the table.

"Deb, this is Tara," Ben said. "Tara, this is Deb—" A loud grunting cut him off, and Deb jumped out of the way just as Persephone the pig charged into the kitchen and straight at Ben. Instead of moving out of its path, he turned to face it then knelt so he was closer to its height.

"Missed me, did you, Persephone?" He allowed the pig to nuzzle him with its snout then petted its head as if it were a dog or something.

Seriously weird farming technique, Ben. Half-amused, half-disgusted, Tara watched as he lavished attention on the animal.

Deb must have noticed her staring, because she tried to explain. "Persephone is very possessive of Ben. Watch this." She held out her hand to the pig, palm up, a piece of candy plainly visible. "Here, Seph. I've got a treat for you."

Instead of accepting the treat, as Tara guessed Ham would have in a second, a low grumbling rose from Persephone's chest, and she swung her gaze around to Deb, a kind of fierceness in her eyes.

"Intense pig," Tara said. *And that's some intense rock on your finger.* It was impossible not to notice the brilliant diamond sparkling on the third finger of Deb's outstretched left hand.

"If you think that's bad," Deb said, "you should see her if I touch Ben. Seph goes nuts."

"I thought she was going to eat Deb alive last week." Ben stood again. "Naughty pig." But his voice didn't sound reprimanding as he looked down on Persephone.

"I'll remember to watch myself around her," Tara said. *Not that I'll be touching you again anytime soon.* Her happiness had deflated a bit with Deb's arrival.

"Let's get the rest of the food so we can get dinner started. I'm starved," Josh said.

"What else is new?" Deb teased. Josh elbowed her.

"Can I help you bring something in?" Tara asked.

"That's okay. We've got it." Deb gave a dismissive wave as she headed back outside. Ben and Josh followed, the latter whispering louder than he probably realized after they'd left the kitchen.

"Craziest thing you ever did, kissing a woman in the middle of a Colorado—"

The front door closed, cutting off the rest of Josh's sentence.

Tara pressed herself further into the wall, wishing she could disappear into it. That wasn't an option, but leaving quickly was. She needed to be alone, to think things through. She still wanted Ben to baptize her, but she couldn't talk to him right now, couldn't ask him in front of other people. She wasn't sure she *should* ask him, as he was obviously in a relationship, and Tara wasn't sure how Deb would feel about Ben flying across the country to baptize some other woman.

I probably wouldn't be okay with it, she admitted to herself.

Rising from her chair, Tara picked up her glass then took it to the sink. Out the window she could see Ben and Josh hefting bags of feed from the truck. Several feet away, Deb was busy collecting tomatoes from the garden.

With a last glance around the quaint kitchen and front room, Tara went outside. Ben and Josh had disappeared. Tempting though it was to leave without saying good-bye, Tara thought she'd better do at least that. And maybe Ben could call her later.

Maybe I can still ask him. For weeks she'd been imagining herself in white, walking toward him in the baptismal font the missionaries had shown her. She'd known, ever since Jane had suggested seeing him again, that Ben was the one she wanted to baptize her. And though he would be the one doing something for her, she felt in some small way it might do something for him as well. He needed to know that last December he'd touched her life. He'd shown her a glimpse of an honest, caring man, and she hadn't been able to forget that. *Or him.*

The door of a shed near the house was ajar, so Tara headed toward it, hoping she'd find Ben there. As she got closer, she heard the men's voices again.

"She's the last thing I need right now," Ben said. Tara froze.

"She's exactly what you need," Josh said. "A smart, savvy, easy-on-the-eyes woman to—"

"She may be easy on the eyes, but it ends there," Ben said. "I'd have to be insane—"

Josh appeared in the doorway, saw Tara, and held up his hand, cutting the rest of Ben's sentence short.

It didn't matter. She'd heard enough. Turning away from them, she began walking quickly, toward the front of the house, the driveway, her car.

"Tara," Ben called.

She ignored him and hurried faster. She reached the Jeep and climbed in. She had the key in the ignition and was putting it in reverse when Ben appeared at her window. He leaned in, hands resting on the side of the car, reminding her of the time he'd talked to Cadie the night before Ellen and her family moved.

"I'm sorry you overheard us," Ben said. "It's just that I never expected to see you again, and I'm not good with surprises."

"Is that supposed to be an apology?"

He glanced toward the porch where Josh and Deb stood talking. "I think it better be, if I want Deb to let me back in the house."

"Have fun sleeping outside." Tara put her foot on the gas and looked over her shoulder to back up.

"Hey, wait a minute. You can't just leave."

"Watch me," Tara mumbled as she began backing down the drive. From the corner of her eye, she saw Ben step away. A few seconds later he'd come around the front and was on the passenger side, running next to the Jeep.

"Go away," she yelled.

He moved closer and grabbed the door handle. She pushed down on the accelerator. Ben shouted then dropped out of sight.

"Ben!" Tara slammed on the brakes. She leaned across the gearshift, trying to see him. "Ben? Are you okay?"

When he didn't answer, she put the car in park and scrambled across the seat to stick her head out the open window. Ben sat on the ground, one leg stretched out in front of him.

There's no blood. Relief rushed through her.

He had an incredulous look on his face. "You ran over my foot."

"You were trying to climb into my car."

"You *ran* over my foot," Ben said again. "In fact, you're still on it."

Horrified, Tara glanced down and saw that Ben's shoe was in fact under her front right tire.

"Oh!" she gasped. She pulled herself back into her seat and drove forward. Instead of getting out, she leaned over the wheel and closed her eyes, wishing—as she had so many times in her life—for a do-over. *Well, he certainly won't want to baptize me now.*

"Where are we going?" Ben opened the passenger door and climbed into the car, taking extra care as he did so.

"To the hospital for an X-ray?" She pressed her lips together and braced herself for a well-deserved verbal tirade.

"Nah. I think it's all right. You just got my toes. Don't need those for much except balance," he teased. "My tailbone hurts though. I fell kind of hard when my shoe caught."

Serves you right. Saying those things. "I'm sorry. You're certain you're okay?"

Ben nodded.

"Good," Tara said. "Then please get out of my car."

"You drive a Jeep? Really?" Ben moved his head around and turned in his seat, checking out the interior. "I would have thought you're more the Lexus type or—"

"You don't know a thing about me," Tara said. "So get out. Go back to your pigs."

"Ouch." Ben brought a fist to his chest like he'd been stabbed. "Look. I'm sorry you overheard Josh and me. A while ago I'd told him about you, and—it's just that you're about the last person on the planet I expected to see."

"Yes. You said that already." *I'm the last person he* wanted *to see.* Tara leaned her head back against the seat. "I should have just sent a letter."

"That might have been helpful," Ben said. "After all, the last time I saw you—*ten months ago*—you practically attacked me in the cab of the truck then jumped out and snuck away without even saying good-bye."

"You were busy unloading. And I sent a thank-you card with the cashier's check," Tara reminded him.

"The check that was for way more than it should have been?"

Tara waved away his argument. "I'm sure I was $500 worth of trouble to you that weekend."

"In that case, it should have been at least a thousand."

She glared at him. He grinned back. She laughed. She couldn't help it.

"I've missed you, Ben. No one else is quite as much fun to argue with."

He shrugged. "Just like old times."

"Yes—*no*." She shook her head, remembering why she had come all this way to see him.

"It isn't like old times. It's apparent that a lot has happened to each of us this year." She glanced toward the porch.

"Whatever happened to you, it must be good." Ben studied her for a moment, as if really seeing her for the first time. "You look great. Your hair and your clothes, and you're much . . . *calmer* . . . than before. The Tara I met last December would have cussed me out, shoved me out of her car, and really run me over if I'd insulted her the way I just insulted you."

"Good suggestions, all."

He turned to her. "But you're really here. In a million years, I never would have imagined you in jeans and a T-shirt—"

"This isn't a *T-shirt*," Tara said. She might not be wearing the best brands and latest fashion trends like she used to, but she definitely hadn't stooped to the common T-shirt yet. *Ever.*

"It's also not some hot-pink-leopard-skin print thing." Ben grimaced.

He remembers what I was wearing?

"But here you are, sitting in my driveway like—" He stopped abruptly.

"Like what?" She wasn't sure she wanted to hear the answer.

"I don't know." He shrugged. "Like any other normal person."

"Was I that bad? Never mind. Don't answer that." She remembered well enough the way she'd acted on that trip. *And many, many other days of my life.*

"No—not bad." Ben was trying to backtrack. "Different. We move in different circles. Can you imagine me on my tractor in LA? That's all I meant. This place doesn't seem like you, that's all."

"It's not as weird as I thought it'd be," Tara said. "And sometimes things change—people change."

"Circumstances change?" Ben asked, a questioning edge back in his voice.

"I suppose," Tara began, "but that's not why I came. I want to ask—"

"Ben," Josh yelled from the porch. "Ham's wedged himself in the cellar door again."

"That pig," Ben muttered. He opened the car door. "Sorry. I've got to go, and this could take a bit. Last time we had to lather Ham down with cooking oil to get him out. He goes after the apples I store down there. I put two twenty-five-pound bags of flour on top so he couldn't open the door, but I guess he figured a way past that."

"Smart pig." *Wait*, Tara wanted to say. *Just give me one more minute. I have something really important to tell you—to ask.* But Ben was already getting out.

"Stupid pig. One of these times I might not be able to get him out of the predicaments he gets himself into. O—ow." Ben stood slowly, a pained look on his face.

"Is it your foot?" Tara asked. "Is it hurt worse than you thought?"

Ben started to shake his head then stopped and began vigorously nodding. "Yeah. It's my foot. I think a couple of toes might be broken."

"You know where liars go," Tara said.

"What?" He bent down, giving her a peculiar look.

"Nothing." *Now who's lying.*

"My foot's okay, but my tailbone *is* pretty sore. I'm probably going to have a hard time getting Ham unstuck."

"There's always your Boy Scout tool," Tara suggested.

Ben grinned. "Why don't you come in and help me? You can stay for dinner afterward. It's the least you can do for running over my foot."

"The least I can do to alleviate your guilt for so rudely talking about me, you mean."

"That too," he had the decency to admit.

Their eyes met as he waited for Tara to decide. Part of her was still ticked and hurt at what she'd overheard by the shed. The other part of her had immensely enjoyed their conversation the past ten minutes. A few minutes—few hours—more, and she'd be able to ask him for sure.

Tara pulled the keys from the ignition. "Who am I to turn down the once-in-a-lifetime opportunity of seeing you wrestle with a slippery pig?"

"It'll be good," Ben promised. "Though probably not so entertaining as seeing you scared by a jackrabbit."

Thirty-Eight

HAM, AS IT TURNED OUT, had done a fine job of getting himself stuck and was literally hanging, caught around his rotund middle and squealing, in the opening of the basement storeroom when they reached him.

"Stay here. You two grab his front legs," Ben said to Josh and Deb. "I'll crawl through the basement window and push him back up. Tara, there's cooking oil on the bottom shelf of the pantry. We may need it." Ben ran out of the kitchen, and a second later the front door banged shut.

Deb took one hoof, and Josh the other, and they held on to Ham, trying to relieve some of the pressure around his abdomen.

Tara entered the well-stocked pantry and located the oil. She brought it over to the trio—Josh, Deb, and Ham.

"Okay. I'm here," Ben called from below. "On the count of three. I'll push; you two pull. One. Two. Three." Amid numerous grunts, most of which were *not* from the pig, Tara watched as Ham budged about a quarter of an inch.

"Tara," Ben called. "We're going to need some oil. If you could help with that—"

She looked at the jug in her hands. *He can't be serious.*

"And hurry, please." Deb's face was red, her breathing heavy. "Unless you need me to do it . . ."

The old Tara would have said, "It's all yours, sister," and walked off, but the implication that she was above such things or incapable of helping Ben bothered her enough that she began unscrewing the cap. Tara stepped forward between Deb and Josh and poured a generous amount of oil onto Ham's back. *Disgusting.* She grimaced then placed her hand on the pig, slathering the oil into his skin and hair. Giving up pork forever was definitely not going to be a problem.

She continued the process on his sides where, to make matters worse, he was covered with flour. He'd chewed through the bags then pawed the flour out, getting it all over himself and the kitchen in the process.

Ham was now slippery enough that he began sliding back into the cellar—despite Ben's heroic efforts to hold him up.

"My fingers are slipping," Deb complained. Tara set the oil aside and hooked her arm beneath Ham's leg, just as Deb let go and the pig went rocketing downward, taking Tara with him.

Tara shrieked. Her free arm flailed in the air, her legs bounced down the steep, narrow stairs, before she and Ham both landed on Ben and a couple bushels of apples. Flour rained down, topping things off.

"Are you all right?" Josh knelt over the opening, peering down at them.

"I'm okay." Ben sounded as if he'd had the wind knocked out of him. "A broken rib or two, maybe. It'll go well with my tailbone."

Unsure if he was serious or not, Tara rolled away. "I'm fine," she said, feeling anything but. Her shin was killing her, and her hair was tangled in the side of a basket of apples. She was covered in oil and flour and—*pig*. She pushed Ham aside with her foot. He began running circles around them, squealing. This made the DI shopping trip with Ben seem like a completely normal activity.

"You *look* fine." Above them Deb snorted with laughter. Tara frowned, wondering if this had been part of Deb's evil plan all along. *Make the unwelcome visitor look like an unattractive idiot.*

Josh joined her laughter. "Yeah. You two look great together."

Pushing the hair back from her face, Tara struggled to sit up. She glanced over at Ben a foot away. He was still lying flat but raised his head to give her a lopsided grin.

"Here on the farm, we believe that true once-in-a-lifetime opportunities involve participation."

* * *

"The bathroom is on the right." Deb pointed to the door across the hall. "You can shower first. I think you got the worst of it."

You think? "Thanks," Tara said, both annoyed by and appreciative of Deb.

Why does she have to be so nice? Tara didn't think she would have been if the tables were turned and some woman happened by in her territory. But since the pig incident, and since Ben had invited her to stay for dinner and then stay the night, it seemed Deb was doing her best to be kind and make her feel welcome. Though she couldn't seem to help flashing her diamond around while she did it.

"You can take that bed." Deb pointed to one on the far side of the room beneath the eaves. "I'm glad you're staying." Tara's eyes narrowed as she hoisted her suitcase on the bed and began unzipping it. *I'm glad you're staying? Who is she kidding? No one can be that nice.*

"I wasn't planning on it, but I don't have much choice." Tara glanced down at her shirt, covered in a sticky mixture that was part oil, part flour, part pig. *Ruined, no doubt. Oh well. At least I'm used to getting rid of clothes.*

Deb left the room, and Tara collected her things for a shower. On a whim, she selected the pink sweater Ben had purchased for her last year. She doubted he would remember it, but somehow the thought of wearing it around him again seemed right.

After she'd showered and changed and dried her hair, she came downstairs to the smell of fried chicken. Ben, wearing a clean pair of jeans and a different flannel shirt, stood at the stove, turning the chicken. Josh was busy mashing potatoes, and Deb pulled a pan of perfect-looking biscuits from the oven.

Of course she's a great cook. Tara felt a pang of something more than sadness or jealousy as she stood in the doorway watching the scene before her. It reminded her of standing in the hospital doorway, looking in as Peter and Jane held their babies. The closest thing she could think of to describing the feeling was homesickness. *I'm sick of not having a home like this. People to be with and care about.*

Ben noticed her standing there and beckoned to her. "Would you mind setting the table?" He asked the question almost as if he were afraid of offending her.

"Not at all," she said, grateful he'd asked her to do something inclusive. "Where is your silverware?"

He pointed out the drawer and the cupboard that held plates and cups, and Tara got busy, doing as much as she could with her menial task. *Nothing to compete with compared to those biscuits. That's okay. I'm not competing. Never was. I came here to ask Ben to baptize me.* That thought, and all that it meant, all the change that had occurred in her life over the past months, came clearly into focus, and a sense of peace and contentment settled over her.

How wonderful it will be when I can feel this all the time, when I receive the gift of the Holy Ghost. She longed to ask Ben now, to tell him all that had happened in her life since December. When they sat down to eat, she folded her arms, closed her eyes, and bowed her head. After Josh said the prayer, Tara looked up to find Ben giving her a peculiar look, much as he had earlier when she'd almost quoted him the scripture about lying from the Book of Mormon.

She ignored him, determined not to get into another argument— fun though those sometimes were—for the rest of the evening.

"So how long have you all been in Ohio?" Tara asked.

"Five years," Ben said.

"I was raised here," Josh said.

"I've only been here since February," Deb said. "I needed a change of pace, and Ben had invited me several times, so I finally decided to come see for myself what all the fuss was about." She favored Ben with a pretty smile.

"It's very beautiful here," Tara said, working to push down a spurt of jealousy trying to surface. "I can see why you like it."

"Ohio has been very good to me." Deb stared across the table at Josh, busy digging into an enormous helping of mashed potatoes.

"Where are you from?" Deb asked.

"Los Angeles," Ben said, answering for her.

"Seattle," Tara corrected him and kept her annoyance to herself. "That's where I was raised and where I live now. I left Los Angeles last spring."

"Job transfer?" Josh mumbled as he chewed.

Tara shook her head. "Not exactly." Purposely being evasive, she bit into her biscuit. She didn't want to say any more right now. Later, she hoped, she'd get the opportunity to talk alone with Ben and to make her request.

"You weren't let go, were you?" Ben put his elbow on the table and leaned forward, as if suddenly eager to hear her life story. "The economy's awful everywhere, but I imagine the real estate market in LA must be extra tough."

"I wasn't laid off." *So much for later.* "I quit when I was asked to fire several other people."

Josh whistled. "Bet that took guts."

She smiled at him. "Thank you. It turned out to be a very wise decision." She attacked her chicken again, hoping the conversation was closed.

For some reason, Ben persisted in keeping it open. "What are you doing now?"

You'll never believe it. Tara kept her explanation as simple as possible. "I sell things online," she said. "It started as kind of a fluke. I had a bunch of clothes I was getting rid of." *Long story, that.* "And I did very well pricing them and selling them on eBay. Then I figured out that I could list things for other people and take a cut. Often people are simply too busy to sell things themselves." She stopped, uncomfortable with the look Ben was giving her.

"That's your *job*? eBay?"

"What's wrong with that?" Tara asked, unable to keep the defensive tone from her voice. "It's not stressful like real estate was. I may never be rich doing it, but I'm not doing badly. I have everything I need."

"Like your old Jeep?" His voice held a hint of scorn.

Tara stared at him. "It's not mine. A friend offered to let me use it."

"To drive all the way across the country?" Ben whistled. "Nice friend."

"I left my BMW for her to use," Tara said, wondering just what he was getting at. "I wanted something a little more . . . rugged . . . for the trip." *And so I wouldn't show you up when I arrived at your humble farm*, she wanted to add but didn't. Try as she might, it didn't seem she and Ben could have a conversation without emotions and tempers involved. Now she was the one who couldn't let it go.

"What does it matter what kind of car I'm driving or where I work?" she asked. "Last December you mocked me because of my big-city, pampered-girl lifestyle. I'm not like that anymore, but I guess I should have realized that just because I've changed doesn't mean you did. You still look down on me and think you're so much better." She stood and pushed back her chair. "You know what? I didn't come here to argue." She threw a quick glance to either side of the table, to Deb and Josh's shocked faces. "Sorry."

"Why *did* you come here?" Ben asked. He stood, facing her across the table. "What on earth *possessed* you to drive clear across the country—in an old, borrowed car?" His tone of voice told her he didn't believe her story.

Does he think I'm down on my luck or something?

Tara felt tears building behind her eyes as she met his gaze. "Nothing," she said quietly. "There was nothing on *earth* that could have done that. It was a much greater power. One that you hold." She paused, not wanting to say this now. Not wanting to ruin what she had hoped would be a wonderful, remember-for-the-rest-of-her-life moment. But it was too late. She'd already ruined everything. Again.

"I had hoped you would use it to baptize me."

Thirty-Nine

IMMEDIATELY FOLLOWING TARA'S DEPARTURE, SILENCE descended on the kitchen. Even Josh had stopped eating, though he still held his fork aloft, clutched in his unmoving hand. They all stared at the empty doorway in a dazed sort of way. Deb was the first to recover and find her voice.

"You." She pointed her knife at Ben. "Are a total jerk."

"*Baptized?*" Ben was sure his face revealed the shock he felt. "Tara wants me to *baptize* her?"

"Not anymore, I'd wager." Josh put down his fork, picked up a drumstick, and bit into it.

Deb wrinkled her nose and frowned at him. "How can you eat at a time like this?"

"Like what?" he mumbled through a bite of food.

"That poor woman is upstairs, crying, no doubt, and you're stuffing your face like some—"

"Pig?" Josh grinned at her.

"She's not some poor woman," Ben said. "Don't let her act fool you. She's critical and bossy and vain, and I *can't* believe she really wants to be baptized. There's something else going on. She's after something."

"You?" Josh suggested.

Ben shook his head. "In the past, she's made her opinion of farmers—or anyone vaguely related—clear. Very uncouth in the company she keeps."

"What makes you so sure she isn't telling the truth about getting baptized?" Deb asked.

"Because I know her," Ben said. "She's the complete opposite of what a Latter-day Saint is supposed to be. She's selfish and worldly and temperamental and spoiled. I can't imagine the things that would have had to happen for her to want to join the Church."

"She sure didn't seem to be any of those things today," Josh said.

"People can change, Benji." Deb reached for his hand, but he pulled away. "You've got to stop letting your mom taint every relationship you're in."

"My mom has nothing to do with this," Ben said. "And I never had a relationship with Tara."

"He just kissed her." Josh winked at Deb.

Ben glared at him. "That's one mistake I won't be making again."

* * *

An hour later, when the dinner dishes had been washed, dried, and put away, and he'd swept the floor and wiped down the counters and done every other chore he could think of, Ben headed up the stairs to his room. Tara had not left the house, but she also hadn't come downstairs again. He worried she'd sneak out sometime during the night, leaving him without a chance to apologize. And he wanted to apologize. While he still didn't believe her, he also couldn't deny that he'd been rude and unkind during dinner. He needed to tell her he was sorry. He wanted to feel as if he were in the right of things again.

He wanted to know what Tara was really up to.

Ben trod carefully on the steps, hugging the wall as he went, so as not to put weight on any of the squeaky boards. Maybe if Tara thought he was still downstairs, she'd get tired waiting to leave and fall asleep. Then, in the morning, he could figure out what this was all about. If she really did need help, well . . .

It won't be the first time.

He thought of the ten thousand he'd emptied out of his bank account five months ago and all the promise for the future he'd felt when doing it. To this day he still didn't completely regret the decision. McKenzie and her two children had needed help. And he'd been only too happy to give it. Too happy to fly them out to Ohio, to have them close by for a couple of months. To pretend for a short while that they belonged together.

To start to believe he could fall in love again.

To remember that women—his adoptive mom and sisters being the only exceptions he could think of—were not to be trusted. Ever.

Especially one he'd seen in action before. Tara had been able to turn on the tears at will last December. The months since then would have only given her time to perfect her technique.

Ben's face was grim as he passed her door. He wasn't going to fall for it, for her. No matter how much he'd thought about her—*and that stupid kiss*—since last December, he wasn't going to let himself be used again. He'd find out what she needed, and then he would help— or not—on his terms.

On my terms. He liked the sound of that, the thought of being in control again. Exactly what he hadn't felt all afternoon since seeing Tara seated at his kitchen table.

Forty

DEB RETURNED FROM SHOWERING AND flopped onto her bed. She glanced over at Tara, lying perfectly still in the bed across the room beneath the eaves. "I've never seen Ben like this. I'm sorry he was so rude tonight."

"I bring out the worst in him." Tara rolled to her side, facing the wall. She hoped Deb would take the hint and leave her alone. She didn't feel like talking to anyone right now. She would have gone somewhere else for the night, but she didn't trust herself not to get lost this far out in the country in the dark.

"Why is that, do you suppose?"

"I'm lucky that way," Tara said sarcastically. *What does she expect me to say to that?* "I seem to bring out the worst in just about every man I've ever known." *Maybe if I'd had a dad around, things would've been different. I'd have had a role model, someone to help me figure men out.*

"Do you?" Deb asked. "Do you have other guys scattered around the country who are as madly in love with you as Ben is?"

Tara made a sound somewhere between a snort and a sob. "Ben isn't in love with me. You don't need to worry. I'm leaving tomorrow morning. You'll never see me again, and you guys can go on and have your wedding and your happily ever after."

"*What?*" A few seconds later the mattress sagged, and Tara rolled over to find Deb sitting on the edge of the bed. "Ben's my brother."

"That's not funny," Tara said. "In fact, it's sicker than naming a pig Ham."

Deb threw her hands up in the air. "All this time—today—you thought I was marrying *Ben.* Eeww."

"You were grocery shopping together," Tara said. "And there was that whole bit about you touching Ben and the pig being jealous. You've got that rock on your finger. You *live* here."

"Like I could do that if we were engaged," Deb said.

Tara stared at her, realizing she told the truth. *Ben* isn't *engaged.* For a brief second she felt almost giddy. Only Deb's eyes narrowing suspiciously kept Tara from laughing out loud.

"If you were a member of our church or had investigated it, you'd know two unmarried people can't live together." Deb's voice was accusatory.

"I'd forgotten," Tara said. "To the rest of the world, living with someone is perfectly acceptable. I forget everything that's taboo sometimes."

"That's kind of a big one," Deb said, still skeptical. She rose from the bed, bent over, and removed the towel from her hair.

"It is, isn't it?" Tara said, disturbed by how easily she'd forgotten. If she'd thought about it, then much earlier she might have realized Ben wasn't engaged, and her emotions might not have been running so high. *I might not have blown my one opportunity to ask Ben to baptize me and to make amends for the way I acted last December.*

Though Ben had been rude, Tara felt the most disappointed with herself. *I should have waited. Should have tried to explain things better.*

Twelve days and 2,400 miles for nothing.

"But you are engaged?" she asked, hoping to change the subject and take her mind off her misery. "Or are diamonds that size standard accessories for farmgirls in Ohio?"

Deb was still towel-drying her hair, but she turned her head to the side so she could see Tara.

"I'm engaged to Josh. I'd have thought that was pretty obvious. I kissed him on the porch in plain sight this afternoon, and we were flirting shamelessly during dinner. I guess you didn't notice those things?"

"No." Tara grimaced. *Now that we've established I am an unobservant, forgetful idiot.* "Congratulations," she said sincerely. "When's the wedding?"

Deb finished drying her hair and stood up. "We haven't decided on a date yet. We'd like to get married soon, but . . ."

"What?" Tara asked, knowing full well that Deb wanted her to ask.

"I'm worried about leaving Ben all alone. It's bad enough he talks to the pigs when I'm around. If he's here by himself, I'm afraid things will get even worse."

"Worse—how?" Tara asked. She leaned up on one elbow and gave Deb her full attention.

"I'm worried his depression will come back," she said. "Summer was rough, and I'm not sure he's completely recovered. Which is why Josh and I haven't set a date."

"Why was summer rough?" Tara asked. *Bad crops?* It couldn't be the pigs. Josh had as much as told her that Ben had the best around here.

Deb tossed her towel on the back of a chair and climbed into her own bed. "It's not my place to say anything. If Ben wants to tell you, he will." She twisted the knob on the hurricane lamp on her night table, leaving the room in darkness.

"I'll be surprised if Ben tells me so much as good-bye tomorrow morning," Tara said.

"We'll see," was Deb's only reply.

I wanted to see, Tara admitted to herself. *I wanted to see Ben again, to see if my changing made any difference at all.* She frowned into the dark as a new, unwelcome thought crossed her mind.

Maybe that's why everything went so wrong tonight. Had she wanted Ben to baptize her just to show him she'd changed, that she was better than she'd been when he last saw her?

Yes, a tiny voice inside admitted. Tara stared up at the ceiling, hating the guilt she suddenly felt. All this being honest with herself all the time was hard. Especially since *herself* wasn't always such a great person—like right now.

"Daa-rn it," she muttered under her breath. *It's more than that. I know it. Everything I felt this summer. The things I read and learned. It's about something much more, much bigger than Ben or me.*

Tara flipped back the covers and quietly got out of bed. Kneeling beside it, she bowed her head, folded her arms, and closed her eyes.

Heavenly Father, she began then poured out her heart, thanking Him for every blessing she could think of. That she was healthy, she had good friends, she'd made it here safely. That she'd seen Ben again and asked him what she had planned to. Tara stopped, taking a moment to gather her thoughts and her courage. Now came the hard part.

Please forgive me if my motives were wrong. Forgive me for confusing Thy love with—other feelings. I'm sorry. Again. At least she was getting good at that. Since she'd started praying every night, she'd yet to have a day when she hadn't made mistakes—usually in multiples. *And please bless Ben that whatever was rough about his summer will get better.*

She ended her prayer but stayed by the side of the bed, her head on the mattress while she listened. The missionaries had told her this was the most difficult part of prayer and communicating with Heavenly Father. They'd said that most people, when it came to praying, forgot that a conversation went two ways—that part of the time you had to listen.

Tara never forgot. This was her favorite part, the quiet moments after her prayer when a spirit of peace and comfort filled her soul. It was then she felt that someone—a Father—was listening to her.

Bless Ben, she thought again. *Help me be better than I am. Help me have better motives.*

The floor was cold, so Tara climbed into bed, determined to do the rest of her listening there. Just before she dropped off to sleep, she felt the comforting warmth of the Spirit envelop her again, just as surely as she was tucked in the folds of the quilt. The faintest whisper seemed to brush by, an answer to all of her earlier pleas.

I will.

Forty-One

Tara carefully pushed her easel and canvases aside and loaded her suitcase into the back of the Jeep. She reached up to close the hatch and discovered Ben's hand already there—stopping hers.

"Hi." She looked up at him, squinting against the early morning sun.

"I thought you didn't ever get up before ten," he said.

She shrugged. "I usually sleep better these days." In spite of yesterday's turmoil, she'd slept like the dead last night.

"Good thing I was up early myself." Ben kept his stance, hand braced against the Jeep's hatch.

"Milking your cows, I suppose," Tara said then grimaced inwardly. Somehow that comment had sounded snarky. Why was it so hard to be nice around him?

"No cows. Just pigs," Ben said.

"You milk pigs?" That one had been too much to resist.

A corner of his mouth quirked up. "Haven't tried that yet. Don't think I want to, either. Not with Persephone's temper."

Tara glanced at the hatch. "Do you mind?" she asked, after several awkward seconds had passed without either of them speaking.

"I do, actually," Ben said. He released the hatch but reached in the Jeep to retrieve her suitcase. One corner caught on the easel, and he moved it aside. He turned to Tara. "Do you draw?"

"Paint," she corrected. "Though this trip is really the first time I've done much in years. I'm pretty rusty."

"Let me judge?" Ben lifted her suitcase from the back of the Jeep and set it on the ground.

She shrugged. "Go ahead." Her work was far from perfect, and of course she'd yet to finish any of the paintings she'd started this trip, but it didn't really matter what Ben thought. He'd made his feelings clear last night, and she didn't think anything else he said could hurt any more.

Ben picked up the closest canvas. He took it from the car, turned it over, and stared at her painting of the Nauvoo Temple.

Tara watched as, once again, fleeting expressions crossed his face. Surprise—obviously. She'd known he hadn't believed her last night when she'd asked him to baptize her. Something akin to remorse or chagrin followed his surprise, and then . . . *respect?*

He looked up. "I owe you an apology."

"Yes. You do." She folded her arms across her chest as her eyes met his. "It would have meant more if you'd offered it before you saw that painting."

Instead of continuing with his apology, Ben leaned into the back of the Jeep, put the canvas inside, and grabbed another, this one her rendition of Parley Street in Old Nauvoo. "You're good," he said after he'd studied it a minute.

"That one is my favorite." Tara's eyes flitted from his face to the painting. "I imagine you know the history, but when I was there last week, I learned they used to call that street the Trail of Tears but changed it to the Trail of Hope. Yet there were an awful lot of tears shed there."

"Did you read all the signs?" Ben asked.

"I did." She knew exactly what he was talking about. All along Parley Street, down to the waterfront, where the pioneers had crossed the frozen river, were plaques that told of the people who'd left their homes and possessions behind and with faithful hearts had followed Brigham Young to an unknown West.

"Reading them was heartbreaking—and inspiring. Those people had so much faith." Right after she'd finished, she'd gone to her car, gathered her art supplies, and spent the rest of the afternoon and much of the next day down by the river, sketching and then painting that street as she imagined it looked when the pioneers walked it for the last time. Just remembering the feelings she'd felt there brought her fragile emotions to the surface again.

She was grateful that Jane had convinced her a day at Nauvoo would be well worth a few hours' detour and her time. Tara had kept her promise to stop there, intending to spend an afternoon. Four days later, she'd finally left, only the thought of seeing Ben able to tear her from the overwhelming spirit she'd experienced in that sacred place.

Ben put the painting back in the Jeep and closed the hatch. Her suitcase was still on the ground beside the car.

"I think you forgot something," Tara said, nudging the bag with her toe.

"I've forgotten a lot of things." Ben shoved his hands in his pockets and looked at her. "Like the fact that people can change and the gospel is for everyone and you're a nice person who I had a lot of fun with last December."

"Mmm. That last one might be stretching it a little." Tara made eye contact, wanting him to believe her this time. "I was telling the truth last night, Ben. I drove all the way here to ask you to baptize me. And—" *The truth. The whole truth, and nothing but the truth so help me*— "Because I wanted to see you again," she admitted. "When I moved back to Seattle, I ended up staying with my friend Jane—the one I mentioned to you last December. She's a great person, and a member of the LDS Church. She started teaching me, and then I spent four months taking the missionary discussions. During that time some things happened—Jane had her babies early. She was in a coma and almost died. It was a rather life-changing experience."

"Wow," Ben said. "Is she okay now? Are *you* okay?"

The genuine concern in his voice warmed Tara's heart. This was the Ben she knew. The one she remembered. The one who, like King Benjamin in the Book of Mormon, cared about others.

"I'm fine," she said. "More than fine. Better than I've ever been in my life." She wished her words were more eloquent, that she could better express what she'd learned and felt. "I'm not the same woman you offered to help at the airport last year. And in a way, it's your fault."

"I wish I could take credit," Ben said. "But you're the one who sought your friend out again, who made the changes in your life."

"Yes, but you planted the seed—so they say, or sing, if you're in Primary."

"Must have been some gardener who took over afterward," Ben said.

"You could say that." Tara smiled at him, both relieved and grateful that he seemed to believe her. "Jane is actually an amazing gardener. Her yard is like something out of *Better Homes and Gardens.*"

"Not quite what I meant." He chuckled, then his face grew serious again. "I really am sorry about the way I acted last night. I jumped to conclusions. I had no right—"

"No, you didn't," she agreed. "And yes, you did seem to jump to some conclusions about my visit. Care to share those with me?"

"Not really." He looked past her, out to the distant cornfield. "Though I suppose, to be fair, I should."

"Go on," Tara urged. Some part of her knew it would have been better, more Christlike, to tell him he didn't need to explain, that she forgave him already, but that other part of her—the one that always wanted to know all about what was going on with people—took over. *More repenting tonight.* She glanced at her watch. It was barely eight o'clock in the morning. At this rate, she was in for one long evening prayer.

"I was in a relationship earlier this year," Ben said, still not looking at her. "It ended badly. I lost in more ways than one." He paused, as if considering what to say next. "I guess, yesterday, with the way the conversation went at dinner, and thinking about how you showed up here out of the blue—" He pulled his gaze from the field back to Tara's face "—I thought you might be here because you wanted something. You know, money or—"

"Ahh," Tara said, beginning to understand. "I can see why Jane's old Jeep and my new business didn't impress you."

"But that's not all," Ben hastened to add. "I had no idea that you'd come to ask me to baptize you. But that you had traveled all this way to see me sort of implied . . ."

"I see," Tara said, and she did and suddenly felt very foolish. "It's not like that, Ben. I know we had those . . . moments . . . in Colorado, but I didn't come for romantic reasons." *Mostly I didn't, anyway.*

"Good." His smile was one of relief. "Because right now I'm not looking for a relationship. Nothing serious, I mean."

"I promise to be completely *un*serious," Tara said. "Except for right now. I'm sorry about last night too. After I went upstairs, I spent the evening chastising myself for losing my temper."

"I hope your mental flogging didn't last as long as mine," Ben said. "I hardly slept. I haven't felt that lousy about anything since—" He stopped abruptly. Tara almost missed the flash of hurt in his eyes.

"So anyway," Ben continued, "I was hoping to make it up to you. You've come all this way. You could stay for a day or two and—" He shrugged. "I don't know. See the place?" He nodded toward the car and her paintings inside. "If you're interested in Church history, I could take you up to Kirtland."

"I'd like that," Tara said. "And will you consider—" Now she was the one having trouble finishing her sentence. She'd already asked once if Ben would baptize her, and she'd completely botched it. Maybe now wasn't the time to ask again, but this was what she'd come for. She wanted to know. She didn't expect or want him to baptize her here. She needed to be back in Bainbridge with Jane and Peter and the missionaries. But she wanted to know if Ben would at least think about it, if he truly believed her.

"You let me know when and where," Ben said, as if he'd heard her thoughts. "And I'll be there. Dressed in white."

"Thanks." To Tara's dismay, her eyes filled with tears.

"I'm honored you would ask." Ben started to reach for her suitcase then stopped. He hesitated then took a step forward, put his arm around Tara, and pulled her into an awkward embrace.

"Welcome to Ohio, Sister Mollagen."

Forty-Two

BEN TOOK TARA'S SUITCASE UPSTAIRS while she waited in the kitchen. As he stepped into the bedroom, he almost ran into Deb, who was just coming out.

"What's that you've got there?" she asked, a teasing smile on her face.

"Don't start," he warned. The last thing he needed was Deb on his case, playing matchmaker.

"Tell me you apologized properly, and I'll leave you alone," she said.

"I apologized. I don't know if it was proper, but I'll make it up to her today."

"Good," Deb said. She followed him into the hall. "I'm glad you talked her into staying another day."

"Could be more than one." Ben started down the stairs. "We didn't discuss specifics."

"Smart man." Deb pushed him from behind. "Now hurry up. I'm starving."

Josh was at the stove already, flipping pancakes. "How many does everyone want?" he asked as they entered the kitchen.

"Six," Ben said. "I didn't get any sleep last night and am gonna need some serious carbs to make up for it today."

"You'll get some serious pounds if you eat that many." Deb crossed the room to Josh, turned him away from the stove, and planted a long, juicy kiss on his lips. "See?" she said turning to Tara, when at last the kiss ended.

"I'd have to be blind to miss that one," Tara said.

"Enough of that in my kitchen," Ben said, irritated with his sister's ridiculous behavior. "Did you make orange juice yet, Josh?"

"Nope." Josh flipped a pancake and caught it perfectly on the center of the pan. "You expect me to do everything around here?"

"You *eat* everything around here." Ben pulled a can of frozen juice from the freezer.

Deb took a stack of plates from the cupboard and handed them to Tara. "Josh doesn't really live with us," she said, as if that needed explaining or something.

"He just *lives* here," Ben said.

"Hey." Josh pointed the spatula at Ben. "Cut me some slack. I've been doing my best to persuade her to leave you and those pigs. I even promised we could get a dog or something."

"You know I like you better than the pigs," Deb said.

"I don't know." Ben shook his head as he watched Josh take a sausage from a plate on the counter and down it in one bite. "Sometimes there isn't much difference."

* * *

Ben slowed his steps so Tara could keep up as they walked across the grass toward the cornfield. He was pleased the shoes she wore were far more sensible than the heels he remembered her wearing last December. But though she was trying to fit in, she still had *city girl* stamped all over her. The way she was picking her way across the yard—side-stepping areas that appeared wet or dirty—amused him.

Oh the fun I could have. Possibilities for practical jokes and fun at her expense rolled through his mind before he could stop them. *But I will stop them,* he vowed. Tara wasn't the same woman he'd met last December who needed taking down a notch or two. Instead, Ben worried he was the one in need of self-improvement.

He glanced at her from the corner of his eye. She caught him looking and smiled. A new happiness seemed to radiate from her. She seemed younger, as if she'd shed years of burdens and had discovered the joy of life.

Noticing all this, Ben swallowed uncomfortably. Most of the joy he'd previously known seemed to have fled in the past few months. He'd been able to ignore the loss pretty well—until yesterday. Having Tara around had opened up his wounds again. She reminded him of what he would never have.

There's no reason to take it out on her. Silently, he vowed to be nicer, to display whatever good she'd seen in him ten months ago.

"You chose a great time of year to visit," he said. "October is the absolute best month here."

"Why?" Tara asked. "Because of the weather or the harvest?"

"Neither," Ben said. "The weather is nice, but October is nice in a lot of the country. And I don't do much with crops. Just the garden mostly. October is the best because of Halloween."

"Huh?" Tara followed him as they left the lawn and headed up a dirt road to the corn.

"My favorite holiday," Ben explained. "And it's only gotten better since I've been an adult and had my own place."

"Aren't you a little old for trick-or-treating?" Tara asked.

"Never." Ben's mouth quirked mischievously. They reached the corn, and he stepped aside, his hand held out, gesturing for her to go ahead. She stepped through the wide gap between stalks. Ahead of them four separate paths led off in different directions.

"It's a maze." A look of wonderment lit her face as she walked deeper into the rows. "I've heard about these, but I've never actually been to one."

"I have to use that tractor I bought for something," Ben said. "This is my fourth year. It's getting to be pretty popular. We've already had a lot of traffic and it's only the first week of October."

The sound of an approaching ATV drowned out his voice. He and Tara watched as Deb drove up to the entrance. She killed the engine and climbed off, a clipboard in her hand.

"So today we have a preschool coming at ten o'clock then two Girl Scout troops at three. A birthday party at four, and we open to the public at five. Does that sound about right?"

"I think I said yes to a youth group this afternoon too." Ben tried to remember when, exactly, the All Saints Community Youth had said they were coming.

"Be-en," Deb whined. "You can't do that. You've got to write this stuff down. You know we can't be three places at once. And are any of those groups paying?"

"The birthday party is," Ben said. "And it's a big group. Fifteen, twenty kids."

"Well that's something," Deb said. "Though, if you keep letting groups in for free, we're never going to make enough."

"You worry too much," Ben said. He'd pledged five thousand to the Ohio Family Care Association this year, to help with recruiting and training foster families. Last year he'd made just under $3,500 during the month of October, with the cornfield and other Halloween activities he'd set up. With the new things they'd added this year, plus word of mouth, he felt certain they could donate that much more. "Just watch. We'll do fine."

"I hope you're right." Deb held up the key to the ATV. "You want to do a drive-through or should I?"

"That depends." Ben looked at Tara. "Want to ride around in the maze on an ATV? We go through every morning, just to make sure there are no surprises inside."

"Or at least not ones we didn't put there," Deb said, a sly grin on her face.

"What sort of surprises *do* you have in there?" Tara asked.

"The usual." Ben grinned. "Snakes. A skeleton or two, Big Foot, guy with a chainsaw . . ."

"And preschoolers around here enjoy that sort of thing?" Tara was giving him her you-are-so-sick-and-twisted look again. The same one he'd gotten at breakfast when he allowed Persephone to sit beside him at the table.

"The younger kids take the left fork," Deb explained. "It's completely tame. There are silly ghosts and decorated pumpkins. And, of course, *Farmer Ben* is there to guide them."

"It's a chance to be a kid again," Ben said defensively. He wondered what Tara would think if she saw him being goofy with the little kids. That act had never won him any dates before, though most preschool moms seemed to appreciate his corniness. Somehow he didn't think Tara would. Maybe if he were lucky, she'd be off painting or something during that time.

"What do you think? Will the maze be too much for your claustrophobia?"

Tara glanced uneasily at the paths that disappeared into the twelve-foot-high corn. "I guess it might be okay. If we keep moving . . ."

Deb started walking toward the house. "Call me if you need me," she said. "Otherwise I'll see you a little before ten."

"You'll see to the pigs?" Ben asked.

"I'll try. Seph is in a temper again."

"Thanks," Ben called.

"Thanks?" Tara asked. "You just sent your sister to milk the pigs—or whatever you do with them—and all she gets is a 'thanks'?"

Ben stroked his chin as he studied her. "I'm wrong again. Thought for sure you were one of those equal rights types."

"When it comes to farm work, I think a little chivalry is in order. After all, your sister baked the biscuits last night. She's already doing the feminine thing. Why should she have to do both?"

"*I* baked those biscuits," Ben said. He'd noticed how Tara had seemed to be enjoying them—before he'd driven her away from the table, that is.

"It's actually important for Deb to work with the pigs. Persephone thinks we're married or something," Ben grumbled. He walked over to the ATV and Tara followed.

"You almost treat that pig like you are. So of course she expects it." She waited for Ben to get on then climbed on behind him. "You let her sit beside you at the table. You rub her belly. You feed her treats and pamper her. You even let her sleep in your bed!"

He turned around to see her face. "How do you know that?"

A slight blush crept up Tara's cheeks. "I went the wrong direction in the hall this morning. It was early. I was still half asleep. Your door was partway open, and for a minute I thought it was the bathroom."

"Good thing I was decent," Ben said.

"I wouldn't have known if you weren't," Tara said. "Aside from your hair and forehead, all I could see was this huge pig covering the bed."

"She's had a rough life," Ben said. "So what if I do baby her a bit."

"A bit?" Tara choked.

Ben frowned. "Nothing wrong with it. Pigs are God's creatures too."

"I know," Tara said. "I'm just saying—"

He started the engine. "You're saying if I treat her differently, she'll act that way?"

"Yes." Tara had to shout to be heard above the motor. "The way you treat people—or pigs, apparently—is important. Kindness will be returned with kindness and the like."

"Really?" Ben thought back to the all-about-me Tara he'd known last December. He'd witnessed firsthand her being more than a little *un*kind to a couple of unfortunate airline employees. A lot must have happened to change her so much.

If, indeed, she really was changed. He still wasn't completely convinced.

"Hang on." He clutched the gas, and they zoomed forward, down the third path, the one with the most snakes—some that dropped on you.

"Let me know if you're getting uncomfortable, and we'll turn back."

"Okay." Her arms tightened around his waist and she scooted forward, pressing up against his back. Before a minute had passed, Ben was acutely aware of every part of her that was touching him. It wasn't that it was unpleasant—the opposite was true. But it bothered him all the same.

He'd invited Tara to stay because Deb was right. He had been a jerk last night, and he wanted to make up for that. But he didn't want to think about Tara as more than a visitor. He didn't want to *feel* anything for or about her—a near impossibility at the moment.

He would do as she advised and be nice and hope it came back to him. *Though sparring with her is kind of fun.* But it ended there. He had no desire to start something, to get involved when it would surely end badly.

He'd treat her nice. He'd go to Seattle. He'd baptize her. Then they would part ways.

For good.

Forty-Three

THE SECOND NIGHT OF HER stay, Tara found herself waiting up for
Deb, wishing she'd hurry and finish lingering longer on the porch
with Josh. When his truck finally pulled away, Tara stepped back from
the window, letting the lace curtain fall in place. She jumped into bed
but sat up with a book, so it would be apparent she was still awake.
Yesterday she hadn't wanted to talk; tonight she could hardly wait.

A few minutes later Deb came in, changed into her pajamas, and
sat on the bed. "Did you have a good day?" she asked.

"Yes," Tara said. "Ben showed me most of his property, and seeing
him in action with the preschoolers was . . ." *Highly amusing.* "Fun."

"Just stay away when he's playing Freddy Kruger," Deb advised.
"If you ask me, Ben gets a little *too* into that role, sticking that creepy
hand out of the corn and grabbing kids."

Tara grimaced. "I'll be sure to stay far away when the teen groups
are around." She closed her book and set it on the floor beside the
bed while pondering how best to lead into what she wanted to talk
about. She was glad that Deb showed no sign of planning to go to
bed right away but had started folding a basket of laundry.

"We had a nice picnic today too," Tara said. "Up on the back
ridge—or whatever you call it. I guess it's not actually very high."

"Slope," Deb suggested. "It is nice up there. And high enough
you can see pretty far."

"It was a good way to get acquainted with the place," Tara said.
"Ben pointed out just about everything up there. I even got the scoop
on all your neighbors."

Deb laughed. "'Cause they're such an interesting bunch—not."

What she said was true enough. Ben's closest neighbors—distant specks from the vantage point of the back slope of his property—were mostly older families who had farmed for generations, were set in their ways, and stuck to them. Josh was the most interesting person who lived close by. But earlier in the year, McKenzie had been here too. Ben had let that slip out accidentally when telling Tara all there was to know about the homes and families in the area.

She decided just to throw the name out there now and see what reaction she got from Deb.

"Ben told me about McKenzie," Tara said. *Not a* complete *lie.*

"Oh?" Deb's voice and brow rose together. But she said nothing else and continued hanging shirts in the closet.

Tara tried again. "I see why he was so upset and suspicious last night. Nothing like having two women from the past show up out of the blue in the same year."

"McKenzie didn't show up out of the blue. Ben invited her." Deb's lips pursed suspiciously.

"I didn't mean here." Tara hurried to cover her blunder. "I meant last December. At Dallin's house. Ben wasn't expecting her then."

"Oh." Deb seemed to consider for a second then went back to the laundry basket and the pile of loose socks on the bottom.

"I can see why he'd be bitter," Tara said. "I had a guy do something similar to me once. Before I'd realized what had hit me, he'd cleaned out my bank account."

"Ten thousand hardly cleaned Ben out," Deb said. "But he was really hurt." She looked up at Tara. "He still is."

So be careful. Tara read the warning in Deb's eyes. "I'm sorry to hear that," Tara said. She was more than sorry. She was mad too—at McKenzie for messing with Ben's heart again. *For messing it up for me.*

Tara couldn't think of a way to get any more out of Deb, so she knelt by the bed and said her prayers then got back under the covers. A few minutes later, Deb turned out the light.

"Good night," she called across the dark room.

"Night," Tara said. All was quiet for several minutes, and Tara felt herself beginning to drift off to sleep when Deb spoke again.

"Ben will be okay eventually," she said. "It's his pride that was hurt as much as anything."

"How so?" Tara asked. Since Deb had initiated the conversation this time, it didn't seem wrong to pry a little.

"Well, McKenzie *did* take his money," Deb said. "But more than that, she used him. Ben knocked himself out to help her and her children, when all the while McKenzie was just playing him. Ben was part of a ploy to get her husband back."

Kids were involved? Her husband? *She was still married?* Tara realized this was a lot bigger deal than she'd thought. *Poor Ben.* "Poor Ben," she said out loud.

"Yeah," Deb agreed. "But like I said, he'll be all right." She sighed and rolled away from Tara. "It's just a good thing he didn't really love her."

Forty-Four

HIKING ALL OVER BEN'S PROPERTY must have worn her out more than she realized, because it was nine thirty before Tara woke the next morning. She rolled over in bed, surprised by both the sunlight streaming through the window and the numbers on her travel alarm clock.

After getting dressed and doing her hair and makeup, she ventured downstairs, only to find the house empty. There was no sign of breakfast. Deb, Ben, and Josh were nowhere to be seen. Not even Ham was around. Tara fixed herself a piece of toast then headed outside to find Ben.

Hands on hips, she stood in the yard and looked toward the shed, the garden, and the cornfield. Ben didn't appear to be anywhere near the first two, and after Deb's warning about his Freddy Kruger impersonation, Tara intended to avoid the cornfield for the remainder of her stay. This left only the barn as a possibility—the one place she had yet to explore.

Because I so love pigs. Ugh. With a resolute sigh, Tara headed off on a well-worn path leading to the huge red barn. She wasn't exactly sure what kind of pigs she'd see in there—all Josh's talk about Ben beating out everyone at the fair made her a tad nervous—but she supposed it was time to find out. *Love Ben; love his pigs.*

She stopped abruptly, unsure where the thought had come from. *I don't love Ben—do I?* Regardless of the answer, thinking about it was off limits. But yesterday, being with him again, being *here*, had been even better than she'd imagined it could be. After the cold beginning to her visit and the awkward start to their morning, both the weather and their friendship had warmed considerably as the day went on. By the time they'd returned to the house at sunset, Ben had seemed,

once more, like the tender, caring guy who had kissed her on top of a
Colorado mountain.

Tara hoped that, to him, she seemed much better than she'd been
back then.

She approached the barn with caution. The immense door was
slightly ajar, helping her decide it was okay to go ahead and walk
right in. She pulled the smooth, polished crossbar, opening the door
enough to squeeze through. She stopped just inside, waiting for her
eyes to adjust to the dim light. Before they did, Ben was at her side.

"Morning, Sleeping Beauty."

She looked at him and saw that he wore overalls similar to those
she'd given him a bad time about last December.

"Nice duds." She smirked. *If he can tease, so can I.*

"*Practical* duds," he said. "Look at all these pockets." He pulled at
the one across the center of his chest and pointed out others on the
side. "I keep all kinds of tools in these. Helps me get my work done
faster if I don't have to get up to find stuff."

"What kind of *stuff* are we talking about?" Tara asked warily.
What upkeep do pigs require, before they go—

"Files, clamps, blades." Ben pulled a large metal file from a side
pocket of his overalls and pointed to a clamp hanging off the side loop.
"Convenient."

"So I see." She swallowed and tried not to imagine what part of a
pig might need clamping. *And a blade?*

"Want to see my shop?" Enthusiasm oozed from his voice.

"That's why I came," Tara said. *Must be positive. Must be positive,*
she chanted to herself. *Everyone has to do* something *for a living.*

Ben moved aside. "Watch your step," he said, holding out his
hand for her to go ahead.

Tara saw that he had been blocking a set of three wide, wooden
steps, flanked on either side by rustic-looking rails. Holding on to
one, she quickly climbed the few stairs then gasped when she reached
the top and the interior of the barn came into view.

It wasn't really a barn at all—in the traditional, filled-with-animals
sense, anyway. A knotty wood floor covered the entire, vast space.
Bright lights hung suspended from a ceiling also made of that same,
rustic wood. On the far side of the barn, a large stone fireplace blazed.

And scattered around the room were varied and assorted machines and tables, none of which resembled any farm equipment she'd ever seen.

There were a lot of hand tools as well. And wood. Lots and lots of wood.

Ben stepped around her, heading for some of that wood, and she followed him into the belly of the barn.

"Where are your pigs?" Tara turned a slow circle, noting as she did the pungent smell of sawdust, a far cry from the manure she'd expected.

Ben shrugged. "I'm not sure. Persephone was with me for a while, but she hates the noise of the saws and won't hang around when I'm using them. Ham's probably out in the cornfield, searching for left-over candy."

"What about your other pigs?" Tara asked. "Like the one who beat out all the others at the fair."

"I didn't enter a pig at the fair." Ben's eyebrows drew together in a perplexed sort of way. "What made you think that?"

"Because Josh said . . ." *What had he said, exactly?* Tara tried to remember but could only recall the part about no one else around here being able to touch what Ben had in his barn. *Josh didn't actually say it was a* pig. "You don't raise pigs?" she asked hopefully.

A grin spread across Ben's face as he shook his head. "Took you a bit to figure that one out."

"You tricked me." She punched him in the arm. "Last year, at Ellen's house, you said—you led me to believe—"

"Ah, ah." He wagged a finger at her. "All I said was that I *had* pigs on my farm. I didn't say how many or what kind. *You* were the one who jumped to conclusions."

"But you made it sound like—"

"You wanted to believe the worst," Ben said. He took a step back and leaned against a sawhorse. "You were sure that I was some poor, backward farmer."

"Who raised filthy, disgusting pigs," Tara said. *I did want to believe that. I* thought *it. I'm awful.* "Guilty," she admitted.

Ben's grin turned smug. "Thought so."

She pointed a finger at him, jabbing the pocket of his overalls with her long, polished nail. "You believed the worst about me too. In fact, you *still* believed it at dinner the other night. The whole *big city girl* thing."

"Touché." Ben saluted her.

"Oh, don't go speaking French to me," Tara said. "You're completely messing with my head here. You're not at all who I thought you were."

"Neither are you," Ben said, all traces of teasing gone from his voice.

"Are you disappointed?" Tara held her breath, waiting for his answer. It was slow in coming.

"I've never been so glad to be wrong."

Beneath her blouse, her heartbeat felt erratic. She couldn't bring herself to look away, could hardly keep from stepping forward and closing the space between them.

"Are *you* disappointed?" Ben asked, a hint of vulnerability in his question.

Nothing about you disappoints me, she wanted to say. "Well, I had hoped for some really great bacon while I was here," she teased instead. Ben laughed, and the momentary spell between them was broken. Tara worried a little that her heart might be too.

Nothing serious, she reminded herself. *I promised.*

* * *

An hour later, Tara had completed her tour of Ben's workshop. She'd never known anyone who worked with wood before, had never been to a shop where furniture was made, but she knew artistic ability when she saw it and craftsmanship and talent. Ben was blessed with an abundance of all three.

"May I?" she asked, running her hands over the arms of a newly completed rocking chair.

Ben nodded. "Go ahead. I've got a couple of frames to finish up, but feel free to stay as long as you'd like."

"Thanks." Tara sat in the rocker and was pleased to find it as comfortable as it was pretty. Ben went back to work, using a tool he'd called a router, making intricate grooves along the pieces of oak he'd previously cut.

Tara rocked contentedly for a few minutes, enjoying the warmth near the fire. Then she got up to wander around again. Ben had explained each of his tools in detail, but he hadn't spent much time showing off his completed work. Most of it was at the far side of the barn, so Tara headed that direction. With an artist's eye and appreciation, she looked over each piece. Ben had used a variety of different woods, each with a unique and beautiful grain. He'd shown her hickory, maple, oak, cherry, and walnut, and explained their different qualities. She tried to remember those now, guessing which piece was made out of what wood.

He'd told her his work was patterned after the old style of furniture making, with the pieces fitted together in the mortise-and-tenon style. The process had sounded tedious to her when he'd described it, but the end result was extremely well-made pieces of furniture. Tara ran her fingers over the curved backs of chairs, opened and closed drawers on a dresser, and even rocked a cradle back and forth.

Ben and his wood, indeed. This is amazing.

She was admiring a dining table when he called out to her. "Time for lunch break."

Tara returned to the bench where he'd just finished putting clamps on two picture frames.

"What do you think?" Ben asked, stepping aside so she could see both frames laid out on his workbench.

"Very nice," Tara said. "They'd look good above a mantel."

"Good idea. Do you have one?" Ben asked.

"No," Tara said. "Why?"

"Because these are for you—to frame your paintings of Nauvoo."

"Oh, Ben." She heard the catch in her voice and stopped speaking before her emotion became even more apparent. In her previous life she'd received numerous gifts from men. Many had cost a lot of money. Several had been given as an apology. None had taken much thought. *No guy has ever taken the time to* make *me something*, she realized. "I don't have anything to give you," she said, wishing fervently that she did.

"You've already given it." Ben put his hands in his pockets and looked past her. "You're here."

Forty-Five

DEB PULLED ANOTHER COSTUME OFF the rack. "How about this one?" She held it up to Tara. "It looks fairytale-ish."

"No, thanks." Tara walked along the row of costumes, running her fingers over them as she passed. Ben and his sister—*especially his sister*—were trying to talk her into staying a few more days to attend their annual barn dance. It was the event that brought in the most money for the charity Ben donated to every year, and according to them both—*and Josh and the mailman and everyone we talked to at church*—it was *the* event of the year.

Behind her, Deb sighed. "This is the only costume shop we've got around here. I'm afraid you're going to have to be a little less—picky."

Tara stopped then turned around to face her. "These are all great." She touched a red velvet cape. "I just don't think I should stay." *Dancing with Ben . . . isn't a good idea.*

"Why not?" Deb challenged. "You were able to do some office work on your laptop the other day. Isn't travel flexibility one of the perks of being self-employed?"

"It's not just work," Tara said. "Though I do need to get serious about that and put in some real hours soon. Designer labels—even secondhand designer labels—are apt to move more quickly during the holiday season."

Deb waved away her argument. "That's over a month away. We're talking about three more days." She pulled a green dress off the rack and held it up to Tara. "This one looks great with your eyes."

"It also looks too modern to belong to a fairytale character," Tara said. *Not to mention it's way more modest than anything I've ever worn to a costume party.* She wondered what Ben's barn dance *would* be like. *What do people do at parties when there is no alcohol?* Curious though she was, Tara knew Ben's dance wasn't the place to find out. She'd just have to ask Jane sometime.

"I guess you're right. The collar looks out of place." Deb put the dress back. "But you will stay? It's been nice having another woman around, and there's always so much to do to get the barn ready."

"I can help you today and tomorrow," Tara compromised. "Then I have to go." She took a step toward the exit. Deb grabbed her arm.

"You'd leave my brother without a date, just before the dance?"

"You make it sound like we're a couple," Tara said, frowning. "And you know that isn't true."

"I know Ben has seemed happier since you arrived than he did the previous six months—and that includes the time McKenzie lived here." Deb dropped her hand back to her side. "I know you like him too."

"Is it that obvious?" Tara bit her lip.

"No more so than Ben's feelings for you," Deb said kindly. "He's crazy about you. It's as plain as . . . as Persephone is pink."

Tara rolled her eyes. "He's crazy about his pigs."

"Only because he hasn't had anyone else to love," Deb said. "Pets can help fill a need. Why do you think so many people treat their pets like family?"

Tara tilted her head to the side, considering. "Maybe I should look into getting a dog when I'm back home."

"You should look into getting *Ben.*"

* * *

Ben finished helping the band get everything set up on the stage then ran around taking care of other last-minute details before they opened the doors for the dance at eight. A string of lights had gone out, and he had to figure out which bulb was bad and replace it. He did a last check of the change in the money boxes and went over, one more time, the procedure for ticket sales and money collection with the volunteers from the young men and young women in his ward. He swept the steps and set out the tickets for the coat check area. At seven fifty-nine, everything was finally ready.

With less than a minute to change into his costume, Ben stepped into the storage area of the barn, where he'd arranged the items waiting to be shipped out or picked up by customers. He hadn't had much time to figure out a costume this year, but it didn't really matter. The theme they'd gone with was fairy tales, and his favorite flannel shirt and jeans would have to suffice for the woodcutter from Little Red Riding Hood. Tara and Deb had teased him about dressing Persephone up as the wolf, to add a little authenticity to his character, but Ben knew the pig wouldn't come anywhere near the barn tonight with this many people around.

He was just glad Tara had decided to stay one more night. More than he had any other year, he was looking forward to the evening.

People were already streaming in when he returned to the main floor, and a quick glance outside told him that parking was filling up quickly. Deb and Josh were directing the cars and would be in later. Ben took his spot by the door, greeting people and thanking them for coming and for their generous donations to Ohio's foster care program. It was a charity close to his heart, and someday he hoped he might participate in more than a monetary fashion.

You've got to have a wife before you start thinking about kids, Ben remembered his mom telling him on more than one occasion when he'd told her he was going to grow up and foster a bunch of children too.

That hasn't really worked out so well, Mom. He stared out past the open barn doors to the dark house where Persephone was probably hiding while Ham likely took advantage of free rein in the kitchen. *At least I have the pigs.* He'd started fostering orphaned potbellied pigs shortly after he'd moved here and found one by the highway. Now Piggy Pals was his second-favorite charity. *If I can't save a child, at least I'm helping out some animals.*

Ben stayed at the door another half hour greeting couples, families, teenagers on dates, and a few curious passersby who'd seen all the traffic and wondered what was going on. The band was going strong by then, playing a lively swing tune when he saw Tara leave the house and start toward the barn. A cloak billowed out behind her, and as she drew closer, the details of her previously secret costume—a girlish billowy dress, a cloth-covered basket, and a red cloak—came into view.

"What's in your basket, Red?" Ben asked when she came to the door.

"Wouldn't you like to know?" Tara said coyly. She pushed the red hood back from her head and turned around in front of him, flipping her braids as she did. "What do you think, Mr. Brave Hunter?"

Taking a cue from her flirting, Ben leaned close and whispered in her ear, "I think the wolf was crazy not to devour you on the spot the first time he saw you."

Tara laughed. Ben linked his arm through hers.

"Come on. Let's dance."

He guided her up the steps and onto the dance floor. Tara tugged him to the side momentarily, so she could set her basket down, then allowed him to pull her back to the center of the already-packed floor.

"This is fantastic," she said. "You must have a couple hundred people here, easily."

"Three hundred nineteen at last count," Ben said. "We're going to make our goal." He beamed.

She gave him a hug. "That's great, Ben. *You're* great to go to all this work to do this."

"Show me how great I am and dance with me." He took her hands and started into a basic swing step.

"Uh-oh." She shook her head and took a step back. "I don't know how to dance like that."

"You will soon." Ben grabbed both her hands and showed her the footing slowly. "Slow, slow, quick, quick." He exaggerated the steps so she could follow.

"I don't know," Tara said skeptically. But Ben wouldn't let her leave. He continued teaching her, going slow until she had it down. The band played another swing number then switched to a waltz.

Tara groaned as she glanced at the couples around them who obviously knew what they were doing. "I just figured out the first dance."

"No worries." Ben pulled her close, placing her hands on his shoulders and putting his arms around her waist. "There's only half an hour until the DJ replaces the band and we get top forty. We can dance however we want then. In fact, we can dance however we want now. No fancy steps needed for this one."

"But you do know how to do that?" Tara inclined her head toward a couple waltzing around the outskirts of the floor.

"I do," Ben said. "Remember how I said my parents were big into Scouting?"

Tara nodded.

"Well, they were big into dancing, too. They'd been on a team together when they were young. So all of us kids had to learn, of course."

"Of course," Tara repeated. "Do you realize how unusual you are? Men these days don't dance and build their own furniture and take care of stray pigs and—"

"I'm part of a true dying species," Ben said sarcastically. "And the way you make me sound, I'm thinking that's a good thing."

"You didn't let me finish," Tara said. "Not a lot of men out there are nice and genuine and helpful the way you are. You're a good person, Ben, and I'm better for knowing you."

"Thanks." He didn't know what else to say to such a nice compliment, so he pulled her close, enjoying the way her head came to rest against his shoulder. It reminded him of the last time he'd held her this close, when snow had swirled all around them, and her lips had been blue.

Don't go there, he warned himself. But it was too late. He'd gone there at least a dozen times since he'd first seen her sitting in his kitchen last week. If he were truthful with himself, he'd never really *stopped* going there. He'd thought about Tara—and that kiss, their connection—off and on throughout the year. He'd thought of her most when McKenzie had been here. He hadn't realized it at the time, but that was probably what had saved him from getting any closer to McKenzie, from getting hurt more than he'd already been.

The song ended, and Tara pulled back, looking up at him with shining eyes. "You saved my life, Ben Whitmore."

He smiled. "I'm glad." Ben wondered if it were possible that she could save his.

Forty-Six

IT WAS AFTER MIDNIGHT WHEN the last car pulled away and Ben locked the barn for the night. Along with Deb and Josh, Tara had been a trooper, staying with him and cleaning up till the very end. Now she yawned and pulled her cloak tight around her as he walked her toward the house. Josh had left five minutes before, and Deb had already gone inside.

"Stars are pretty tonight," Ben remarked, looking up at the sky.

"I can't believe it—I almost forgot." Tara craned her neck back, staring upward. "Jane expects a full star report from Ohio. She's really into that stuff."

"In that case, I've got an idea," Ben said. "Wait here." He dashed past Tara, up the steps, and into the house. He ran to the front closet and pulled out a quilt his mom had made from old jeans years ago. It was one of the things he'd wanted when she passed away. Ben ran back to the yard and Tara, standing exactly where he'd left her.

"Come on." He grabbed her hand and pulled her toward his pickup truck. "This won't be quite as posh as your BMW, but the stars will look the same." He put down the tailgate, tossed the quilt inside, and climbed up. When he'd spread it across the bed of the truck, he reached down to help Tara. She climbed up after him. Ben lay down on the blanket and patted the spot beside him. "Great view from here."

"If I can keep my eyes open long enough." Tara yawned again then lay down beside him.

"Oh, wow. You're right. This is even better than the view from Jane's house."

"There's something to be said for living in the middle of nowhere," Ben said.

"I suppose you know the names for all those." Tara pointed at different constellations.

"Most," Ben said. "Learned them in Boy Scouts."

"Every kid ought to be a Scout." She put her hands behind her head and sighed.

"What was that for?" Ben asked.

"Just thinking," Tara said. "Since I've known you—and Jane—I've learned so much, and I'm grateful."

"She taught you the constellations?" Ben asked.

"No." Tara sounded mildly exasperated. "Do you remember what you said to Cadie the night before we left Utah?"

"Um—" Ben racked his brain but couldn't remember much about that night, aside from fighting with Tara at the DI.

"Cadie was whining about having to move, and you pointed out how lucky she was to have her family, and especially her Father in Heaven, to love her."

"I guess I sort of remember," Ben said.

"You told her she ought to 'thank her lucky stars,'" Tara said. "I didn't get that then, didn't understand what you meant, but now I do. Right now, this very moment, I'm thanking my lucky stars—for you. For Jane. For all you've both taught me. For a Father in Heaven. For the knowledge that He created all these stars."

Ben reached up and took Tara's hand. He twined his fingers through hers, squeezing gently. "The woman I met last year wasn't grateful for much outside of a new tube of lipstick or a pair of shoes."

"I know." Tara's voice was forlorn. "She really didn't have much else *to* be thankful for. She didn't know any better."

"I'm glad she does now."

"Me too. But it's still hard. Sometimes, like now, I feel over-whelmed with gratitude. But other times, being around you or Jane makes me realize how much I've missed. So many experiences other kids have when they're growing up that I never did. Like your Scouts."

"Don't think it was all good," Ben said. "And I doubt a lot of other kids shop at the DI and are forced to learn to waltz."

"I'm sure you're right," Tara said. "But it's more than that." She sat up and hugged her knees to her chest. "You had parents who cared about you, who did stuff with you. They *loved* you."

The hurt in her voice made his chest tighten. How often had he envied others because he felt they had that same thing—someone who cared about them—when he didn't? *But I've had far more caring in my life than Tara has.* He sat up and reached for her. She turned her face to his, and he read the surprise in her expression.

One kiss. Just one to show her I care. Ben leaned forward and brushed his lips across hers. She didn't pull away but seemed to hesitate for a few seconds, then she reached out to him and almost shyly put her arms around his neck. He took her face in his hands and deepened their kiss. She responded in kind.

Do unto others. He thought of their conversation in the cornfield the other day. "Tara." He breathed her name as they broke apart. Her eyes were swimming with tears, but she was smiling.

"You're not going to run off and ride with Ellen now, are you?" he teased.

She shook her head, but the words she spoke were upsetting. "I am leaving tomorrow morning."

In all the chaos of the evening, somehow he'd forgotten that minor detail. Tara didn't belong here. She didn't belong to him.

But she could. His mother's voice again. This was one time he didn't want to hear it.

"What if I come with you, drive you home?" Ben asked the question before he'd fully thought it through. Hope flickered in Tara's eyes.

"Are you serious?" Her question immobilized both of them. Ben knew she'd been referring to the trip, but the deeper meaning bled through. The status of their relationship was on both their minds—and had been for days.

"I'm serious," he said, going against everything he'd told her when she'd first arrived, against everything he'd tried to tell himself since then. Ben leaned close once more, his lips seeking hers, in an affirmation of what he'd just committed to.

She didn't let him down. In less than a minute he was lost in the tide of emotion flowing between them.

One kiss? Who was I kidding?

Forty-Seven

TARA PARKED HER CAR IN the nearest stall she could find at the airport then dashed inside, her three-inch heels clicking as she ran. *Not the day to be late,* she berated herself. What were the chances Ben would believe her if she told him she'd just barely arrived because she'd been babysitting?

Well, not really baby*sitting. Why do they call it that, anyway?* Kid sitting sounded better. At six, Maddie was much less frightening than her baby brother and sister, each of whom Tara had yet to hold. *No way I'll ever stay with them. No, thank you.*

She made it to the baggage carousels in under five minutes and without breaking her neck. The arrival board said Ben's plane had already landed, so Tara looked around, wondering if he was still at the gate or had made his way here yet.

"Hey, would you mind giving a stranger a ride?" a voice behind her said. "The woman who was supposed to meet me seems to have forgotten to pick me up."

"Ben!" Tara whirled around and saw him at last, sitting casually, one leg propped up on the other, his arms across the back of the bench.

"Oh, you *are* here," he said, acting surprised.

"I'm so *sorry.*" She walked over and held her hand out, intending to pull him up. He pulled her off balance and onto his lap instead.

"What are you doing?" Tara felt herself blush as she noticed several people looking their direction.

"You're not . . . *embarrassed,* are you?" He made no move to let her go. "Used to be—about a year ago—you had no problem making a scene in an airport."

Tara cringed. "I know. I was positively wretched that day. Is this my punishment for that or being late?"

"Neither. This is." Ben leaned forward and kissed her soundly, really throwing her off balance. She hadn't been sure what the climate between them would be like on this trip. The last time she'd seen him, when they'd said good-bye at the end of their weeklong cross-country drive to Seattle, he hadn't said much about the status of their relationship. Their road trip had been amazing—a true romantic adventure—but a month had passed since then, and Ben was a man of few words when it came to e-mail.

At last he released her, and she stood, smoothing her knee-length skirt. *It's* almost *to my knees, anyway.* "Should we get your luggage?" she asked when he'd stood and thrown a duffel over his shoulder.

"This is all I brought," Ben said. "Can't trust the airlines not to lose your stuff. I knew this woman once whose luggage was lost. Made her kind of nuts."

"If I didn't know you better," Tara said, "I'd be suspicious that you've been drinking something other than soda or juice on the plane." She started toward the exit.

"Can't a guy be happy?" Ben asked, walking beside her.

She stopped, turning to him as she did. "I hope so." The goofy grin on his face reminded her of the time they'd been in the moving van, right after he'd eaten a pint of Ben & Jerry's. "They didn't happen to have ice cream on your flight, did they?"

Ben gave her a puzzled look. "No. Why?"

"Just wondering." She was the one smiling now, remembering what he'd said that day when she'd asked him why he was so happy when they were stranded on a cold mountaintop.

It's Christmas Eve, I'm in a beautiful canyon, with a pretty woman, and I just had some awesome ice cream.

"It's going to be a great weekend," Tara said, her heart feeling lighter than it had all month. *After all, it's two days before Thanksgiving, we're headed to beautiful Bainbridge, I'm with a good-looking man wearing a flannel shirt, and the day after tomorrow we'll eat lots of pie.*

Ben took her hand in his.

And the good-looking man, the man of my dreams, is going to baptize me tomorrow.

Forty-Eight

TARA PAUSED AT THE TOP of the stairs leading down into the baptismal font. On the opposite side, Ben waited for her. The jumpsuit they'd given him to wear was too big, and the legs were already puffing up as pockets of air formed while he stood in the water.

He'd never looked better, never appeared quite as handsome as he did in that very moment, as he stood there in white, waiting—

For me. Their eyes lingered on one another for a few seconds, then he waded into the water and held a hand out to her. Tara descended the stairs carefully and made her way over to him. His hand was firm on hers, warm and reassuring.

Ben helped her keep her balance, and she placed one hand on his arm, the other ready to plug her nose when he lowered her into the water. She glanced up at the full room and at her two witnesses— Peter and Brother Bartlett, the Sunday School teacher whose lessons had helped change her life.

Ben began speaking. "Tara Ann Mollagen, having been commissioned . . ."

She closed her eyes, hanging on to every beautiful word he said. The simple prayer was over all too fast, then she felt him lowering her gently into the water. She leaned back to help him and felt the water reach her hair then cover her face, body, legs. Every last particle of her.

Washed clean.

Ben lifted her, and she opened her eyes to look at him. He wore the most amazing smile, and he gave her hand a squeeze. She turned and hugged him, right there in the font.

"Thank you."

Forty-Nine

THANKSGIVING AT THE HOME OF Jane's parents the next day was total chaos. Tara had barely stepped through the door of the Warners' home when she started having serious reservations about coming at all.

She was clean now, perfect for a little while. *Well, probably not anymore, because I was vain enough to think that.* But, at the least, she didn't want to seriously mess up by losing it with some kid just a day after her baptism.

And there were kids *everywhere*.

Tall ones, short ones, babies, teenagers, and the really weird ones in between. All together, this many people younger than eighteen years old was nothing short of terrifying.

"Feels just like home," Ben said, settling right in on the sofa. He propped one leg on the other, put his arm across the back of the couch, and beckoned for Tara to join him.

"Go ahead," Jane said. "Peter and I are going to put the babies down for a nap in one of the bedrooms. Be back in a few minutes."

As she sat, Tara eyed the group of medium-sized boys who had previously infiltrated and were hiding in various spots, each with some sort of play weapon in his possession. Every now and then, one of them popped out from behind a wingback chair or the overturned piano bench, and a foam arrow went flying.

Two little girls—older than Maddie but not yet to that awkward middle stage—sprawled on the floor in front of the fireplace, playing a board game. Tara's eyes flitted from them to the boys to the various people filtering through the room. She leaned back into the cushions and tried to relax, as a teenager talking a mile a minute on a cell phone came in and perched on the arm of the sofa. A toddler with a bottle hanging from her mouth followed him. The tiny girl teetered on unsteady legs then fell headlong into Tara's knees. Tara quickly set her upright and tried to hush her crying. The noise must have annoyed the teenager because he took off. To Tara's relief, the toddler followed.

Grateful for the respite, she leaned forward, head in her hands. "Isn't having this many people in one house against fire code?"

"Hey, do you mind getting up for a minute?" One of Jane's brothers stood over them. "I lost my keys and think they might be in the couch."

"Sure." Ben stood then pulled Tara up and to the side. A Nerf ball whizzed by her face.

"Sorry," some kid yelled as he ducked behind a chair.

"You doing all right? Need some air or anything?" Ben asked.

She took another deep breath then exhaled slowly, looking around the room. Being shot at aside, so far nothing bad had happened, and these were just kids, right? *Smallish people, like Maddie. Nothing to freak out about.*

"I think I'll be okay," she said after a minute, "but thanks." She smiled at Ben as he squeezed her hand. How great it was to have someone looking out for her. It was a feeling she could get used to.

"Game's on in the other room," Peter announced as he and Jane returned.

"I'm there." Ben started to go after him then stopped at a nearby chair so Maddie and her cousin could piggyback.

Where did they come from? Tara wondered as she waved at Allison, who seemed to have grown exponentially in the months since Tara had seen her.

"How are you doing?" Jane asked. "Kids driving you crazy yet?"

"Not too much," Tara said, proud that she could say that. "So far the worst has been almost getting hit by a Nerf ball." She raised her eyebrows at the owner of the gun that had shot that ball, who was angling his way around the love seat.

Jane beckoned with her hand. "Come in the kitchen. No balls or weapons allowed in there." She turned back the way she'd come, and Tara followed, half-expecting an attack as she retreated.

The kitchen was a flurry of activity, with Jane's mom issuing orders to the mostly female population. The one exception was Ben, just taking his place at the stove to stir gravy.

Seeing her perplexed look, he shrugged. "I always made the gravy at my house. So I asked Sister Warner if she'd mind."

Jane handed two baskets of rolls to Tara and took another two off the counter. "Mom never turns down help. You'll have a standing invitation here the rest of your life."

"That's what I was hoping." Ben sniffed the air appreciatively. "Any kitchen that smells like this is one I want to be welcome in."

Tara helped Jane and her sisters finish putting the food on the tables—butter and rolls, salad dressings and boats of gravy, trays of olives and nuts. Two platters of turkey, three bowls of mashed potatoes, four different kinds of salads. *And I thought setting up the caterer's delivery took time.* Tara's mouth watered, anticipating what was likely going to be the best home-cooked meal she'd ever enjoyed. The kitchen held a counter full of pies. A ham still warming in the oven was almost forgotten. Tara sent a sideways glance at Ben and wondered if he'd be eating any. There were certainly enough other foods to choose from.

Things got crazier after that. Jane's dad called everyone to dinner. Bodies crammed into the space as everyone found their places at the tables—three of them, end to end. Tara guessed that together they must run close to thirty feet.

"My mom doesn't believe in a separate children's table," Jane explained. "We've always eaten together. I just hope they made this room big enough."

"I don't know," Tara said. "If you and Peter have as many kids as your brothers and sisters have . . ."

"Not possible," Peter said. "Remember?"

Tara covered her mouth, horrified she could have forgotten something as significant as the tragedy that accompanied the twins' birth last summer.

"I'm sorry." Tara touched Jane's arm. "I didn't mean—"

"That's all right." Jane's smile was reassuring as she looked from Tara down into her baby's face. "There's always adoption. Peter and I had talked about it before I got pregnant, and I think it's something we'll talk about again at some point."

"Just not. Right. Now." Peter placed his hands on Jane's shoulders.

"Not now," she agreed, laughing as she tilted her head back to look up at him.

"Adoption's great," Ben said, joining the conversation. "The only way to go. You guys could still have fifteen kids, easy."

"*Easy?*" Jane said. "I don't think so."

Her mother had arranged the seating so that everyone sat in families. Tara was relieved to find that she and Ben were beside Jane, Peter, and Maddie. Jane's father said the blessing, which was immediately followed by at least two dozen hands reaching for the food.

"Remember," Brother Warner boomed, "no one leaves this table until we're done with the thanking. If that happens, then next year we'll have to return to the way things were years ago, before a couple of naughty little girls—" He looked from Jane to her sister, Caroline, then back to Jane again— "convinced us that eating first was prudent."

"Here's to naughty girls." Caroline's husband raised his glass in a toast. Caroline elbowed him, but Tara didn't miss the flirtatious look that went along with it.

"I think we're missing a story here," Ben said.

"I know we are." Tara took the potatoes from Jane. "But don't worry. I'll get it out of her later."

Even with the number of people at the tables, dinner was mostly uneventful. The volume rose throughout the meal as people talked over each other, and three different times children spilled their drinks. *But not on me*, Tara thought happily. Laughter was plentiful, teasing between Jane and her siblings even more abundant, and everyone around her, with the exception of a cranky toddler and one of Peter and Jane's twins, seemed happy.

Thinking about her last Thanksgiving—spent alone in her apartment in Los Angeles—compared to this one—surrounded by people who accepted and cared about her—Tara felt an overwhelming rush of gratitude for the experiences of the past year, along with an all-too-familiar lump forming in her throat.

Attentive as always, Ben noticed. "You okay?" He placed his arm around the back of her chair and leaned in close.

Tara nodded. "Just thinking. Does this being weepy ever get better? I mean, am I going to be this emotional the rest of my life now?"

His expression grew tender. "I hope so. It means you're feeling the Spirit, and that's—"

"A good thing," Jane concurred, reaching over to give Tara's hand a squeeze. "I love that you're here with us, Tara. *You* are what I'm thankful for this year."

"Me?" Tara said. "Oh, please. Peter came home safely. You've got two beautiful new babies—"

"Who wouldn't be here without you. Neither would I," Jane reminded her.

Tara waved away her praise. "Someone else would have stayed with you."

"Maybe," Jane said. "Maybe not. But the point is, the Lord sent *you* to help me. And you listened."

"I listened," Tara repeated, thinking back all those months ago to that lonely February night, when she'd curled up on her sofa and had a dream about Seattle—and coming home. Had that been the Lord directing her life? The answer came quietly to her heart.

He was listening, even when I didn't know He was there, didn't know any better. Heavenly Father was watching out for me.

Fifty

DINNER WAS OVER, AND THANKS had been expressed. Too much thanks from some members of the family, in Tara's opinion. Jane had a sister who wouldn't shut up. The dishes were mostly done and dessert consumed when Jane's father announced it was time for Great Dalmuti.

"It's one of the Warners' traditions," Peter explained before Tara or Ben could ask. The three sat on the couch in the front room, Peter and Ben each holding one of the twins. "This family is big on traditions. Football at eleven o'clock sharp every Thanksgiving. Boys against girls. Losing team has dishes." He lifted the baby to his shoulder. "Dalmuti is part of every holiday, and some regular Sunday dinners, depending on everyone's mood. Just be glad you don't have to participate in the annual family photo shoot next week."

"I heard that." Jane's mom smacked him on the head with a roll of paper towels as she walked by.

"What *is* Dalmuti?" Tara asked, wondering if the missionaries had forgotten to tell her about some important Mormon custom.

"A card game," Peter said, "that Jane's family takes to the extreme."

As if to prove his point, Brother Warner carried a giant plastic tote into the room. Before he'd had a chance to take off the lid, the teenagers swarmed him.

"I call Dalmuti first," one yelled.

"Nice try," another said. "You know we don't pick that way."

"And doesn't asking mean you're automatically the peon?"

"Each card represents a different hierarchy," Peter said. "The Great Dalmuti is like the king, then there are merchants, right down to the lowest peon, who has to collect the cards at the end of each round." He rose from the couch, careful to support Ella's head. "Jane's mom and sister made hats to go with the cards. It's kind of crazy but also a lot of fun."

Tara thought that was an apt description of the entire evening. Or maybe "really crazy but kinda fun" would have been a better fit. At any rate, she was surprised and pleased at how much she had enjoyed herself. She was grateful for the game, strange though it might be, because it promised the night would last a little longer.

Thinking about tomorrow was depressing. Friday was Ben's last day here, and then . . . She didn't know. Could they continue a relationship long distance? Where did they go from here? She had to believe that, since she'd first seen him again seven weeks ago, his feelings about getting serious with anyone had changed. But she wasn't positive. Ben remained a man of few words as far as feelings were concerned, though by his actions alone, she knew he cared about her.

How much? was what she couldn't figure out how to answer.

Her own emotions were easy enough to decipher. She'd been head-over-heels in love with him long before she'd even realized it. Even more than that, she respected him. He was honest, hard-working, kind, generous. And that only scratched the surface of his noble character. Which worried her. If LDS singles ran *The Bachelor,* Ben could be the star. He could have any woman he wanted.

So why would he want me?

It was a question she didn't care to dwell on.

Aside from her relationship with Ben, life was entering a new rhythm far better than the previous. Unfortunately, she feared it still forecast a lot of lonely days.

She hoped that at least Christmas would be good this year. Since picking Ben up at the airport, she'd been toying with the idea of asking him to return at the end of next month. She planned to pitch the idea as a way for her to make up for how awful she'd been the previous December. With a little luck, it might just work.

Tara watched as Ben held Jane's baby like a pro. He had the makings of an excellent dad. It really was too bad things hadn't worked out for him and McKenzie.

Who am I kidding? I'm thrilled it didn't work out for them.

Tara sighed as she felt a little more of her perfect cleanliness wash away. *Bummer that even our thoughts count against us.* She stood and followed the guys into the other room.

"Look who's here." Jane came in a minute later with two people Tara hadn't met. More family, no doubt, though there were already too many here for Tara to begin to keep track. The newcomers didn't quite seem to fit in with the rest of the family. They looked younger than most of Jane's siblings and didn't appear to have any kids with them. They made a striking couple, though completely different in looks, with her blonde hair and fair complexion beside his darker hair and looks. When they greeted the family, Tara thought she detected a slight accent.

"Hi, Jay. Sarah." Peter set Ella in her car seat on the table and came over to shake their hands. "You made it."

"We did," Sarah said. "Actually, we flew in last night. We spent the day going through Jay's storage unit."

"We're shipping what we want to keep and getting rid of the rest," Jay explained.

"Which means you're not returning to Seattle anytime soon," Jane guessed.

"Probably not," Jay said. "And this trip is short. We needed to work on the unit today because Sarah has to be back for a concert Saturday night."

Jane turned toward Tara. "Tara, Ben, these are our good friends Sarah and Jay. They live in Boston but occasionally remember those of us out West."

"*Occasionally*, as in most major holidays for the past couple of years." Jay stuck his hand out to shake Ben's.

"Jay was my law intern the summer before he graduated," Peter explained. "We keep hoping we'll get him here permanently."

"We may get back here someday," Jay said. "But right now Sarah's having some fantastic opportunities with her music, and we've got to pursue those dreams first."

Tara greeted each of them, deciding as she did that it wouldn't be too awful a breach of etiquette to mix business with social tonight. "If you've got things in your storage unit you'd like to sell or just want to get rid of, I can help you."

"That would be great," Sarah said enthusiastically. "We hardly have any time to go through it, but we'd like to clear it out so this is our last month of rent."

"We're buying a house," Jay announced, grinning.

"Kill my hopes," Peter said, shaking his head. "But that's great. Quickest way to a woman's heart—" he took Jane's hand— "is to buy her a house."

"With a *yard*," Jane added.

"You may have to come out and work on ours," Jay said. "It's an older home, but the front room is big enough for a grand piano."

"When we can afford it," Sarah said, though her eyes sparkled with excitement at the possibility.

"Let me help you earn some cash for that piano," Tara said. "I'm pretty good at selling things to local stores and online. Remind me to give you a business card before you leave."

"I will, and thanks," Sarah said then followed Jay around the room to say hello to the rest of Jane's family.

Tara noticed that Jane's sister Caroline was the only one who didn't give a warm welcome to Jay. She thought that was a little odd, but then, from what she knew of Caroline, she'd always been her own, outspoken, opinionated person.

Kind of like me. The thought was comforting. *Maybe the gospel really is for those of us who are less than perfect.*

Jane's dad stood at the head of the table and explained the rules of the game. Then he turned to Tara and Ben. "Since this is your first time as our guests, you get the honor of sitting at the head of the table and being the Great and Lesser Dalmutis first."

"But not for long," one of Caroline's sons called out.

"That's what you think." Ben stood then held his hand out for Tara. "Come, my queen. Leave the peasants behind." They walked to the end of the room, and Ben pulled a chair out for her. "Ladies first. You get the greatest honor."

"Why, thank you." Tara sat and stared haughtily at her royal subjects. "Isn't there supposed to be a back massage or something with this position?"

"Hey, you're off the bench, aren't you?" Peter yelled. He and Jane were at the far end of the table, seated on one of the hard, backless benches.

Ben took the chair beside Tara, and Jane's dad reached into the plastic tub. "For you." He placed a Burger King crown on Ben's head.

Tara could tell where fake jewels and sequins had once adorned it. She laughed.

"Our kingdom must be poor."

"We'd better increase the taxes," Ben said.

"And for you, milady." Brother Warner removed an equally appalling cone-shaped purple princess hat. Tara tried to place it on her head, but it fell off—twice.

"First day on the job, and your head is already too big," Ben teased.

Tara glared at him. "We'll see who stays a Dalmuti longer."

"We need to find something else for you to wear." Ben stood and pulled her up. He removed his crown and set it on the person nearest him. "Start without us. We'll jump in next round." He towed Tara toward the front room. "I know just the thing. It'll be much better. It's *you*."

"Back in a minute," she called over her shoulder.

"I doubt it," Peter said.

"Take your time," Jane called, sounding amused.

Ben led her to the now-deserted front room and pulled a book-sized cardboard box from the top of the piano. "I saw this at a thrift store, and I thought of you."

"You know, that hat in the other room wasn't so bad." Tara imagined the sort of atrocity Ben likely held in his hands. He'd only been in Seattle since Tuesday, and *already* he'd had time to find a thrift store? "If it's going on my head, I hope you at *least* disinfected it." She sighed loudly, remembering the Minnie Mouse fleece he'd crowned her with last December. "Let's get this over with."

"What? No tantrum, no tears? No 'Forty-seven bucks and an hour at Sears is abuse' line?'"

Tara folded her arms and shook her head. "We're not talking about buying underwear. It's a *game*."

"You've changed, Tara." Ben lifted a hand, as if to reach out to her and pull her close but hesitated at the last second. "And this isn't a game anymore. Peter and Jane just helped arrange that convenient setup." He opened the box and took out a sparkling silver tiara.

She gasped and reached for it. Ben handed it to her. It was heavier than she'd expected, and examining it closely, she noticed a slight tarnish on some of the inner curves. *Sterling silver?*

"If you're finding this kind of stuff at thrift stores, we need to go shopping together. This diamond looks real."

"Could be," Ben said casually. "I bought the tiara at an antique store the week after I flew home from Seattle."

"You made an incredible find." Tara stared at him. "It's stunning, Ben. Absolutely beautiful."

"Like you."

She didn't know what to say to that but felt herself flush with pleasure.

Ben set the box aside and took one of her hands in his.

"As I said—this isn't a game." All teasing was gone from his voice, and the tender expression he'd worn earlier was back.

"Ben?" *What're we doing here?*

"Once, I told you your name should be Tiara, because you were—"

"A spoiled princess," she whispered, ashamed by the memory.

"It was an awful thing for me to say," he hurried on. "But I still think you should have a tiara, because as you've discovered this year, you are a daughter of God—a princess who stands to inherit all the many blessings He has in store."

Tara felt tears building behind her eyes. Her embarrassment fled, replaced by a rush of love for Ben, the one who really deserved a crown, the one who'd been named after a noble king and exemplified so many of the characteristics of his namesake.

"If it wasn't for you, I might never have discovered that," she said.

Ben gave her a wry smile. "I remain astonished that, in spite of me, you *did*."

She laughed then pressed her lips together to quiet her nerves.

"Tara, will you accept this tiara from me and consent to be *my* princess, my bride?" He paused, searching her face for an answer. "My wife."

Your wife? She tried but couldn't find her voice to ask the question, to be certain he was real, that he'd just asked her to marry him. Moments like this only happened to people like Jane. Good, deserving people who wore flannel nightgowns and were always honest and never longed for a drink and hadn't done all the hundreds of awful things—

"You want to marry *me*?" Tara blurted.

"There's no one else around here." Ben's smile was wide as he looked around the room.

"But I'm so—*flawed*." And though she'd been baptized just yesterday, though she'd been washed clean, she knew that what she said was true. Her thoughts weren't always pure—or even charitable. She was still impatient and temperamental. She'd probably mourn the loss of her old wardrobe the rest of her life. She didn't think she could handle being a mom to half a dozen kids—maybe not even one. She wasn't *wife* material.

"I love your imperfection," Ben said. "It matches my own."

She snorted. "You don't come close."

He took the tiara from her hands and placed it on the piano.

"You don't know," he said, quietly serious again.

But she did. She knew all that Ellen had confided to her during that long ride to Denver. Ben had problems too. Like her, his past was full of pain and difficulty. Those things had haunted him before, and someday they might again. But that didn't matter to her, not in the least. If there ever was another time in the future when Ben was sick or hurting, she wanted to be there for him.

"I do know," she said. "Ellen told me everything. About your mom and your engagement . . . All of it." She stopped, aware of the pain filtering through his eyes.

"I see." He stepped back in a weary, defeated sort of way.

"Wait," Tara said. "What, exactly, *do* you see—besides me and all my imperfections that you love?"

He shrugged. "I've got a family history of—instability. It's asking a lot—too much—for someone else to live with that. It's probably for the best if I face up to that and am content to spend my life living with pigs."

Tara poked a finger at his chest. "Don't go comparing me to a pig."

"Don't mess with me, Tara. I was serious about this—about us. I wanted to tell you everything about my past. I wanted to take it slow, for both our sakes."

"*Wanted*? What's not to want now? I am serious about us. You didn't give me a chance to say so, to say yes." She paused, willing him to look at her.

Ben picked up the tiara and held it in his hands, his fingers running over the curls and curves and pieces of glass. "You were right. This one is real." His thumb brushed over a princess cut diamond in the center of the tiara. "I picked it out for you, but I didn't want to put it in a ring yet." He met Tara's surprised gaze. "I knew we both still needed some time. But I wanted you to know, I wanted us to start—"

Tara reached out, touching both the stone and his hand. "It's beautiful." She blinked back tears and prayed for the right thing to say, to make this better. *Only I could botch what should have been the perfect proposal.*

"I would be honored to be your wife, Ben. If you can love me, in spite of knowing me when I was at my worst, then I think I should be allowed to love you, even though I've heard about the hardest part of your life." She paused, waiting for him to acknowledge her acceptance of his past, to say something romantic or to kiss her. He did neither.

Tara tried again. "Ben, we're not going to be like your parents or the Warners—or even Jane and Peter. I'm high maintenance, and you may have to deal with anxiety or depression sometimes, but we can be *us* with each other. And we can be happy. I know it."

A corner of his mouth lifted, and Ben looked up at her, nodding his head slightly. "Yeah. I know it too." He raised the tiara, and she bent forward so he could place it on her head. Then he stepped back to look at her.

"Even more beautiful on you."

Tara reached for him, grabbed the front of his shirt, and pulled him close, covering his lips with hers. But her kiss was soft and gentle and sweet, just like that first kiss he'd given her on the mountain. She felt the magic again, much more than the chemistry between them, but all the deep, abiding love he felt for her and she for him.

When their kiss ended, Tara's cheeks were wet with tears, and she kept her arms around Ben, hugging him tight. "When did you first think you loved me?"

"Um—at the barn dance?"

"It took you *that* long?" She reached up, pretending to take off the tiara.

"When you ran over my foot." He grabbed her hand, stopping her. "I'd wondered before then—when I couldn't get you off my mind for months. And then, when I saw you in my kitchen, it all came to the surface. But when you ran over my foot and didn't yell *at me* for it, I said to myself, 'Ben, this woman has changed. You'd better not let her go this time.'"

"I first loved you when I kissed you in the moving truck," Tara said.

"Why then?"

"It was the first time I cared about you," Tara said. "I didn't realize it until months later, but I kissed you because I knew what you'd be facing that weekend with your ex, and I wanted to give you a boost of confidence before you went into the lions' den."

"Barely a convert and talking in parables already," Ben said. "Amazing." He pulled her to him again, resting his chin on top of her head.

Tara closed her eyes, reliving a similar moment from eleven months earlier. It had opened her eyes and heart to possibilities she'd never before considered. How happy she was now, how grateful for her newfound knowledge and understanding, how in love with Ben. Modern-day miracles, indeed.

And oh, how she thanked her lucky stars.

Epilogue

JANE CLOSED THE DOOR OF the nursery and tiptoed down the hall. It had taken her almost a year and a half, but she finally had the twins' nap schedules coordinated. The hour they slept in the afternoon allowed her to have some time alone with Maddie when she came home from school each day.

Grabbing a sweater from the back of a chair, Jane headed toward the front door. She went outside and down the walk to wait for Maddie's bus. She opened the gate and walked to the mailbox. While she waited each day, she sorted through the mail, a particularly enjoyable task during the past few weeks, with friends' Christmas cards arriving daily.

As she stood by the gate, she shuffled through the envelopes, setting aside bills and ads to look through later. The second-to-last envelope—with a return address from Ohio—brought a smile to her face. Jane turned it over and tore it open then pulled a photo card out. She laughed at the faces staring up at her.

Ben, in overalls and holding a pitchfork, was doing his best to look somber but couldn't entirely hide the mischievous twinkle in his eyes. Beside him, Tara wore a high-collared, old fashioned dress that Jane would have bet a million bucks two years ago that Tara wouldn't ever touch, let alone wear. Her face attempted equal somberness, but she too betrayed a hint of amusement. A large wooden picture frame bordered the couple, as if they were a painting on the wall.

A small caption at the bottom confirmed Jane's suspicions.

American Gothic: a Whitmore Halloween Production

On the side of the card, in the space reserved for holiday greetings, there was one word.
JOY.

About the Author

MICHELE HOLMES SPENT HER CHILD-HOOD and youth in Arizona and northern California—often with her head in a book instead of out enjoying the sunshine. She has been married to her high school sweetheart for twenty-three years, and they live in Utah, having traded the beach for the mountains.

Michele graduated from Brigham Young University with a degree in elementary education—something that has come in handy with her five children, all of whom require food, transportation, or help with their homework the moment she sits down at her computer. In spite of all the interruptions, Michele is busy at work, with more story ideas in her head than she will likely ever have time to write.

Michele's first published novel, *Counting Stars*, won the 2007 Whitney Award for best romance. The companion novel, a romantic suspense titled *All the Stars in Heaven* was a 2009 Whitney finalist. *My Lucky Stars* continues the series. Michele also enjoys writing historical romance. Her first, *Captive Heart*, was published by Covenant in 2011 and is a Whitney finalist.

To learn more about Michele's writing, please visit her website at michelepaigeholmes.com You may also contact her via Covenant email at info@covenant-lds.com or through USPS mail at Covenant Communications, Inc. P.O. Box 416 American Fork, UT 84003-0416.